TROUBLED WATER

A LARK CHADWICK MYSTERY

JOHN DeDAKIS

13-digit ISBN 978-1939-5210-7-1
10-digit ISBN 1-9395210-7-6

For Cindy

Advance Praise for Troubled Water

"Troubled Water is the latest page-turner from John DeDakis, featuring no-nonsense journalist Lark Chadwick. The thriller novel is a masterful adventure that rings true to life. DeDakis really understands how reporters work, women think—and how killers kill."
Kitty Pilgrim
Journalist/Author

****

"How John DeDakis can write so compellingly about the world of journalism is no surprise. But how he can write so convincingly about a woman in the field is astounding! I can't wait to find out what happens next in the world of Lark Chadwick."
Diane Dimond
Journalist/Author/Syndicated Columnist

****

"As a young female journalist, I spent most of this novel wondering how John DeDakis got into my head. *Troubled Wate*r is sharp, suspenseful and—most importantly—utterly believable."
Jenna Troum
Reporter, WSPA (CBS) – Greenville, SC

Praise for Fast Track

"*Fast Track* is one of those rare novels that you simply can't put down. I was hooked on page one and it was non-stop until the very end – an emotional roller coaster."
Wolf Blitzer
CNN Anchor, "The Situation Room with Wolf Blitzer"

***

"From a heart-breaking opening to a heart-stopping finale, this story kept me turning pages. A well-crafted and exciting novel."
Patricia Sprinkle
Former National President, Sisters in Crime
Author, *Thoroughly Southern* Mystery Series

***

"Another Hemingway, but better. John DeDakis writes with clarity, sensitivity, and passion."
Patricia Daley-Lipe, Ph.D.
National League of American Pen Women

Praise for Bluff

"I raced right through it. Definitely hard to put down! John DeDakis is a masterful storyteller who has adroitly woven several story lines into this fast-paced page-turner. With true-to-life characters and an insider's knowledge of the world of journalism, the second of DeDakis' Lark Chadwick mysteries will not disappoint fans of *Fast Track*."

Charlene Fu
Former Veteran Foreign Correspondent for the Associated Press

***

"Lark is like an old friend. I'm glad she's back and as fierce as ever. *Bluff* is a good, fast read…I can't wait until the next adventure."

Carol Costello
Anchor, CNN's "Newsroom with Carol Costello"

ACKNOWLEDGMENTS

I'm frequently asked how it is that I'm able to write as a woman. Perhaps the key reason is that I'm blessed to have so many wonderful women in my life, beginning with my wife Cindy and daughter Emily. They do a lot of talking and I *try* to do a lot of listening.

In addition, there are a number of women who read all or some of the earlier drafts of the novel and then gave me their honest feedback on what worked, and – more importantly – what didn't. These are the women to whom I'm most indebted: Carla Babb, Carolyn Cremen, Dana Davidsen, Cindy and Emily DeDakis, Diane Dimond, Sarah Elliott, Darcy Geddis, Emily Gowor, Karen Hallacy, Jillian Harding, Karen Hoel, Cindy Hoyt, Sarah Marx, Barbara Mays, Jo McDaniel, Carolyn Presutti, Amanda Tatem, Jenna Troum, Becky Perlow, and Lindsay Perna.

Troubled Water would not have been possible without the expertise, assistance, and influence of several people. A huge thank you to:

- My CNN colleague Wolf Blitzer and Mike Ruane of the Washington Post for their door-opening abilities
- Former medical examiner Steele Lipe for helping me create an authentic crime scene
- Alan Audet for his insights
- CNN's Carol Costello for her friendship
- Karen Hoel for helping me understand how 911 operators do their jobs
- Friends and mentors Lowell Mays and Jim Hoyt for their constant encouragement
- Psychiatrist, writer, and friend Dr. Paul Dobransky for allowing himself to be interviewed by my heroine Lark Chadwick
- Ashley Perkins of GameVortex.com for her constructive reviews of my first two novels—*Fast Track* and *Bluff*
- CNN Political Producer Peter Hamby for his insights on covering presidential campaigns
- Ben Holden of the Ledger Enquirer in Columbus, Georgia for being a generous host and tour guide of his newsroom.
- Reporter Alan Riquelmy of the Ledger Enquirer for helping me understand how he does his job
- Garry Dinnerman of Beverly Grant Associates in Atlanta for continuing to believe in me

I want to give a special thank you hug to my wonderful agent and editor Barbara Casey. Barbara fell in love with my first novel *Fast Track* in 2004 and we've been together ever since. Barbara is always just an e-mail or phone call away, standing by with a generous supply of wisdom, expertise, and encouragement.

Finally, to the scores of friends – and strangers – who took a chance on this relatively unknown author, and then encouraged me with your enthusiastic response to *Fast Track* and *Bluff*, a gigantic thank you. You keep me inspired.

John DeDakis
Washington, DC
July 2013

ONE

THE LILAC SPRIG I clutched in my right hand had long since lost most of its spring-fresh scent. Three days earlier, as I began driving from Wisconsin to Georgia, I'd cut it from a lush lilac bush that shaded the graves of my parents. I never knew them. They died in a car accident a quarter century ago when I was an infant. Annie, my father's younger sister, raised me. We were like sisters. Now, she's buried next to them—and that lilac bush.

Every few miles, I'd take another deep whiff so that spring in Wisconsin would stay with me—and in me—as I drove farther and farther into the Deep South. I'd never been to that part of the country before, so I had all kinds of preconceived notions of what life would be like living "down there." Actually, I'm ashamed to say I haven't traveled very much at all. So, after a long heart-to-heart with my friend and mentor, Lionel Stone, publisher of the *Pine Bluff Standard,* we agreed it was time for me to leave my reporting job at his paper and spread my wings.

Through Lionel's contacts, I landed a job as a cops and courts reporter at the *Columbia Sun-Gazette*—a daily paper in west central Georgia about a hundred miles southwest of Atlanta and just across the river from Alabama. Lionel told me the paper had a reputation for scrappy investigative journalism that led to Pulitzer Prizes for reporters who then went on to prestigious publications like the *New York Times* where Lionel recently retired as the paper's National Editor.

"It'll be a good place for you to park for awhile, kid, until you're ready to go on to the big time," Lionel had said to me a couple weeks earlier when I was weighing the paper's offer.

Lionel won his Pulitzer in the early 1970s when he was the White House Correspondent for the *Times* during Nixon's presidency. Lionel had also covered the Civil Rights Movement, so he insisted that I stop in Memphis on my way south and tour the National Civil Rights Museum located in the old Lorraine Motel where Martin Luther King, Jr. was assassinated in 1968.

On my drive south, I also made a detour to the King Center in Atlanta to see MLK's tomb, tour the neighborhood where he grew up and see the Ebenezer Baptist Church where he and his father preached.

About nine-thirty on this Saturday night, I was cruising down I-185 closing in on Columbia, but still in the boonies and having a heck of a time staying awake. I'd had so much caffeine that I was facing the law of diminishing returns—it seemed like the more coffee I drank, the sleepier I got. To entertain myself, I kept hitting the scan button on my radio to see what kind of nonsense could be strung together by the brief bursts of audio snippets. One particularly amusing string sounded like this:

"Governor Gannon's presidential campaign got a boost today when he won the endorsement of — *[ffffttt]* — JAY-zuss.

Thank you, Lord. Thank you, Lord for your — *[fffftttt]* — Dodge Charger. It comes fully-equipped with — *[fffftttt]* — your own personal banker. That's right. I'm here to — *[fffftttt]* — got a line on you, babe, yeah — *[fffftttt]* — I can't get noooo…sat-is-FACK-shun. No, no, no — *[fffftttt]* — are you SAVED by the blood of the LAMB?'"

After awhile, that got boring, so I called Lionel because I can always count on him to keep my mind energized. We'd been yakking for a few minutes when my bladder began competing for my attention.

"Lionel, if I don't stop this car right now, I'm gonna wet my pants."

"You should've worn a diaper, Lark," he chuckled.

"What are you talking about?"

"Don't you remember the story about the former astronaut who drove cross-country wearing a diaper?"

"That must've been before my time."

"She was in such a hurry to confront the 'other woman'—her romantic rival—that she didn't want to take rest stops, so she—"

"Lionel!" I barked.

"Whuh?"

"I can't talk any longer. I've gotta pull over. Now!"

"Oh, alright," he sighed.

"I'll call you right back."

"Okay."

I hit *end call* on my iPhone and peeled off the interstate at the very next exit—exit 252—Skunk Run Road. On impulse, I turned right at the bottom of the ramp, the hyper-caffeinated urine in my bladder pressing urgently for release.

There were no gas stations or fast food joints. Traffic was sporadic. I needed to find someplace more private. I turned right again at the first road that came along. It was narrow and had no shoulder. Trees and shrubs crowded the pavement. There was no place to pull over.

I pressed on the accelerator and Pearlie, seeming to understand my plight, lurched forward. Pearlie is my yellow VW Beetle. We've been through a lot together.

"I've gotta go, Pearl. Help me out here."

We rounded a curve. Down the road, I saw four pairs of headlights. At first, it looked as though one car was passing another. Quickly, however, I realized the lights weren't moving toward me at all. The four lights looked like two small cars parked side by side on a narrow bridge.

"What the hell, Pearl. Are they about to drag race right at me?" I eased back on the accelerator.

Suddenly, the car lights darted forward, swerving in tandem into my lane.

I hit the brakes and eased Pearlie to the right, trying to get over as far as I could without smashing into the dense hedges that hugged the edge of the road. Branches slapped against the side windows and scraped along the side door.

Then, just as unexpectedly as the lights had veered toward me, they lurched back into the other lane.

I felt my brow furrow as I squinted to get a better look. As the lights sped closer, I could now see that it wasn't two cars going side by side, but one car with an unusual quad headlight configuration.

I honked and shot an annoyed glare at the driver as the car swished past, but I couldn't get a good look at who was behind the wheel.

I turned my attention to the road ahead—and my insistent bladder—accelerating as I got to the bridge. Just beyond it, I saw a road to the left. I took it. The road sloped down. On the left was a clearing with a picnic table. I turned in. It seemed to be the perfect out-of-the-way place to pee.

I turned off my lights, threw the lilac branch I'd been holding onto the passenger seat, grabbed a flashlight and some tissues from the glove box, and raced to a sandy spot among reeds and tall grass along the edge of a rushing stream—as out of the way as I could get from the road. I didn't want to be caught with my pants down if someone else suddenly stopped by.

Before undoing my jeans, I swung the flashlight around to make sure some guy and his girlfriend weren't making out nearby. Satisfied that I was alone, I turned out the light, shoved down my jeans and underwear, squatted, and then . . . blessed relief!

It seemed to take forever. The warm, humid May night surrounded me like a heavy blanket. My eyes had still not adjusted to the darkness, which made me feel claustrophobic. The sound of the churning stream next to me blended with the riotous chirping of cicadas and crickets. It was so loud I feared I wouldn't be able to hear the rustle of grass if someone just then decided to sneak up behind me. That thought instantly made me feel frightened and vulnerable.

I finished as quickly as I could. I didn't want to be exposed a second longer.

Hurriedly, I wiped myself as daintily as I could with a tissue, stood and pulled everything up. Just as I was buckling my belt, I felt something bump my foot. Alarmed, I switched on the flashlight and aimed it straight down at whatever it was that had just given me that gentle, but unexpected nudge. I hoped it would be nothing more than some harmless night creature out for a stroll.

But what I saw caused me to scream in terror.

TWO

AS I SCREAMED, I jumped backward, bobbling and then dropping my flashlight. It plunked into the sand and went out. I groped wildly for it in the dark before I latched onto it a few seconds later. I clawed at the switch. The light came back on, but my hands were shaking so badly I needed both of them to aim the beam. At first, I couldn't see what had startled me, but I was sure my mind wasn't playing tricks—I knew I'd felt and seen *something*.

The air was saturated with the cacophony of thousands of cicadas. They shrieked at me as I brushed aside reeds and tall grass and crept closer to the gurgling water.

Then I saw it again—a right hand, palm up, bobbing gently against the sand at the water's edge. I gasped and clamped my left hand over my mouth to keep from screaming again. I tried to catch my breath, but couldn't. The sound of my heart thudding in my ears was deafening.

I bent closer and pushed aside more of the tall reeds. The hand was attached to a thin, grayish, bare arm.

"Oh, Jesus," I kept repeating under my breath.

A slight breeze pushed a reed into my face. I brushed it away with my free hand and continued to focus the light. It slowly revealed more. Floating face up in the eddying current was the body of what looked like a teenaged girl, her mouth open in a silent scream, her eyes wide and bloodshot.

"Oh, God!" I jumped back.

My breaths were coming fast and shallow. I felt light-headed, my body tingling as if a strong electrical current pulsed through me. Everything inside me ordered me to turn and run away, but somehow I resisted the urge to panic.

I'm no stranger to death. On two separate occasions, I was the one who was the first to discover the dead bodies of people I loved dearly. Now, it had happened again—a young girl, staring wildly at the night sky. She had died violently, or so it seemed, perhaps not too far from here.

I took several deep breaths to try to calm myself, but it wasn't easy because I was afraid the murderer might be nearby, perhaps watching me.

I shined the flashlight in all directions. As near as I could tell, I was alone. The thrumming of the cicadas and crickets continued unabated, blending with the rushing water of the stream.

I thought about running to the car and locking myself in, but something inside urged me to stay put so as not to contaminate the crime scene. Quickly, I dug my cell phone from the front pocket of my jeans and stabbed 911.

"Nine-one-one. State your location and your emergency," came the reassuring voice of a woman.

"My name is Lark Chadwick and I've just found a dead body."

"What's your location, ma'am?"

"I'm not sure. Don't you have GPS?"

"You're on a cell phone, so I can't pinpoint you. What's your location?" Her voice was steady. No emotion. No nonsense.

"I'm . . . I'm not sure. I was on the interstate and got off to go to the bathroom."

"Take a deep breath and try to calm down, ma'am. I need you to be more specific in case your call gets dropped."

I gulped some air, but my heart was still pounding.

"Were you on I-185?" the woman prompted.

"Yes," I said, getting my wits. "Northbound. No! Southbound. I was going south when I got off."

"Do you remember the exit number?" She was trying to sound patient, but I could hear exasperation seeping into her voice.

I shut my eyes and tried to concentrate. "Yes," I almost shouted. "It was exit 252."

"Okay. Thanks." There was a pause. "I've got someone heading that way now. Which way did you turn after you got off the interstate?"

"I turned right, then right again at the very next intersection. Then I turned left on the other side of a small bridge."

"Okay, okay. Slow down," she said. "I'm looking at a map. You would have gotten off onto Skunk Run Road--"

"Skunk Run. That's right. I remember."

"Creek Road is the first intersection. You turned . . . right?"

"Yes."

"How far did you go down Creek?"

"Not even half a mile. I went over a small bridge--"

"That would have been the east branch of the Chattahoochee River . . . ."

"Uh huh." *The what-a-hoo-chee?*

"And then you made a left?"

"Right. I mean, yes. I turned left."

"Okay. That's River Road. Then how far'd you go down River?"

"Not even a hundred yards before I found a clearing off to the left and turned in."

"There's a picnic table there, right?" she asked.

"Yes. Yes."

"Good. That's what I thought. I've been there."

"How soon will someone be here?" I pleaded, my voice shaking.

"In just a few minutes. I want you to stay on the line with me while I update the responding units, alright, hon?"

"Okayyy. I'm getting a little sp-spooked."

The line was quiet for a moment, but soon the dispatcher came back on. "Are you sure the person is dead, ma'am?"

"Yes, I'm pretty sure," I said, taking a tentative step closer to the body.

"Are you near the body now?" she asked, seemingly indifferent to my growing fear.

"Y-yes. Just a few feet away."

"Can you tell if the person is definitely dead?"

"I think so."

"I'm sending an ambulance, but I need to know for sure. I might need you to do CPR."

I felt my stomach tighten, but heard myself say, "Okay, lemme check."

I pressed the phone against my ear as I slowly approached the body. I held the flashlight as far out in front of me as I could. The girl was bobbing in a portion of the stream that had carved itself into the riverbank. Her corpse was slowly swirling counterclockwise in an eddy formed by the gnarled roots of a huge tree on the downstream side of me to my right. In just the few minutes since I'd found her, the strong current had caused the body to rotate nearly 180 degrees so that now the water was pushing her left side up against the sand where I stood. I assumed her hand must have brushed against my foot on an earlier rotation.

An expression of terror seemed frozen onto the girl's face. She wore a sleeveless checkered sundress, her long, blonde hair was splayed out like a sunburst behind her head. I picked up a stick and gently poked her side. She didn't react to my prodding.

"I just poked her with a stick," I told the 911 operator. "She's not moving at all. She's just lying on her back, eyes open, with an awful expression on her face."

"Okay. I'm going to update the units. Stay on the line, please." She must have put me on hold because I could no longer hear any background noise in my ear.

I continued to stare at the girl's body, trying to notice more details. As near as I could tell, there was no blood, but there were some angry bruises around her neck and at her throat. The girl's skin was ashen, but there didn't seem to be any decomposition. I looked for bullet or stab wounds, but saw none. Then something shiny alongside her head caught my eye. I leaned down to get a closer look.

A silver, tear-shaped earring dangled from her left earlobe. It resembled a fishing lure. I pointed the beam of my light at the right side of her head, but noticed that the other earring was missing. As I bent closer—my head directly over hers—I could see that her right earlobe was ripped in half, making me wonder if perhaps a fish may indeed have been attracted to her other earring. There didn't seem to be any blood oozing from the ragged flaps that had once been joined together to hold in place the now missing earring.

Suddenly, I remembered the strange lights of the car that had been parked on the bridge and had nearly run me off the road as I approached. Was that the murderer? Had he just finished dumping the body into the water when I came along? I hadn't gotten a good enough look at the car to be of any help to the police, but did the killer know that?

My mind began to spin macabre scenarios: Did the killer fear that he'd been recognized? Had he doubled back? Was he sneaking up behind me right now, getting ready to kill the only person who could put him at the scene of the crime?

"Hello?" I shouted into the phone to the 911 operator. "Are you there?"

She wasn't. The line hissed.

I was alone . . . except for a dead body lying at my feet in the dark.

THREE

JUST BEFORE I thought I'd lose it, I heard the comforting sound of a siren—actually a chorus of them. They got louder by the second. Soon the area was alive with blue, red, and white strobing lights and the crackling of police radios.

"Over here!" I hollered and waved my flashlight at the first cop to arrive as he got out of his car.

He hustled to me. I was surprised at how young he looked. I'm 27 and he seemed way younger than me. He reminded me of Rolf, the 17-year-old Hitler youth in the classic movie "The Sound of Music."

I pointed my light at the body. "Here she is."

Rolf pulled a flashlight from his belt and shined it onto the girl's face.

"This is 13 on the scene," he said into his radio. "She's definitely 10-7."

I knew from my days listening to the police scanner at the *Pine Bluff Standard* that 10-7 meant "ending tour of duty." It was a discreet way for the cops to communicate that they had a death on their hands, without prematurely tipping off the news media and having a swarm of reporters descend onto the scene. They rarely get their wish.

Rolf turned his attention to me. Before he spoke, he looked me up and down as if mentally undressing me. This happens to me a lot—and I hate it. "You're the one who called it in?" he asked, gazing admiringly at my ample chest—not my eyes.

"Um . . . I'm up here, officer," I said cocking my head and bending my knees to bring my eyes in alignment with his.

He lifted his gaze to meet my stare, but frowned, clearly annoyed that he'd been busted—so to speak. "You called it in, right?" he asked.

"That's right."

"And you are . . . ?" He took a small notebook and pen from his pocket.

"Chadwick. Lark Chadwick."

"Lark?" He raised his eyebrows like it was the dumbest name he'd ever heard. "Like the bird?"

"Something like that."

"Address?"

"I don't have one yet. I'm in the process of moving here from Wisconsin."

"Uh huh." He slapped his notebook shut. "I'm going to ask you to wait over here until the detectives arrive." Gently, but firmly, he took me by the arm and led me to his patrol car and opened a rear door.

"You're treating me like I'm under arrest." I'd been in that position before and it's no fun. "Am I?"

"No, ma'am." He paused for effect. "Not yet, at least." He gave me a twisted smile, as if he liked inflicting psychological pain. "The detectives will be here in just a few minutes."

Reluctantly, I climbed into the back seat of his car. He slammed the door. There were no handles on the inside and a wire mesh separated me from the front seat. I was locked in. Trapped.

"Great. Just frigging great," I muttered to myself.

Rolf walked back to the dead body, joining a few other cops standing there looking down at the girl. He must have said something funny because they all laughed and one guy slapped Rolf on the back. He'd probably made some wise-ass comment about taming the shrew. After a moment, they got to work unrolling yellow police tape, cordoning off the crime scene.

My reporter instincts kicked in. I dug into the front pocket of my jeans and pulled out my iPhone. I had the number of the newspaper preprogrammed from when I was interviewed for the job a few weeks earlier.

"Metro desk," said a harried female voice.

"Hi. This is Lark Chadwick. I'm your new cops and courts reporter."

She brightened. "Oh hi, Lark. I'm Marcie Peck. We haven't met yet, but I heard you were coming. What's up?"

"I know I'm not supposed to start until Monday, but I've got a story for you. I just discovered the body of what looks like a murdered teenage girl."

Marcie's affable voice suddenly became all business. "Where are you?"

"Just off the interstate near exit 252 on River Road."

"Okay," she said. "I'll send a photog. Where should I tell him to go?"

"Take Skunk Run to Creek." I paused so she could take notes. "Okay."

"Right on Creek."

"Uh huh."

"Go over a little bridge, then a quick left onto River Road . . . ." I waited for her next prompt.

"Then what?"

"Then another quick left into a picnic area beside the east branch of the Chatta-something River."

"Chattahoochee."

"Whatever."

She laughed. "You gonna handle the reporting from the scene?"

"Right. What's your deadline?"

"We've got about 45 minutes before the paper goes to bed, but we can get something on the website right away. Gimme a couple lines. I'll punch it up and get it out there."

"Let's see," I said, quickly trying to come up with a lead. "The body of what appears to be a teenage girl was discovered to-night—" I stopped. "What's the name of that river again?"

"Chatt-ah-HOO-chee," Marcie said, as if talking to an addled child. "It's Native American for 'let's see if we can trip up the *Sun-Gazette's* new cops and courts reporter,'" she chuckled.

I laughed. I liked Marcie. "You'll take care of the spelling, right?"

"Got yer back. Go on."

" . . . was discovered tonight along the banks of the Chatta-whichever River."

Marcie giggled.

"How far from Columbia am I, anyway?" I asked her.

"You're at the far northwest edge of the county. Still in our circulation area. 'Bout twenty miles north, I'd say."

"Okay. Thanks. Where was I?"

"Lost somewhere in the middle of your lead sentence along the banks of the Wherever River. Should I read it back to you?"

"Yeah. Thanks."

When she finished, I continued, "Police are on the scene now. There were no obvious bullet or stab wounds on the body, but bruises on the throat suggest the girl may have been strangled."

"Okay. Good stuff. I'll get this onto the website right away and we'll make a hole for it on the front page."

I made sure she had my cell phone number before we hung up, then I slumped back against the seat and watched, helplessly, as Rolf and his cop buddies finished cordoning off the area.

Soon a crime scene unit arrived. A photographer methodically took pictures of everything, including the body from almost every angle imaginable.

After a bit, Rolf and a man wearing civilian clothes came back to the car. Rolf opened my door. "Ma'am, would you step out of the vehicle, please?"

He didn't have to ask twice. I nearly dove out of my claustrophobic cage.

"This is Detective Benson," Rolf said. "He'll take it from here."

"Has she been locked in the back of your car all this time?" Benson asked Rolf.

"Yes, sir."

"Why? Is she a suspect?"

"I don't know, sir."

"You don't know?"

Rolf looked uncomfortable. "I started to interview her, sir, but when I learned she's not from these parts, I thought it best to park her in here until we had the crime scene secured and you had a chance to make the proper disposition."

"I see. Thank you, officer . . ." Benson looked at the cop's nametag. " . . . Hardin. That will be all."

"Yes, sir. Thank you, sir." Rolf, chastened, actually saluted before backing away, turning around and walking away from us as fast as he could.

Detective Benson held out his hand to me and I shook it. When he spoke, it was in a slow drawl. "Hello, Ms. Chadwick."

"Hi."

"I'm sorry for the inconvenience."

"Thanks."

He wore a sport coat over a polo shirt, khaki slacks and Docksides boat shoes. His hair was short, dark, and wavy, combed back. His chiseled good looks reminded me of Dick Tracey— without the hat. His eyes were sad as if he'd seen way more than a human being's normal allotment of suffering. I guessed him to be in his early forties.

"And your first name is Lark?"

"Yes."

"They tell me you're the one who discovered the body."

"That's right."

"Who were you here with?"

He's good, I thought to myself. He assumes I was here with some guy and by asking the question that way, he thinks he can trick me into revealing something.

"I was by myself," I replied.

"Why were you here by yourself in the middle of the night?" Benson asked, his dark eyes boring into mine.

I thought he was different than Rolf, but now he was pissing me off. "Am I a suspect?"

"At this point, everyone's a suspect."

"Do I have the right to remain silent?"

"Yes, you do." He showed his teeth, but it wasn't a smile. "And I have the right to take you downtown and hold you until we get this thing sorted out."

I considered that, but resisted the very strong temptation to dig in my heels just because I didn't like his style.

"That won't be necessary," I said wearily. "Let's just get this over with."

"So, why were you here?"

"I had to pee."

For the first time, his lips betrayed genuine mirth. "Uh huh."

"I didn't want anyone to see me, okay?"

"Of course," he smiled. "Before you discovered the body, did you see or hear anything suspicious?"

"Yeah, come to think of it." I told him about the car I'd seen on the bridge that sped away crazily, nearly running me off the road.

"Show me."

As we walked toward the road, Benson called to Rolf. "Have some of your guys come up here with us. We have to tape off another area."

We didn't speak during the few minutes it took for us to walk in the dark along River Road to where it intersected with Creek. A chorus of cicadas and crickets filled the silence.

As we got closer to the bridge, Benson said, "Tell me what you saw."

"I was coming from that way." I pointed down the road and across the bridge. "As I got closer to this bridge, I noticed a car parked right here." I pointed to the right side of the bridge next to a crumbling stone guardrail. I started to walk to the spot, but Benson grabbed me firmly by the arm.

"Don't go any farther," he said, sternly. "We don't want to contaminate the scene." Then, to Rolf and the three other cops who'd accompanied us, Benson said, "Cordon off the whole bridge, stem to stern, plus all the way back down to River Road."

"You got it," Rolf said, then he and the others walked to the intersection of River and Creek where a cop car was spurting blue light into the night. They opened the trunk and got more yellow tape.

Detective Benson turned his attention back to me. "Tell me more about what you saw."

It was an open-ended question, just the right kind to let the interviewee spill her guts.

I started to describe what I'd seen, but then stopped abruptly. "Aren't you going to take any notes?" I asked.

Benson tapped his right temple with his index finger. "It's all right in here." His eyes held mine. Pulsating lights from the nearby police car flashed kaleidoscopically across his face.

After I finished describing what I'd seen as I was driving toward the bridge, the detective spoke again. "Okay. Let's go back over that slowly," he said. "How far away were you when you first saw the vehicle?"

"It was almost immediately after turning off Skunk Run—maybe half a mile."

"How fast were you going?"

"Thirty or forty."

"Exactly how were the car's headlights configured?"

I closed my eyes, trying to get the image in my mind. "I see four headlights, almost evenly spaced, all in a line. At first, I thought it was two cars, side by side."

"Okay, good." He paused, thinking. "And you say the car pulled into your lane?"

"Right. It was like the driver was in such a hurry to get going that he briefly lost control and lurched into my lane before correcting and swerving back. At first, I thought he was trying to run me off the road."

"You had to take evasive action, correct?"

"Yeah. I started to. I slowed down and eased over as far as I could. The branches from that hedgerow scraped along the right side of my car," I said, pointing at the brush that hugged the edge of the road.

"What about when the car went past you? What did you notice?"

"Nothing. It was a blur. I tried to see into the car, but it went by too fast."

"Was there anything distinctive about the engine noise?"

"No. I don't even remember hearing any."

He took a flashlight from the pocket of his sport coat and walked slowly toward the side of the bridge, combing the pavement with the white light. If he found anything significant, I couldn't tell.

"Did you hear the sound of squealing tires?" he called over his shoulder.

"No. I was too far away and had my windows up. Did you find some skid marks?"

"Not sure what I've got here, yet. We'll have to wait and see what the crime scene geeks come up with." He walked back to me and turned off his light. "Let's go back down to the body." He pointed at Rolf and said to him, "C'mon."

The three of us retraced our steps in silence—except for the deafening night-country noise of the insects—but soon we became aware of a helicopter hovering overhead.

Detective Benson looked up and scowled. "Re*po*rters!"

"Got something against reporters?" I asked.

He didn't answer.

By the time we got back to the body, the crime scene was bathed in so much high-intensity light it was like high noon. All of Pearlie's doors were open, as well as the trunk, and at least three people were combing through the contents of my car.

"Hey!" I shouted. "I didn't give you permission to do a search."

"We don't need your permission, Miss," Rolf said. "We found it parked at the scene of a murder. That gives us probable cause to check it out."

"I told you. I stumbled onto the body by accident."

"Yes. You did *tell* us that," Rolf said. "And now they're checking out the accuracy of your statement. If there's any evidence the victim was ever in your car, you've got some serious explaining to do."

I fumed. "You're not gonna find anything." To prove my point, I stomped over to where the technicians were going through Pearlie. It felt as though they were violating a close member of my family—and in a way, they were. "So. Guys. What have you found?"

"Nothing, so far, ma'am," said one of the men. "Seems clean."

"There you have it. Satisfied?" I stood with my arms folded stubbornly, daring Rolf to respond.

"Any paint scratches on the passenger side?" Benson asked the technician.

"Yes, sir."

"Take some pictures, okay?" Benson said, "and then let's let Miss Chadwick have her car back."

"Yes, sir," the guy said.

Rolf's face darkened.

Benson turned to me and asked, "Do you mind looking at the body again?"

I scowled.

"You don't have to if you don't want."

"I don't mind," I said. I tried to sound nonchalant. It wasn't easy.

We walked to the body, now drenched in light. The thing that immediately struck me was how death profoundly changes the way a person looks. The young girl's skin seemed almost gray, ashen. Only a few hours earlier, she may have been laughing with friends. Now her face was hideous, contorted. One of her earlobes was torn in two, her neck badly bruised. I wondered who she was and who could have done this to her. And why.

"What can you tell just by looking?" I asked, trying to turn the tables on Benson.

"I try not to jump to quick conclusions," Benson said, slowly drawing out the long "U" in conclusions. "I just take it all in and let my subconscious go to work."

"Looks to me like she may have been strangled," I said, blatantly leading the witness.

He nodded. "Could be. Could be." He uprooted a blade of long grass and sucked thoughtfully on the bottom end. "Show me where you, ah, did your business just before you found her."

"You're standing on it," I smiled.

He jumped off it quickly and swore under his breath. In my terror when I discovered the body, I'd forgotten to bury the tissue I'd used. It was stuck to the bottom of Benson's Docksides. "What's this?" he asked, disgusted, peeling it from his sole and holding it up.

"It's what I, ah, wiped myself with."

He grimaced and dropped it. As it fluttered to the ground, he turned to the crime scene photog who was taking pictures. "Make sure the coroner analyzes this *litter*,"—he gave me a look—"and the sand to see if, indeed, it's a puddle 'o pee."

"Yes, sir," the guy replied.

Benson turned back to me and took out a notebook. "I'm gonna need to know how to reach you," he said.

I gave him my cell phone number. "Do you have a card?" I asked. "I may need to contact you, too."

He dug his wallet out of his back pocket, opened it, extracted a business card and handed it to me.

I studied it. "Don't you have email at the . . . " I looked at the card again, "Columbia County Sheriff's Department?"

He took the card back from me, wrote something on it, and handed it back. "I put my cell phone number on there, too," he said, "in case you think of anything else you want to add. But I'm not on Twitter just yet. Sorry."

I looked up at him.

He was smiling. "One more thing," he said. "What's your address?"

"I don't know yet."

"Excuse me?"

"I'm moving down here from Wisconsin to start my new job on Monday. Was gonna get a hotel room tonight and begin looking for an apartment tomorrow before I start work at the paper Monday."

"The paper?"

"At the *Sun-Gazette*."

"You a secretary?"

"Nope. Try again."

"You're not a reporter, are you?" he snarled.

"Cops and courts," I nodded—and grinned.

"Oh, shit."

"What's wrong with that?"

"It changes everything."

"Why? You gonna arrest me *now*?"

His smile had faded and storm clouds furrowed his brow. "We need to set some ground rules here."

"What do you mean?"

"You know way more details than any other person in the community, reporters included." He looked disparagingly at the chopper still hovering overhead.

"I kind of like those odds," I smiled.

"There are some details you know that only the killer does. And there are other details about the crime that the killer doesn't know that we know."

"What do you mean?"

"Like the car on the bridge. If the killer knew you saw a car, your life could be in danger."

"Why do you say that?"

"Witness elimination. If he thinks there's a chance you recognized him . . . ." He didn't finish the sentence, but ran his thumb across the front of his neck. "Next—the earring. Let's say that he killed her in his car during a struggle and the earring came loose and fell to the floor, but he doesn't know it. If he reads your story and finds out there's a missing earring, it could tip him off to clean out his car. You following me?"

"Uh huh."

"And then there are the bruises on her neck."

"What about 'em?"

"Let's say she was strangled."

"Okay."

"The killer knows that cuz he did it."

"Right."

"The police know it cuz it's fairly obvious."

"Right."

"But no one else knows."

"So?"

"Two things: there's less of a risk of a copycat to gum up the investigation . . . and, two—if, by some miracle, somebody confesses, we'll know we have the right guy because he'll have the inside info that only the killer possesses. See?"

"Right, but you're a little late on the strangulation thing."

"What do you mean?"

"I already called in the initial bulletin on my cell phone while I was trapped in the back seat of that cop car," I said, jabbing a finger at Rolf's cruiser. "The story's probably on the Web by now."

For the first time, Benson raised his voice. "Are you trying to botch this investigation?"

I took a step toward him. "Are you suggesting I shouldn't do my job?"

"You can do your job, but you need to do it responsibly."

I glared at him.

"Reporters," he spat.

FOUR

TWO HOURS LATER I was sipping a glass of wine with Marcie Peck in the living room of her downtown apartment. When I'd called the paper again from the crime scene to update my story, she'd invited me to crash on her couch until I could find a place of my own.

Marcie lived in a cozy one-bedroom apartment above a hundred-year-old furniture store on Broad Street. Loud music pulsed from several bars—a typical Saturday night

"Doesn't all the noise keep you awake at night?" I held aside a white sheer curtain and looked down onto the clots of young people roaming the street below.

"Nah. Lots of times I'm right down there in the thick of it," she laughed.

I shuddered. "Not me." I let the curtain drop back into place.

"Why not?"

"It's such a meat market." I turned away from the bay window and flopped onto the couch in front of it. Marcie sat across from me in an easy chair with robin's-egg blue stripes that matched the accent color of the wall to my left, on which hung a Degas print of a delicate ballerina.

"A meat market?" She looked offended.

"Yeah. I much prefer a deep, one-on-one conversation rather than some frat boy's superficial pick-up lines."

Marcie sighed. "Sometimes, I long to hear just one pick-up line."

"Oh, come on. You're just being modest."

"Look at me, Lark. I could certainly stand to lose a few," she pouted.

She had a point. She was a little thick in the middle, had flabby arms, chipmunk cheeks, and the beginnings of a double chin.

"You have a pretty face and great curves. I'm sure there are a lot of guys who find you quite bewitching." I smiled at her hopefully trying to bring her out of her self-induced funk, but when she frowned into her wine glass I realized I'd just said a stupid thing and instantly regretted it.

"Refill?" she asked, diplomatically changing the subject. She lifted the half-full bottle of Riesling off the coffee table between us and angled the neck toward me.

"Sure. Thanks." I held out my glass and she topped it off.

"Got a boyfriend?" she asked as she poured herself more wine.

"I did, but it . . . um . . . ended." I took a sip, hoping she'd change the subject.

"Awww. That's too bad." She set the wine bottle on a coaster. "You get dumped?"

"He was murdered," I said simply.

Marcie's eyes widened and her mouth fell open. "Oh my God. How horrible." She leaned forward and rested her elbows on her plump knees. "How did it happen?"

Her abruptness made me wince. "The short answer is he was pushed off a cliff."

She leaned closer, a look of genuine concern furrowing her brow. "Oh, Lark. I'm *so* sorry." Her voice was soft. Caring.

"Thanks," I said, taking another sip that bordered on being a gulp.

Marcie sat back. "You seem so upbeat and confident. I *never* would have suspected anything so traumatic had just happened to you."

"Well, it's been a year."

"Ah," she said, relaxing. "Time does heal, doesn't it?"

"Oh, I'm not so sure. It's still pretty painful."

She nodded and sipped her wine. "Did they catch the guy who did it?"

I gave her a curt nod, but I knew that if we got much deeper into this, I'd begin weeping.

"What was your boyfriend's name?" she asked gently.

"Ja—" Tears instantly flooded my eyes. I clenched a fist. "Jason," I finally managed to whisper. It was the first time in months that I'd said his name out loud.

"Ohhh . . . ." Marcie moaned. "Here." Quickly, she handed me the cocktail napkin she'd been holding.

I took off my glasses and dabbed my eyes, then held up a hand like a traffic cop. "I really don't want to talk about it, Marcie. I'm sorry. Maybe some other time?" I gave her a weak smile.

"Sure. Of course. I'm sorry."

We sat in uncomfortable silence. The only intrusion came from the thumping bass of a band playing in the bar across the street. Finally, after collecting myself, I asked, "What about you? Got a boyfriend?"

She flinched and pursed her lips. "Sort of."

"That doesn't sound too encouraging," I managed a chuckle to lighten the mood, but it felt mirthless.

"Things were serious for awhile, but lately he's gotten . . ." she paused, looking for the right word, "inattentive."

"Oh, that's too bad." I shook my head sympathetically. "How'd you meet?"

She sat thoughtfully for a moment, gazing into space, her face curtained by her long, dark hair. She gathered a fistful of it and absentmindedly stroked it with both hands. "Long story," she said, finally. "Another time, maybe."

"Sure." I couldn't tell by her tone if she was genuinely putting me off—or putting me down by throwing my own words back at me. I chose to assume the former.

The steady *thumpetta-thumpetta* from the street below got me thinking about Madison again. "Even though I never liked the bar scene," I said, trying to fill the silence, "I miss Madison."

"What was it like working with Lionel Stone?" Marcie leaned forward "That must've been awesome."

"How'd you know I worked with Lionel?"

"Oh, they sent around a big memo about you, telling the staff that you'd been hired. You're a big deal here, Lark. Your exploits precede you."

"Uh oh." I made a face. "No pressure having to live up to my advance billing, huh?"

We both laughed.

"So, tell me," Marcie pressed, "what's Lionel Stone really like?"

I smiled. "Lionel's wonderful."

"But what's he *like*?"

"Grumpy is the first word that comes to mind," I laughed.

Marcie placed her finger delicately on the lip of her wine glass and slowly circled the rim. "Did he ever come on to you?" She looked at me coyly.

"Eww. No." I wrinkled my nose. "Not even close. He's got to be in his seventies, Marcie. And he's married."

"Doesn't matter." She arched one eyebrow and waved her hand dismissively. "All men are cretins."

"Many," I corrected. "Maybe even most, but definitely not all." It was reassuring to hear myself say that. Five years earlier, when I'd been assaulted by my English professor, I would have readily agreed with Marcie. But Jason and Lionel had helped me see that good men are still out there. They're just hard to find. I began to have at least a bit of hope I might find someone as good as Jason in this fresh start in a new city.

"And don't call me Marcie. Call me Marce. Everyone else does." She smiled and took a swig.

"So, Marce," I said, "I don't hear much of a Southern accent. Where'd you grow up?"

"Raised in Ohio, but my folks moved to Atlanta when I was in high school."

"Where'd you go to college?"

"University of Georgia."

"In Atlanta?"

"Athens. It's about an hour-and-a-half east of Atlanta."

"Journalism major?"

She nodded. "This is my first job. Did an internship here during the last semester of my senior year. They hired me as a freelancer when I graduated. Entry level. No benefits."

"How long ago was that?"

"Two years. It took a year before they brought me on fulltime."

"You're what? Twenty-four?"

"Uh huh." She gave me an appraising look. "You're older, though, right?"

I frowned. "Does it show?"

She laughed. "God, no. You're gorgeous."

"Good recovery," I chuckled.

"You just seem so . . . mature."

I smiled. "Thanks. If you must know, I'm twenty-seven." Saying my age out loud caused me to shudder. "Geez," I said, more to myself. "I'm closer to thirty than to twenty-one."

Marcie nodded, a thoughtful, forlorn look on her face. "Did you major in journalism, too?"

"Nope. English. But I needed some time away from the books," I said, deftly sidestepping having to explain the assault. "Took a year off before graduating. Waited on tables and wrote a novel."

"Really? A novel?" Marcie leaned forward again.

I nodded and laughed. "It sucks so bad, no one wants to publish it. One rejection letter calls it 'an anti-male rant.' Another says I have serious 'trust issues with men.'"

"Welcome to the club," Marcie said, ruefully.

We both laughed and clinked our glasses together.

"So, how'd you get into journalism?" Marcie drained the rest of her drink, then poured the remainder of the bottle equally into our glasses.

"I stumbled into it. I met Lionel when I was doing research into the car accident that killed my parents when I was an infant."

"Oh my God. You're an *orphan?*"

Her bluntness took me aback. "Well, yeah. I guess. I mean, I've never defined myself in such stark terms."

Marcie waved her hands, palms forward, trying to erase her words as they hung between us. "Sorry. Lemme back up. That didn't come out right. It's the headline writer in me, automatically looking for the grabbiest way to summarize a story."

"That's okay," I smiled. I didn't want to let Marcie deeper into my private life by telling her about the carbon monoxide poisoning that took the life of Annie, my dad's sister—the woman who raised me. Finding her body—and Jason's six months later—were two of the lowest points of my life. I quickly changed the subject. "I know you do more than write headlines. What exactly is your job description at the paper?" I asked.

Marcie made a face and stood up. "I'm sort of a glorified desk assistant." She picked up her glass and the empty wine bottle and walked to the kitchen.

I stood. "What's a desk assistant?" I picked up my nearly empty glass and followed her.

She dropped the bottle into a recycle bin where it clanked loudly against several other discarded wine bottles. She opened a cupboard door and surveyed the shelves. It looked like a well-stocked liquor store with bottles of various sizes and colors. "Let's try some Cabernet." She removed a bottle. "A desk assistant. Let's see . . . ." She took a corkscrew out of a drawer. "I'm on call twenty-four/seven . . . I answer the phones . . . I do what I'm told . . . ."

"Sounds like you're not thrilled with it," I said, taking a sip from my glass.

She shrugged and dug the metal spiral into the cork, then began vigorously twisting. "It's not that I don't like it. I get to write and at least do some newsgathering, but it's not enough and it's all from the desk." She made a little grunt as she pulled the cork from the bottle with a *pop*. "Ready yet?" She held the bottle out toward me.

"Sure." I downed what was left of my Riesling, then gratefully held out my glass as she sloshed the blood-red liquid into it, then poured herself a generous refill. "You want to get out of the office and into the field?" I asked as she poured.

She nodded decisively.

"Why won't they let you?"

"Ed says I need more 'seasoning.'"

"Who's Ed?"

"Ed Richards." She scowled. "My boss. He's the Metro Editor—and your boss, too, come to think of it. Didn't he hire you?"

I shook my head. "I was hired by Elmer Wiesenthal."

"Ah. Mister Big." Marcie raised her glass in a toast. "The publisher himself. How'd you manage to swing that?"

"Lionel put me in touch with him. They go way back. We talked on the phone and before I hung up, I had a job offer."

"Nice," Marcie said without much enthusiasm. "It's all about who you know."

I could tell she was getting a little buzzed, so I let the remark pass.

"Do you like working at the paper?" I asked.

Marcie furrowed her brow and squinted her eyes, but said nothing.

"Uh oh. Did I make a mistake taking this job?"

She shrugged. "I'll be honest. Things aren't good. It's a snake pit right now. There've been layoffs and there are rumors of more."

"How can that be? I just got hired."

"Sam Erickson, the guy you're replacing? He'd been on the police beat for more than twenty years. They bought him out and brought you in to replace him. I'm sure you're way cheaper than him. No offense."

"Geez, I had no idea." I'd been spoiled working for Lionel Stone at the tiny *Pine Bluff Standard,* where there's no political intrigue, just Lionel, his wife Muriel, and a great learning experience. This would be much, *much* different.

As I pondered my nearly empty wine glass, I wondered what the future would hold—and worried.

FIVE

Marcie and I called it a night about two in the morning. Even though I was exhausted, I had trouble sleeping. I couldn't get the image of the dead girl's face out of my mind. Her particularly gruesome expression didn't help: eyes and mouth wide open in horror. I thought at the time that I was tough enough to handle it, but in the predawn darkness, her image haunted me.

By seven, I was up, restlessly searching Marcie's kitchen. I found what I needed and made coffee. What I really needed was a handful of aspirin—my head was throbbing from all the wine we drank just a few hours earlier.

While the coffee was brewing, I padded down the hardwood stairs to the street level entrance and found that the paper had been delivered. I slid off its plastic covering and scoured the front page to see if my story was there. I found it above the fold, upper left. I'd had very little information by the time the paper went to bed, so there wasn't too much substance in my piece. It was similar to what I'd written for the Web, but the style was more formal and there was one notable addition:

GIRL'S BODY FOUND

By

Lark Chadwick

Sun-Gazette Staff Writer

The body of a young girl was found along the banks of the Chattahoochee River about 10 o'clock last night.

Police said it did not appear that the girl had been dead for very long.

The body was discovered by *Sun-Gazette* reporter Lark Chadwick in a picnic area on River Road near the Skunk Run Road exit off I-185 about 20 miles north of Columbia, just downstream from a narrow bridge on Creek Road. (See map)

It was cool to see my name in the byline, but I was a little irked that someone, Marcie I presumed, inserted my name as the person who'd discovered the body. I saw that as a tidbit the killer might find useful, perhaps to my detriment. I resolved to ask Marcie about it later.

Marcie had worked with graphics to come up with a basic map that showed the place where the body had been found. A picture I'd taken of the scene—a wide shot of the police at work—accompanied the story. The caption read, *Police investigate the death of a teenage girl whose body was found along the Chattahoochee late last night.* I also got a "photo by Lark Chadwick" credit.

The name of the girl has not been released pending notification of next of kin.

It appeared that the girl was in her mid-to-late teens. Bruises on the throat suggest the girl may have been strangled.

Detective Matt Benson of the Columbia County Sheriff's Department would not speculate on the cause of death until the results of an autopsy are complete later today.

The picture and the map, plus the large headline, gave the impression of more substance than there actually was.

After reading the story while sitting on the stairs, I bounded back up to the apartment, satisfied that I'd gotten my first byline at my new job on a big front-page story, yet troubled by the death of such a young girl. I quickly showered, threw on my jeans and a denim work shirt, poured myself a mug of coffee, and hit the street. Since Marcie was still asleep, I left the brewer turned on so she'd have hot coffee when she got up.

Driving back to the scene to take some daylight pictures, I felt a tinge of guilt as I passed people dressed in their Sunday finery heading to the many churches I passed. I was raised Episcopalian, but ever since my Aunt Annie's tragic death, I hadn't been on speaking terms with the Almighty—unless I was in a jam—then we were really tight. And I seemed to get into tight spots all the time, so I guess you could say we kept in touch regularly.

Even so, I'd hoped that my move south could also result in a fresh start with me finding a church home, but it wasn't going to happen on this beautiful Sunday morning. I wanted to check out the crime scene and see if the cops had identified the girl yet—and maybe even found the killer.

The area was still cordoned off with yellow tape and guarded by a police car when I arrived. This time the cop keeping an eye on things from behind the wheel wouldn't let me cross the threshold into the crime scene even though I told him I was the one who discovered the body. The fact that I'm a reporter didn't help much, either. When the cop realized I was with the

Sun-Gazette, he unceremoniously closed his car's power window, stopping the frigid flow of his air conditioner from chilling the already-humid morning.

I took a few pictures of the cop car and the taped off area, and also got a wide shot of the taped-off bridge.

My cell phone rang as I was heading back toward Columbia. I didn't recognize the number, but answered anyway: "Lark Chadwick."

"Hey, Lark, it's Ed Richards," said a jovial voice.

"Oh, hi!"

"I'm the editor of the Metro page at the *Sun-Gazette*."

"I know. It's good to finally speak with you."

"I just wanted to thank you for the great work you did for us last night."

"Thanks." I suddenly felt tongue-tied.

"You went above and beyond the call of duty, young lady. I know you're not even supposed to start work until tomorrow."

"That's okay. I figured I'd stumbled onto a big story, so I just did what came naturally and called the desk."

"Good job."

"Th-thanks," I managed to stammer.

"So, where do things stand now? Do we have an ID on the girl yet? What are the cops saying?"

"You're reading my mind. Those are the questions I'm trying to answer right now. I've already been to the scene and taken some pictures."

"That's great. Email 'em to the desk right away so they can get them onto our website."

"Okay."

"Once you find out who the girl is, go talk to the parents."

"Are you serious?"

"Deadly."

"But that's—" I paused. The first word that popped into my head was ghoulish, but it didn't seem very diplomatic. "It's kind of, um, invasive, don't you think?"

"Not if you're sensitive about it. You'd be surprised. Some people find that talking at a time like this is very therapeutic."

I wasn't convinced, but he was the boss. "Okay." I tried to sound upbeat so Ed wouldn't think I was being a diva.

"Oh. And one more thing: If you're able to score an interview with the family, keep an eye on the dad."

"How come?"

"He could very well be a suspect."

"Ya think?"

"Sure. The cops are looking at all kinds of different angles, including the possibility that she was in an abusive situation."

"If you say so . . . ."

"You have any plans for later this afternoon?"

"Depends on what I find out, I guess."

"Come by the house about five. My wife and I are throwing a little barbecue. It'll give me a chance to introduce you to some other members of the staff before you hit the ground running tomorrow, your first *official* day at work," he chuckled.

"That would be great. Thanks."

I pulled over to the side of the road to write down the directions he gave me.

"Do you need me to bring anything?" I asked.

"Nope. Just yourself. It's BYOB, though."

"Okay. See you tonight. And thanks for the call."

I hung up feeling a sense of satisfaction, encouraged that I was working for an organization that at least *seemed* to value me.

SIX

AFTER HANGING UP with Ed Richards, I sat behind the wheel for a moment and thought about what my next move should be. Pearlie and I were parked along Veterans Highway at Townline Road. Traffic lights dangled above the intersection that was busier than I expected. Services at the Baptist church on the corner had just ended and a policeman was on Townline directing traffic so that cars could get out of the church parking lot.

I decided to phone Matt Benson, the detective. He answered on the first ring.

"It's Lark Chadwick at the *Sun-Gazette*, Detective. Sorry to bother you on a Sunday morning." I glanced at my watch—ten o'clock. "I hope I'm not calling too early."

"Nope. Been up for awhile." He drew out the "while" syllable so that it sounded like *whahhl*. "What can I do for ya?" He sounded tired and distracted.

"Has the girl's body been identified?"

"Yep. I'm at the morgue where the dad just made a positive ID."

"What's her name?"

I could hear him rustling through papers. "Let's see . . . . Luanne Rae Donovan, age 15."

"Awww. So young."

Benson grunted, in agreement, I assumed.

"Can you spell the name for me, please?" I asked.

He did.

"Got a cause of death yet?"

"Not yet. Autopsy's due to start any minute."

"How long do you think it'll last?"

"Couple hours, maybe."

"Can I watch?"

Benson burst out laughing. "No. But nice try."

"Was she sexually assaulted?"

"Dunno. That's another one for the coroner to answer."

"What's the girl's address?"

"Oh, um, I meant to give you that, too. It's . . . . " More paper rustling, "2217 Longview Trail. It's a trailer park at the north end of the county, not too far from where you found her."

"Anyone in custody? Any suspects?"

"No one in custody. No comment on suspects."

"Got leads?"

"Yes, we're tracking down a few."

"Can you be more specific?"

"Yes."

Silence. Crickets.

"*Will* you be more specific?" I pressed.

"No."

"Why not?" I tried not to sound petulant.

Benson's voice took on an edge. "C'mon. Do I need to spell it out for you?"

"A girl can ask," I laughed, trying to break the tension. "Had . . ." I flipped back a page in my notebook, "Luanne Rae Donovan been reported missing?"

"Yes. She'd been sent to the store to get a gallon of milk. When she didn't come back, her mother got worried and called the police."

I scribbled as fast as I could in my long, thin reporter's notebook, hoping I'd be able to decipher my notes later. "What time did she leave home and where did she go to get the milk?" I asked, still writing.

"She left home about nine o'clock last night and went to the 7-ELEVEN near her home."

"What's the address of the 7-ELEVEN?"

Benson sighed. More paper shuffling. "Intersection of Skunk Run and Route 155."

"How'd she get there?"

"Walked. It's about a quarter mile from her house."

"Did she get to the store and buy the milk?"

"She did. She arrived there about nine-twenty."

"How do you know?"

"Um . . . ." Benson hesitated.

"Surveillance tape?" It was a guess.

He snorted. "You're good."

"What does it show?"

"It shows her making her purchase and leaving the premises."

"Anything unusual on the tape?"

"There doesn't appear to be, but we're still studying it."

"Can I have a copy?"

"We're not planning to release it."

"Why not? Maybe someone out there might see something significant."

"Maybe, but we're not ready to put it out there."

"But you might?"

"Maybe. That's as far as I can go."

"Did you find the gallon of milk?"

"Negative."

"What do you think happened to it?"

"The killer probably took it home and drank it."

I sighed. "Okay . . . . Um . . . ." My mind raced. I was trying to come up with the perfect question to get Benson to divulge the key clue that would solve the mystery. My mental inventory came up blank, so I settled for nuts and bolts: "Are you the lead investigator?"

"I am."

"How many other people are working with you on this?"

He chuckled. "That's classified, but let's put it this way—enough to find the bastard."

"Was Luanne last seen at the 7-ELEVEN or were there later sightings?"

"As far as we know, no one saw her after that."

"When was she reported missing?"

"Around eleven, which was about an hour after you found the body."

"How come her mom waited so long to call the cops?"

"The mom says she got worried about ten when her daughter hadn't gotten home. First, she made phone calls to neighbors and the girl's friends, and then she went out looking on her own before she called us."

"Did the dad join in on the search?"

"As far as I know, yeah."

I hesitated, then plunged ahead. "Is the dad . . ." I paused . . . "a suspect?"

"No comment on suspects, remember?"

"Won't confirm. Won't deny." I said in a voice that let Benson know that's what I was writing in my notebook.

Matt Benson's voice turned icy. "No, Miss Chadwick. I specifically said *no comment*." He spoke the last two words slowly and distinctly, pausing for emphasis between "no" and "comment."

"Okay. Gotcha. Thanks for clarifying." I scratched out what I'd written and scrawled his exact quote, then circled and underlined it.

"Any idea how long the girl had been dead when she was found?" I asked.

"The coroner might be able to give us something more definitive, but probably not all that long. Less than an hour's my guess—but it's just a guess."

"Was she strangled or did she drown?"

"I'll let the coroner make that call."

"Maybe she was strangled *and* drowned?"

"Dunno. We all just have to wait and be patient." Ironically, Benson's voice was beginning to take on a tone of exasperated *im*patience.

"Okay." I'd run out of questions, anyway. "This is all very helpful, Detective Benson. I'll check back with you later, after the autopsy." Before I could say thank you, he'd hung up.

It was already dawning on me that the pace of working for a daily paper in Georgia, a place I'd always assumed was slow and backwards, was going to be much faster than at a weekly newspaper in Pine Bluff, Wisconsin. Quickly, I pulled my laptop out of my messenger bag and typed up my notes. I had to slide my driver's seat way back to have room to work. I decided to leave out Benson's "no comment" to my question about Luanne's dad being a possible suspect. Instead, I wrote, "Columbia County Detective Matt Benson said police are 'tracking down a few' leads, but he had no comment on any possible suspects."

After about fifteen minutes of writing, I was done. I called the desk to see how to go about filing what I had. As it turned out, I didn't have all the necessary equipment I would need to file from the field, but I was right outside a Starbucks that had Wi-Fi, so I was able to duck in there to email in my story for the website. I also emailed the pictures I'd taken at the scene earlier that morning.

While I was on the phone with the desk, I told the editor—I think his name was Paul—that I was going to go out to Luanne Donovan's house and try to interview her parents. He assigned me a photographer.

"You'll be working with Doug Mitchell," Paul said. "You're lucky he's on-call today. He's our best."

I gave the editor the address of the Donovans' trailer and told him I'd meet Doug Mitchell there. I gave Paul my cell phone number and he gave me Doug's.

After hanging up, I typed the Donovans' address into my iPhone's GPS and got a routing on how to get there from where I was. I'd been in that general area earlier and now had to backtrack.

Twenty minutes later, I found a place to park a little ways down the street from the Donovans' trailer. I decided to wait for Doug Mitchell rather than charging in on my own. Besides, I was very uncomfortable having to do this angle of the story at all. Too many times in my life, *I'd* been the next of kin or the grieving loved one. At those times, I just wanted to be alone, free to wail and curse and generally lose it. But, when Jason died, Lionel and Muriel had been there for me because I could barely function at all.

Part of me hoped Luanne's parents would simply say they didn't want to talk and would I please go away. But the other side of me—the side personally invested in this story—*needed* to know who Luanne Rae Donovan was. I would never know her as a living being, but now part of my job would be to bring her to life for my readers—and myself. And, perhaps just as importantly, to find out who had the audacity to believe they had the right to bring that life to such a sudden and violently premature end.

I checked my hair in the rearview mirror. Chia Pet, as usual. But the stern expression on my face surprised me. That's when I knew I was deeply committed to finding Luanne's killer.

SEVEN

The trailer Luanne Rae Donovan called home was at the end of a dusty street at the edge of a field, just off Route 155. I'd passed the 7-ELEVEN on my way and made a mental note to return with my photog after talking with the family.

The day was already getting hot, so I sat in Pearlie with the engine running, the windows up, and the air conditioner going full blast. While waiting for Doug Mitchell, I watched as small groups of people came and went from the home. Most people carried what looked like casserole dishes. Many of the women who left the trailer were wiping their eyes. I got the impression that people here stuck together.

My stomach churned as I contemplated approaching the home of complete strangers going through the worst crisis anyone can imagine—the violent murder of a child. I sat there slightly annoyed at Ed Richards, my new boss, for pointing me in this direction. I feared the family would think I was a vulture. And I was also still stewing about what Marcie had said about the *Sun-Gazette* being a "snake pit." I was beginning to have second thoughts about my impetuous decision to abandon my comfortable job working for Lionel Stone so that I could advance my career.

The bleating of my cell phone brought me back to the present.

"This is Lark," I answered.

"Hey, Lark, it's Doug, your photog *du jour*. Where are ya?"

His upbeat voice was pure velvet. A fleeting image of a hot-bod lifeguard flashed through my head. "I'm parked in front of the Donovans' waiting for you. Do you have the address?"

"Yeah. Do you drive a yellow VW Beetle?" Doug asked.

"Right. How'd you know?"

"Turn around."

I looked into my rearview mirror, but only saw the grill of a vehicle parked directly behind me.

"To your left," the voice said.

I turned.

A bug-eyed face, contorted and grinning maniacally, filled the driver's side window just inches in front of me.

I recoiled and let out a frightened yelp.

The man's face, cell phone pressed against an ear, burst out laughing.

I turned away and caught my breath. My momentary terror turned to anger as I mashed my finger against the red *end call* bar. I turned off the ignition, quickly composed myself, and shoved open the door, wearing an exaggerated smile on my face.

Doug, still laughing, stood back as I got out. "Sorry. Didn't mean to give you such a scare."

"Yes, you did." I was grinning, but there was ice in my voice.

He shrugged. "I like to make a memorable entrance." He held out his hand. "I'm Doug. Truce?"

To make him uncomfortable, I waited a few beats. "I'm Lark," I said, coolly. Finally, I shook his hand. "We'll see about the truce." His hand was warm and rough, but I was thankful for the gentle rather than bone-crushing grip I was expecting.

"My gear's back here," he said, ambling toward the olive green Jeep Wrangler parked directly behind Pearlie. He walked with a slight limp.

I noticed right away that he filled out his Army T-shirt in all the right places. His thick, dark, wavy hair was parted down the middle and swept back at the top of his ears. Form-fitting jeans and hiking boots completed the ensemble. In short, he looked as attractive as he sounded. I just wished he wasn't such a creep.

I waited for him in the no-man's land between our two vehicles while he pulled his camera out of a bag in the back of the Jeep.

"Thanks for coming," I said.

"It's my job." Still grinning, he put a Nikon around his neck with a thick strap that looked like a Native American beaded belt of white and turquoise.

I guessed him to be about ten years older than me. He stood a foot taller than my 5'2" frame, had chocolate brown eyes, a stubble beard—and no wedding ring.

As he walked toward me, Doug looked me up and down, then, with a flirty, Matthew McConaughey drawl, said, "So, you're the new hotshot reporter from the North." Then, more to himself, he added, "*Definitely* an improvement." He stopped a few feet from me, looked me in the eye and beamed, "So, what's the plan?"

I turned away in disgust at being objectified by a man yet again and led him toward the driveway. "For starters," I said, pointing, "we need an exterior shot of the house." I turned around and, walking backwards as he followed, asked with a condescending edge, "You do know what the story is, right?"

"Yep. Follow-up to the body you found last night, right?"

"Right." I turned my back on him and continued walking and pointing. "This is where she lived. I'll wait until you get a couple exteriors, then we'll see if the family will talk." I stopped, turned to him, and put my hands on my hips. "Any questions?"

"Nope." He glided past me toward the driveway, his head cocked toward the Donovans' white doublewide as he sized up his shot. He stopped, crouched and squeezed off a few frames. It looked to me like he had the mailbox in the foreground and the house behind it.

I walked closer and read the name *Donovan* on the mailbox. A Confederate flag was painted on the side. "Looks like you got a good shot," I said. "I really don't want to intrude on these people."

"I know. It's the worst part of the job. But ya just gotta suck it up and do it."

"Don't you just feel like a voyeur?" I asked as we walked slowly up the driveway.

"They pay me to look at stuff, so I'm okay with it."

I knocked lightly on the screen door. A middle-aged woman wearing a gray running suit opened it. Her eyes were damp and red.

"Mrs. Donovan?" I asked.

"Yes."

"I'm Lark Chadwick from the *Sun-Gazette*. I'm SO sorry to bother you at a time like this. May I ask you a few questions about Luanne?"

She hesitated, a look of alarm on her face.

"I'm the one who discovered Luanne's body last night," I added, hoping that connection might win me some points.

Quickly her hand shot to her mouth and she bit her knuckle to keep from sobbing. "Come in," she said softly, opening the door.

"Thank you." We stepped inside. "This is Doug Mitchell, my photographer."

Doug touched her hand. "I'm sorry for your loss, ma'am."

"Do you have to take pictures?" she asked plaintively.

He shook his head. "Not if you don't want us to." His voice was gentle.

"We can just talk," I added.

"Can I get you anything?" she asked.

"No, thank you," I said. "We really don't want to intrude."

"Come and sit down." Mrs. Donovan led us to the living room.

The trailer was more spacious than I expected—and immaculate. The dining room table had dozens of casserole and fruit salad dishes on it, left by the parade of people I'd been watching come and go. An air conditioner in a picture window blasted mercifully cool air into the living room. The window allowed in plenty of light, and the white walls helped make the place cheerier. This family was going to need a *lot* of brightness, I thought to myself.

A florid man lounged in a huge recliner in a corner of the living room facing a bald man and a plump woman who sat on a large sofa. The couple looked as though they'd just come from church. He wore a brown sport coat and tie and she wore a conservative light blue two-piece suit.

As we entered the living room, the man and woman stood. They seemed relieved at having an excuse to bolt from a socially awkward situation. "We'll get out of your way," the woman said to us, then turned to Mrs. Donovan. "We just wanted to stop by to let you know we're praying for you." She embraced Mrs. Donovan and the two women hugged and cried for a long moment.

The man in the recliner didn't get up, so the guy wearing the sport coat stepped to the chair and the two men grimly shook hands.

The couple nodded briefly at Doug and me and then let themselves out.

"This is Buddy, my husband," Mrs. Donovan said, gesturing in his direction. "They're with the newspaper," she said to him.

Buddy shook hands with us. He wore a tattered short-sleeved shirt and faded trousers. A tattoo of an eagle in flight sprouted from his left forearm. He looked to be about 40. His two most prominent features were his large belly and his flushed face, roadmapped with numerous broken capillaries. He held a can of beer in his hand.

"I'm so sorry for your loss, Mr. Donovan," I said.

He shrugged listlessly. "Can I getcha a beer?" He looked mostly at Doug.

"No, thanks," Doug said.

"Please sit down," Mrs. Donovan said, gesturing toward the couch.

Doug and I sat next to each other. Mrs. Donovan sat on the edge of a chair just to my left.

"Do you think Luanne suffered?" Mrs. Donovan asked me immediately after sitting down. Worry lines etched her face, and she leaned toward me, anxious for any detail I could supply.

I heaved a heavy sigh. I didn't want to lie, but I didn't want to add to the agony of the girl's parents, either. "Maybe," I said. "But I hope that if she did suffer, it was mercifully brief."

"But why? *Why* did this happen to our little girl?" Her voice was earnest, pleading.

"I wish I knew." I shook my head slowly. "I think finding Luanne has given me a special connection to her. I really want to get to know her and I want our readers to know her, too. What can you tell me about her?"

"She was a wonderful girl," Mrs. Donovan began.

"Do you mind if I tape record our conversation?" I asked, pulling my iPhone out of my pocket. "I'll be able to quote you more accurately."

"Yes. That's fine."

I found the Voice Memo app and pressed *record*. "What can you tell me about your little girl?"

She immediately buried her face in her hands and sobbed, "My little girl. Oh, my little girl." Her whole body shook.

I wanted to reach out and touch her, but she was just out of my reach, so I simply sat there helplessly, waiting, feeling awkward and uncomfortable.

After a moment, she heaved a sigh and removed her hands from her tear-streaked face. I snatched a tissue from the box on the coffee table and handed it to her.

"Thank you," she said. "I'm sorry."

"That's okay," I said. "I can only imagine how excruciating this must be for you."

She dabbed at her eyes and then blew her nose.

When it looked as though she was a bit more composed, I tried again. "Did Luanne know what she wanted to be when she grew up?"

Her mother smiled wistfully. "That depended on the day of the week. One day she wanted to be a famous writer, the next a ballerina, but she kept coming back to detective. She seemed to want to go into law enforcement."

"Where do you suppose that idea came from?" I asked.

Mrs. Donovan slowly shook her head. "I haven't the slightest idea. She liked reading mysteries, so maybe it was there."

"What was her personality like?"

"Happy go lucky. Upbeat. She was always making new friends. I think she had a couple thousand friends on her Facebook page—including me."

"You sound surprised that Luanne friended you."

She nodded and smiled. "Pleased, too."

"Why?"

"It tells me she that she trusted me as a friend and that she didn't mind me seeing what she was up to."

"Did she have a boyfriend?"

"I think something was brewing," Mrs. Donovan smiled. "But she wouldn't tell us much. Said she didn't want to jinx it by broadcasting it online—or to us."

I nodded. "I know what you mean. She was only fifteen, though. Had she dated a lot?"

"More than I was comfortable with. She'd had puppy-love crushes in middle school, of course. But only one serious boyfriend—"

"The *African-American*," Mr. Donovan snarled with exaggerated sarcasm. He clearly would have preferred to use the N-word.

"Hush, now, Buddy. She broke up with him. Remember?"

"Thank God." He took a swig from the can and swished the beer around in his mouth before swallowing.

"She'd been dating Tyrone Jackson, the quarterback of the football team," Mrs. Donovan explained to me.

"Why'd she break up with him?" I asked.

Mrs. Donovan shrugged. "She never said. But I was relieved, too—and it had nothing to do with Mr. Jackson's skin color." She shot a reproachful look at her husband, who seemed more intent on reading the side of his beer can.

"Why were you relieved?" I asked.

"I was worried the relationship would go too far too fast. But I think Luanne was able to put on the brakes before things got out of hand."

"What else can you tell me about Luanne and what she was like?"

For the next several minutes, Mrs. Donovan talked lovingly of her daughter, painting a picture of a vibrant, gregarious young woman who had a bright future.

About fifteen minutes into our conversation, Doug asked the Donovans, "Would it be all right if I took some pictures while you keep talking? You won't even know I'm here." His soft voice and gentle tone made even me want to curl up in his lap.

"I suppose that would be okay." Mrs. Donovan looked over at her husband. "Buddy, what do you think, dear?"

"Sure. I guess," Mr. Donovan's mumbled response echoed in his beer can.

Doug got up from his perch on the couch and began to snap away.

"Do you have a picture of Luanne?" I asked Mrs. Donovan.

"I have oodles." She got up and fetched a family photo album from a nearby bookshelf. She brought it to me then sat next to me on the couch and opened the book so that we could look at it side by side.

"This is her school picture," Mrs. Donovan said, pointing at a photo in the album.

Luanne Rae Donovan was pretty. She had straight, blonde, shoulder-length hair, a wide smile and bright blue eyes. I nearly gasped at the contrast between the exuberance radiating from her picture, and the grotesque, lifeless form I'd stumbled upon just twelve hours earlier. The picture and the hideous corpse bore almost no resemblance to one another.

"May I get a shot of that?" Doug asked.

"Okay," Mrs. Donovan said.

Doug changed lenses and took close-ups of Luanne's picture. "This way we won't have to borrow it from you," he explained as he squinted through the viewfinder.

I turned to Luanne's father who sat brooding, quietly sipping from his beer can. "What do you do for a living, Mr. Donovan?"

"Unemployed," he replied, curtly, then got up to fetch another beer from the fridge.

"Buddy's a mechanic," his wife said, watching him sadly, as he popped the tab and returned to his place in the recliner. "He got laid off last week."

"I'm sorry to hear that," I said. "And what do you do?" I asked her.

"I'm a pediatric nurse at County General."

"I have just a few more questions and then I'll get out of your way," I said. "Take me back to the last time you saw Luanne. What can you tell me about that?"

Mrs. Donovan took a deep breath and let it out slowly. "It seemed so ordinary. I asked her to go to the 7-ELEVEN to get a gallon of milk. I gave her some money and she walked out the door. If I'd have known it was going to be the last time . . . ." Her voice trailed off and she began to sob.

I reached over and touched her hand, but knew there would be nothing else I could do to comfort her. That kind of visceral grief is a painful and lonely experience.

Mr. Donovan made no move to comfort his grieving wife. He merely sat in his recliner quietly sipping from his beer can.

During the uncomfortable moment, I glanced at Doug, who'd changed lenses again and was still busily snapping pictures. But to my surprise—and annoyance—I realized that the latest series of pictures he was taking were of ME.

"So, what was *that* all about?" I asked Doug as we walked down the Donovans' driveway, heading back to our cars. I was pissed.

"What was *what* all about?" Doug sounded genuinely surprised.

"You know what I'm talking about."

"No, actually. I don't." Now *he* sounded pissed.

We got to his Jeep and he put his camera into its bag in the back. I waited, arms crossed, as he continued fumbling with his gear, his broad back to me. Finally, he turned around, the expression on his face was wide-eyed innocence with just a touch of an insouciant smile.

"I'm waiting . . ." I said.

"Waiting for what?"

"For an explanation."

He furrowed his brow. "You need to be more specific."

I sighed and rolled my eyes. "Why were you taking pictures of *me*?"

"Um, because you were there?"

"Not good enough. Try again."

"C'mon, Lark. What's with you?" He walked past me.

I followed him to his driver's side door.

He turned to look at me. "I always take shots of the whole scene—and that includes the reporter. What's the big deal?"

"I'm not the story," I jabbed a finger into my chest, forcefully emphasizing each word.

He shrugged. "Maybe yes, maybe no."

"What do you mean by *that?*" My voice went up an octave.

"You discovered the body, right?"

"Yeah. So?"

"That makes you part of the story."

"That's not for you to say."

"Not in the end, maybe, but if an editor wants to include a shot of you in the story, he'll be on my case if I didn't provide him with one."

I scowled. Doug had a point. Maybe I was just being paranoid, I told myself. But I was torn. For too long, men had been coming on to me and I was sick and tired of their unwanted advances. My experience with men had not been particularly good, so I was extremely wary. Too wary? How many times, I asked myself, had my anger and suspicions caused me to lose out on an opportunity to have a good guy friend? I'd probably never know. But I liked being a lone ranger. I was comfortable being on my own. I didn't need some guy to define who I am.

"But you got plenty of shots of the Donovans, right?" I asked, my tone a tad more gentle.

He rolled his eyes and stormed back to his stowed gear. He jerked his camera out of its carrying case. "Here. Take a look," he said sternly. He stabbed at some buttons then thrust the back of the camera toward me so I could see what he'd shot. Quickly, he scrolled through the pictures. As he did, he maneuvered himself next to me so that we could look at his handiwork together. I could feel the heat radiating from his body.

I watched as, one-by-one, his pictures popped into the viewfinder. He was good. Very good. His ability to capture the Donovans' unguarded expressions was uncanny and brilliant. With each new picture that appeared, I became increasingly impressed with the variety of what he'd been able to shoot. His photos included wide shots that showed me talking to the Donovans, but also extreme close-ups of each of them, including a powerful shot of Mrs. Donovan wiping away a tear.

"You're good," I whispered. "*Really* good." I felt like a heel.

"Yes. I am," he replied curtly. He continued jabbing a button that kept the pictures advancing. He breathed fiercely through his nose. Soon he got to the shots of me that he'd been taking when I'd looked up at him during the interview. His pictures of me were pretty good—considering what he had to work with, especially my wild frizzy-wavy-curly hair that I could never get to behave.

When he got to my images, he pressed the advance button more slowly. His breathing slowed, too. Finally, he spoke. "But I have to admit—you're very easy on the eyes." He gave me a gentle nudge.

My blood pressure went down a notch. "I'm sorry I went off on you," I said softly.

He shrugged.

I held out my hand. "Friends?"

He pried his eyes away from the last picture of me he'd taken and turned to look at my hand. "Sure," he said brightly. "That's even better than a truce." He took my hand, wiggled his eyebrows, and gave me a dazzling smile. "Ever pose nude?"

"You're *terrible!*" I yanked my hand from his grasp and socked him in the shoulder. Hard.

EIGHT

AFTER DOUG AND I finished at the Donovans', we stopped by the 7-ELEVEN where Luanne Donovan was last seen alive. While Doug took exteriors of the place, I went inside to talk with the clerk.

The guy behind the counter was stocky, about thirty, with dark, unkempt hair. He was just finishing ringing up a customer when I approached.

"Hi. I'm Lark Chadwick with the *Sun-Gazette*," I smiled.

He looked at me blankly.

"I'm working on the story about the girl who was found murdered not far from here last night."

He nodded. "The cops already talked to me about it."

"What did you tell them?"

He shrugged and raked his stubby fingers through his hair. "Nuthin' much to tell."

"Do you remember waiting on the girl?"

"Oh yeah. She was a fox."

"Did you know her?"

He shook his head. "Not by name, but she'd been in here a lot."

"What can you tell me about last night?" I dug into my messenger bag for my iPhone, whipped it out, and turned on the Voice Memo app. "I'm recording you so I can quote you accurately," I explained when he looked questioningly at the device cupped in my hand.

"There's not much to say. She came in, bought a gallon of milk and left."

"What time was it?"

"Nine-fifteen…nine-thirty. Somewhere in there."

"Was she alone?"

"Uh huh."

"Did she talk with anyone?"

"Not really. The guy standing behind her in line tried to strike up a conversation with her."

"What did he say?"

"Something lame like 'hot enough for ya?'"

"Did she respond?"

"She just laughed, said 'yeah,' and then I rung her up."

"What did the guy buy?"

"Cigarettes."

"What brand?"

He thought a minute. "Marlboro."

"Did he pay cash?"

"Yeah."

"What did he look like?"

"I already told the cops all this," the clerk said impatiently, looking at the person behind me. "I've got customers."

I stood aside while he waited on a middle-aged woman in curlers who plunked down a ten-dollar bill to buy some aspirin.

The clerk gave her change, then turned back to me. "I already went over all this with the cops."

"They don't always tell reporters everything, so that's why I appreciate all your help so far." I flashed him my best megawatt smile.

He scowled.

Doug came into the store and ambled over to me, camera dangling from the strap around his neck.

"What's your last name, Johnny?" I asked, nodding at the nametag the clerk wore on his red and black uniform shirt. I held out my hand. "I'm Lark."

"Right. Lark. I know. You told me. Lark, like the bird." Johnny ignored my hand. "I don't want my name in the paper. Or my picture, either," he said sternly to Doug, who'd raised the camera but hadn't yet started snapping away.

"That's cool," Doug said, holding up a hand, palm out, and letting the camera drop against his chest. He shuffled over to the magazine rack and began browsing.

"Anyway," I said to the clerk. "What did the man who talked to the girl look like?"

Johnny sighed. "Average."

"Had you ever seen him before?"

"Not that I can remember."

"Was he your age?"

"Older by maybe ten years."

"White? Black? Hispanic?"

"White."

"Hair?"

Johnny rolled his eyes. "Yes. He had hair."

"C'mon, man. Help me out here. Was his hair long? Short? Dark? Light?"

"Dark and short. Thinning."

"Thank you. How was he dressed?"

"Average."

I sighed and gave Johnny a look.

"Polo shirt, as near as I can remember."

"Did he and the girl leave together?"

"No. She bought her milk and left. The guy left about a minute or two later."

"Did you notice if he caught up with her in the parking lot?"

"Nope. Didn't notice. It was Saturday night. I was busy."

"Did the cops seem interested in the guy when you told them about him?"

"Oh yeah," Johnny nodded vigorously. "That's when they wanted to see the surveillance tape."

After Doug and I finished at the 7-ELEVEN, I called Matt Benson from the parking lot while Doug put away his camera gear.

"Is the autopsy over?" I asked the detective.

"Just ended," Benson said.

"Drowning or strangulation?"

"Right now we're going on the assumption she was strangled."

"What about sexual assault?"

"That's a negative."

"Really?"

"Yeah. Kinda surprises me, too, but that ruling could change if toxicology tests turn up something. We should get the results back in a day or two."

"Was there water in her lungs that would indicate drowning?"

"Nope. She was dead when she hit the water," Benson said.

"I just talked to the clerk at the 7-ELEVEN who waited on Luanne," I said, hoping it would prompt Benson into telling me something.

"Uh huh."

I tried again. "He says some guy waiting in line behind her tried to chat her up."

"Uh huh."

"'Uh huh,' meaning 'yes, that's true,' or 'uh huh, I'm listening?'" I asked.

"The latter."

"You mean Luanne didn't talk with anyone in the store other than the clerk?"

"I didn't say that."

"What did you say?"

"I said 'Uh huh.'"

"Did I just hear an echo?"

"Uh huh," Benson laughed.

"C'mon, Detective. The guy on the surveillance tape might be the killer. Don't you think you should release the tape so the public can help find the guy?"

"We might. It could also be some innocent bystander about to be fingered as a suspect in a murder investigation. But I'll take your suggestion under advisement. I gotta go."

I thanked him and then called the desk to update the web edition of the story I'd written earlier. I supplied Paul, the editor on duty, with quotes from Benson, Mrs. Donovan, and Johnny the Clerk, and let Paul know what Doug had shot.

I hung up and began fiddling with my iPhone.

"Who you calling now?" Doug asked, slamming the door of his Wrangler.

"I'm checking an app that will show me where the nearest Wi-Fi hotspot is so I can file my piece after I write it."

"Don't you have an air card?" Doug asked, fishing what looked like a thumb drive from his pocket.

I shook my head. "What's that?"

"It gets you onto the web from anywhere. Standard issue at the paper."

"I don't officially start until tomorrow."

"Oh. Right. You're new here," he chuckled. "There's a good diner about a mile from here. It's got Wi-Fi. You can write and file your piece from there while we get a bite. My treat."

"Thanks, but I'll pay my own way. I'm a big girl."

I got into Pearlie and followed as Doug led the way to the diner—a shiny, chrome monstrosity. The place was teaming with people, many wearing their Sunday best after having been to church, but we were able to find a booth and began to set up shop with our computers and Doug's camera gear.

We each ordered a burger and Diet Coke then worked steadily—and mostly in silence—between bites and sips.

I found Luanne's Facebook page online, but her privacy settings wouldn't allow me to see any of her pictures, nor did it give away any sense of who she was as a person. I wrote up my story for the Monday morning paper. The story included the identity of the victim whose body I'd stumbled upon the night before. Sprinkled throughout were the facts given to me over the phone by Detective Benson. I also wrote a sidebar that was my interview with the parents. I reviewed Doug's pictures with him. We chose shots, captioned them, then emailed them to the desk, along with my story. Doug's pictures included the head-and-shoulders portrait of Luanne; an exterior of the Donovans' home, with the mailbox in the foreground; a two-shot with the mother and father looking longingly at the picture of their daughter; a close-up of the mother crying; and an exterior of the 7-ELEVEN where Luanne Donovan was last seen.

Several hours later I was pushing my shopping cart down an aisle at the grocery store not too far from Marcie's apartment. I paused by the dairy case and picked up a carton of soy milk and placed it in my cart. The mundane act of shopping allowed my unconscious mind to kick in as I found myself thinking about the next steps I would need to take to investigate the "Murdered Girl" story—the topic slug given to it by the desk.

As I wondered what my first official day at the paper would be like, my mind suddenly slipped a groove and I found myself thinking about Doug. He'd tried to strike up a conversation with me at the diner after we finished working, but I'd kept things superficial, not wanting to be sucked into his vortex until I'd at least had a chance to quietly consult my heart.

No doubt he was yummily handsome, but I'd been deceived by good looks before. I'd accepted his explanation for why he'd been taking candid shots of me during the interview with the Donovans. When I remembered his cheeky question about whether or not I'd ever posed nude, my mouth curled into an involuntary grin. I knew he was kidding, so I didn't even bother to take his crack seriously. I'd never posed nude—and never intended to.

In spite of myself, however, I liked his confident audaciousness. He was good and professional at his job and, though I could tell he was attracted to me, he exuded a self-confidence that seemed to say, *Look, I like you. Let's have fun. But if you don't want to, no big deal—I'll just move on.*

I found myself realizing that Doug Mitchell had the potential to be a fun friend. But nothing more. That's because I could tell he was a player and I'm not *any*one's plaything.

I threw a few more basics into my shopping cart, then stopped by a vast beer display. I chose a Wisconsin beer, Old Milwaukee, to bring to the Richards' barbeque.

At the check-out line, the clerk had a clump of hair hanging directly into her eyes. She was overweight, slack-jawed, chewed gum with her mouth open and, frankly, looked like a moron. Part of me—the grown-up part—inwardly rebuked the judgmental me. But I couldn't help myself—even as I was ashamed of myself.

As the clerk rang me up, she came to an abrupt halt when the six-pack of beer slid into her line of sight. "You can't buy that," she barked at me officiously.

"Excuse me?" I said.

"I said, 'You can't buy that.'"

I get really pissed really fast whenever someone tells me what I can't do.

"Like hell I can't," I said, jutting my chin toward her aggressively. "I'm way over twenty-one."

"You're not from around here, are you?" she said, accusingly.

"What's that got to do with anything?" I could feel my pulse quickening. An inner voice warned me that if I wasn't careful, this conversation could go downhill very fast.

The line behind us was getting longer with impatient people wanting to get on with their lives.

The check-out clerk—*Denise*, according to her nametag—proceeded to clue me in as to "how it is" in the great state of Georgia. "You can't buy alcohol on Sunday," she said, nose in the air.

"Why the hell not?" I said, my voice getting louder and more impatient every time Denise opened her mouth.

"You just can't," she said, unhelpfully.

"It's one of Georgia's myriad stupid laws." The voice belonged to the bag boy standing at the end of the counter.

When I looked at him, he smiled and rolled his eyes. "Actually," he continued, "things are changing. Most localities in Georgia have finally repealed the archaic ban on Sunday alcohol sales, but, sadly, not this one."

His empathetic and informative intervention helped calm me down a little, but I was still annoyed. "I'm going to a picnic and I need to get something to bring," I said to him.

"How about a liter of Coke?" He turned and hefted one from a display case behind him. "Will one be enough?"

"Yeah. That's fine. Thanks."

Denise set aside the six-pack of beer and finished ringing me up.

"Let me help you carry this stuff to your car," the bag boy said, picking up the four plastic bags that he'd just finished stuffing.

"Sure. Thanks," I said.

He walked ahead of me through the automatic doors into the parking lot, but stopped to wait for me when a blast of hot air caused my glasses to fog up momentarily—they'd been chilled by the store's highly effective air conditioning.

When I finally caught up to him, he fell into step beside me.

"You really aren't from around here, are you?" he asked, but there was something about his gentle tone that made me want to carry on an adult conversation with him instead of doing combat with Denise.

"Is it that obvious?" I asked.

"For starters, you don't have an accent."

"Neither do you."

"I'm from Rhode Island."

I stopped to look at him. He was short, only a few inches taller than me, had thick dark hair, bright, intelligent eyes, a kind face and a pleasant smile. And he wasn't really a boy. I gauged him to be in his early forties.

"How'd you end up here?" I asked him.

A shadow came over his face. "The job."

"This one?" I asked, incredulously. "That's a long hike to be a bag boy. No offense."

"Different job," he smiled sheepishly. "It's a long story. Maybe some other time."

We continued walking slowly toward Pearlie, parked in a far corner of the lot.

"What brings you here?" he asked, " . . . and from where?"

"I just moved here from Wisconsin," I said. "I officially start my new job at the *Sun-Gazette* tomorrow."

"No kidding!" His eyes widened in what seemed like genuine enthusiasm. "I used to—" he paused, coughed uncomfortably, and recovered. "I used to write a little."

"Fiction? Non-fiction? Both?"

He waved me off. "Non-fiction. But some people would dispute that. It was a long time ago," he said wistfully.

This guy clearly had a lot more going for him than Denise. It occurred to me that he seemed smart enough to run the store, yet here he was bagging groceries. *What's up with that?* I wondered to myself.

"What'll you be doing at the newspaper?" he asked as we got to Pearlie and he began placing the plastic bags in the back seat.

"I'm their new cops and courts reporter," I explained. "In fact, I've already been working."

He looked quizzical.

"I've been working the story of the murdered girl whose body was found in the river last night."

A light of recognition clicked on behind his eyes. "I read about that," he said. "Are you Lark?"

"Guilty," I laughed.

"Forgive me. I forgot your last name, but Lark is certainly a distinctive first name and I remembered that from your byline. Good piece."

"Thanks. And tell me who you are," I said, holding out my hand.

He grasped it. "I'm Augie." He smiled and his eyes held mine briefly, but then he looked down, shyly. "I've got to get back inside, but it was great t-talking with you," he stammered.

"Thanks for rescuing me from Denise," I said.

"No problem. It's my mission in life," he laughed, seeming to relax and gain more confidence the farther away he got from me.

As I drove out of the lot, I saw Augie rounding up a conga line of shopping carts and guiding them to the front door like a tugboat pushing a barge down the Mississippi River.

The river reminded me of Wisconsin, and that reminded me of Lionel, and thinking of Lionel made me realize I missed him. I needed to give him a call to bring him up to date.

NINE

I WOULD HAVE BEEN more apprehensive about Ed Richards' barbecue had I not been with someone I knew at least a little bit. Marcie and I got there after four in the afternoon.

Ed lived in a spacious house in the historic district on Columbia's south side. We skipped ringing the front doorbell and followed the lure of classic rock wafting to us from Ed's backyard. As we ambled along the side of the house to join the crowd in the back, we passed the Richards' open garage. I couldn't help noticing two Jaguars parked side by side—one hunter green, the other midnight blue—each with matching *HIS JAG* and *HER JAG* license plates.

"Pretty fancy," I said to Marcie. "How can Ed afford a Jag on a journalist's salary?"

"His wife's loaded. She's a partner at a posh corporate law firm downtown."

The music blared from a boom box perched on Ed's back deck. The yard was filled with people, but I only recognized Doug. He was sipping from a half-full bottle of Corona and talking with a barely-legal bleach blonde nearly half his age.

Marcie nudged me and nodded toward the center of the yard. "That's Ed," she said under her breath.

Ed, a portly, balding, middle-aged man stood sweating in front of a smoky-sizzling grill. He wore a Georgia Bulldogs apron and wielded a pair of tongs in one hand and a spatula in the other as he turned hotdogs and flipped burgers.

Marcie and I made our way to Ed to say hello. He saw us coming and gave us a tired smile and a jaunty tong-salute.

"Hey there, Marce!" he called out, then turned his attention to me. "And are you *the* Lark Chadwick?" His southern drawl was smooth and refined.

"Actually, there's another Lark Chadwick who lives in Montana," I said, shaking his hand, "but I'm *the* Columbia, Georgia Lark Chadwick."

"It's good to finally meet you in person, Lark." His beer breath and glazed eyes gave me the sense that his joviality was largely alcohol-fueled. "You're already doing great work."

"Thanks," I blushed. "And thanks for the invite." I held up my liter bottle of Coke. "Where do you want me to put this?"

Ed called to an attractive woman nearby. "Honey, come meet our new star reporter."

The woman turned and gave me a stiff, cold smile. She was about 40 and wore a yellow sundress so revealing that it screamed boob job. As she came my way, Ed continued, "Lark, this is my wife Joyce. Honey, this is Lark Chadwick."

Joyce took my hand by the fingers and gave it a jerk-twist so that my hand was palm up and hers was in the power position. "Bless your heart. It's wonderful to finally meet you, Lark," Joyce smiled icily. Her exaggerated Southern Belle accent made me think immediately of Scarlet O'Hara on steroids.

"Same here," I said, weakening my grip and subtly trying to shake her hand loose.

"And you already know Marcie," Ed said to his wife.

"Yes. Hello," Joyce said dismissively, barely looking at her. "Thanks for coming."

Marcie held up a liter bottle of root beer. "Where should we put our beverages?"

"Over there," Joyce said, finally dropping my hand and sweeping her fingers toward two coolers sitting next to each other on the deck near tables where various side dishes were arrayed.

"Joyce is quite the ice queen, isn't she?" I whispered to Marcie when we were out of earshot.

"Oh yeah."

"How come?"

"She doesn't like you."

"Why not?" We placed our soft drinks in a cooler.

"You're hot, young, and a potential rival."

"For Ed? Eww. I don't think she has anything to worry about."

Before Marcie could reply, we were interrupted by the sound of Ed clanging his tongs against the hood of the grill.

"Can I have your attention, everyone?" he called out above the noise. "Will someone kill the music for just a second?"

The music stopped and the back yard became silent except for the sizzle of the meat cooking on Ed's grill.

"Now that the guest of honor is here," Ed continued, "I want to introduce her to the rest of you." He gestured grandly toward me with his tongs. "This is Lark Chadwick, the newest edition to our staff."

I gave a shy wave in response to a smattering of polite applause.

"Lark comes to us from Wisconsin. She may be a Yankee, but don't hold that against her."

Several people chuckled.

"Even though her first official day with us doesn't begin until tomorrow, she's already gotten an early and strong start. By now you've probably read her work on the Murdered Girl story she broke last night. As you may know, she got into journalism working with the legendary Lionel Stone, the Pulitzer Prize-winning author and journalist."

There were a few murmurs of surprise and approval.

"Anyway," Ed said, "we're honored and delighted to have you with us, Lark."

More clapping.

"Thank you," I bowed slightly.

"So, everyone," Ed concluded, "make sure you introduce yourself to Lark. Otherwise," he smiled impishly, "there's no food for you."

Everyone laughed, the music came back on, and the buzz of dozens of conversations resumed.

It took me another half hour to make my way to the food tables to get something to eat because people kept coming up to introduce themselves. I was impressed by their friendliness, but felt bad because I forgot most of their names as soon as they said them.

But a few names and faces stood out. An attractive Asian woman named Priscilla Lee told me she was an intern at the paper, but before I could learn more about her, we got interrupted by a pudgy guy named Tom who said he worked in tech services. An overweight woman named June introduced herself as Ed's secretary. There were many, many others. All friendly.

At one point I saw Doug—still chatting-up the bleach blonde—watching me from a distance, but he made no move to come my way. Finally, Marcie and I were able to pile potato salad, chips, and burgers onto our plates. I led us to a place off to the side where we could survey the crowd.

"So," I said to her. "What's your commentary on the who's who of the assembled multitude?"

"Let's see," she said, looking around. "Ed's been with the paper about ten years. He's about fifty and he's been under a lot of pressure lately."

"How come?"

"Not sure. He's in Elmer's office all the time and usually comes out of those meetings looking pretty grim. I think his job's on the line and he's feeling the pressure to increase circulation."

I pursed my lips and worried yet again that I might be in for a bumpy ride.

Doug passed near us, his hand resting lightly on the shoulder of Bleach Blonde.

"What's with Fabio?" I asked Marcie after Doug was safely out of earshot.

"Ah, Doug," she said dreamily. "He's bagged just about everyone at the paper." She looked longingly at him as if wishing she were next.

"Including you?" I teased.

"That's classified," she smiled, demurely.

"What about your inattentive boyfriend? Is he here, too?"

Marcie gave me a curt nod, but said nothing. Her eyes pleaded *let's not go there.*

I let it drop. Later, I saw her looking longingly again at Doug.

TEN

THE NEXT MORNING, Monday, my profile of Luanne Rae Donovan was the lead story—upper right, above the fold, accompanied by the picture Doug took of Luanne's parents gazing at her picture.

It was also my first official day on the job. The first few days of any job—at least for me—are disorienting. Which is ironic, of course, because they're supposed to orient you to your new surroundings.

The offices of the *Sun-Gazette* were located just north of the main part of town along the banks of the Chattahoochee River. Unlike the *Pine Bluff Standard*'s storefront office on Main Street, the *Sun-Gazette* stood five stories and looked like a warehouse from the outside.

The main newsroom was on the third floor. The printing presses and shipping area were on the first; Sales and IT shared space on the second; the people who ran the website occupied the fourth floor, along with graphics and accounting; and the executive suites were in the rarified air of the top floor. Each floor had a centralized kitchenette complete with a coffee machine—and free coffee.

Erica Canalway was the unit manager of the newsroom. Her job was to make sure the moving parts ran smoothly—that included making sure the copy machines had paper, everyone's computer worked, the temperature was comfortable, and she handled the orientation of new hires, like me.

For the first few hours, Erica had me filling out numerous forms for direct deposit, 401(k), health benefits, etc., etc., etc. It was mind numbing. Then she took me on a tour of the building, some areas of which I would probably never visit again. Near the end of the day, she issued me a BlackBerry, a laptop computer with an air card like Doug's, and a box of business cards. The final stop was a meeting with Ed Richards in his glassed-in office just off the newsroom on the third floor.

When Erica dropped me off, Ed was sitting at his desk, chair swiveled so that his back was to me. He was looking out the window at the Chattahoochee, the dividing line between Georgia and Alabama.

"I'll leave you here with Ed," Erica said. "I think you're going to like it here, Lark."

"Thanks for everything, Erica."

Ed swung his chair around to face me. He looked terrible, like he hadn't slept all night—quite a switch from the hospitable affability he'd displayed the day before at his barbecue.

"Have a seat," he said, waving at one of the two chairs in front of his desk.

"Thanks again for inviting me to your party yesterday," I began. "I had a great time."

He smiled wanly, barely listening.

"Rough day?" I asked.

He shrugged and smiled ruefully. "They're all rough these days. But this meeting isn't about me, it's about you." He stood and walked around to my side of the desk and perched on the edge. "I'm very proud of you, Lark. You're off to a great start. You've learned from Lionel Stone. He's the best. Now, you're being groomed for the *New York Times*. Maybe you'll get there. All I can do is help—the rest is up to you."

He pushed himself away from his desk and sat in the chair next to me. "The newspaper industry is going through a lot of changes right now. As you know, a lot of papers are going out of business."

"Is this one at risk?" I asked.

He shot me a glance and scowled.

"I am a reporter, after all. How bad are things here?" I persisted.

"That's no concern of yours."

"It is, actually. I quit a job I loved and moved a thousand miles away from all my friends, and now I hear rumors about possible layoffs. Is the ship sinking, captain?"

He grunted. "I'm not the captain. Just a hired hand. The captain and his mates are up on the fifth floor," he said, looking at the ceiling, then back at me. "Who knows?"

Ed got up, walked behind his desk and took a long look out the window, his hands in his pockets, jingling his change and his keys. After a moment, he turned to look at me and leaned against the windowsill and crossed his arms. "To be honest, times are rough. The pressure's on to turn out a good product. The Internet is the future of journalism so they're putting a lot of emphasis our web edition. It used to be that a reporter had all day to work on a story and had the luxury of cultivating sources and tracking down leads. Now, every *minute* is a deadline. Subscriptions are shrinking. So's advertising revenue. We're in uncharted territory."

"Newspapers had to change and adapt when television came on the scene," I reminded him. "The *Sun* had to merge with the *Gazette* when evening papers were killed off by the nightly TV news, so it's not like this hasn't happened before."

"True enough. But it's still a scary and uncertain time. That means that I'll be riding you hard for results. Of course there's the Murdered Girl story. That's your baby and I want you to stay ahead of everybody on that one—and so far you are—but you've got other duties, too."

I nodded.

"You'll need to be at the police station every day to get leads for new stories. You'll need to keep an eye on the court dockets and cover any important trials that come up."

"Right. I was planning on doing that."

"But I also want you to write a daily blog for the Web."

"That I *wasn't* expecting. I thought reporters aren't supposed to be the story. I really intended to keep myself out of the Murdered Girl story, but the desk wrote me into it because I literally stumbled onto her body."

"But this is part of what's changing about journalism. Now it's not just driven by the news, it's driven by personalities."

"You mean it's showbiz, like TV?"

"To a certain extent, yes."

I frowned and winced.

"I know. I feel the same way you do about it, but I think there's a middle way."

"And what might that be?"

"Your blog doesn't have to be your opinion. I want it to be a vehicle by which readers come to know the person who's their link to the news of the day. Because you're new here, you can start fresh by introducing yourself to your readers and building a personal relationship with them. Who knows? You might even get leads for future stories as readers get to know you—and you get to know them."

"This is the first time I'm hearing about having to write a blog. It's one thing to have a Facebook page where I can keep in touch and share pictures with a small circle of friends. It's quite another to open up a two-way street with a bunch of faceless strangers."

"You won't know unless you try. And you get your first chance to try right now."

"What?"

Ed pushed himself up from against the windowsill. "Starting right now, for the web and tomorrow's paper, I want you to begin writing a daily blog."

"Weekly."

"Excuse me?"

"I said, 'weekly.' I'll write it once a week."

Ed scowled.

"I think it's too much to ask for me to crank out something thoughtful on a daily basis in addition to all the reporting I have to do."

He walked to his desk and stood next to it looking down at me. "It doesn't have to be long."

I stood and matched him scowl for scowl. "Tell you what. Let's compromise. How about at *least* once a week, but more frequently if I have something to say. Who knows? Maybe I'll warm to the idea and end up doing it daily."

Ed nodded. "That's reasonable, but your first one is still due tomorrow. Don't worry about what to name it—our marketing folks will come up with a way to brand it. Just write from the heart and connect with the readers." He held up a finger to emphasize his point. "That's the key word, here, Lark—*connect!*"

I felt like holding up a finger, too.

ELEVEN

I left Ed's office feeling dazed and overwhelmed. I still needed to find a permanent place to stay, but his hints about the uncertainties of the paper's future made me wonder—and worry—about the wisdom of signing a lease and putting down roots here. I was still rooming temporarily with Marcie, but now I had no time to search for a place of my own because I felt so overwhelmed getting my footing at this new job.

When Ed said I should "connect," my first instinct was not my new blog. I called Lionel, instead. I thought about phoning him from my newly-assigned, cramped and barren cubicle in the newsroom, but there would be no privacy there, so I went outside and connected with him on my cell from a park bench overlooking the Chattahoochee. It was our first conversation since before I found Luanne's body. He picked up on the second ring.

"Hey. It's me," I said.

"You sound tired."

"I'm shot."

"You done for the day?"

"Not yet. My editor just told me I need to begin writing a blog."

"That's great."

"So you say."

"Don't you want to?"

"I have no idea what to say, plus he wants me to do it *every fricking day*."

"You'll come up with something."

"I was kind of hoping you'd tell me what that something is."

"That's for you to decide. Nice try."

I laughed. It felt good.

"At least I got him to compromise," I said. "He still *wants* me to do it every day, but he settled for at least once a week, but maybe more."

"Uh huh." There was a pause, then Lionel added, "You've been busy."

"How do you know?"

"You haven't called until now, plus I've been reading your stuff online."

"Really?"

"Sure. Let's call it 'gentle stalking.'"

I laughed. "Well, that saves me having to bring you up to date."

"You've stumbled onto a big story right out of the gate. Nice goin'."

"Yes, but at a young girl's expense. She had her whole life ahead of her, Lionel."

He sighed. "You don't have to tell *me* that." His voice quavered.

"Too true. I'm sorry, Lionel." Lionel's daughter Holly had died three years earlier in a fall from a cliff along the Inca Trail in Peru. He'd had to identify the body, and I'd helped him find the reason for her death. But losing Holly produced a crisis in Lionel and Muriel's marriage they were still working through.

It took a moment for Lionel to compose himself. I waited patiently—I was used to his "moments"—as he called them—little, sudden grief pangs that broke out from time to time when something reminded him of his "little girl," even though she was in her early twenties when she died.

"So," he said, finally. "Got any hunches or leads?"

"I feel a little hinky about Luanne's dad."

"Yeah. I read that between the lines. Think there's anything there?"

"Maybe. He drinks. Has no social skills. He's unemployed. The mother is the one trying to keep it all together."

"Do you suspect sexual abuse?"

"It's one theory I need to check out. Maybe Luanne was gonna tell on him, and her dad freaked."

"Yeah."

"Or it was just random—wrong place, wrong time."

"Snatched?" Lionel asked.

"Uh huh. The 7-ELEVEN had a surveillance cam, but the lead detective won't let me see it."

"What's your take on the detective?"

"He seems to know what he's doing, but I don't think he trusts me—or maybe he just hates all reporters. How can I soften him up?"

"It's a naturally adversarial relationship, so you have to work hard to build up trust—and that takes time."

"So far, I'm honoring his wishes to keep some details I know out of the story. He said he doesn't want the killer to know what the police know."

"Yeah. He's right about that. Honoring those wishes—at least for now—helps you build up some good will."

"What do you mean, 'at least for now'?"

"There may come a time when all bets are off."

"Like when?" I asked.

"Like when you feel you're being stiff-armed and shut out. If that happens, you can tell him you're gonna go public with what you know."

"But that's blackmail."

"No. It's leverage. It's what'll make him come around. But, if you play things right, you won't have to go nuclear."

"That's what I was thinking, too."

"You have to take it one step at a time. Try not to be antagonistic—a challenge for you, I know."

Lionel's tone was teasing, but I winced. He knew me and my impulsive impatience all too well.

"But don't just roll over, either," Lionel continued.

"What do you mean?"

"You still have every right to work the story on your own and not just get your cues from him."

"Information is power, right?"

"Right."

"But the cops have resources I don't."

"Yes. But they can't be everywhere, so they need you, too."

"Bargain and negotiate?"

"Yes. Make it a two-way street. Name it trust."

"Good advice." I watched the river froth as it rushed past boulders near the shore. "I wish you were here, Lionel," I sighed.

"No. I wish *you* were *here*. But I'm only a phone call or an email away."

"I'm having second thoughts about having left you, Muriel, and *The Standard*."

"Good. You should," he chuckled.

"I'm serious."

"It'll pass. It always feels the worst at first because you're still getting stabilized. Everything's new. That's why you called. I'm the old familiar. I get it."

"How's Muriel?" I got up and paced in front of the bench.

"She's good. We're still in couples' therapy and it's going well. She's gotten my attention and I think I'm mellowing in my old age."

"Yeah. I agree. I can hear it in your voice. You seem more relaxed."

"If you say so."

On the other end of the phone line, I heard what sounded like ice cubes clinking in a glass. "A nightcap, Lionel?" I glanced at my watch. "It's barely five-thirty."

"Busted." Lionel's laugh was low and deep. "Jameson on the rocks."

"Why so early?"

"It mellows me out before I head home."

"But you're drinking alone."

"No I'm not. *You're* here."

"But I'm not drinking yet. And I've still got work to do." I began a slow amble away from the park bench and toward the *Sun-Gazette* building.

"How do you like the South?" Lionel asked.

"Not my cup o' tea." I waited for a car to pass, then loped across the street.

"Why not?"

"Let me count the ways: First, even though it's spring, it's hotter'n hell. Next, half the time, I can't understand anyone because their accents are so thick. And, Lionel, the Civil War ended more'n a hundred fifty years ago, but they're *still* fighting it." I was feeling my blood begin to boil. "Want me to go on?"

"Nah. I hear ya. Got a boyfriend, yet?"

I laughed. "There's a photog who seems interesting, but he's a real player. Hot, but dangerous."

"Dangerous?"

"He'll break my heart as soon as I give in to him, so I'm just not gonna go there. I've had my heart broken enough."

"True. But you *have* thought about giving in . . . haven't you?"

I paused.

"That's what I thought. Remember, Lark: back in the day, I used to be just like him."

"Dangerous?"

"And hot."

I laughed. "You're still both, Lionel."

He grunted. "That's what I keep trying to tell Muriel. You be careful, kiddo."

"I'll try," I said weakly.

It felt good to call Lionel. He was definitely the "old familiar" and talking with him was just what I needed to help me get my bearings. After hanging up, I got myself situated in my cubical on the third floor newsroom and began to write my first blog as a staff writer for the *Columbia Sun-Gazette*.

T W E L V E

My blog was posted on the paper's website Monday night and appeared on page two of the Metro Section Tuesday morning, along with one of the pictures Doug took of me while I was interviewing the Donovans. The picture was tightly cropped so only my face was visible. I was listening intently to the Donovans, a pensive, thoughtful look on my face. I had to hand it to Doug—he had a good eye.

I kept my first blog short:

> Moving to a new city for a new job can be a bit daunting, but here I am. I grew up in Wisconsin and for the past two years I was a reporter at the *Pine Bluff Standard* near the state capital of Madison.
>
> I had the good fortune to be mentored during that time by Pulitzer Prize-winning journalist and bestselling author Lionel Stone. But now it's time to branch out on my own.
>
> I'm thrilled to be in Columbia and I hope there'll be times when my path crosses yours.

During my time with you, I'll be covering law enforcement and the judicial system—or, as we call it in the biz: cops and courts.

Journalism is more than just giving you the facts—it's storytelling. It's putting those basic facts into a coherent whole in a way that connects you with the wider world of other people's lives.

Or, in all too many cases, their deaths.

I've already had to relay one sad story to you: the tragic death of Luanne Rae Donovan, 15. Her funeral will be later today and you'll be able to read an account of it this evening on our website.

Police are still looking for leads. They think she was strangled, but toxicology results aren't back yet following her autopsy.

Who could have killed her? I intend to find out—perhaps with your help.

First thing Tuesday morning, I found my way to the police department in downtown Columbia, just two blocks from the newspaper office. I spent most of the day going from office to office introducing myself to secretaries and schmoozing with whoever would talk to me. The courthouse was in the same building, so I made the rounds there, too, concentrating on the various courtrooms, checking in with secretaries, exchanging email addresses, and generally getting acquainted.

I found the coroner's office and checked to see if they were ready to release a copy of Luanne Donovan's autopsy report. Actually, I wasn't allowed to review the full report, merely a press release giving a sanitized version for public consumption. Obviously, the cops were still holding back some details of what they had so as not to jeopardize their investigation.

The official cause of death was strangulation. No drugs or alcohol were found in her blood and she had not been sexually assaulted. I walked down to the area of the building where Matt Benson worked, but he wasn't there. I called him on my cell.

"Benson," he said gruffly when he answered.

"It's Lark."

"Hey," he said without much enthusiasm.

"I just got the news release on Luanne Donovan's autopsy."

"Uh huh."

"Does it surprise you that she wasn't sexually assaulted?"

"Nothing surprises me any more."

"Was she a virgin?"

"No comment . . . but why does it matter?"

"If she was sexually active, there could be a connection to a possible suspect."

"We're looking into that."

"So, she was sexually active?"

"I didn't say that."

"You implied it."

"You're pissing me off, Miss Chadwick."

"Alright. Alright. Lemme back up. Got leads?"

"Yes."

"Care to elaborate?"

"No."

"Is the dad a suspect?"

He paused a long, telling moment. "We have leads, but we haven't zeroed in on any one person."

"Is the dad among the leads?"

"Not gonna go there."

"Why not?"

"Too highly speculative, which does no good."

"If your leads pan out into something more substantial, when do you think you'll make an arrest?"

"I don't know, and I certainly don't want to speculate and get people's hopes up or down. We are pursuing a vigorous investigation and we are confident that we will find Luanne Donovan's killer very soon. Beyond that, I don't want to speculate."

"Should the public be concerned that there's still a killer on the loose?"

"The public should be vigilant. If people follow common sense procedures—don't get into a car with strangers, be aware of strangers who are near you, don't go out alone—then there should be no cause for alarm."

I paused, trying to collect my thoughts. "Can we slip off the record and just talk informally for a sec?"

"I'd rather not. I don't know you well enough to know if I can trust you. No offense."

"Fair enough. How can I earn your trust?"

"Play it straight. Be careful that in your zeal to catch the guy— and sell more papers—you don't screw up the investigation and make matters worse. I'll know if I can trust you if you play by the rules."

I wasn't sure exactly what rules he had in mind, and decided not to let him set them. Right now we were working in the same direction, but I'd already had plenty of experience with public officials who were less than honest, so as far as I was concerned, all bets were off if Benson started lying to me or misleading me. Then the relationship would become adversarial. That's okay. I was comfortable with that. Maybe *too* comfortable.

"I appreciate what you've been able to tell me so far," I said. "As long as you're up front with me, we'll get along fine."

"Okay then." His voice sounded like he was ready to move on.

"You gonna be at her funeral today?" I asked.

"Yeah. I thought I'd stop by."

"Paying your respects or checking out the mourners?"

He chuckled. "Little o' both."

"See you there."

We hung up and I immediately wrote up my notes and filed them with the desk. His comments, along with the coroner's report, would be on our website within ten minutes.

Luanne's funeral was held late in the afternoon at a Baptist church on the northern outskirts of town. I got there early, but sat near the back so I could watch the crowd. The place filled to overflowing. I sat on the aisle next to two teenage girls who spent most of the service hugging each other and weeping. At one point, I contributed a tissue to the cause.

Luanne's closed mahogany-looking coffin stood at the head of the center aisle in front of the pulpit. A large choir dressed in flowing burgundy robes sat spread out behind the pulpit. Luanne's parents sat in a front pew. They were led into the church through a side door just before the service started. Luanne's mom, clutching a hanky to her mouth, wore a plain black dress. Her dad, still florid, wore an ill-fitting dark suit. He looked uncomfortable. Probably, I thought to myself, because he had to put down his beer can.

The choir sang "Amazing Grace," plus some other hymns I didn't recognize because they weren't in the Episcopal hymnbook I grew up with. I did not participate in the service because I was there to observe, but I prayed silently for the young girl I'd only met after her life had been snatched away. I prayed for her parents. And I prayed that the killer would be caught soon.

But even as I prayed, I kept my eyes moving. The family did not want cameras in the church service, but a battery of television cameras—along with Doug, my still photog—waited out front. In addition to the music—which was moving and heartfelt—a parade of people came to the front to share their memories of Luanne. I took good notes.

I learned that Luanne was on the track team at her school; I learned that she had amassed 2,600 friends on Facebook; I learned that she loved chocolate, sad movies, and even sadder songs; I learned she was a good listener and was fiercely loyal to her friends. One kid, a hulk of a guy who looked like a thick-necked football player on steroids, concluded his talk by looking at someone in the front pew and saying, "Don't be sad for Luanne, Tyrone. She's in a better place now."

The comment drew a snort of derision from the girl sitting closest to me.

I leaned over to her. "Who's Tyrone?" I asked. I already knew the answer—Luanne's parents had already told me—but I wanted to get the girl next to me talking.

"Tyrone's her loser EX boyfriend, but he never got the message," the girl hissed.

"What do you mean?"

"Luanne broke up with him last week, but he refused to believe it was over."

"Which one is Tyrone?" I asked.

She half stood to see better. I half rose to get to her level. She leaned her head close to mine and pointed. "He's the black dude in the front row," she whispered.

He wasn't hard to spot. He was the only African-American in the church.

The minister began his sermon by talking quietly and lovingly about the Luanne he knew: raised in the church, accepted Jesus at age eight, member of the youth group. But then he quickened his intensity as he broadened his message, speaking ominously about how life can end suddenly and long before we may be ready. He ended with a passionate and earnest appeal to "get right with Jesus before it's too late."

Part of me resented and rebelled against what I considered the minister's emotional manipulation of the congregation, yet on another more rational and objective level, I couldn't disagree intellectually with his admonition to make sure you're on the positive side of God's ledger when life ends. Only trouble was, I could never be sure where I stood with Him—or Her—or Whoever.

I'd been looking for Matt Benson, but didn't see him until I filed out of the church behind the casket. He was across the street near the news photographers, busily snapping pictures of the congregation as we filed out. As near as I could tell, he was shooting indiscriminately, not focusing on any one person.

The procession circled to the side of the church to an open grave among rows of granite headstones. The minister said a prayer, the casket was lowered into the ground, and Luanne's sobbing mother threw a white rose into the hole. Mr. Donovan did nothing, either to comfort his grieving wife or otherwise.

The girl I was sitting next to dabbed at her eyes. "Thanks for this," she said, nodding at her now-soiled tissue.

"Sure," I smiled. "Something to remember me by." I gave her my business card identifying me as a *Sun-Gazette* reporter. "How well did you know Luanne?" I asked.

"We grew up together. She was one of my best friends," she said, her chin trembling.

"What's your name?" I asked.

"Tracey Meadows. Is my name gonna be in the paper?"

"Do you mind?"

"No. That's okay, I guess."

"What's the most important thing you want people to know about Luanne?"

Tracey's chin stopped trembling. She gritted her teeth and said, "That she would never hurt anyone and did not deserve what happened to her."

"Do you have any idea of who could have done this to her?"

A panic-stricken look came over Tracey's face.

"No names," I said.

She nodded toward Tyrone who was just passing near us as we stood on the front steps next to a white pillar. "He was pissed that she'd dumped him," Tracey whispered.

"Had he threatened her?"

Tracey shrugged.

"Had they dated long?"

"A long time. Maybe a month."

"Had they, um, gone all the way?" I asked.

"Of course," Tracey smirked, "but don't put *that* in the paper."

"How do you know?"

"Like, she told me?"

"When?"

"A week ago. He'd been trying to do her for weeks, but she held out. She told me that as soon as she'd done it with him, she knew it was a mistake. That's when she tried to end it."

"Tried?"

"Like I said earlier, he wasn't too accepting of the idea."

"In what way wasn't he accepting? Did they have a fight?"

"Uh huh. Friday after school."

"Did you see it?"

"Yeah. Me and Luanne was walking together to the bus when he came flying up behind her and grabbed her by her collar."

"Did he hit her?"

"No, but he yelled at her."

"What did he say?"

"He called her a 'bitch' and kept screaming, 'How can you do this to me?'"

"What did she say or do?"

"She kept walking and told him to leave her alone."

"Did he?"

"Not right away."

"What got him to stop?"

"I pushed him and told him to back off or I'd go to the principal."

"Did you?"

"No."

"Why not?"

"Cuz he backed off."

"Did he threaten her?"

"Not really, other than just by being a prick."

"Have you told your story to the police?"

She shook her head. "I spoze I should, huh?"

"Probably wouldn't hurt. Do you know her parents very well?"

"Oh sure. Her mom's real nice."

"What about her dad?"

She looked at me sideways. "No names?"

"No names." I hate going off the record with a source because I have to work twice as hard to confirm the information some-place else.

"Her dad gives me the creeps."

"How come?"

"He looks at me funny. Can't keep his eyes off my boobs. Tells me I'm really cute."

"Did Luanne ever tell you he'd molested her?" It was a shot in the dark.

Tracey pursed her lips and inhaled deeply through her nose. She nervously raked her hair behind her ears. "Yeah," she said tersely.

"When did she tell you?"

"Two weeks ago. She said it had been going on for a couple years."

"What prompted her to tell you?"

"She said she was fed up. Was gonna move on."

"What caused her to want to bring it to an end?"

"She met a new guy in school."

"Who?"

"A guy named Bob Black. Real tall."

"What did Bob have to do with Luanne wanting to blow the whistle on her dad?"

"I think it's because Bob's real nice. Not like Tyrone or her dad. Bob seemed to like her for who she was, not what he could get from her. I think being around Bob gave her self-respect—helped her see that not all guys are mean control freaks."

"Did Luanne tell Bob about what her dad was doing to her?"

"I don't know."

"What's your best guess?"

"If she hadn't, she would have pretty soon. They were only just getting started when . . . ." Tracey's voice trailed off and she put my tissue to her mouth.

I placed my hand gently on her back and rubbed it lightly. In a moment, she'd composed herself.

"Did you see Bob here today?"

"Yeah, he was here," she said looking around, "but I don't see him now."

Out of the corner of my eye, I saw Tyrone talking to a couple of his buddies in the church parking lot. I wanted to talk with him before he left, so I quickly wrapped things up with Tracey.

"You've told me some very heavy stuff, Tracey, and I appreciate it. I'll use your name when I mention the nice things you said about Luanne, but the other stuff I'm going to check out a little more first, and I'll keep your name out of it. You've given me some important leads. Maybe your information will help nail the bastard who killed Luanne."

Tracey's eyes welled up again. I asked for and she gave me her cell phone number and email address.

"I want you to meet someone, Tracey." I took her by the hand and led her to where Matt Benson was standing by his unmarked car.

"Tracey, this is Detective Matt Benson. I want you to tell him everything that you told me." I looked Benson in the eye as I said to Tracey, "I *trust* that Mr. Benson will know what to do with the information you're about to give him. I *trust* that," I repeated, making sure he got my point.

THIRTEEN

DEADLINE URGENCY. I was feeling it big time. The funeral service had been over for nearly half an hour, but I still hadn't filed my piece for the website because Tracey had been such a goldmine of information, plus I didn't want Tyrone to get away before I'd had a chance to talk with him.

I left Matt and Tracey to get acquainted and hurriedly crossed the parking lot. Tyrone was leaning against the trunk of a bright red Mustang GT, a toothpick in his mouth. He wore a tight-fitting red polo shirt and black slacks. Two young men stood on either side of him. One was Steroid Boy, the guy who'd talked lovingly of Luanne and had encouraged Tyrone to be strong.

I knew Tyrone saw me approach, but he pretended not to notice me. When I got to him and his friends, I hesitated for a minute as they talked, but then broke through their exclusionary circle.

"Those were nice sentiments you expressed about Luanne," I said to Steroid Boy.

"Th-thanks," he stammered, embarrassed.

"I'm Lark Chadwick with the *Sun-Gazette*. I'm going to quote you in the paper, but can you tell me your name?"

"It's Jim," he said.

"Jim what?"

He paused, seeming to consider whether or not he wanted his name in the paper, but decided to go for the glory. "Mason," he said, simply.

"M-a-s-o-n?"

He nodded.

I wrote it down, then turned to Tyrone. "And you're Tyrone?"

"Yeah," he said.

"I'm sorry for your loss," I said, touching his beefy forearm. It was rock solid.

"Yeah. Whatever," he mumbled, toying with his toothpick.

"Were you her boyfriend?"

The other two guys snorted and shuffled.

"Yeah. Sorta." He gave his friends an ominous stare.

"How'd you meet?" I was trying to soften him up, get him talking, get him to relax.

"In the lunchroom. She let me sit by her."

"When was that?"

"Month ago, I guess."

"I never knew her. What was she like?" I asked.

"She was a bitch," Jim Mason said under his breath.

Tyrone glared at him, then turned to me. "She was nice. Mostly."

"What do you mean?"

He shrugged.

Tyrone, I could tell, was going to be a tough interview. Quickly, I composed a question that wouldn't result in a monosyllabic yes/no response. "For people who didn't know Luanne, what's the most important thing you'd want them to know about her?"

Tyrone shut his eyes for a moment and bit his lower lip. When he opened his eyes, they glistened. "Um . . . " he said softly, then coughed and looked down at his Reeboks. "She was real nice. She was kind. She was understanding." He looked up at me, his wet eyes fierce. "Y'know what I'm sayin'?"

"I do. That's what I'm hearing from others who knew her, too. When was the last time you saw her?"

He shrugged and looked down again. "I dunno. Friday after school, I guess."

"What did you talk about?"

"Nuthin' much. Stuff." He gave me a furtive glance. "Y'know?"

"What kind of stuff?"

He pinched the bridge of his nose and winced as if the memory was too painful.

Mason spoke. "Stuff like that she'd been cheatin' on you," he said to Tyrone. "Go on, dude. Tell her what you told us."

Tyrone pushed himself away from the trunk, flashed his friend a hot glare and shoved him. "You shut your face. You hear me? *Shut* it!"

Mason backed up a few steps. He looked hangdog-chastened.

"Did you have a fight with Luanne after school on Friday?" I asked Tyrone, then held my breath and waited for his answer.

His face morphed from rage at Jim Mason to remorse over Luanne's death. "Maybe," he mumbled.

"What was the argument about?" My voice was tender, nearly a whisper.

Tyrone bared his teeth at me. "That's none o' yer bidness. It's *personal*."

"I'm sorry. I know this is a difficult day for you, Tyrone. I'm just trying to help our readers get to know her."

"She's dead," he said vehemently, throwing down his tooth-pick. "Let her rest in peace. Let *me* have some peace." He pushed past me. "Let's get the hell outta here," he said to his buddies.

They each got in the car. I followed Tyrone. As he opened the driver's door, I touched his cement bicep. "Talk to me, Tyrone. Tell me about Luanne."

He shook off my hand as if I had major cooties, plunged behind the wheel and revved the engine to a throaty growl.

"Please, Tyrone . . . ."

He ignored me, backed rapidly out of the parking space, and threw the car into first gear. As he squealed away, he thrust his left arm out the window, hand held high in a middle-finger salute.

FOURTEEN

TRACEY MEADOWS AND Matt Benson were still talking by his unmarked Crown Vic when Tyrone sped away. Benson was taking copious notes as Tracey chattered on. I dashed past them and got into my car.

Pearlie was roasting in the late afternoon sun. I rolled down all the windows, started the engine, then switched on the AC to blast out the hot air. I slid back my seat, got out my computer, set it on my lap and splayed open my reporter's notebook on the seat beside me. I also placed my iPhone on the seat. When I was ready to write, I rolled up the windows so that the whooshing-cool air would stay inside.

I closed my eyes, collected my thoughts, and then began composing my story about the funeral of Luanne Rae Donovan.

I've been blessed with never having been crippled by writer's block. I start with a lead sentence that slowly comes to mind as I'm still gathering the facts of the story, so that by the time I sit down to write, I have my lead. Everything else just flows naturally from there.

Lionel's voice was always guiding me. "Just accept it, Lark: The first draft is gonna suck. It's a given. Just get something down. You can always go back and tweak."

That advice always took the pressure off having to write a perfect piece the first time because my expectations suddenly became more realistic. The irony, however, was that often the first draft bore a close resemblance to the end product.

The rule I set for myself was to write the first draft hot, then let it simmer while I went back through my notes—and/or the tape recording—to see if I'd missed anything. Then I'd read it through with my editor's cap on, looking at it critically for holes, inconsistencies, awkward or clunky writing, misspellings—and always, *always* looking for ways to tighten and streamline the copy. I never filed the piece with the desk until I could read it through at least twice without changing anything. At *The Pine Bluff Standard*, Lionel rarely had to futz with my copy.

I worked steadily for at least half an hour. I described the funeral service, mentioned some of the hymns, quoted from the testimonies, the pastor's eulogy, and the interviews I did with Jim Mason, Tyrone Jackson and Tracey Meadows. I was tempted to use Tracey's account of Luanne's run-in with Tyrone the day before she died, but I felt that there was too little to go on. I decided that suggesting Tyrone might have killed his ex-girlfriend—juicy though it was—would open me up to a major libel suit if it turned out not to be true. I decided to see if the information Tracey gave to Matt Benson might eventually yield some fruit. It certainly gave me a few things to look into on my own.

While I was busy writing, I glanced up to see Tracey and Matt shake hands and go their separate ways, but I decided not to chase after him just yet to pump him for information. I thought it best to give him time to track down Tracey's leads. Besides, I was on a deadline.

The sun had just gone below the horizon when I finally hit *send*. I closed my eyes, leaned back against the headrest, and let out a satisfied sigh.

Suddenly, a loud rapping on my window startled me. I turned to see the angry face of a man filling the window. In the dim light, I could only tell that he had dark features and relatively short hair.

Quickly, I locked the door.

The man took a step back so that I could see him better. He wore a dark sport coat, an open-necked white shirt and jeans. I didn't recognize him. He gestured for me to roll down my window. I did, but only a crack.

"Who are you and what do you want?" I demanded.

"I want to talk."

"Who are you?"

"I'm the guy you replaced at the *Sun-Gazette*."

"Look, that's not my fault . . . ."

He waved his hand dismissively. "I know."

"What do you want to talk about?"

"I just want to get acquainted. Can I buy ya a drink?"

I laughed at his audacity. "Maybe some other time."

"Just so you know, the *Sun-Gazette's* a snake pit. I can help you. I know where all the bodies are buried," he said.

He had my attention. I was definitely tempted to get the inside scoop on the paper, but drink invitations from men I don't know made me leery. "Thank you for the offer to help, but I'd rather figure that out on my own instead of having some stranger poison the well for me before I've even had a chance to make up my own mind."

"We don't have to be strangers." He tried to smile, but it was crooked, awkward.

I shook my head. "Sorry."

The man shrugged. "Suit yourself."

"Do you have a card?" I asked.

He took his wallet out of his back pocket and fumbled in it before he found what he was looking for. "Just got these printed up," he said, extracting a card. He slipped it to me through the inch-wide crack in my window.

I looked at it. *Sam Erickson* was written in bold letters across the front. Below his name in smaller letters were the words, *The Police Beat.* A web address took up the lower left portion of the card; the lower right gave Sam Erickson's cell phone number. The card contained no street address.

"What's 'The Police Beat?'" I asked.

"My crime reporting blog," he said proudly.

"So, we're competitors," I said.

Sam shrugged again. "It doesn't have to be that way."

"Are you proposing we work *together?*"

"I'm not proposing anything."

"You just—"

"I just wanted to say hello," Sam said, finishing my sentence.

I rolled down my window a little farther and held out my hand to him—actually, I just held out a few fingers. "Okay, then. Nice to meet you, Sam Erickson."

He gripped my fingers, squishing them together, causing me to wince. "Is it true that you discovered Luanne Donovan's body?"

"Yes."

He let go of my fingers. "I don't suppose you'd be willing to tell me anything about the condition of the body or things you observed at the crime scene."

"You suppose correctly." I made a mental note reminding myself to scold Marcie about writing me into the story.

He smiled, broadly this time. "It was worth a try."

"Looks like we'll be seeing a lot of each other," I said.

"Welcome to Columbia, Lark. I wish I could say that you're gonna like it here." With that, he gave me a salute, turned and walked toward his car, a dark sedan, parked a few spaces down from me. He got in, started the engine, backed out, and flipped on his lights. As he drove past me, he gave his horn two light taps.

I shuddered as he turned out of the church parking lot and into traffic. Something about his car didn't seem right. Then it hit me. His headlights were closer together than usual. His brights, even though turned off, were positioned on the outside edges of the front of his car. That meant, I realized, that if all of his headlights had been on, his car might have looked like the one that nearly ran me off the road just moments before I found the strangled and dead body of Luanne Rae Donovan.

FIFTEEN

MY CELL PHONE bleated as I watched Sam Erickson drive out of sight. Caller ID told me it was Lionel.

"Hey," I said.

"Good piece on the kid's funeral."

"Is it on our website already?"

"Uh huh. I get email alerts whenever you file."

"Don't you have anything better to do?" I chuckled.

He laughed. "Always. But you're a great distraction."

"It's nice to see that you're remaining in the twenty-first century, at least technologically speaking." I'd been teasing him about his slowness to adapt ever since he'd finally—and grudgingly—upgraded the computer system at the *Standard*.

"Yeah. What I wouldn't have given when I was your age to have the electronic tools you take for granted now."

"But the downside is so many newspapers are going out of business." I put Pearlie into gear, eased out of the church parking lot, and transferred Lionel to speakerphone.

"Too true," he said. "How are things at the *Sun-Gazette*?"

"Dicier than I was led to believe."

"Oh?"

I told Lionel about the rumored layoffs, Ed's distracted and bedraggled demeanor, and the unsettling meeting I'd just had with Sam Erickson, the guy who, until recently, had been doing my job for the past twenty years.

"Classic," Lionel said.

"What do you mean?"

"Give the expensive old-timer the heave-ho and bring in someone young and cheap to do the same job. Classic age discrimination."

"But isn't that just good business?"

"How so?" He sounded defensive, on the verge of belligerent.

"Newspapers aren't charities. They can't be expected to pay killer salaries in a recession."

"Right. So they pay the old guy a big enough severance, he goes away and doesn't make a stink. Age discrimination."

"Is that why you left the *New York Times*?"

"No comment," he mumbled.

I noticed I was going forty-five in a thirty-five-miles-an-hour zone and eased back on the accelerator. No need to get a ticket when I'm not in a hurry.

"You getting any closer to solving the girl's murder?" Lionel asked.

I sighed. "I don't think so. I'm just accumulating more suspects to choose from."

"It's not just the dad anymore, huh?"

"Nope." I told Lionel about the argument Luanne got into with her ex-boyfriend Tyrone Jackson. I also mentioned the unsettling feeling I'd just had meeting my competitor Sam Erickson and his car's resemblance to the one I saw near the Donovan murder scene.

"What possible motive would the reporter have?" Lionel asked, his voice dripping with skepticism and maybe a bit of defensiveness for members of his chosen profession.

"Good question. I haven't thought that one through yet. Maybe Sam Erickson has a porn problem that's been under control, but then he suddenly loses his job, which triggers him to act out in sexually deviant ways."

"I love it when you speak in psychobabble," he snorted.

"Lionel! Don't mock me. I'm just thinking out loud here."

He grunted.

"But the more I think about it," I said, more to myself than to Lionel, "the more I'm wondering if it might be worth tracking down and interviewing a shrink who deals with this kind of stuff."

"Remember, though, that the girl wasn't sexually assaulted."

"True. Good point. But maybe she was about to be assaulted, fought back, and was killed before anything sexual could happen." I turned Pearlie into the parking lot of Publix because I needed to pick up some supplies. "I've just gotten to the grocery store, Lionel, so I'm gonna sign off. It's good to know you're reading my stuff and it's *always* great talking with you."

"You're doin' a great job, kid. Keep up the good work."

"I miss you."

"Good. Keep that up, too."

I parked the car just as Augie, the bag boy who'd rescued me from the gracious and talented Denise, came past me pushing a cluster of rattling grocery carts.

"Hey, Augie," I said, getting out of Pearlie and locking her with a beep.

His face lit up when he saw me. "Lark! How's it goin'?"

"I wish I had your energy. I'm wiped out. It's been a long day."

"I've still got a couple hours to go," he said.

Just then my cell phone went off. I checked the caller ID. It was the desk.

"Lark Chadwick."

"It's Marcie." A police monitor crackled in the background.

"I'm at the grocery store getting supplies. Need anything?"

"Drop everything." Her voice had an agitated edge.

"Why? What's up?"

"It's happened again."

"What has?"

"They've found the body of another young woman."

"Oh my God. Where?"

"Almost in the same place where you found Luanne Donovan."

"You're kidding! When?"

"Just now. I heard the chatter on the police monitor and followed up. All that the cops will say is what I just told you."

"I'll head to the scene right now." I ended the call and unlocked Pearlie.

Augie's expression morphed from upbeat enthusiasm to genuine concern. "What's wrong, Lark? You look alarmed."

"It's happened again," I said, echoing Marcie. "Another woman's been found dead near where I found Luanne Donovan."

Augie's face fell. "Now it starts," he muttered to himself. "Now it starts."

SIXTEEN

I DROVE AS FAST as I could back to Skunk Run Road, but kept a worried eye on my rearview mirror to make sure I wasn't going to be pulled over for speeding. Before I'd left Wisconsin, my driver's license was hanging by a thread because I'd been stopped so many times while rushing to or from a story. The Wisconsin State Patrol hadn't cut me any slack—I didn't want to test the tolerance of the Georgia cops just now.

Long before I arrived at the murder scene, I could see where it was: two news helicopters hovered over the site, lasering down bright beams of light. I turned off Skunk Run onto Creek, but the road was blocked off at the bridge by a police cruiser parked sideways across the road, its lights strobing blue, red, and white. Several cars and news vans were parked alongside Creek Road and a gaggle of reporters was clustered between the police car and yellow crime scene tape that stretched across the road from one side of the bridge to the other.

I parked Pearlie behind a news van and gathered what I thought I'd need: iPhone, ballpoint, and notebook. I got out and took a quick picture of the cop car and the small crowd gathered nearby, emailed it to Marcie on the desk, then followed up with a phone call.

"*Sun-Gazette*. This is Marcie."

"Hi, Marce. It's Lark. I'm on the scene. Just sent you a picture. It's nothing much, but at least you can get it up on the website."

"Thanks, Lark. I'm on it."

"Got any more info for me?" I asked.

"Nope. The coroner is on the way, but that's it. No arrests. I'll let you know if anything changes."

"Okay. Thanks. I'll see what I can pick up here. In the meantime, can you get graphics to put together a map of the area? Also pull up the headshot we have of Luanne Donovan and any background info we have so we can plug that into my piece."

"Already on it."

"Cool. Thanks. I'll be in touch."

I hung up and walked toward the nearby gaggle of reporters. On the way, I stopped to talk with the cop who was sitting in his patrol car. He rolled down the window as I approached. A frigid blast from inside the car cooled the humid air around me.

"I'm Lark Chadwick with the *Sun-Gazette*. What can you tell me?"

The cop gave me a bored look. "Nuthin,' but thanks for askin'."

"Is Matt Benson on the scene?"

He nodded. "Him and a million others."

"Can I go down there to talk with him?" I knew it was a long shot.

The cop laughed and shook his head. "Nice try, babe."

"Oh well," I smiled. "Thanks." I backed away as his window silently slid up.

I speed-dialed Matt. Thank God he picked up.

"Hi, Lark."

"We have to stop meeting like this."

He chuckled.

"Does this seem familiar, or what?" I asked.

"Eerily so."

"What have you got?"

"We'll be making a statement in a few minutes."

"I'm on a deadline," I said. "Can you give me just a tidbit so I can file something on the web?"

He hesitated, then said tersely, "White female. Caucasian. About twenty-five. How's that?"

"That's good. Thanks. Witnesses? Suspects?"

"We'll make a statement in a minute."

"Okay. How far from where Luanne's body was found was this one found?"

"Exact same spot," he said.

"Thanks, Matt. There are a bunch of us waiting on the other side of the bridge. Are you gonna make the statement there?"

"It'll be the sheriff, but I'll be with him."

"What's his name?"

"Max Parrish. We'll be there in a little bit."

"How little?"

"Wait and see. Gotta go, Lark."

"Thanks, Matt," I said, but he was already gone.

Quickly, I dialed Marcie and gave her what little more I had. She was thrilled because no one else was reporting any of those details. She told me the TV stations were doing live reports, consisting of little more than speculation—no hard facts.

After I got off the phone, I ambled toward the cluster of reporters talking and laughing by one of the news vehicles. Many of them were TV photographers, but Doug was among them. He sidled over to me when he saw me approach.

"Hey," he said. "I just got a shot of the Medical Examiner's van and the ambulance going in. And I got a few long shots of the cops down there." He pointed. From our side of the bridge, we could see the picnic area across the river where I had discovered Luanne's body. High-powered police lights bathed the area, giving it a stark, white pallor. A yellow tarp screened the body from our prying eyes, but we could see plenty of activity as police and plainclothes detectives combed the area for clues. I thought I could see Matt Benson among them.

"Have you sent the pics to the desk yet?" I asked.

"Was gonna do that now."

"Good." I took Doug by his muscled forearm and gently pulled him away from the others and lowered my voice. "I've already gotten a jump on everybody else. The cops are gonna make a statement up here in a few minutes."

"Okay. I'll get that, too."

I let go of his arm, but then he grabbed mine. "Oh," he said softly. "I love it when you whisper."

Before I could protest, he dropped my forearm, turned and walked toward his Jeep. Just then, I saw the lights of another car approaching along the road where I'd just come from.

"Doug," I called.

"Yeah?"

"Do me a favor and squeeze off a couple quick shots of the car that's coming. I've got a funny feeling about those headlights."

He shrugged. "Sure. No problem." Gracefully, he brought the camera up, made a couple of adjustments, aimed and rattled off a series of shots. "Is that enough?" he asked, glancing at me.

"Sure. Thanks."

"What's this all about?" he asked.

"I'll tell you later. No need to file those with the desk, but if you can email them to me, that would be great."

"I was *hoping* you'd give me your email," he smiled. "Now I don't have to ask." He continued walking to his Jeep where he fished a notebook and pen from his camera bag. "So, what is it?" he asked.

"What's what?" My attention was on the approaching vehicle. Its headlights were closer together than on most cars.

"Your email address." Doug's pen was poised to write it down in the notebook.

"Oh," I laughed. "It's Lark dot Chadwick at SunGaz dot com."

"I meant your *home* email."

"This one will do just fine, Mister Mitchell," I mock-scolded.

He scowled, but wrote it down, then fumbled in his equipment bag for a cable, which he connected to his camera and laptop so that he could send his pictures to the desk.

The approaching car pulled off to the side of the road and parked behind Pearlie. The lights went off and the driver got out and strolled down the dark road toward us. It wasn't until he'd gotten close that I recognized him. Sam Erickson.

"Looks like we've got a serial killer on our hands," he said to me. He was creepily jovial.

"Could be," I said. I'd already decided that I was not going to share with him any information I was picking up. At all.

"What do we have?" he asked.

"I just got here myself."

"Hey, Sam," Doug called out as he continued to fiddle with his gear. "How's retirement?"

"You mean banishment?" Sam snapped.

"That's one way of putting it, I guess," Doug shrugged. He continued to work on sending the pictures to the desk.

Sam turned his attention back to me. "We meet again, Miss Chadwick."

"Yes. Apparently so."

"This is becoming a habit."

"The habit is yours." I smiled, but felt uncomfortable.

Just then, there was a flurry of activity as Matt Benson, accompanied by a burly man, approached us from the other side of the bridge. The TV photogs hefted their cameras to their shoulders and flipped on the lights mounted just above their lenses. We all walked to the yellow police tape where the two men came to a stop. The reporters who were there, about five of us, held out microphones and tape recorders.

The man next to Matt cleared his throat. He wore a brown uniform with a *Columbia County Sheriff's Dept.* patch on his right shoulder. "Y'all ready?" he asked.

"Just a second, sheriff," said one of the photogs. He made a quick adjustment. "Okay, sir. Rolling."

"About nine o'clock this evening, a picnicker found the body of what appears to be a young Caucasian woman, mid-twenties, washed up along the shore of the Chattahoochee River. The body was found in almost the exact same location where the body of Luanne Rae Donovan was found on Saturday night. We don't have a positive identification yet. The coroner tells me he believes the victim has been dead for a day or two. That's about all I've got, guys."

"Why was someone picnicking here?" I asked. "Wasn't it still a crime scene from the Donovan murder?"

"Nope," the sheriff answered. "We cleared the scene about mid-afternoon on Sunday.

"Any witnesses?" someone asked.

"No."

"How was she killed?" Sam asked.

"Gonna leave that up to the coroner to decide."

"Suspects?" I asked.

"There are several leads we're following."

"Does this look like the work of the same person who killed Luanne Donovan?" I asked.

"Possibly, quite possibly. We're proceeding under that assumption."

"So, it would appear that a serial killer is on the loose?" I asked.

"That's affirmative," the sheriff replied.

At that instant, I knew I had my lead: *A serial killer is on the loose in Columbia County, police say.*

"Who found the body?" Sam asked.

"The girl who found the body is a minor so I'm not going to release her name."

"Was she with her parents?" Sam asked.

"Yes."

"So how 'bout releasing their names?" Sam pressed.

"That would be the same as releasing hers," the sheriff answered.

"No it wouldn't," Sam snarled, his voice rising.

"Any other questions?" the sheriff asked.

When no one else spoke up, the sheriff ended the informal presser. "Well, okay then. Thanks, ever'body."

He and Matt turned away, but I stepped forward to the yellow crime scene tape. "Sheriff?" I called.

He turned to look at me.

I held out my business card. "I'm Lark Chadwick with the *Sun-Gazette*. Do you have a card?"

"Sure." He fumbled in his pocket and came up with one. "Here you go," he said, handing the card to me and taking mine. He turned and walked away looking at my card, but then stopped abruptly and turned around. "C'mere," he said, crooking his beefy forefinger at me.

I ducked under the police tape and hurried to his side. He put his arm on my shoulder and walked me out of earshot of Sam and the other reporters.

"Ain't you the one who discovered the first body?"

"Yes, sir."

"Walk with us."

I fell in step between him and Matt Benson, who continued his silence.

"You've been doing a fair and responsible job reporting this story, Miss Chadwick," the sheriff said in a low voice.

"Thank you, sir."

"I want you to take a look at the murder scene."

"Okay."

"But on one condition."

"What's that?"

"No pictures. And you can't report any details about the body."

"That's two conditions."

"Whatever."

"I've got no problem about the pictures," I said, "but why no reporting about the body?"

"We don't want the killer to know what we know."

"Then why do you want to show it to me?"

"I want you to look at the scene and tell me if you see any similarities or differences with the Donovan crime scene."

"Okay. Sure. I'll try to be helpful."

Within two minutes we were back at the spot where I'd found Luanne Donovan. The body of the latest victim was face down, half in the water and half on the sand at the water's edge, fully clothed in a waterlogged sleeveless yellow dress, but barefoot.

"This is right where I found Luanne's body."

"Right," he said.

"Does that mean their bodies could have been placed here on purpose rather than being thrown from the bridge?"

"Not necessarily."

I could tell he was in a talkative mood, but I had to get him to take off the muzzle he'd placed on me or I wouldn't be able to use anything in my story that he was about to say.

"We're not talking about the victim's body any more, so can we go back on the record?" I asked.

He gave me an indignant look. "Not on your life. We're talking about the theory of the case. That car you saw could be the breakthrough we need."

We stood glaring at each other for a moment before I blinked. "Okay," I sighed. "We're still off the record. Go on."

He looked at me a beat longer, deciding. Finally, he turned away and pointed toward the bridge. "If both bodies were dropped from the same place on the bridge, then the strong current could have taken both of them to this spot where we are now. When the river bends to the left, the current sweeps up against the bank here." He pointed to the gnarled roots of two trees that had fallen into the river. "These trees act as sort of a bay or cove that snags objects floating downstream."

"I see," I said. "So you're assuming the body was dumped by the same person from the same location on the bridge?"

"That's one theory. Yes."

"Does it make sense?" I asked.

"Sure. It makes sense to dispose of the body in water because fibers, fluids and other evidence have a better chance of being washed away. It also makes sense because the killer remains in his comfort zone. He's chosen a remote location he's apparently familiar with. Maybe he hoped that the body would have gone farther downstream. I don't think he planned for the second body to come to rest in the same location as the first."

"However, both girls could have been killed right *here.*" I said.

"Yes. Maybe. But there's no sign of a struggle."

"Could they have been killed in a car or someplace else and then dumped here?"

"There's no sign the body was dragged."

"She could have been carried."

"No footprints."

"Are you kidding? Cops were walking all over the place for hours after I found Luanne."

"I'll amend that. No *fresh* footprints."

The sheriff was shooting down all my ideas, but his tone of voice showed that he had respect for the way I was thinking. I liked that.

"Before I forget," I said. "I've just now seen the front end of a car whose headlight configuration resembles the car I saw on the bridge just before I found the body."

"Oh? Tell me more," the sheriff said.

"The car belongs to Sam Erickson."

"No shit? Pardon my French, ma'am. Sam Erickson, the *reporter?*"

"Yes. I have no idea if he killed Luanne and no objective reason to believe he did, but I do have a possible theory."

"I'm listening," the sheriff said.

Matt took out a notebook and looked at me expectantly.

"Look, I don't want to get him in trouble, but it occurred to me that the stress of losing his job at the *Sun-Gazette* might have caused him to snap. I've only talked with him briefly twice, but he seems to have anger issues, plus his car looks familiar. That's all."

"Okay. That's helpful." He nodded thoughtfully and exchanged a look with Benson. "We'll check it out."

"Thanks. But keep my name out of it, okay?" I said to both of them.

"Sure. No problem." The sheriff turned his attention toward the body at our feet. "Let's flip her over," he said to Benson.

Together, Matt and the sheriff bent over and gently rolled the body of the girl onto her back.

I let out a surprised yelp. I recognized her. The dead girl was the bleach-blonde Doug had his arm around at Ed's barbecue.

SEVENTEEN

❚❚DO YOU RECOGNIZE her?" the sheriff asked, surprised.

As I stood looking down at the corpse, a thousand thoughts careened through my head. My first reaction was panic at the realization that perhaps Doug was the killer. But that didn't compute. Maybe he was a player, but he was a damn good photographer and didn't seem to be particularly creepy—not nearly as creepy as Sam Erickson, Tyrone Jackson, or Luanne's dad.

My next instinct was to tell the truth and say immediately that I'd seen the dead woman with Doug Sunday night.

That thought was then crowded out by a selfish desire to lie to the sheriff and protect Doug because, damn it, I was attracted to him and, on a purely carnal and irrational level, I didn't want to believe that he was a murderer. I wanted to protect Doug so that he could still be available to me in case some of the sparks that flew between us got fanned into something hotter. That wouldn't happen if he became the prime suspect in a serial killer investigation.

As the seconds ticked by and the sheriff waited for my response, yet another thought peeled through my mind: What would happen if I lied to the sheriff and he later discovered that both the victim and I were at the same picnic?

Finally, my thoughts circled back to the first one: What if Doug Mitchell really was the serial killer?

"Miss Chadwick?" the sheriff barked.

I pried my eyes away from the dead body and looked at the sheriff and Matt Benson peering at me quizzically.

"Sorry. What?" I asked, stalling for time.

"Your reaction indicates to me that you either know or recognize the victim," the sheriff said.

"Um, what makes you think that?" More stalling from me.

"Because you're a tough cookie. You've already seen one dead body and you didn't barf. And you took this murder scene in stride—until we turned over the body. Seems to me you know her."

"I-I don't know her," I said. It was true. I didn't. So far, so good.

"But?" he prompted.

"But what?"

"But you *might*?"

I pursed my lips, trying to decide what to do. I tried humor. "Objection. Leading the witness."

"C'mon, damn it. I don't have all night. You *might* know her—or recognize her?"

"Yes. I might. She looks familiar."

"Now we're gettin' somewhere. Got a name?"

I shook my head.

"How do you know her?"

"I told you—I don't."

"Christ. Don't make me play twenty questions. Where have you *seen* her before?"

"I-I saw her Sunday night at a barbecue at my boss's house."

"Who was she with?"

I bit my lower lip.

"Miss Chadwick, withholding information from the police about a murder investigation is an obstruction of justice. It's a very serious crime." He paused between the last three words and enunciated each one elaborately.

"I know." I took a deep breath . . . and deeply regretted my next words. "I saw her with Doug Mitchell, my photographer." I looked up sheepishly at Sheriff Parrish, trying to gauge his expression. It was blank. "Do you know him?" I asked.

"Not by name, but I might recognize him if I saw him."

"He's my shooter tonight."

Matt chimed in. "I know him, sheriff. He was at the news conference just a few minutes ago."

"Good lookin' guy? Long hair?" the sheriff asked.

"Right," Matt and I said simultaneously.

"Yeah. I know who you mean." He nodded at the body. "Did they leave the picnic together?"

"I don't know," I answered, honestly.

"Are you and this Doug guy an item?"

"No."

"You sure?" He hunched his eyebrows at me.

"Believe me, I'd know it if we were."

The sheriff grunted and took Matt by the arm. "Excuse us for just a second, Miss Chadwick." He and Matt walked several paces away from me until they were out of earshot.

The sheriff leaned his head close to Matt and did most of the talking. As he talked, the sheriff pulled a round tin of what looked like chewing tobacco out of his back pocket, took off the lid, dipped his thumb and first two fingers in, pulled out a pinch and stuck it between his cheek and lower side teeth. As he chawed, he closed the tin and returned it to his pocket, all the while continuing to talk animatedly. Matt listened and mostly nodded. After a few minutes, they ambled back to me.

"How well do you know Doug Mitchell?" the sheriff asked me, his cheek now bulging like a tumor.

"I just started working with him. He's good."

"Does he trust you?"

"Yeah. I think so. Why?"

"We want to put a wire on you."

"A wire?"

"A listening device. We want you to get him alone and try to have him talk about his relationship with the girl. It's dangerous, but you'd be safe because we'd be monitoring the signal, and you'd be surrounded with armed officers who would swoop in and make an arrest if anything goes wrong."

I could hear Lionel in my head screaming at me. "That's a frigging conflict of interest, Lark! You can't work for the police AND objectively report the story."

I found myself having a conversation with Lionel in my head—okay a flaming argument—but before it got nasty, the sheriff interrupted.

"Miss Chadwick?"

"I'm thinking. I want to be helpful. Really, I do, but it would be a conflict of interest for me to, in effect, be an agent of the police force."

"We have two murders on our hands, ma'am," the sheriff said, his voice rising. "Other people's lives may be at risk because the murderer may be a serial killer. When the next body shows up, do you want it on your conscience that you refused to help us?"

My mind was racing. He had a point. But so did I. I wracked my brain, trying to find a way out.

"Why don't you or Matt question him, sheriff?" I asked. "Why do you need me to do your job for you?"

"Because, Miss Chadwick, I don't have enough to go on yet. If we question him now, it might spook him. I don't want him to know we're on to him. By putting a wire on you, he might say something incriminating, then: *bam.*" He clapped his hands. "We nail him."

"He might also get suspicious and make me victim number three."

"Yes. He could try to do that, but, as I say, that's when the calvary comes riding to your rescue, we get our man, the killings stop, justice is done, and the community is safe once again." He rubbed his hands together to show how simple, neat, and tidy his solution would be.

His misuse of the word calvary for cavalry did not inspire my confidence in him. "Look. Sheriff," I said. "I understand what you're saying. But do you see my point?"

"Frankly, no. I don't. I think catching killers trumps freedom of the press every damn time. Hands down."

"I'm all for catching whoever did this," I replied, "but I can't, in good conscience, abdicate my responsibility as a reporter. I've been around too many crooked cops to know it's why the Founding Fathers created the first amendment and a free and unfettered press—the fourth estate, if you will—to be a check and balance on government officials."

"Spare me your sanctimonious lecture about the constitution, *Justice* Chadwick." He spat a stream of tobacco juice that landed just inches in front of my feet. He was red in the face. In a moment we'd be having a shouting match over a dead body.

Matt touched the sheriff on the arm. "Maybe there's some middle ground," Matt said.

The sheriff turned and glared at Matt. "What do you mean?"

"I can attest that Lark here is a good citizen *and* a trustworthy reporter."

"Oh?"

"First, you said it yourself: She's been doing a responsible job covering this story. For example, she's refrained from mentioning anything about the missing earring in any of her reporting."

"Yeah? So?" The sheriff was still irked, but at least he was listening to Matt.

"And, this afternoon, Lark came across a female witness who claims to have seen the ex-boyfriend confront the Donovan girl Friday afternoon, a little more than a day before her death."

"So?"

"After interviewing the young woman for the newspaper, Lark brought her to me so that I could interrogate her. Miss Chadwick didn't have to do that."

The sheriff's face softened and he rubbed his chin thoughtfully. "Yeah. I see what you mean." He turned and looked at me sternly. "Okay, here's the deal." He was not in a negotiating mood. "If you don't want to wear a wire, that's fine, but it royally pisses me off. That said, by refusing to do so, I want it understood that you are putting your life in danger by associating with a person who may have killed twice and won't hesitate to kill you if he suspects you know too much."

"Wouldn't I be putting myself at the same risk by wearing a wire?"

"Sure, but there'd be heavily armed calvary ready to ride to your rescue."

I winced.

"Without the wire, you're pretty much on your own." He paused. "Do you own or carry a weapon?"

"No and no."

"You sure you don't want to rethink that?"

"Positive. I hate guns. I know they're necessary sometimes, but they just make me nervous."

"Back to what I was saying: You're at a greater risk knowing what you know about this guy, but not cooperating with us. Can I at least get a promise from you that if you come across anything else that may help this investigation—*anything*—that you won't hesitate to bring it to our attention?"

"I don't have a problem with that, so long as I'm not hindered in any way from doing my job."

"Then I think we understand each other." He lasered me in the eyes with his glare, but I returned his stare until he finally looked away.

A few minutes later, the three of us were walking back up the road and toward the bridge.

The sheriff broke the silence. "I think I'll bring our boy Doug down there to look at the body. What'dya think, Matt?"

"Works for me, sheriff."

But when we got to the bridge, Sam and Doug were gone.

EIGHTEEN

There's a joke I heard once that goes like this:

A good-looking guy walks into a bar. He's dirty, disheveled, and looks like he hasn't slept in days. He says to the bartender, "I just killed my wife. Gimme a double."

The bartender complies and the guy gulps it down.

Slamming the empty glass onto the bar, the mess-of-a-guy says, "Gimme another double."

The bartender obeys.

As the confessed wife-killer is downing his second stiff drink, an attractive woman sidles over to him.

"Excuse me," she purrs in her most alluring voice. "Did I just hear you say you're *single*?"

As I drove away from the murder scene to find Doug, that joke was playing in my head because, like the foolish floozy in the joke, I was drawn to Doug Mitchell in an illogical way I couldn't explain.

The good and wise Lark Chadwick of my inner dialogue kept harping at the foolish Lark Chadwick:

GOOD LARK: Run the other way, girl.

FOOLISH LARK: Why? Doug's hot and I want him.

GOOD LARK: He's a player.

FOOLISH LARK: I can tame him . . . and I'll have fun doing it.

GOOD LARK: He's dangerous.

FOOLISH LARK: Indeed.

GOOD LARK: He might be a killer.

FOOLISH LARK: The only reason I want to talk with him is either to confirm him as a murder suspect—or exonerate him.

GOOD LARK: Yeah. Right.

FOOLISH LARK: Zip it. I'm sick of your virginal sanctimoniousness.

Foolish Lark won the argument. Why? Because she ignores wise counsel and impulsively does whatever she wants.

I fished my cell phone out of my bag and called Doug.

"Hey there," he said jovially.

"Where are you?"

"Marcie dispatched me to the scene of a bad accident on the other side of the county."

"Is that where you are now?"

"Yeah. Just finishing up."

"We need to talk."

"Excellent. I'm on my way home. I'll meet you there."

"No. There's an all-night diner near the paper. I'll be there in about twenty minutes."

"Dino's, right?"

"Right."

"Fine. See you there."

We hung up.

GOOD LARK: Slut! Slut! Slut!

FOOLISH LARK: Shut up. We're just gonna talk.

GOOD LARK: So you say.

As I drove slowly back toward town, I called the desk. Marcie picked up.

"Hi, Marce. It's Lark."

"Hey, Lark. Sorry I had to pull Doug. We're short-handed. Did you get what you needed from him before he had to go?"

"Yeah. Thanks." I dictated my serial-killer-on-the-loose lead and the few extra details I had about the latest murder. What we had was pretty sketchy until the police could make a firm ID and pinpoint a cause of death, which would be a long time after the newspaper had gone to bed.

Doug was waiting for me at the diner when I arrived, sitting in a booth sipping a cup of coffee. The place was brightly lit and nearly empty. I slid into the booth, my heart beating wildly. Stupidly, I hadn't calmly thought through my line of questioning. I was winging it.

"Looks like you scored a coup," he said after I ordered coffee.

"How so?"

"It's not every reporter who gets invited by the sheriff to view a crime scene."

"Yeah. Lucky me."

"Why you?"

"Dunno. I'm as surprised as you are. I think it's because the body was found where I found the first one and he wanted my impressions."

"And what are your impressions?"

This wasn't going well. I was supposed to be the one asking the questions, but Doug had swiftly and skillfully taken control, throwing me off balance.

"I don't want to talk about it right now," I said. "Tell me about the accident."

He shrugged. "Head-on collision on a county road. Killed both drivers."

"Any passengers? Injuries?"

"Nope. They were the only two in the cars. Cops think they might have been playing chicken. Lots of empty beer cans in both vehicles. Not pretty."

"Did you phone in the details?"

"Yeah. The desk can track down the rest."

"I'll follow up on it tomorrow. That chicken angle is kind of interesting."

There was an uncomfortable silence. The guy behind the counter brought me my coffee and I doctored it up with my usual cream and sugar.

"So, how long have you been at the *Sun-Gazette*?" I asked Doug.

"Couple years."

"What were you doing before that?"

"I was in the Army."

My eyebrows raised involuntarily. "Really? Doing what?"

"Shooting."

"With a gun?"

He laughed. "Nope. Combat photography. Did two tours in Iraq."

"Why'd you join the Army?"

"Patriotic, I guess."

He had me completely off balance. I never would have suspected Doug was the military type. I found it hard to picture him with extremely short hair.

As I tried to gather my thoughts, Doug asked, "So, what about you? What were you doing before here?"

I brought him up to date as briefly as I could about working with Lionel, but I found myself babbling on and on about what a good teacher he is. As I talked, Doug seemed mesmerized by my story. He sat listening intently, cupping his chin in his hand, elbow resting on the Formica tabletop.

"I'm talking too much," I said, finally.

"No you're not. You're fascinating."

I felt myself blush.

The waiter came and refilled our coffees, then left us alone again.

"I can't believe I've only been at the paper a couple days and already so much is happening," I said.

"Yeah. It's really gotten busy." He took a sip. I noticed he drank it black. "How do you like the paper so far?" he asked.

"I like it, but I'm a little spooked about all the talk about layoffs."

He nodded.

"Did you know Sam Erickson well?" I asked.

"Sure."

"That's not a ringing endorsement. Care to elaborate?"

"You know the old saying, 'If you can't say anything good about a person, don't say anything at all.'"

"Humor me."

"Let's just say he has a tendency to cut corners."

"What about Ed?"

Doug shook his head. "Good guy, but he's under incredible pressure from the fifth floor. I think his job's on the line."

"And Marcie?"

He smiled knowingly while absentmindedly fingering the lip of his coffee mug. "Marcie's . . ." he paused. "Marcie."

"That's diplomatic."

"Hey. She's your roommate. I plead the fifth."

"Oh, I've been meaning to ask you: Who was the girl you were with at Ed's barbecue?"

He shrugged. "One of Ed's neighbors. Met her that night."

"What's her name?"

He arched his eyebrows, amused. "Want her number, too? I didn't know you played for the other team."

"Seriously, what's her name?"

"Why do you want to know? I try to keep my personal life personal."

"You don't know her name, do you?"

He looked down at his coffee sheepishly and contorted his lips. "Busted."

I waited until he looked up at me. "I just saw her tonight," I said.

"You did?"

"At the murder scene."

He looked confused. "How could I have missed her? What was *she* doing there?"

"She was the center of attention."

He furrowed his brow and shook his head slowly. "I'm not following you, Lark."

"Doug, the woman you were with the other night is the latest victim."

NINETEEN

DOUG'S JAW DROPPED and his eyes bugged out. Until this moment, he'd been the master of his emotions. Joe Cool. Now he looked genuinely stricken.

"Oh my God," he said. "Are you sure?"

I nodded. "I saw her, Doug."

He brought both his hands to his face and kept them there for a moment. When he finally put them down, it looked as though he'd just aged ten years. His fingers trembled as they rested on the table.

"How well did you know her?" I asked gently.

He shook his head. "Hardly at all."

"Did you leave with her?"

He nodded. "Walked her home. She lives in the neighborhood."

"Was she married?"

He shook his head. "Lives alone."

"Did she invite you in?"

"Oh yeah."

"Did you go?"

"Nope. Wanted to, but I'm trying to change my ways. We just made out a little."

"What do you mean that you're trying to change your ways?"

"Playing the field's getting old. I'm looking for something more long-term."

"Did you see her again?"

He shook his head. "She gave me her number and begged me to call, but I didn't."

I wanted to believe him, but I still wasn't sure. "How good's your alibi?"

He looked up sharply. "What do you mean? You don't think I killed her, do you?"

"It doesn't matter what I think. If she's been dead a couple days, then you might have been the last person to see her alive."

"Jesus," he said. His face drained of all its color and his eyes got deer-in-the-headlights wide. "After I dropped her off, I went home and watched TV before bed. I was home alone."

I shook my head, sympathetically. Just then, the door behind me opened and I heard someone enter. The wide-eyed look on Doug's face caused me to turn around.

The sheriff and Matt Benson were walking swiftly in our direction. They had stern looks on their faces and the sheriff's hand rested on his holstered gun.

"Are you Douglas Grant Mitchell?" the sheriff asked.

"Y-yes," Doug managed to reply.

"We'd like you to come with us, sir. We have some questions we'd like to ask you about the murder of Luanne Rae Donovan and Polly Lorraine Arceneaux."

"Am I under arrest?"

"Not if you come peacefully."

Doug, his face ghost-white, slowly slid out of the booth and stood before the two men. Matt took him firmly by the arm, but did not handcuff him, and hustled him to the door as a swarm of police cars, lights flashing, converged on the scene in a massive show of force.

The sheriff stayed behind. "Evening again, Miss Chadwick." He tipped his Smoky the Bear hat. "Nice of you to lead us to the suspect. We'll take it from here."

Before I could say anything, he turned and walked toward the door.

TWENTY

HEY!" I CALLED after the sheriff's retreating hulk. "What about me?"

He stopped at the door and gave me a look. "What about you?"

"Don't you want me to come along, too?"

He scowled and shook his head. "That won't be necessary. You're more valuable to me on the outside, doing *your* job by showing that the sheriff is doing *his*." He gave me a self-satisfied chuckle and followed Doug and Matt down the front steps of the diner.

I watched as Matt eased Doug into the rear seat of an unmarked Crown Vic. When Matt and the sheriff sped off, the other cop cars gradually dispersed, their flashing lights turning off one by one.

Quickly, I dialed the desk. Marcie picked up.

"Take this down," I ordered.

"Geez, Lark. I knew I shouldn't have picked up. I was just leaving. I'm exhausted."

"This is important. You ready?"

"Go ahead," she said heavily.

I began to dictate: "A suspect has been taken in for questioning in the case of the young woman found dead tonight along the shores of the Chattahoochee River.

"In a massive show of force, several police cars, along with Columbia County Sheriff Max Parrish and County Detective Matt Benson swarmed Dino's Diner in downtown Columbia just before midnight and took in a man for questioning.

"One witness describes the man as about 35 with long hair and an athletic build. Police made it clear the man is not under arrest, but is wanted for questioning in tonight's death investigation, as well as the strangulation death last weekend of Luanne Rae Donovan, 15."

I asked Marcie, "Have police released the name of the victim yet?"

"No."

"Her name is Polly Lorraine Arceneaux. I'm not sure of the spelling. But don't go with this unless police confirm that they've notified next of kin and they give the okay to go with the name, okay?"

"Gotcha. Do you have the name of the suspect?"

"I do, but since he hasn't been charged, it might be considered libelous to go with it just yet."

"Okay. What else?"

"I think that's it for now." I paused to think. "Oh! Give me Ed's home number."

"Now? It's almost midnight. He'll kill you."

"I have to take my chances. It's important."

Marcie gave me Ed's number and we hung up.

Ed answered on the fourth ring. "Hullo?" His speech was slurred as if he'd been drinking, not sleeping.

"Ed, it's Lark Chadwick."

"Wh-who?"

"It's Lark, your cops and courts reporter."

"Oh. Hi, Lark."

"Listen, I'm sorry to call so late. I hope I didn't wake you up."

He grunted. "No. I had to answer the phone."

"We have a problem, Ed."

"We do?"

"The police have taken Doug Mitchell in for questioning."

"Doug? Our photographer? Wh-why?"

"Another young woman's been found dead. They think he might have something to do with it."

"No. Not Doug."

"Yes. Doug."

"Our Doug?"

"Yes."

"Why?"

"Long story. The bottom line is I think the paper needs to get its attorney down to the county jail as quickly as possible. Doug may be a bit disoriented. He needs to have a lawyer there to stick up for him. I think the cops *might* be barking up the wrong tree."

"What's the right tree?" Ed was sounding more coherent now.

"Dunno. I'm just saying Doug needs legal help and he needs it now before he says something that can be used against him unfairly. I'm pretty sure the cops are anxious to file murder charges and get this serial killer case closed as soon as possible."

"Doug's involvement doesn't make any sense to me, but okay. I'll get right on it. Thanks for the tip, Lark."

"Sure thing. Thanks, Ed."

I'd done about as much as I could do. I decided to head to the apartment to get a little sleep. It might be my last chance to sleep for awhile.

TWENTY-ONE

I **LEARNED AN IMPORTANT** lesson that night: whenever I *try* to sleep, I can't. When I got to the apartment, Marcie hadn't gotten home yet, so I slipped into my sweatpants and a U.W. T-shirt and tried to fall asleep on what was my temporary bed—the living room couch. I mostly tossed and turned and was still wide awake half an hour later when I heard Marcie trudging up the stairs.

"Rough night, huh?" I asked putting on my glasses as she came through the door.

"Rough fits," she said, trying to smile.

"Thanks for your help tonight."

"Sure. No problem." She paused. "Should I pour us a nightcap?"

I sat up. "That would be great. Maybe it'll help me get to sleep."

I wandered into the kitchen behind her.

Marcie came to a stop in the middle of the room, looking undecided. "Red or white?" she asked, her hand at her chin.

I thought for a minute. "Do you have white?"

"I do. Shall we do another Riesling?"

I nodded vigorously. "Very refreshing."

Marcie opened the fridge and brought out a bottle that had been chilling. As she did that, I went to the cupboard and took out two glasses.

"You seem bothered about something," she said, simply.

"Remember the thirty-five-year-old guy with long hair and an athletic build I told you about tonight, the one the cops took in for questioning?"

"Uh huh."

"I didn't want to tell you over the phone, but the guy is Doug."

"You're *kidding!*" She stopped twisting the cork and looked at me, stunned, her hands still cupped at the top of the sweating wine bottle. "Doug's been *arrested?*"

"Not 'arrested' as in handcuffs and 'you have the right to remain silent,' but 'come with us downtown, sir.'"

"Oh, my God." Her face had gone ashen. "Do you think he's . . . ."

"The serial killer?"

She nodded dumbly.

"Don't know, but my gut tells me no."

She gave me a hopeful look. "How good's your gut, normally?"

I let out a little laugh. "Not always so good."

"Well, *my* gut tells me he could *never* have done it!" Marcie's voice was resolute, but her hand trembled as she resumed her job of taking out the cork. She poured us both a generous portion. All the while she seemed lost in thought and deeply troubled.

"I didn't mean to drop such a bomb on you," I said. "Are you two close?"

"Wh-what?" She refocused on me, the dazed look on her face beginning to fade.

"I said, 'are you two close?'"

She took a deep gulp of wine. "That depends on how you define 'close.'" She picked the bottle up by the neck and led me into the living room. "Music?" she asked, turning off all the lights, but one—a lamp on an end table.

"Sure. Got any smooth jazz?"

"Do you like Sade?"

"I *love* Sade. She's my favorite."

Marcie fiddled with her iPod, found what she was looking for, and in seconds, Sade's velvet voice was flowing into the room. Marcie turned the volume down so that the music was background sound, allowing us to continue our talk. She flopped onto the striped easy chair by the couch, and I sat in a chair by an ottoman. We both put our feet up on it.

We sat quietly listening to the music before Marcie spoke: "Are we close?" she asked, repeating my question. "Yes . . . and . . . no."

"Care to elaborate?"

"No."

When I remained silent, she added, "It's complicated and I'm too tired."

"You've known him longer than me. Why don't you think he's capable of killing one or both of the women?"

She took a sip and shrugged, "Anyone's capable of murder under the right circumstances." She paused, considering my question, then frowned and shook her head. "I've never gotten that kind of vibe from him. He *seems* pretty normal."

"From what I've read, Ted Bundy seemed pretty normal too."

Marcie winced, but then nodded thoughtfully.

The sounds of "Smooth Operator" oozed into the room. It reminded me of other times I'd trusted—and fallen for—men who'd turned out to have been just that: smooth and crafty manipulators who tried to use me to get what they wanted.

I took a sip of wine and let it cool and soothe my parched throat. Marcie was good company. I liked her and appreciated that she'd opened her place to me. I set my glass on an end table and let my thoughts drift.

I must have been dozing because suddenly my eyes flew open. Marcie was sitting up. Her feet were planted firmly on the floor, no longer sharing the ottoman where mine still rested. Her elbows were on her thighs, chin resting on her two palms, fingers balled at her cheeks. She was looking at me intently.

"Sorry," I said, rubbing my eyes. "I must have been dozing. Did you just ask me something?"

She smiled. "I said, 'what's your plan for tomorrow?'"

"Oh," I laughed. "I haven't figured that out yet."

"I wish I could be in the field covering this story," she said. "You're so lucky. I'm trapped on the desk."

"Your time will come."

She frowned.

"What would you do if you were me?" I asked.

"First, I'd go to the morning meeting."

"At the paper?"

She nodded. "It's at nine in the fifth floor conference room. That's where they map out the day's coverage."

"Can anyone go?"

"Uh huh. It's mandatory for the editors of the various sections, but anyone's welcome. Reporters show up now and then."

"Good. I'll go. You gonna be there?"

"I try not to miss it."

I looked at my watch. It was after one in the morning. "Geez. I should try to get some sleep."

Marcie laughed. "Actually, you'd already gotten started. You were just beginning to drool."

I laughed and drained my wine. "Thanks for the nightcap."

"You're welcome. We should do this more often." She stood.

"Here," I said, standing and taking her empty wine glass from her. "I'll take that off your hands for you."

"Thanks." She headed toward her room. "G'night, Lark."

I put our glasses in the dishwasher then crossed back to the couch, switched off the lamp on the end table and slid under the quilt. I fluffed my pillow and curled into the fetal position, fully expecting blessed unconsciousness to follow immediately. It didn't. I rolled onto my back and stared at the ceiling, watching as light from cars going by on Broad Street played across the molding from one side of the room to the other.

As I lay there, I went over the day's events in my mind. Luanne's funeral seemed eons ago and already there was another dead girl. Now my coworker Doug was in jail and under suspicion. My thoughts turned to the other possible suspects: Luanne's dad, Tyrone Jackson, Sam Erickson—and then returned to Doug. Which one had a connection to both women?

I know I slept, but my unconscious dredged up troubling images of faceless murderous men and helpless female victims.

TWENTY-TWO

WAS UP BY seven and out within thirty minutes. I hadn't been to my desk at the paper for at least a day and was beginning to feel overwhelmed and disoriented. The pace at a daily paper is MUCH faster than at Lionel Stone's weekly in Wisconsin.

As I sat at my desk, I sketched out a to-do list that included checking with the cops to see if they had notified the next of kin so that I could release the name of the latest victim. I also made a note to check into last night's fatal head-on car collision that Doug told me the cops thought was a deadly game of chicken. In addition, I needed to make my daily beat calls to the other law enforcement agencies—and try to come up with an idea for my next fricking blog.

My mind kept coming back to the serial killings. I felt I needed to find a shrink to interview who was an expert on these types of things to help me—and the public—get a better idea of how a killer thinks. I also wanted to do a profile on Matt Benson who was the lead investigator of the serial killings.

Oh. And Doug. I needed to find out what was up with him.

I scanned the wires for the latest news. The police had released the name of the victim overnight: Polly Lorraine Arceneaux, age 21. She worked as a secretary at an insurance firm. Police believed she'd been sexually assaulted. She, too, had been strangled. The story was on the national wire, so my competition had just increased exponentially.

About eight-thirty I called Matt.

"Mornin', Lark," he mumbled.

"Ain't caller ID grand?" I laughed.

"It can be. I took your call, didn't I?"

"Yes. A good sign and I appreciate that. Thanks."

"My pleasure."

"So, do the wires have the correct information?" I read him the AP story about the murder.

"Yeah. That pretty much sums it up."

"There's no mention of Doug. What's his status?"

"Questioned and released."

"Not charged?"

"No."

"Why not?"

"No comment."

"Is he still a suspect?"

"Not officially."

"*Un*officially?"

"No comment."

"I think I just got my answer."

"Think what you want, Lark, but he's a free man."

"Does he still have his passport?"

"No. We're keeping an eye on it for him."

"Can he leave town?"

"He can still do his job, so long as it doesn't take him very far away. We might need to question him again."

"Can we go on background?"

"I'd rather not."

"C'mon, Matt. I helped you out yesterday by giving you that girl, Tracey, at the church after the funeral."

"And I helped you out with the sheriff at the crime scene, so I'd say we're even."

I sighed. "I want to do a profile on you, now that you're the lead investigator."

"Not gonna happen."

"Why not? The taxpayers should get to know who their champion is."

"Since you put it that way, I'll think about it."

"That's a start. Thanks." I paused to collect my thoughts. "Did Tracey give you any helpful information?"

"She might have."

"Have you questioned Luanne's father and Tyrone, her ex-boyfriend?"

"Yes."

"Are they suspects?"

"No comment."

"Okay," I laughed. "Maybe you'll be more talkative once you've had your morning coffee."

He chuckled. "I'm on my third cup."

"Thanks, Matt. I'll talk to you later."

I strolled into the morning editorial meeting at 8:55. The glassed-in conference room was claustrophobic. Several men and a couple women sat in easy chairs around an oval table. Less comfortable chairs lined the two side walls. Younger employees, many of them women—interns, I assumed—sat in those. People were still filing in. I sat in a chair in a corner against the back wall at the far end of the conference table.

Most people were focused on their BlackBerrys, but there was some low-key bantering, too. A guy sitting to my left was talking to a woman next to him. I overheard just the tail-end of his conversation: "...she's so litigious that she'll sue if a comma's out of place, so I decided to write the piece without any commas."

The woman snickered and touched his sleeve.

I noticed Marcie wasn't there, but it didn't surprise me. She'd worked a long, grueling day yesterday. I assumed she wasn't scheduled to come in until later. Lord knows she deserved to sleep in.

Ed was among the stragglers. He looked terrible, like he hadn't slept. He carried a Starbucks coffee and his hands seemed to be trembling.

Elmer Wiesenthal, the publisher, was the last to enter the room. I'd seen pictures of him, but the only time we'd spoken was the day he hired me over the phone. Elmer was a big man, bald, probably in his late sixties. He wore a dark blue suit, white shirt, and burgundy tie. He took a seat at the head of the table. Ed sat to his left.

The room hushed and Elmer got the meeting started. "Okay, what have we got? Ed, start us off."

"Metro has the serial killer story that Lark Chadwick's been covering. Not sure what she'll be working on today." Ed sounded exhausted, his voice a bored monotone.

I piped up. "I'm here in the corner, Ed, so say nice things about me."

Several people laughed as Ed twisted around to look at me. "Oh, hi, Lark. I'm glad you're here. What have you got?"

Before I could answer, Elmer cut in. "I just want to say, Miss Chadwick, that you've been doing a stellar job. You hit the ground running even before your official start date and you haven't let up."

"Thank you, sir."

"This serial killer story is now national, Lark," Elmer continued, "so the pressure's on us to get it right and take the lead. This could really be what we need to get our circulation numbers up."

Elmer's comment sent a jolt of panic through me. There wouldn't be enough hours in the day to adequately cover this major story and still do all the more menial aspects of the job necessary to ferret out other stories.

Elmer must have been reading my mind because he looked at Ed and added, "I think we need to break Lark free from her other duties so she can devote herself fulltime to this story, don't you think, Ed?"

Ed flushed a little. "That leaves her entire beat uncovered."

"No it doesn't," Elmer said, testily. "We can have the desk make beat calls and write up most things, or we can put a general assignment reporter on anything big that comes up."

Ed sighed. "Okay."

Elmer turned to me. "What are you working on, Lark?"

"I've got lots of different directions to go," I said. "Matt Benson is the lead detective on the case. I'm trying to convince him to let me do a profile of him."

"Having any luck?" Elmer asked.

"Limited, so far, but I remain hopeful."

"What else?" Ed asked.

"I want to interview a shrink to see if we can get into the mind of someone like this. Find out why he kills."

"Maybe he's just horny," chortled a guy sitting at the end of the table near me. He looked like a young, hotshot investment banker: cocky, gelled hair, broad shoulders beneath a blue designer shirt.

A few people laughed.

I didn't. I leaned toward Snark-Boy and said evenly, "Sex, though an element of the attack, seems less a motivating factor than power and *dominance*."

"Who made *you* the expert?" he whispered, his mouth a sneer.

I squinted my eyes at him and in a voice so low even he could barely hear I said, "The guy who once tried to rape me. He's in prison now." I bared my teeth at him in a humorless grin.

He looked down at the table. All of the snark was now gone from the boy—or so I thought.

I summarized what I knew about the two cases, mentioning that the police had questioned several people, but made no arrests. I decided not to mention that Doug had been questioned. Was I protecting him? Yes, I realized.

"Wasn't Doug Mitchell one of the people arrested last night?" Ed asked.

Several people gasped.

"Doug Mitchell? One of our photographers?" Elmer asked, his eyebrows wide.

"Yes, sir," I said.

"W-why? I don't understand," Elmer said. "I didn't read his name in your piece."

"He was never formally arrested or charged, sir. He was taken in for questioning and I just learned this morning that he's been released."

"Why was he taken in?" Elmer asked.

"He was one of the last people to see the latest victim alive," I said softly.

Elmer turned to Ed. "And how did *you* know about this?"

"Lark gave me a heads up phone call late last night and urged me to get a lawyer for Doug," Ed replied.

"I see." Elmer rubbed his chin thoughtfully. "And why did you leave his name out of the story, Lark?" Elmer's tone was calm, nonthreatening, but he was putting me on the spot and making me feel defensive.

I tried to keep my voice calm and steady as I answered. "I felt that since Doug hadn't been arrested, naming him could turn his colleagues and the general public against him unfairly."

"That's admirable," Snark-Boy chimed in, this time with a vengeance, "but it makes *me* wonder if you're covering up for him." He wiggled his eyebrows suggestively and glared at me.

I felt my cheeks flush and my blood pressure spike, but did my best to keep my voice level. When I spoke, I ignored Snark-Boy and looked directly at Elmer. "I felt Doug's reputation would have been tainted, perhaps unfairly. He's not a public figure and had not been charged. He could have sued successfully for libel." I paused, hoping my response would end the matter.

Elmer looked at me, unconvinced. "Oh? How so?"

Just as I was about to panic, I remembered something I'd learned when I took Lionel's journalism class at the University of Wisconsin. "I felt naming Doug prematurely could put the paper at risk in the same way the *Atlanta Journal-Constitution* was at risk in their coverage of the Olympic Park bombing in Atlanta in 1996." I paused.

"Go on," Elmer prodded.

"As you may remember, sir, the FBI named security guard Richard Jewell as a 'person of interest' in the case. Reporters hounded him mercilessly, but he was never charged. Eventually, Eric Robert Rudolph was tried and convicted of the crime. The FBI ended up publicly apologizing to Jewell and exonerating him, but Jewell sued several news organizations, including the Atlanta paper, and probably made millions in out-of-court settlements."

"I'm impressed, Miss Chadwick," Elmer said. "I must admit I'd forgotten some of those details. Thank you for protecting the paper, as well as Mr. Mitchell's reputation." He gave me a dignified nod.

I felt myself blush. "Thank you, sir." I shot a victorious look at Snark-Boy, but he was busy fiddling with his BlackBerry.

Elmer said, "You've got a lot on your plate, Miss Chadwick. Need any back-up?"

I thought a minute. "Marcie Peck and I have become a pretty good team, sir. If you could break her free to work with me, that would be great."

"Consider it done," Elmer said.

Ed threw down his pen in disgust. "Geez, with all the layoffs, we're spread way too thin already."

"Let's you and I talk more about this privately, Ed," Elmer said softly, but firmly.

Snark-Boy spoke up, reading from his BlackBerry: "The wires are just now reporting that the governor and his wife will be in town this afternoon at three to make a major announcement on the murders."

Elmer rubbed his hands together. "Delicious. Now the story is part of the presidential campaign." He turned to Snark-Boy. "Make sure Lark gets credentialed for that event, Glenn."

"On it," he said, thumbing his BlackBerry.

Elmer gripped both sides of the table, his arms wide enough to encompass everyone in the room. "I want all hands on deck for this serial killer story. What Lark needs, she gets. Is everyone clear on that?"

I was thrilled.

Several people nodded or murmured their assent. Ed, I noticed, stared morosely into his coffee cup.

TWENTY-THREE

THE MORNING MEETING droned on. When they got to discussing the sports section of the paper, I knew they didn't need me any more, so I quietly slipped out the door and headed down to my desk in the third floor newsroom.

My head was spinning. I checked the wires and realized immediately it was going to be a busy day. The sheriff had scheduled a news conference for eleven, and the governor's campaign rally was set for three.

I tried calling Doug, but got no answer. Decided not to leave a message. I spent the next ten minutes simply staring at my computer. To the casual passerby, it probably looked like I was being a slug, but my mind was on overload—it needed to drift until it got its bearings. So much had been happening that I had to force myself to pause, regroup, and be quiet so that whatever was in my subconscious had a chance to bubble to the surface and get my attention.

As my mind wandered, I flipped open my reporter's notebook and jotted notes to myself as ideas and thoughts popped into my

head. After another ten minutes, I had a lengthy list of questions
I wanted to answer:

*What kind of cars match the description of the headlight configura-
tion of the vehicle I saw on the bridge?*

What kind of car does Sam Erickson drive?

What's up with Doug?

Did Polly have a Facebook page?

Any other clues on FB or online? Memorials?

Did any of the suspects know both women?

Does Luanne's friend Bob Black have any insights into her death?

Profile Polly.

Where did she work?

What do her coworkers say?

Find shrink to interview

Talk to Ed about creating a serial killer task force

What's up with Doug?

When I realized I'd put Doug on the list twice, I could see
that my mind kept looping back to him. For a reason. I called
him again. Still got no answer, but this time I left a quick message: "Hey, Doug. It's Lark. Just checking to see how you're
doing. Gimme a call." I was about to hang up, but then added,
"Oh. One more thing. Remember those shots I asked you to
get of the car arriving at the murder scene last night? Would
you mind emailing them to me?" I gave him my email address
again. "Thanks."

I looked at my watch. Ten-fifteen. I had about half an hour
before I needed to head to the sheriff's presser. I rummaged in
my bag and found the sheriff's business card. I entered his number into my iPhone's contact list then gave him a call.

He picked up on the first ring. "This is the sheriff," he said,
all business.

"Morning, sheriff. It's Lark Chadwick at the *Sun-Gazette*."

"Hi, Lark." He sounded jovial, not annoyed—a good sign.

"I know you have a presser within the hour, but I need to file something quickly for the web. What's on the agenda?"

"Come and see."

"I'll be there, but can you give me a preview?"

"You want special treatment?"

"No, sir. I want to keep this story alive so that people will continue to follow your investigation."

"It'll probably be fairly short. Just a quick update on what we've got."

"What'll be your headline?"

"That we're gonna find whoever it is that killed those two young women."

"So, you're still assuming that a serial killer is on the loose?"

"That's affirmative."

"Thanks, sheriff. I'll see you in a little bit."

Quickly, I banged out a story for the web. It began, "Police are voicing determination to find a serial killer who has murdered two young women in this area since Saturday. Columbia County Sheriff Max Parrish will be holding a news conference within the hour (11 a.m.) during which he plans to update reporters on the status of the investigation."

After I wrote my short piece, I still had fifteen minutes before I had to leave. I checked my email. Nothing from Doug, but I got an email from Sam Erickson. "Something that might interest you," was the subject line. The body of the email just contained a link. I clicked on it. It took me to his blog.

CONFLICT OF INTEREST FOR NEW SUN-GAZETTE REPORTER?

By

Sam Erickson

Lark Chadwick, the new hotshot reporter brought in to beef up the Sun-Gazette's sagging bottom line, is once again where she's the most comfortable—as the center of attention.

She hadn't even arrived in town to start her new job when she conveniently stumbled onto the body of Luanne Rae Donovan—Lark's first big scoop as the Sun-Gazette's new star cops and courts reporter. So, what does she do? She writes herself into the story.

Lark, Lark, don't you know that rule number one in journalism is that you're NOT the story?

Next, she covers up for her hunky photographer, Doug Mitchell, who police took in for questioning last night in the death of Polly Arceneaux, the latest victim. You can scour the pages of the Sun-Gazette and its website and not find one word about Mitchell's brush with the law.

One wonders if Lark is covering up for her friend. Is he more than just a friend? Mitchell has a well-earned reputation as a lady's man at the paper—is Lark his latest lady? I'm just askin'.

According to sources close to the investigation, Mitchell was with Arceneaux, the night she is believed to have died. He has not yet been charged with her murder, but sources say he is "a person of interest."

I was seething after reading Sam's wise-ass insinuations. I was also annoyed with myself for neglecting to ask Marcie if she'd been the person who inserted the line in my initial report that I'd been the person who found Luanne's body.

My first impulse was to call Sam and give him a piece of my mind. My next thought was to dash off an equally snarky rejoinder as a comment on his blog—or, better yet, on mine. Finally, I thought about blasting him with a personal email protesting my innocence and explaining that someone else put my name in the story, and my reasoning for leaving out Doug's name—at least for now. But I quickly backed away from all those options because I realized Sam was just trying to push my buttons and get me to react. Any response I made would play into his hands and keep his vendetta alive.

I also thought about calling Marcie, but knew I was too agitated. I feared that my tone would put her on the defensive. After all, I was still a guest in her apartment, and I didn't know for sure exactly who was responsible for slipping my name into the piece.

As I walked the two blocks to the Columbia City/County Building, I worried that I'd probably be seeing Sam at the presser. Someone inside the department was obviously leaking to him. Not a big surprise—he'd been covering the place for twenty years and probably had excellent connections in every nook and cranny. I decided to do my best to avoid him. I reminded myself of an earlier time in my career when a heated tiff between me and someone else had had disastrous consequences, landing me in jail charged with murder. Not gonna go back there again, I told myself, sternly.

Easier said than done.

Sam Erickson was waiting for me just inside the door of the room on the first floor of the City/County Building where the sheriff was about to hold his news conference.

"Good morning, Lark." Sam was nearly giddy.

I considered ignoring him completely, but decided to take the high road.

"Morning, Sam." I avoided his eyes and looked past him for a place to sit. All seats were taken. I tried to ease into the room, but Sam had planted himself right in front of me.

"Did you get my email?" he asked. I could smell stale cigarette smoke on his breath.

"Uh huh." I looked for a place to stand near the podium where the sheriff would be speaking in just a couple minutes. The room was full and there were at least six TV cameras on tripods near the back of the room.

"What's your reaction?" Sam pressed.

I thought a terse "no comment" would be sufficient, but I couldn't help myself. I glared at him and said icily, "I consider the piece to be the work of a disgruntled former *Sun-Gazette* employee."

"Care to elaborate?" he smiled.

"Nope. But you may quote me." I pushed past him, and made my way to the podium as I fished my iPhone and reporter's notebook from my messenger bag. I put my pen into position just as the sheriff and Matt Benson made their entrance to a flurry of flashes and clicks from the still cameras of several photographers. I checked, but saw no sign of Doug. It occurred to me that if the *Sun-Gazette* had a photog there, I had no idea who he—or she—was. I squeezed off a couple shots on my iPhone, just to be sure I had something.

Matt Benson stood next to the sheriff at the podium. The sheriff adjusted the mic and then looked up to survey the room.

"Y'all set?" he asked, looking at the TV cameramen in the back of the room.

A couple of them gave him a thumbs-up.

The sheriff cleared his throat and began reading from a piece of paper in his hand. "Thank you all for being here. A serial killer is on the loose in this community. The Columbia County Sheriff's Department is vigorously investigating and we feel confident that soon the killer will be in custody and the community will once again be safe."

As the sheriff spoke, I felt my BlackBerry vibrate. I unholstered it and gave it a glance. It was a message from Doug with an attachment. "Lark," it read, "here are the pix you wanted. Thanks for your calls. Sorry I wasn't able to take them, but they mean a lot. Gotta go now, someone's at the door. D."

I turned my attention back to the sheriff. He was giving advice to women about being vigilant and careful during this time. Finally he said, "That's all I've got. Questions?"

"We understand the second victim was sexually assaulted. Were you able to get any DNA?" I asked.

"Yes," he said. "Any DNA on her skin would have been washed away by the river water, but we found some, um, internally."

"What's the estimated time of death?" someone wanted to know.

"Judging from the relative decomposition of the body, the coroner can't be certain. It's believed the victim died either late Sunday night or early Monday, but she wasn't discovered until Tuesday.

"Are you expecting to make an arrest soon?" Sam asked.

"Yes," the sheriff said, confidently. As he was speaking, one of his staff members appeared through a side door and brought a note to the sheriff. He read it briefly, then looked up with a big smile on his face. "As a matter of fact," he beamed, "I've just been informed that we have made an arrest. The name of the suspect is . . . ." he looked down at the note he'd just been given, " . . . Douglas Grant Mitchell, a photographer with the *Sun-Gazette*."

My jaw dropped and the room erupted in bedlam.

Reporters began shouting questions all at once: "What's the evidence against him?" "Is he charged with both murders?" "Where is he now?"

The sheriff held up his hands and raised his voice. "One at a time." The room quieted. "I understand the suspect is being transferred here now. He should be arriving in a few moments."

"Can we get a shot of the perp walk?" a television reporter shouted.

"Sure. He'll be arriving in the usual location. Let's take a break so you can get your shot. We'll reconvene right here after the prisoner arrives."

There was a scramble for the door. The TV photogs killed the lights and shouldered their cameras after unhitching them from tripods. Everyone had obviously done the perp walk drill here before and knew where to go, so I followed the herd.

We rushed down one flight of stairs to the basement garage. Everyone surged into the parking area then dashed to a bank of elevators about fifty yards away. There was much jostling and shouting as people jockeyed for position.

"There he is," someone shouted. "Roll!"

A black, unmarked sedan had entered the garage and was coming down a ramp, heading for the scrum of photographers and reporters clustered by the elevators. The car stopped and a man wearing a sport coat got out of the front passenger side and opened the right rear door of the vehicle. I was standing between the right front fender and the bank of elevators, well positioned to see.

As Doug got out of the car, the barrage of shutter clicks and camera flashes made it look and sound like lightning in a hailstorm. I got a series of shots as two stern detectives walked Doug toward the elevator. His head was down and his hands were cuffed in front of him.

Several people shouted questions: "Why'd you do it?" "Do you have anything to say in your defense?" were two that I heard distinctly.

Doug looked grim, but said nothing. He kept his eyes on the cement floor. The two men who flanked him seemed in no hurry. It was as if they'd been ordered to stall so that we could get plenty of pictures of the suspect. After Doug entered the elevator, he turned around and faced the front. It was only then that he looked up. He scanned the crowd of reporters. Just as the elevator doors slid shut, his eyes locked onto mine. I've never seen a person look so lost and forlorn.

TWENTY-FOUR

KNOW I'VE BEEN wrong about people before, yet this time I had a strong feeling that Doug was innocent. But the feeling stopped way short of being a conviction. It was just a hunch.

As I trudged back to the sheriff's aborted news conference with the other reporters, I felt a heaviness in my heart. I, too, had been wrongly charged with murder once. If Doug was, indeed, innocent, I knew viscerally—and better than most people—what a powerless and infuriating feeling it is. But, in spite of the way I felt, I was duty-bound to treat his arrest like the major story it was.

I called the desk. Marcie picked up.

"Breaking news," I said. "Doug's under arrest."

"You're *kidding!*"

"I wish." Quickly, I dictated a few lines to her and emailed her the picture I snapped with my iPhone of him being led in handcuffs from the police car to the elevators. "Can you get that on the web right away?" I asked.

"Not a problem. I've got to run it past an editor first," she said.

"Can you transfer me to Ed?"

"Sure. What's up?"

"You'll see."

I stopped in the hallway outside the room where the sheriff was about to reconvene his news conference. People were filing past me into the room, so I still had a few minutes before I'd have to slip back inside.

"Hi, Lark," Ed said when he answered his phone.

"Ed, Doug's just been arrested."

"Geez."

"I just filed a quick piece for the website, but I need your help."

"Shoot."

"Remember in the morning meeting when Elmer said I could have what I needed to cover this story?"

"Oh yeah." Ed still sounded peeved.

"I think we need to assemble a war room."

"But the cops just got their guy."

"Um . . ." I lowered my voice and took a few steps down the hall, away from the prying ears of my competitors. "I'm not so sure they did."

"What do you mean?"

"It's just a hunch, but I don't think Doug did it." I looked around to make sure no one was listening.

"Why not?"

"I can't explain it."

"Try."

I took a deep breath. "My gut tells me he's innocent."

"Not good enough, Lark. Try again."

"It feels to me like the cops want to take the heat off themselves by making it look like the threat's over."

"Feelings are all well and good, Lark, but you're a journalist. Gimme some facts. Who do you think *did* do it?"

"There are a *lot* of potential suspects. Too many to get into now on the phone—the sheriff's about to reconvene his presser."

"But what makes you *feel* like Doug's being railroaded?" His voice dripped with derision as he said the word feel.

I tried to ignore his mocking tone and kept my voice level, dispassionate. "One thing that's really weird is they took him in for questioning late last night, but then released him, only to formally arrest him a few hours later, just in time to stage the walk of shame in front of all the cameras. It just smells fishy to me."

"Maybe they were watching him and he did something incriminating."

"Or it's the gang that can't shoot straight."

"What do you mean?"

"It's like the sheriff was out of the loop. If he knew an arrest was imminent, why wouldn't he wait until Doug was in custody before having his presser? It's a pretty ham-handed way to run an investigation, don't you think?"

Ed grunted. "Or, as you say, he did it his way for maximum effect."

I saw my opening and went for it. "So, now that you're coming around to seeing it my way, Ed, can you at least spare five people, plus Marcie, who can help me look into this?"

He swore. "Five people? Who the hell do you think you are?"

"Well, maybe not five, but at least a couple extra bodies?"

He sighed. "I'll see what I can do."

"Thanks, Ed."

"I'm making no promises, Lark" he grumped.

"Okay. I understand. I'll be back in about an hour."

I returned to the presser and reclaimed my spot near the podium just as the sheriff took his place behind it. This time Matt wasn't with him. I assumed he was somewhere in the building grilling Doug.

"Where were we before we were so rudely interrupted?" the sheriff chuckled.

"Has the suspect been charged with anything yet?" I asked.

"Not yet. We can hold him for seventy-two hours before formally charging him."

"So why are you holding him?" I asked.

"To keep a killer off the streets, Miss Chadwick."

"But—"

Sam Erickson's voice drowned out mine. "What led you to arrest him?"

"I can't get into that. The investigation is ongoing."

"Where was he when he was arrested and did he resist?" Sam asked.

"The suspect was at home and came willingly. Meekly, is probably a better word," the sheriff answered.

A radio reporter asked, "Does he have an alibi for the times when the women were killed?"

"He says he was at home alone during both murders."

A TV reporter: "Did he make any other statements?"

"None that I'm aware of."

"Does he have a lawyer?" The middle-aged woman asking the question had an *Atlanta Journal-Constitution* logo on her laptop case.

"He does have a lawyer, so the suspect's not talking to us any more."

"Who's the lawyer?" the woman followed up.

"I'm sure he'll come forward if he has anything to say."

"So his lawyer is a he?" she asked.

"That is correct."

"Then why can't you tell us who he is?" she persisted.

"Because we're not interested in helping with his defense. If his lawyer has anything to say, then he will come forward. Or you can all meet him at the arraignment."

"And when will that be?" she asked.

"Don't know yet. As I said, we haven't formally charged him with anything. And we don't have to until the end of the week. Stay tuned."

Several voices shouted to be heard, drowning out the Atlanta newspaperwoman's attempt at yet another follow-up. The sheriff pointed to a young man in the back of the room standing next to one of the TV cameras.

"Is the suspect connected to both murders?" the reporter asked.

"We believe so."

I blurted out, "You *believe* so? Are you *sure?*" The tone of my voice surprised and alarmed me because I knew I sounded as if I was defending Doug. But I couldn't help myself.

"We believe so," the sheriff repeated, already looking elsewhere in the room for a questioner other than me.

"If you believe so, why haven't you charged him?" I tried to sound calmer and more reasonable. The question was the closest I felt I could come to challenging the sheriff without fueling another one of Sam Erickson's innuendo-laden blogs.

The sheriff didn't answer my question, he just turned and glared at me.

"Can the community relax?" someone asked.

"The community needs to remain vigilant. There's always the danger of a copycat killer."

"Does the suspect have a record?" Sam asked.

"A couple speeding tickets, paid in full. That's all."

"Do you consider this case closed?" I asked.

"We believe so." He looked around. "Anyone else? I need to see if I can spend some quality time with the suspect." Taking advantage of the brief silence, he added, "Thanks, ever'body." He turned to leave, but several reporters shouted additional questions at him, which he ignored.

As the sheriff left the podium, a guilt-pang shot through me. I'd been the one who'd told the sheriff that I'd seen Doug with Polly just before she was murdered. Part of me now regretted that.

Suddenly, I found myself surrounded by a swarm of reporters sticking mics and tape recorders in my face. It was like being a vulnerable salamander at a convention of sharks. Lights flashed in my face and questions were shouted at me. "What can you tell us about Doug?" "How well do you know him?" "Could he have done it?"

"Guys! Guys!" I held up my hands. "Lemme get my bearings. I'm as surprised by this as the rest of you."

"Do you think he did it?" asked a stunning blonde with a Fox News logo clipped to her microphone.

"No. That seems pretty hard to believe."

"What's he been like to work with?" she asked.

"He's a really good photographer."

"But what's he like as a person?" she pressed.

I thought better of asking her if she wanted me to book a room for them at the no-tell motel. Instead, I answered, "Any one of you could probably answer that better than me. I've only known him for a couple days. This is my first week on the job."

Just as quickly as it started, my mini news conference broke up and everyone scattered when they realized I didn't have much to add to the story.

But Sam Erickson stayed behind.

"So, you don't think he did it? Tell me more," Sam purred as he walked alongside me toward the door. His tennis shoes squeaked on the marble floor.

"I have nothing to add." I stared straight ahead.

Sam got to the door first and turned around and planted himself in front of me.

"Excuse me." I tried to push past him.

Sam stood in the doorway, blocking my path. "Why do you think he's innocent?"

"Do you mind?" I tried to go around him, but he wouldn't move.

"It's a simple question."

"I'm not required to answer."

"What are you hiding?"

"What are you getting at?"

"The truth."

I rolled my eyes.

He continued to stand in my way.

"You're holding me in this room against my will," I said.

"No I'm not. You're free to go." He didn't budge.

"Do I have to push you out of the way?"

"Probably, but that would be assault." He grinned. "And this place is crawling with cops."

"Look. Sam. I'm sorry you lost your job."

"Me too, but what's that got to do with anything?"

"You tell me. I seem to be the focus of your anger lately."

"Anger?" His smile widened.

"It's like you've taken up a crusade against me just because I got the job you used to have."

"Is that what you think?"

"Is that what's going on?"

He was about to speak when one of the TV photogs came from behind me lugging his camera and tripod. Sam stepped out of the way to let him pass.

I saw an opening and bolted through the door on the heels of the photog. I jogged past him and down the hall to the entrance of the building, pausing only to glance back as I went through the front doors and onto the street. I was relieved to see that Sam had apparently decided not to chase me.

On the street, I slowed my pace to a brisk walk. The sun beat down mercilessly. I was still agitated by the confrontation with Sam and found myself wondering if he could be the serial the killer, not Doug. Sam's car resembled the one I saw the night of Luanne Donovan's murder, but that's all I had to go on. Even so, I resolved to stay as far away from Sam Erickson as possible and never allow myself to be alone with him.

As I walked, I called Marcie on the desk and filled her in with the latest shards of information from the sheriff's presser.

Before hanging up Marcie asked, "Lark, did you tell Ed you wanted me to be part of your war room?"

"Yeah. Did he talk to you?"

"He told me to get four people, including myself, and assemble in the fifth floor conference room when you get back."

"That's great. Who'd you get?"

"Well, um . . . ."

"What's wrong?"

"Ed said that because of what he called 'budget limitations,' we can only use the interns."

"Are they any good?"

"Too soon to tell. They've only been with us long enough to go through their orientation."

"Okay. Round 'em up and I'll see you in the fifth floor conference room in a few minutes."

"Oh, Lark?"

"Yeah?"

"Thanks. I owe you."

"You don't owe me anything, Marcie. You've been kind enough to give me a place to stay. I'm just glad to be able to do something to return the favor. But I do have a question I've been meaning to ask you."

"Sure. What is it?"

"Remember when I filed my initial report from the scene when the first body was found?"

"Uh huh."

"I don't remember writing that I was the one who discovered the body. Do you know how that sentence got in there?"

"Oh," she said. "That was Paul, the editor on duty that night. He asked me how the body was discovered and I told him. He must've dropped it into the piece. Is there a problem?"

"Maybe."

"What is it?"

"Sam Erickson's making a big deal about it in his blog today."

"Ignore him. He's a jerk."

"But now the killer might know."

"Hmmmm. Hadn't thought of that. Are you worried the killer might come after you?"

"I'm trying not to think about it."

Marcie's tone turned sympathetic, almost cloying. "Geez, Lark. I should've caught that. I'm so sorry."

"Don't worry about it, Marce. What's done, is done. Let's move on."

"Okay." She sounded chipper again. "See you in a bit."

We hung up and I began to put together in my head the beginnings of my war-room strategy.

TWENTY-FIVE

FIVE PEOPLE WERE waiting for me in the fifth floor conference room when I got back to the paper. I recognized a couple of them from the morning editorial meeting. A place had been left for me at the head of the table where, just that morning, Elmer Wiesenthal had held forth. Marcie sat in a chair to my left where Ed Richards had sat.

"Hi, everyone," I began. "I'm Lark Chadwick. As you may know, I've been covering the serial murders. Things are moving fast. We need to get organized for this Sunday's paper when we can really go in depth on this story, so I need your help now. First, before we go any further, I'd like to go around the table and get to know you. Tell me your name, where you're going to school, and a little about yourself."

I looked at the woman sitting next to Marcie, but before she could begin, I stopped her. "Sorry. Let's start first with Marcie, just in case you don't all know her."

Marcie blushed. "I'm Marcie Peck. Most of you know me already, or at least you've seen me around. I work on the assignment desk and Lark and I are roommates, at least for now, until she finds a place to stay. I started here as an intern a few years ago, so I think I know a little about what you're going through. Working on this project will be a great experience for you."

I turned my attention to a statuesque Asian woman to Marcie's left and said, "Sorry I cut you off earlier. Go ahead."

"I'm Priscilla Lee. I'm from San Francisco. My parents came to this country from China. I'm a senior at Berkeley, majoring in U.S. history."

"Right. I remember we met at Ed Richards' barbecue last weekend. Why are you doing your internship here in Georgia?"

"I'm fascinated by the civil rights movement."

"Experiencing any culture shock?" I asked.

"Big time."

We all laughed.

She went on. "The culture shock started my first night in Columbia. I'm staying with Billy Bob Foreman's family out on Veteran's Highway. On my first night with them, he asked, 'What's your last name, Priscilla Lee?' I said, 'It's Lee,' prompting him to say, 'Priscilla Lee *Lee?* Now that's just *dumb.*'" Priscilla stretched "dumb" into two syllables as she mimicked what must be Billy Bob's elaborate drawl.

I laughed along with the others. "I'm glad you're with us, Priscilla." I turned to my right and nodded at the lanky young man sitting across the table from Priscilla. He had a buzz-cut, wore a white shirt and tie and had a baby face.

"I'm John. I'm from Indiana. I'll be graduating from Notre Dame in January and I'm an English major."

"Hi, John. And you?" I said, turning to the young African-American man sitting to John's left. He wore a deep blue dress shirt and had the husky good looks of a football player.

"I'm Devon. I'm from Atlanta. I'm a junior at Howard University in Washington."

"What's your major?"

"Political Science."

"Cool. Now you," I said, turning my attention to a shy, petite African-American woman to my right and Devon's left.

"I'm Alicia. I'm from just down the road in Columbus and I go to Columbus State where I'm a senior majoring in communications."

"So this is your neck of the woods."

"Yes, ma'am."

I gulped. "Alicia, I do believe that marks the first time *any*-one has called me 'ma'am.' Thank you for that aging moment," I laughed, then added, gently, "I'm fine with you calling me Lark."

"Yes, ma'am, I mean L-Lark." She let out a self-conscious laugh.

A few of the others chuckled.

"Anyway, thanks for helping us out, Alicia." I looked around the table at the eager faces looking at me expectantly. "Here's where we stand: We've had two murders within a week. The victims are young women and their bodies were found in the same place. One person, Doug Mitchell, is under arrest. He happens to be a *Sun-Gazette* employee, so all eyes are on us to make sure we handle the story fairly. The governor is coming to town in just a few hours to make a major announcement about the case, which means it could become an issue in the presidential campaign. Which one of you is the poli-sci major? Is it you, Devon?"

"That's right."

"I want you to do a Google search on the governor. I need some background info on who he is and any past stands he's taken on crime. Email me what you come up with in the next hour." I gave him my email address.

"Right now?"

"Now. Scoot."

He left.

"Who among you is a car buff?"

John raised his hand.

"Outstanding." I unholstered my BlackBerry and found the pictures Doug sent to me just before he was arrested. "What's your email address, John?"

He gave it to me.

"I'm emailing you a picture," I said while thumbing his addy into my phone. "It's a night shot of the front end of an on-coming automobile that has an unusual headlight pattern. I want you to identify the kind of vehicle it is and see if there are other car models with similar front grilles."

"Okay. Um, how come?"

"I'll tell you later." I attached the picture to John's email. "I'm sending it to you . . . *now.*" I clicked *send.*

"Alicia," I said, looking at the young woman sitting wide-eyed to my right. "You're from around here. I want you to dig through past issues of the paper and find out if there are similar crimes that may have happened in this area."

"When do you want the information?"

"By the time I get back from the governor's event later this afternoon."

"Okay."

"Who's on Facebook?" I asked.

Everyone's hand went up.

"Priscilla, I want you to go online and find out everything you can about the two victims. Were they on Facebook, Twitter? Did they have a blog? Were they part of any on-line forums? Are there any memorial pages set up by their friends? Look for any chatter that might give us insights into who they were as people, and anything that might suggest who might have done this."

"Okay."

"And the rest of you . . . " I looked around the room at everyone. "When you get caught up, help Priscilla with her social media research. Any questions?"

They shook their heads.

"Marcie will be able to help you with anything you need. Thanks, everyone."

After the interns filed out, Marcie and I were alone.

"Thanks for pulling this all together," I said to her. "They seem pretty sharp."

"And thanks for giving me this chance, Lark. I only wish I could get out onto the street."

"I know. This might help you to get that chance. Did Ed give you any trouble?"

She rolled her eyes. "It's clear he doesn't think you need a war room to investigate two murders that are now, essentially, solved, but Elmer has overruled him, so Ed's stuck. It's obvious that he's not going to break free anyone on the staff to work on this, so he coughed up free labor—the interns."

I sighed. "Good thing they seem smart and eager. I think we'll be okay." I looked at my watch. "I need to get to the governor's event. Thanks again for all your help, Marce."

"Not a problem," she said. "I'm glad to help."

But as I left the conference room, the troubled look on Marcie's face left me with the unsettling feeling it *was* a problem and she *wasn't* glad to help.

TWENTY-SIX

WILL GANNON, GOVERNOR of Georgia, is a most impressive fellow. I watched from the roped off "pen" of the press section near the front of a cavernous convention center as the governor made his way to the podium. Applause was thunderous and raucous.

For the past two hours, I'd been standing in the auditorium going over the research that my intern Devon had sent me. I had to be here way before the scheduled event because every one of the thousands of people here had to go through the Secret Service magnetometers set up at the entrance.

Gannon had been running for president for nearly a year and he was in a neck-and-neck race with the Governor of Pennsylvania for the party's nomination. The convention was still a couple months away and neither candidate had enough delegates to clinch the nomination. There was already talk of a brokered convention.

Gannon clearly had charisma. He was deeply tanned and, though only forty-five, he had prematurely graying hair that reminded me of CNN's Anderson Cooper—a heartthrob of mine. As it turned out, Anderson (we're on a first-name basis, if only in my head) was in the press pen with me, but I was too intimidated by his stardom to go up to him and introduce myself. Instead, I buried my nose in my BlackBerry and read up on candidate Gannon.

Gannon, wearing a dark blue suit, walked into the hall hand-in-hand with his thirty-five-year-old Latina wife, Rose. I'd read that they'd been married for ten years and had two small children, a boy and a girl. Rose was mesmerizingly beautiful: Thick, dark hair spilled onto her shoulders and framed her radiant face like a heart. She wore a pink sleeveless shift accented at the neck with Navy blue. Her bronzed arms and legs were sculpted. I noted that she had a full figure like mine, but—unlike me—she seemed comfortable in her skin.

One of the reporters behind me said to one of his buddies, "She's hotter in person than she is on TV."

"Oh yeah," his friend replied.

As the governor and his wife made their way toward their seats on the dais, Columbus State University's jazz band blared an instrumental rendition of Frank Sinatra's "Fly Me to the Moon." The bouncy music competed with the applause and cheers of thousands of people.

The couple shook hands with each of the dignitaries on the stage. Will and Rose Gannon glided down the row, seeming to connect with the people whose hands they shook, but I noticed that each personal transaction lasted no more than two seconds. Yet even within that sliver of time, their eyes laser-focused on the person, all the while holding dazzling smiles of welcome and greeting. They were a good team and seemed to be energized by the experience.

The crowd was still cheering when they got to the podium, so the governor took his wife into his arms and eased her into a graceful, flowing foxtrot. The roar in the room intensified. I'd read that Rose had ballroom danced competitively in college. It was clear that she still had her chops. The dance ended almost as quickly as it began with the governor twirling Rose twice and then dipping her low and holding the pose as the song concluded.

Judging by the enthusiastic clapping, foot-stomping, and cheering, Will and Rose Gannon would have been voted to come back for another week on "Dancing with the Stars."

When the governor was finally introduced, there was another burst of long and loud applause punctuated by sustained whoops, whistles, hollers, and screams. It felt like being trapped next to a whining jet engine.

Eventually, the crowd quieted. Sort of.

"Hello, Columbia, *Georgia!*" All Gannon had to do was stress the name of their mutual state and the crowd went wild again.

"It's sweltering up here," the governor said. "Do y'all mind if I get a little cooler?"

"Oh, you're *already* cool, baby," a woman near me hollered.

Gannon grinned mischievously and slipped off his suit coat to the excited squeals of many of the women in the crowd who delighted in Gannon's obvious GQ charisma. I had to admit: the guy really knew how to fill out his tight-fitting, blue shirt.

As Gannon draped his coat over a chair, a woman yelled, "Take off your shirt, too!"

The crowd laughed.

The governor paused, gave the woman a coy look and slowly loosened his deep burgundy tie.

The alert jazz band drummer thumped his bass drum for a few bars of a suggestive, strip-tease beat.

The crowd's laughter crescendoed into applause and cheers.

I glanced at Rose to see what she thought of all of this. To my surprise, she was smiling and clapping, clearly enjoying the moment right along with everyone else.

Gannon milked the moment. He fingered, then unhitched, the top button of his shirt.

The cheering intensified.

The governor then rolled up his sleeves revealing muscled forearms that would make Popeye jealous. Then, suddenly, he stopped and smiled. "Sorry," he said. "That's as far as I go."

"Awwwww," several people called out.

Gannon beamed as the appreciative audience laughed warmly.

I marveled that in only a matter of seconds, Will Gannon had been able to forge what felt like an intimate bond with everyone in the room, myself included. *This guy's good,* I thought, followed by, *Be careful, Lark.*

When the din finally lowered a little, the governor quickly ran through a list of names of people he wanted to thank, then segued to his speech. We'd been told by one of his press aides that he was going to preface his standard stump speech with remarks about the recent serial killings, so we knew he would be making news.

"It's great to be back here in Columbia," Gannon began, his voice echoing. "Rose and I want to thank you for your warm response and your support during this long campaign. The finish line is in sight and I'm feelin' *good.*"

Another roar from the crowd.

"I wanted to come back to Columbia," he said, lowering his voice, "because y'all have been dealing with a tragedy. The tragedy of young lives snuffed out needlessly and prematurely by the worst kind of predator: A predator who preys upon the innocent.

Today, I'm announcing the creation of a task force that will assist local authorities in the prosecution of these cases so that the person or persons responsible for the two recent murders here will be *punished to the fullest . . . extent . . . of the LAW.*"

The crowd loved it. They knew Georgia had the death penalty and that this governor was not afraid to use it.

The room eventually quieted and Governor Gannon continued. "As you know, Georgia has a part-time legislature and the latest session just concluded. So, rather than wait nine months for lawmakers to come back, I'm calling a special *emergency* session of the legislature and I'm demanding that both houses take immediate action on my Safe Streets Initiative. It's a bill designed to curb and restrict the activities of known sex offenders."

More cheers.

I pulled out my BlackBerry and started a Google search on the topic of sex offenders in Georgia.

Gannon turned to look at his wife. "I'd like my better half to tell you about the bill. Would y'all like to hear from *Rose?*"

The roar was deafening.

Rose stood and walked gracefully to the podium. A guy behind me exclaimed, "Oh yeah! Thank you, Jesus!"

Gannon gave his wife a chaste peck on the cheek, then stepped to the side as she stood at the podium, waiting patiently for the pandemonium to ebb. A few times she tried to speak, but could only smile helplessly as the crowd continued to cheer. Finally, Governor Gannon walked to his wife's side, leaned toward the mic and said as loudly as he could, "Listen up, now. Rose has something *important* to say."

There was another crescendo of cheering, but this time it tapered off quickly.

Rose Gannon spoke without notes or TelePrompter. "I just want to tell you a little bit about the initiative that Will is unveiling today." Her voice was soft, almost Marilyn-Monroe breathy. I had to strain to hear. "As you know, Will and I have two young children. We love Grace and Thomas with all our hearts, so I was thrilled when Will told me about his plans to keep the youngsters of our state safe."

The crowd was quiet now, leaning in, hanging on her words.

"My husband's Safe Streets bill is designed to target sex offenders living among us. These are people who have already been convicted and served time for the despicably selfish things they've done to our precious little ones. Research shows that a person with the kind of psychological disorder that causes him to victimize a young person can never be cured. Ever. And sixteen-THOUSAND of these creeps are currently living among us here in our beloved state of Georgia."

A murmur of disgust rippled through the room.

"The Safe Streets Initiative will do a number of things, but here are the highlights: Known sex offenders will not be allowed to live or work within two thousand feet of a school, school bus stop, park, church, or any place near where children gather. Known sex offenders will be required to provide law enforcement with the passwords for all of their online accounts so that they will no longer be able to use the Internet to insinuate themselves into the lives of innocent victims."

Rose paused, waiting for the applause to die down.

"And finally, the bill will beef up the government's ability to track the whereabouts of known sex offenders and make that information available to law enforcement agencies in other states and available to *you* so that you can keep a vigilant eye on the sick, sex-crazed predators who live among us. If the legislature passes the Safe Streets Initiative, a sex offender who fails to register with the proper authorities could face up to thirty years in prison."

The governor's wife paused and looked deliberately around the room. It seemed as though she was trying to make a personal connection with everyone. I could have sworn that for a nanosecond her eyes even locked onto mine before she took a deep breath and pressed ahead for her big finish.

"So," Rose concluded, "we need to be vigilant. We need to take action." She quickened her pace and her voice switched from breathy to strident. "We need to keep sex offenders in their place. We need to make sure they . . ." and here her voice built to a crescendo, powering through the growing roar of the crowd, ". . . *never, ever harm one of our little ones AGAIN.*" The cheering nearly drowned out her last few words.

As I watched Rose Gannon gracefully relinquish the podium to her husband, I remember thinking two things: *Will Gannon just might be the next President of the United States,* and *Rose Gannon will be one hell of an effective First Lady.*

The governor returned to the podium. He launched into what I figured was his routine stump speech—a recitation of his accomplishments as governor and his agenda if elected president. But I'd tuned him out. My Google search had produced an eye-opening *Wall Street Journal* piece on the challenges facing Georgia's sex offenders after they've served their time.

I was fully engrossed in the story when I felt a tap on my shoulder. I looked up.

Standing in front of me, wearing a laminated I.D. tag that read *GANNON STAFF* was a tall, clean-cut kid who couldn't have been more than twenty years old.

"Are you Lark Chadwick with the . . . " the kid looked at an index card in his hand, ". . . with the *C-Columbia Sun-Gazette*?"

"I am."

"Would you come with me, please?"

"Why? Have I done something wrong?"

The kid laughed. "Today's your lucky day."

"Oh? How so?"

"Our press staff noticed that you're credentialed for today's event and that you're the lead local reporter on the serial killer story. Governor Gannon would like to talk with you after his speech about his Safe Streets Initiative. Are you interested in doing a quick Q-and-A with him and Rose?"

The kid didn't have to ask twice.

TWENTY-SEVEN

I **FOLLOWED AS THE** campaign aide led me to a stern-faced
Secret Service agent standing in front of a blue curtain next to
the stage where the governor was wrapping up his speech.

"She's with me." The kid had to yell at the agent to be heard
over the din of Gannon whipping the crowd into a frenzy of
partisan fervor.

The agent eyed the press credentials hanging from the lanyard
around my neck, looked me in the eye, and, showing absolutely
no emotion, gave us a curt nod and stepped aside.

The kid pushed through a break in the curtain and ushered
me backstage. By this time, the governor had the crowd in such
a froth that I couldn't hear his muffled words distinctly anymore.
People were hollering, stamping their feet, and then I heard the
thumping beat of the jazz band pumping into the hall.

"Let's stand right here," the kid said. "After the governor and
his wife shake hands along the rope line, they'll come through
the curtain right there." He pointed to where we'd just entered
the backstage area. "You'll have five minutes, okay?"

"Sure. Thanks." I realized I didn't have a clue what I was going to ask the governor, but before I could let panic take over, the curtain trembled and through it swept a phalanx of Secret Service agents surrounding a beaming Will and Rose Gannon.

To my disappointment, the governor had put his suit coat back on. The press aide kid stepped forward and with a boldness I certainly didn't feel said, "Governor, this is Lark Chadwick of the *Columbia Sun-Gazette*."

Up close, Gannon was even more imposing than he was on stage. He had a barrel chest and chiseled features.

My mouth was dry and my palms felt as if I'd been holding ice cubes. I held out my hand and the governor clasped it in both of his. His hands were monstrous—they dwarfed mine—but they were comfortingly warm.

"Hello, Lark. I've been following your coverage. Good work."

"Thank you, sir." He towered over me. I had to crane my neck to look him in the eyes. They were a deep and dazzling brown with the hint of wrinkles at the edges that made him seem wise and distinguished.

Gannon turned and held out his arm toward Rose. She stepped forward and let him sweep her into my presence. "This is my wife, Rose," he said, beaming at her as if he'd just met her for the first time. "Honey, this is Lark Chadwick of the *Sun-Gazette*."

"Hi," Rose said simply. We shook hands. Hers was as small and cold as her husband's was big and warm.

"Nice t-to meet you," I managed to stammer. Rose's face looked more angular up close and, although her smile was wide and seemed genuine, her eyes looked tired.

I'd never met or even been this close to anyone famous before and I didn't know what to say or do at first. Of course Lionel is famous, but he's just Lionel. I'd met him before I'd known anything about him or how famous he was. But being in the presence of the man who just might be the next President of the United States was truly daunting. Plus I was supposed to be intelligent, or at least sound like I was.

In that awkward moment, as the possible future president and first lady stood in front of me, my training from being around Lionel kicked in. I realized that I was on the verge of being used by Governor Gannon and his quest for the presidency. Rather than submit to critical questions from reporters who knew him, his positions, and every nuance of public policy, Gannon's ploy was to circumvent them and go to a local reporter more likely to be captivated by his and Rose's obvious star power.

I could see the wisdom of that. Had it not been for the *Wall Street Journal* piece I'd just read, I probably would have been just as swept off my feet as the crowd obviously was when Rose Gannon revealed, for the first time, the governor's attack on child predators.

My hands trembled as I fumbled to turn on the voice memo app on my iPhone. I breathed a quick prayer. *Lord, don't let me say anything stupid.* I decided that rather than trying to sound erudite, I'd just have a conversation with Gannon and his wife.

"Thank you for giving me a few minutes, governor. I understand you wanted to talk a little bit about your Safe Streets Initiative."

"That's right," he said. "I think it's critically important."

"I don't think anyone would dispute the urgency of the problem," I said, "but I'm wondering if it might be a bit, um, draconian."

The governor's smile flickered almost imperceptibly. "Draconian? What do you mean?"

"Let's say if an 18-year-old boy is convicted and serves time for having had consensual sex with his 15-year-old girlfriend, should he *really* be at risk later in life of serving thirty years in prison if he fails to register as a sex offender?"

The governor's face darkened, but his smile didn't fade. "Well, um, I'm sure that wouldn't happen."

"But does your bill specifically guard against that possibility?"

"Well, ah, I'm not sure."

"Another thing," I said. "It seems that severely restricting where a sex offender can live or work could end up having an adverse effect on a person's behavior and ability to make a positive contribution to society."

The governor was no longer smiling.

I charged ahead. "What if a sex offender, after paying his debt to society, gets out of prison and is really trying to mend his ways? By placing so many obstacles in his path on where he can live and work, won't that be so demoralizing that it could sow the seeds for, say, illegal drug use or falling back into crime?"

"Well, that's a hypothetical question." He smiled. "And you know what they say about the wisdom of a politician answering hypothetical questions." He forced a laugh.

Rose stepped in. "I think it's safe to say, Ms. Chadwick, that the governor would be willing to work with the state legislature to iron out any potential problems with the bill, like the ones you suggest."

"Yes. Absolutely," the governor added, then said, "But I think we can't lose sight of the very real problem out there. I mean, you yourself have seen first-hand the horror of what can happen when a sexual predator is loose in society. We have to do something to lower the boom on that kind of sick behavior. I believe the Safe Streets Initiative puts Georgia in the forefront in that fight." He was clearly warming to the topic and was now back on stride. "I would argue that this legislation could end up being a model for what other states would want to emulate."

"I was surprised at your, ah, pseudo strip-tease up there," I laughed, nodding at the stage behind us.

Gannon reddened. "I was, too," he chuckled.

"What do you mean?"

"When I felt the beat, I sort of got 'in the moment,' I guess."

"Looking back, do wish you had a do-over?"

He frowned, thoughtfully. "No. Not really."

"I'm just wondering if some people might think it wasn't very presidential, especially just moments before you unveiled an initiative targeting sexual violence."

At that instant, I could see his eyes squint almost imperceptibly, and I knew the governor regretted his decision to submit himself to my questioning. His eyes darted, then his features relaxed when he saw no cameras.

"I've been in politics a long time, Miss Chadwick," he continued. "Long enough to know I can't please everyone. People will think what they want. But the truly *objective* person—" his eyes drilled mine—"will see that it was a good-natured, fun moment and that I drew the line way before anything unpresidential happened."

The governor's aide, who'd been standing off to the side, stepped in. "We have to be going, governor."

"Anyway, Lark," Gannon said, obviously relieved to be able to extricate himself, "it's good to meet you. Thanks so much for being here. Keep up the good work." He grasped my hand, but his touch was much cooler than it had been just five minutes earlier.

Rose brushed my hand. "Good questions." She seemed to mean it.

And then they were gone, swallowed by the dark-suited Secret Service agents surrounding them.

TWENTY-EIGHT

TO BE IN the middle of the swirl of a presidential campaign is a thing to behold. It's raucous chaos. This was my first experience and I wasn't sure I liked it. Being a quiet, contemplative girl, I much preferred a deep and intense one-on-one, nuanced conversation with an intelligent, interesting person, and the glow of candlelight and wine. What I was experiencing was the opposite of that. The lighting of the auditorium was garish; the blaring band, screaming crowd, and echoing public address system were headache-inducing.

The Gannon campaign provided a "filing center" in another room for the press. There were rows of tables, each with power strips, *lots* of power strips so that reporters could plug in and recharge their cell phones, laptops, and anything else necessary to help a reporter stay in touch with his or her assignment desk.

The traveling national press corps seemed hardened, jaded, and bored. There appeared to be a distinct cultural dichotomy between the print and broadcast journalists. The broadcasters seemed a little younger than their print counterparts. The on-air types had fashion-model beauty and an interchangeable sameness. The male reporters wore sport coats and ties, but below the waist and out of view of the camera, they wore jeans. They were often accompanied by harried women, most of them my age or younger. I assumed they were the reporters' personal producers because they always seemed to have a cell phone at their ear, a BlackBerry in hand, a furrowed brow, and a snarl on their lips. Most wore flats or tennis shoes, but one stunning redhead click-clicked past me in four-inch heels.

The "pencil press," as the campaign referred to us print-folk, seemed a little older than our broadcast counterparts, although I noticed plenty my age—and even a few who were younger. I felt out of place in both camps. A couple of the print guys had been covering presidential elections for decades. They were overweight, middle-aged, and balding. One man, his face flushed, sweated profusely as he was hustled with the rest of us to the filing center.

Lionel had told me about his days covering the McGovern campaign in 1972 and I wondered what it might have been like working side by side with him in the trenches. From what he told me, the highlight of these trips was all the drinking at the hotel bar at the end of the day.

Maybe someday I'd be doing this, I thought to myself, but not now. Not full time. I felt like an interloper. My top priority was the recent murders right here in Columbia, Georgia. I needed to focus on that. But today was instructive about where my career *might* go.

I found a place at a table, unshouldered my laptop, and called the desk while getting set up. Marcie answered.

"It's Lark."

"Hey."

"I just scored a one-on-one with the governor and his wife after he finished his remarks."

"Whoa. Way cool. He's a dreamboat. How'd you manage that?" There was a touch of jealousy in her voice.

"I'll tell you when I get back."

"What's the lead?"

"The lead is that the governor doesn't know the details of his own bill targeting sex offenders."

"Really?"

"Uh huh. I asked him a specific question about his proposed legislation and he replied—and this is a quote—'I'm not sure.'"

"Wow. He's not Mister Perfect after all. You're shattering my illusions, Lark. Sounds to me like your piece might make the AP's national wire."

Until Marcie mentioned it, I hadn't thought about the Associated Press wire service, plus I realized I had the only sound of him on the record commenting on the strip-tease, too, something AP Radio might find interesting.

I filled her in on what Will and Rose Gannon said about the Serial Killer Task Force and the Safe Streets Initiative. Then, together, Marcie and I crafted a lead for the web that highlighted the governor's gaffe followed by the highlights of what he and Rose announced at the rally, including quotes from my interview with them afterwards.

"I'll write up something now for tomorrow's paper that fleshes all of this out a bit more," I told Marcie.

"Okay. Call me when you're ready to send it. Meanwhile, I'll get our piece edited and posted on the website."

For the next few minutes, oblivious to the hubbub around me, I banged out my story on what Governor Gannon and Rose announced. When I was finished, I read it over quickly, correcting misspellings and giving my copy some buffing and polishing before I emailed it to Marcie.

"It's on its way," I told her when I reconnected with her over the phone.

"Got it."

"I'll be back pretty soon. Could you assemble the interns in the War Room right away? We need to regroup."

"Sure thing. No problem."

"K. See you in a few."

I placed a quick call to the AP bureau in Atlanta to give them a heads up about my piece on Gannon that would be on the *Sun-Gazette* website momentarily. And when I mentioned that I had sound of Gannon's "in-the-moment" explanation, the guy on the desk got really interested.

"We've got tape of the crowd reaction," the guy said. "Can you email the audio of your interview?"

"Sure. No problem." I got his email address and he took down all the information he needed from me so he could send me a modest payment for my freelance duties. Sweet.

As I left the filing center, I turned around at the door and looked back. Several reporters were hard at work crafting their stories on their laptops while others lounged and chatted. A few grazed at a table containing sandwiches and fruit.

This was certainly Lionel's vision for me and my career. When he covered the White House for the *New York Times*, he wrote best-selling books about Watergate and Vietnam. The one about Vietnam won him a Pulitzer. He'd been grooming me for the White House beat, but after today's experience, I wondered, *do I really want it? Too soon to tell.*

Back at the paper, the interns and Marcie were waiting for me in the War Room. I looked around for Devon and found him sitting next to Alicia, chatting her up. She was smiling at him admiringly.

"Thanks, Devon, for the background info on the governor. You saved my butt."

"Not a problem," he aw-shucksed.

"Okay, everyone. Where do we stand?" I asked.

Priscilla, the attractive Asian-American from Berkeley, was first to speak. "I've been combing the Web, looking for information about the two victims."

"What'd you find?"

"Both of them were on Facebook," Priscilla said, "but there's not much on Polly, the second victim, because her privacy settings lock out the general public. But there's a lot of activity surrounding Luanne. Someone set up a group page in her memory. It's got lots of pictures and hundreds of people have posted anecdotes and stuff."

"Sounds like it could be a good story. Write up a rough draft and we'll see if we can mold it into something, okay?"

"That's actually what I've been doing."

"Excellent."

Alicia raised a hand and I nodded at her. "I looked through the archives," she said. "There are some unsolved murders in the area, but no young women. Back in 1977, there was a so-called 'stocking strangler' who raped and murdered seven mostly elderly women in Columbus. The oldest was almost ninety."

"Gross," John and Devon said, almost simultaneously.

"Did they catch him?" I asked.

"Uh huh. He's on death row."

"Of course the most important question we need to answer, obviously, is who killed Luanne and Polly?" I asked.

Marcie cut in. "The cops think they already know: It's Doug."

"Maybe so," I said, "but they still haven't charged him with anything. They've arrested him and they're holding him, but that's all. They've got at least until Friday before they have to either charge him formally or release him."

"Why are they waiting to charge him?" asked Priscilla.

"Good question. There are probably lots of reasons: It makes the public less tense, which takes the pressure off the cops. They also might be trying to rattle Doug into saying something incriminating."

Devon spoke up. "Maybe they're waiting to see if there's another murder while he's in custody. If there is, either there are two killers out there, or he's the wrong guy."

"Could be." I said. "Good thinking, Devon."

The conference room had a white wall at one end that could be written on. I walked over to it and picked up an erasable marker from the chalk rail and began making a list of questions on the wall.

"We need to find out as much as we can about both victims," I said. "We know Doug knew the second victim, but did he have any connection to the first girl? That first victim, Luanne, had had a run-in with her boyfriend, Tyrone Jackson, a day before her death. We need to find out more about their relationship."

I thought about telling them that I'd heard that Luanne's dad had been sexually abusing her, but decided against it. Even though these kids were smart and eager, they were unseasoned in handling something so high-stakes delicate. I didn't want to risk having one of them, in their zeal, say something intemperate. A rumor like that could go viral on the Internet faster than a match igniting gasoline.

I decided to work the sex abuse angle on my own by getting to know her friends and making gentle and oblique inquiries.

Maybe, I reasoned, someone would open up. And maybe they'd be willing to put their name on it. Using unnamed sources, especially for something this delicate, was out of the question. But if I could find at least two people willing to go on the record, I could then give the father a chance to respond.

I wrote on the board what we had so far. As I scribbled, another thought came to mind. "We need to find some experts on this kind of crime who can give us insight into the mind of a killer. Who wants to find a couple shrinks for me to interview?"

John raised his hand.

"Thanks, John. As soon as you can, come up with a list of five people, plus their contact info, and a brief backgrounder on each. I'll take it from there."

"I'm on it," he said.

For the next few minutes, we added to our list of questions on the board. Several people volunteered to try to track down friends of the victims who might be willing to talk. We agreed to meet at eight the following morning to regroup.

As people were leaving, Priscilla stayed behind until everyone else had left.

"Is there something you want to talk about?" I asked her.

She seemed nervous, fiddling with the pen in her hand, reluctant to look me in the eye. She glanced around the room. When she was sure we were alone, she looked up at me tentatively. Her dark eyes glistened.

"Uh huh," she said, twirling her long, glossy black hair.

"What is it?" I took a seat next to her and turned it so I could face her directly.

"Well, um . . ." she began, tentatively, "Marcie said the two of you were talking at her apartment last night."

"Uh huh," I said.

Marcie said that while the two of you were talking . . . . " Her voice trailed off and she bit her lower lip.

"Go on, Priscilla. You can tell me. It's just between you and me."

"Promise?"

"I promise."

Priscilla took a deep breath and plunged ahead. "Marcie said you came on to her."

I was stunned, but with all my resolve I managed to maintain a poker face.

Priscilla glanced at me shyly, trying to read my expression.

I felt my face grow hot. I wracked my brain, trying to reconstruct my conversation with Marcie. We'd talked about Doug, we'd talked about her frustrations with her job, she'd suggested I attend the morning meeting, but I couldn't think of a thing I'd said that could possibly have been misconstrued as a come-on.

"That's interesting," I said, noncommittally. "What specifically did Marcie say—and, more importantly, why did she tell you?"

Priscilla fidgeted uncomfortably. "She just said that you came on to her—she wasn't specific—but she said she made it clear to you that she's not gay."

My mind was spinning. This seemed so out of character from the Marcie I'd come to know and like. Before I could compose a response to Priscilla's bombshell, she continued to speak.

"The reason I'm telling you this," she said meekly, "is that even though it's not okay with Marcie, it *is* okay with *me*."

I was reeling. First, I get news that Marcie, a person I like and trust, is telling a lie about me behind my back, followed by a young intern awkwardly coming on to me. I had no idea what to say as my emotions roiled. I tried to think straight. I didn't want to embarrass Priscilla, nor did I want to tell Priscilla that Marcie was—for whatever reason—lying about me.

"I just want to be clear, Priscilla: are you coming on to me?" I said it as gently as I could.

"Uh huh," was all she could muster. She was trembling and seemed near tears. "I've never done anything like this before," she said, "I'm so scared."

I leaned over and was about to touch her gently on the arm, but then thought better of it. "Priscilla, I'm flattered that you might find me attractive. Marcie is mistaken, but even if I was gay, it wouldn't be a good idea for you and I to do anything about it."

Priscilla continued to look at the floor.

"Are you alright?" I asked.

She nodded abruptly, but when she looked up at me, her face was tear-stained and anguished. "I'm so sorry. I don't know what made me think you'd be the least bit attracted to me."

"Please. I'm not rejecting you. This isn't about you. It's about us and our professional working relationship. I like you, Priscilla. I think you're smart. And I'm glad to have your help on this project. But that's where things have to stay." I kept my voice even and firm, but gentle.

Priscilla scowled. "Please don't say anything to anyone, especially not to Marcie."

I wasn't sure what I was going to say to Marcie. Maybe taking her by the neck and throttling her would be enough. Instead I heard myself saying, "I won't."

TWENTY-NINE

MY HEAD WAS spinning as I left the building later that day. I did my best to avoid Marcie. To confront her would put Priscilla in a difficult position and would violate my promise not to say anything to Marcie. But to let it go would perpetuate an injustice. I wanted to clear the air. I wanted to set the record straight. I *needed* to find out why Marcie was undermining me.

I tried calling Lionel in Wisconsin, but he didn't pick up. I was in a funk when I stopped at the grocery store to pick up a few things for dinner. I realized that I'd better move out of Marcie's apartment as soon as possible and find a place of my own. But the thought brought me down even lower because nearly every waking minute had been spent covering the two murders, all while trying to get acclimated to my new job.

Augie was pushing an empty shopping cart across the parking lot toward the store entrance. He greeted me as I got out of my car. "Hey, Lark. Here's a shopping cart for ya." He gave it a shove and it rattled toward me.

"Thanks, Augie." I stopped it and swung it around.

"What's the matter?" he asked, falling in step with me as we walked toward the store.

"Long day," I sighed.

"Nahhh," he said dubiously. "I've seen you at the end of a long day. This is different."

I glanced at him. He had a look of genuine concern on his face. I gave him a wan smile.

"I'm getting off in a few minutes," he said. "I'd be honored to be your sounding board."

I sighed again, unsure of what to say.

"I'll even spring for the wine to lubricate the conversation. Today's Wednesday, not Sunday, so the wine's not off limits and Denise won't give you any hassle."

I laughed in spite of myself and surrendered. "Sure. Why not?"

"I'll see you by the front entrance in a few minutes when you're done getting your stuff," he said as we walked inside.

"Sounds good." I pushed my cart absent-mindedly through the aisles, but only bought a few things: toothpaste, a few cans of soup, and a couple apples.

As promised, Augie was waiting for me just outside the door to the parking lot. He held a paper bag that looked like it had a bottle inside—wine, I presumed.

"Need help with those?" he asked, nodding at the two bags I carried.

"No, thanks. I'm good."

"Your place or mine?" he asked as he walked beside me to Pearlie.

"I think we should go someplace neutral and public," I said firmly. "No offense, but I don't know you very well yet."

He nodded. "That's fine. I know just the spot. I'm parked over there." He nodded toward a far corner of the parking lot. "Follow me."

I put my bags on Pearlie's passenger seat, slid behind the wheel, and cranked the ignition just as Augie drove past my parking place in his red sedan. I pulled in behind him. He led me to a small neighborhood park alongside the Chattahoochee River about a mile or two away from the store. We parked side by side and got out of our cars. We were the only two people around.

"Good thing I decided to get some plastic cups and a cork-screw," he said, holding up his paper bag.

"You think of everything, Augie. Want a medal?" I smiled. I was glad he didn't make a fuss or sound hurt when I suggested someplace public. And I was grateful for a chance to let my hair down.

We found a bench perched on top of a berm overlooking the lazily flowing water and sat down next to each other. The bank on the Alabama side of the river was covered by a ubiquitous vine I'd seen a lot of as I'd driven south from Wisconsin. The vine seemed to take over everything—even the trees on the other side of the river were smothered by an undulating blanket of green.

"What's that vine called?" I asked, pointing at the dense foliage.

"It's kudzu. Basically, it's a weed that was brought over here from Japan in the 1800s to protect against soil erosion. But it grows so fast and is so hard to get rid of that it suffocates everything that gets in its way—plants, trees, you name it."

"You seem to know a lot about the south, but didn't you say you're from up north somewhere? Is it Maine?

"Rhode Island," he corrected.

"Do you like it down here?"

He shrugged and pulled the wine bottle, a corkscrew and two plastic cups from the paper bag. "The south's got its good points and its bad points. What about you?" He handed me a cup.

"I think I like it here so far. I'm not used to it being so hot this early in the year, but then again, I don't think I'll miss fifty below zero next January, either."

Augie laughed and shuddered as he uncorked the bottle, a Cabernet. "I know I won't miss it." He poured us each half a cup of ruby red wine, recorked the bottle and put it back into the bag on the bench between us.

"To your health," he said, raising the cup.

"And to yours." I touched the lip of my cup to his with a light click.

For a moment, we sipped our wine in silence. The days were getting longer, but now the sun was getting low in the sky, painting the wispy clouds ever deepening shades of pink.

"Why so glum, Lark?" Augie asked, finally.

I sighed. "Bad day at work."

"The murders?"

"Not really. I just found out that someone who I thought was a friend is saying untrue things about me behind my back."

He nodded knowingly and pursed his lips. "Office politics. Sucks, doesn't it?"

"Yep." I took another sip. "This is nice," I said. "Thanks for your offer. I needed it."

"You're welcome. I could tell you needed an ear."

"Augie?"

"Yeah?"

"Mind if I ask you a personal question?"

"No. Mind if I don't answer?"

We both laughed.

"You seem like a pretty smart guy," I said. "So, how come you're bagging groceries when you could probably be doing so much more with your life?"

He winced and took another sip.

After an uncomfortable silence, I said, "Never mind. It's none of my business."

"That's okay." He waved his hand dismissively. "It's a fair question. I'm just trying to figure out how to answer it."

"Why? Is it that complicated?"

"Oh yeah." He nodded rapidly and laughed at what must have been some private joke between him and himself.

"What's so complicated about it?"

"You wouldn't understand."

"Try me."

He gave me a raised-eyebrow look.

I raised mine in return, as if to say *bring it on, dude—I can take the truth.*

Augie continued to hold my gaze, studying my face. He seemed to be trying to figure out if I could be trusted. After a moment, he turned away and gazed at the burgundy liquid in his cup. Finally, he spoke. "You're a reporter." He didn't say it with the same derision that was in Matt Benson's voice when he first learned of my profession as we stood over the dead body of Luanne Donovan.

"Yeah. So?"

"I used to be a reporter." He glanced at me quickly.

I sat up straight. "Oh? Where?"

"Here."

"At the *Sun-Gazette*?"

He shook his head. "I was the news director at the NBC affiliate."

"This economy just sucks," I said, angrily. "Why'd they let you go?"

"Long story."

"I've got time."

"Let's just say I went to work for the government for a couple years."

"And then you couldn't get back into journalism because you'd crossed the street to work for the other team?"

"Something like that."

"Were you a CIA spy or something so that if you tell me what you did, you'll have to kill me?" I teased.

He laughed, ironically.

"So, what *did* you do for the government?"

He took a long pause, then a deep drink, then a deep breath. "You could say I made license plates for two and a half years."

I felt myself move involuntarily away from him. "Prison?"

He nodded and looked forlornly into his empty cup.

THIRTY

MUST'VE SAT looking at Augie with my jaw dropped for nearly a minute. He merely sat serenely looking into his wine cup. After a moment, he pulled the bottle out of the brown bag, popped the cork, and poured himself more wine. When he finished, he turned to me, tilting the neck toward my cup, his eyes searching mine.

"Refill?" he asked.

Before I could answer, my cell phone bleeped. I dug it out of my jeans and looked at the display. It was Matt Benson. "Hold on a sec," I said to Augie, "I need to take this."

I got up from the bench and walked a few yards away so that Augie wouldn't be able to overhear.

"Hi, Matt. What's up?"

He was no-nonsense. "We're off the record. Is that understood?"

"Understood." Even as I said the words, I knew I was making my job more difficult because whatever bombshell he was about to drop would mean I'd have to work harder to confirm it.

"Your photographer friend has been released."

My gut reaction was elation. "When? Why?"

"It's happening now. He's being out-processed as we speak."

"Why?"

"The governor's wasted no time in taking over the investigation. His people are now in charge."

"Where does that leave you?"

He grunted. "Not in charge."

"Have you been taken off the case?"

"No. I'm just a cog now in a bigger machine."

"And you don't like it."

"This isn't about me," he said testily.

"Is Doug still a suspect?"

"I can't comment on that."

"We're off the record."

"Still can't comment."

"So, who *is* in charge of the investigation now?"

"The GBI out of Atlanta."

"GBI?"

He laughed, "That's right, you're new here—I keep forgetting. Georgia Bureau of Investigation."

"How can they run it out of Atlanta?"

"They've got an office here in Columbia."

"Who's in charge?"

"Sonny Laskin."

"Is he a good guy?"

"No comment."

"C'mon, Matt."

"Some things you just need to find out for yourself."

"Got a phone number?"

"Look it up."

I sighed. "So, if they released Doug, either they don't have anything on him, or they're keeping an eye on him to see if he does something incriminating."

"I'd go with your second guess, but you didn't hear that from me."

"Okay."

"One more thing."

"Yeah?"

"Be careful about the company you keep."

"What do you mean?"

"The guy on the bench."

"*What*?" I looked over at Augie, patiently sipping from his cup. Then, alarmed, I spun around.

Matt's unmarked Crown Victoria was pulling away from the curb just twenty-five yards from where I stood. Matt, his phone still to his ear, gave me a jaunty wave. "Stay safe, Lark," said the voice in my ear.

THIRTY-ONE

AUGIE MUST HAVE read the inner turmoil written all over my face. "What's wrong?" he asked, concerned. He uncrossed his legs and sat up as I walked slowly in a daze back to where he sat on the bench.

"I-I've got to go," is all I could blurt out.

"Where? Why?" He seemed alarmed.

"It's not about you or anything you said. I really, *really* want to continue our conversation, but there are new developments in the investigation and I need to chase them."

Augie downed his wine in a quick gulp and began packing up our stuff. "Need some help?"

"No. Thanks. But let's keep in touch. Do you have email? A cell phone number?"

"No email—I'm still on parole—but here's my cell."

He gave it to me and I quickly entered it into my phone. As I did, I said, "I don't even know your last name. What is it?"

"Ackermann—with two Ns."

"And Augie is short for . . . . ?"

"August—no E on the end."

"German, huh?"

"*Jawohl.*" He turned to me and took his cell from the pocket of his jeans. "What's your number?" he asked.

I hesitated.

He picked up on it immediately. "Never mind."

"No. It's okay." I gave him my number. "But no stalking, okay?" I wagged a finger at him, hoping he'd take it as a joke. But I meant it.

"Deal," he said, as he punched my digits into his cell.

"Listen, Augie. Thank you for the drink. It was sweet of you."

"You're welcome. Anytime."

"I've got to go now, but I'm serious—I want to talk again, okay?"

"So you say." His voice was sad, resigned—but he smiled.

I jumped into Pearlie and turned on the ignition, my mind in a swirl. I immediately called Doug as I pulled out of the parking lot. No answer. I decided to leave him a voicemail. "Doug! It's Lark. I just heard you've been released. Is it true? Gimme a call."

I made a bee-line for the City-County building which was only a few blocks away. I easily found a place to park out front and ran up the marble steps. The place was locked up tight. I dialed the sheriff's cell as I ran around the building, looking for a way to get inside.

He answered on the second ring.

"Sheriff, it's Lark Chadwick with the *Sun-Gazette*." I was out of breath.

"Hi, Lark."

"I hear you're releasing Doug Mitchell."

"Where'd you hear that?"

"Is it true?"

"Yes. He's a free man as of about half an hour ago."

"Why are you letting him go?"

"Case against him isn't strong enough yet."

"Yet?"

"Um . . . ."

He'd said too much and he knew it.

"How can I get in touch with Sonny Laskin?"

The sheriff gave me Laskin's number with the admonition, "You didn't get it from me."

"My lips are sealed." If my assumption was correct, the sheriff was just as pissed as Matt that the GBI was now in charge, so the sheriff was more than willing to sic a persistent reporter like me onto Laskin.

"Thanks, Sheriff."

"You bet, Lark."

I transferred Laskin's number to the contact list on my phone, then got back into Pearlie and headed for Doug's apartment. As I drove, I speed-dialed Laskin's number.

"Laskin." The voice was no-nonsense impatient.

"Hi, Mr. Laskin. I'm Lark Chadwick with the *Sun-Gazette*. I'm on deadline working the serial killings story."

"Uh huh."

"I just need to confirm a couple things."

"Okay."

"Is it true that the GBI has now taken over the investigation?"

"Yes."

"And why is that?"

"Governor's orders."

"And you're the lead investigator here in Columbia?"

"That's right."

"Did you know that I discovered Luanne Donovan's body?"

"I'm aware of that."

"If you've got a few minutes, I'd like to meet with you face-to-face since I'm working this story full time now."

He paused. "Sure. I guess."

"I'm near the City-County building. Where are you?"

"I'm at the office, but I was just leaving."

"Where's that?"

He gave me the address. It wasn't far. "I'll be the guy leaning against the driver's side of a black unmarked sedan," he said.

For some reason, I pictured a scene from "Men in Black."

"Will your shades be on or off?"

He chuckled. "Off—for now."

The address Sonny Laskin gave me was a nondescript office building in downtown Columbia, a few blocks from the apartment I shared with Marcie. I easily found Laskin leaning against the front fender of his car. My mental picture wasn't too far off—he wore a white shirt, thin black tie and a black suit. All that was missing from the ensemble were a fedora and sunglasses. If he'd had those, he could've passed for one of the Blues Brothers. I guessed him to be about fifty.

I parked behind him and got out.

He looked at his watch as I approached. "I've only got a few minutes," he said. "I've got to pick up my son at baseball practice."

"That's fine," I said as we shook hands. "I won't take much of your time. I just wanted to meet you since we may be spending a lot of time together."

He laughed. "Let's hope not too much. I want to get this thing solved."

I fired up the voice memo app on my iPhone. "How come you released Doug Mitchell?"

"His arrest was, shall we say, premature."

"Is he still a suspect?"

"He's a person of interest."

"What does that mean?"

"We're interested in him."

"Why?"

"He was one of the last people to see the second victim alive."

"Does he have any ties to the first victim?"

"None that we're able to ascertain at this time."

"Does he have an alibi for the time when each of them disappeared?"

"Yes."

"Is it a strong one?"

"He told us where he was."

"Does it check out?"

"No comment."

"Are there any other suspects?"

"None that I care to name, but we're following some leads."

"Care to elaborate?"

"No. But thanks for asking." He smiled.

"Do you have any idea when you might be able to arrest the person or persons you think are responsible for the two deaths?"

"We believe at this time that it's the same person and that he acted alone."

"He?"

"That's our assumption."

"Based on what?"

"Past experience."

"There've been other serial killings here?"

"Not for thirty years, but the second victim was sexually assaulted. That's a guy thing."

"But the first one wasn't."

"True. We haven't ruled out the involvement of a woman, but haven't ruled it in, either."

"How soon before you'll have the case wrapped up?"

He looked at his watch again and pushed himself away from the fender he'd been leaning against. "I don't like to set artificial deadlines. We hope to get this wrapped up soon, but haste makes waste. We want to get it right."

"Anything else you want to add?" I asked as he walked around me and opened his car door.

"Since you discovered the first body, let me ask you a couple quick ones," he said.

"Sure. Go ahead."

"Tell me more about the car you saw driving away from the bridge."

I described the unusual pattern of lights on the front of the vehicle and mentioned that they resembled the cars driven by Luanne's boyfriend Tyrone Jackson and Sam Erickson. He pulled out a notebook and made a few jottings. As he wrote, my cell phone bleeped. I peeked. It was Doug. I sent him to voicemail and prayed he'd leave a message.

As if on cue, Laskin asked, "What about Doug Mitchell?"

"What about him?"

"How well do you know him?"

"Not well. I only met him a few days ago when I started working at the paper."

"Think he could've killed those two?"

I bit my lip. "I hope not. But . . . ."

He pounced. "But what?"

"But . . . I don't know."

"Want some free advice?"

"Sure."

He looked me in the eye, put a hand on my shoulder and spoke slowly and deliberately. "Don't let Doug Mitchell get you alone. *Anywhere.*"

THIRTY-TWO

I **WAS SHAKING BY** the time I crawled behind the wheel. Sonny Laskin had definitely given me something to think about. Before parting, he'd agreed to let me profile him for the Sunday paper. He invited me to his son's little league game on Saturday morning.

Events were going so fast I could barely keep up with them. I urgently needed to file a story before I got scooped by Sam Erickson, yet I knew if I filed prematurely, I might merely tip him off and he'd get to Doug before me. I decided to hold off calling the desk, and deal with Doug first.

I checked my cell phone. It showed I had one voicemail. It, indeed, was from Doug: "Hey, Lark. Got your call. Thanks. Call me when you can. I need to talk."

I hit the *call back* button.

He answered right away. "Hey there," he said breezily.

"Rough day, huh?"

"Geez."

"I'm on deadline. I need a quote."

"Is that all I am to you, a good story?" he chuckled.

"Right now you are."

He sighed.

"I need a quick quote so I can file my story, but I want to talk to you more in depth."

"I want to talk, too. Why don't you come over?"

I felt my blood turn to ice. Twenty-four hours earlier, I might—*might*—have eagerly taken Doug up on his offer. Now, I wasn't so sure. Sonny Laskin's admonition was still ringing in my ears. "Why don't we meet someplace less . . ." I hesitated, looking for the right word.

"Dangerous?"

"I was thinking 'private,' but—"

"But what?"

"But I suppose 'dangerous' fits."

He muttered something profane under his breath. "C'mon, Lark. I'm not a killer, okay?"

"Is that a quote I can use on the record?"

"Geez."

"*You* come on, Doug. You were arrested on suspicion of being a serial killer."

"I'm *not* a serial killer, goddammit. Or *any* kind of killer."

"I'm not saying you are."

"Then what *are* you saying?"

"I'm saying that I'm a reporter and you're a person of interest in two murders."

"I could really use a friend right now."

"Get a dog." I hung up. Then I felt guilty and called him right back.

"Did that feel good?" he asked, his voice mocking.

"Yeah, but only for two seconds. Maybe one."

His voice softened. "Come over."

I shook my head. "I don't think that's such a good idea, Doug."

"I'm not—"

"I know. You're not a serial killer—or any other kind of killer. I heard you the first time. *And* I'm putting you on the record."

He sighed. "So, what's your problem?"

"Do I have to spell it out?"

"No. I understand." He talked rapidly, ticking off each point: "Two women have been murdered. You're a woman. You don't know me very well. Being alone with me in a private setting puts you at risk. I get it."

"So, why are you asking me to put myself at risk?" I asked.

"Two reasons." I could hear the anger in his voice. "One, because I've already been publicly humiliated by the cops, so I'm a little reluctant to be seen in public right now. Two, because I'd like to be able to prove to you that I can be trusted."

I thought about what he was saying. I also thought about the other times in my life when I'd mistakenly trusted men with whom I'd been alone. The first time I'd nearly been raped; the next two times I'd nearly been killed.

"Your silence is deafening, Lark."

"I'm thinking."

"Think about this: the cops are probably camped outside my front door right now. My phone is probably tapped. You can even call the desk and let them know you're coming over to interview me. I'd say being here with me might just be the safest place you could be."

He had a point.

"I need to file my story about your release. I'll be there within the hour."

"I'll order a pizza."

"Fine."

We hung up and I called Marcie on the desk. I gave her a quick heads up about the story I was about to write, adding, "I'm sitting in my car in front of the GBI building. As soon as I file my piece, I'm heading over to Doug's. He's agreed to an in-depth interview."

"You're very, very brave, Lark," Marcie said.

Her tone *sounded* admiring, but after my troubling conversation with Priscilla, I couldn't help thinking that Marcie was being fake. It took every bit of restraint I had not to say something snarky. Instead, I heard myself say, "Either I'm brave, or I'm very, very stupid. Thanks, Marcie."

We hung up, me still unsure how I would handle the seemingly duplicitous Marcie Peck. I fired up my laptop and began to pound the keys.

THIRTY-THREE

TRYING TO TYPE while sitting behind the wheel of a Volkswagen Beetle isn't the most comfortable thing in the world, but when you're on deadline, it'll have to do. I was parked on the street in front of the GBI office where I'd met with Sonny Laskin. I slid my seat back and began writing.

I worked steadily and easily for the next thirty minutes. I began with an umbrella lead, which covered the two main items—Doug's release and the GBI's takeover of the investigation. High up in the story I included Doug's vigorous denial and the broad hints from the sheriff and Sonny Laskin that Doug might still be a suspect. It was dark by the time I put the finishing touches on the story and went back over it.

I didn't use spell-checker because I felt it gave me a false sense of security. Words like *their* and *there*, or *your* and *you're* may be spelled right, but if I'd used one and meant the other, it wouldn't show up in spell-checker as wrong.

When I was satisfied the piece was as good as I could make it, I emailed it to the desk and gave Marcie a quick call to let her know it was done.

"Keep your phone on in case an editor needs to get back to you with questions," she said. "We'll whittle it down, if necessary, for the Web edition."

"Thanks. I'm heading over to Doug's now."

"Stay safe, Lark."

"I will," I replied. But I wondered . . . and worried.

Doug lived in an apartment above a drug store on Columbia's Main Street. He answered the door with a dishrag draped over the shoulder of his sleeveless grey sweatshirt. For an instant my mind flashed back to Madison, Wisconsin and the day Ross Christopher, my English professor at the time, assaulted me.

"Are you just going to stand there?" Doug asked. He stood aside and, with more boldness than I felt, I stepped across the threshold and into his lair.

His apartment seemed more spacious than I expected. The living room was sparsely furnished by IKEA—a white sofa against the right wall was flanked on both sides by easy chairs and floor lamps—both lights were switched on. Newspapers were splayed on an ebony coffee table.

The living room opened into a dining area at the far end of the apartment. The area was dominated by a dark brown, double-pedestal table surrounded by six matching chairs, each backed with a tasteful see-through latticed design.

I was surprised to see prominently displayed above the sofa an imposing portrait of a beautiful brunette painted on black velvet. She was nude.

I walked over to look at the painting. "Who's the artist?"

"Me," Doug said.

"It's really good."

"Thank you. It could have been you."

"I don't think so," I laughed. "Who is she?"

"An old girlfriend."

"How did it end?"

"I moved on."

"Charming. What's her name?"

"I forget."

I gave him a look.

He smiled impishly.

"Did she sit while you painted her?"

Doug nodded. "Sometimes, though, I just take a photo and work off that." He went into the next room—his bedroom. "That's what I did with these," he called.

I went to the bedroom door and peeked inside. He stood next to the bed pointing at several portraits on the walls.

All of the women were nude, painted in oil on black velvet. Their poses were demur and in profile with mostly their backs showing. My attention was easily drawn to the eyes of the women because that's where it seemed Doug had focused most of his artistic energy. Their eyes drew me in. I saw them as people, not objects. But I'm a straight woman.

"The eyes are amazing," I said. "Mesmerizing."

"Thanks."

I turned to him. "So, why do you find it necessary to paint naked women?"

"At least you didn't say 'nekkid,'" he chuckled. "But, to answer your question, I think the female body is a work of art all by itself."

"I can think of many female bodies that aren't. Why not paint those?"

He nodded thoughtfully as he gazed at a painting. "Probably for the same reason that some sunsets are more beautiful than others. It's human to be drawn to beauty."

"But isn't what's considered 'beautiful' relative?" I asked.

"Sure," he nodded, "and it's subjective. Rubens painted pudgy nudes who might seem unattractive by today's standards, but I think he was on to something."

"None of these women look pudgy."

He shrugged. "You have yet to see my entire collection. What *you're* looking at is what I consider beautiful," Doug said, adding, ". . . and what *I'm* looking at." His eyes held mine.

I looked away and felt my face flush, an involuntary thrill raced through my stomach. "I want to be loved for who I am, not how I look," I said firmly.

"Fair enough," Doug shrugged.

"I'm reminded of a joke I heard once," I said, intentionally breaking the mood.

"Oh?" Doug suddenly looked confused, as if his intentions had been unexpectedly derailed.

"It's about a guy in the Army who's just been promoted to sergeant. He's been told he has to work on his people skills." As I talked, I turned and walked away from Doug's bedroom and into the relative safety of his living room.

Doug followed.

I chose a place to stand with my back to the door so I could bolt if I had to and continued telling the joke. "The sergeant's commanding officer tells him he has to find a way to gently break the news to one of his recruits that the guy's mother has just died."

A shadow of a smile began to play at the side of Doug's mouth. He was already anticipating the punch line.

"So," I continued, "the sergeant assembles his platoon and has them stand at attention. Then he announces in his best drill sergeant voice, 'All you men whose mothers are still alive, take one step forward.' Then, as everyone obeys, the sergeant bellows, 'NOT so fast, Johnson.'"

Doug burst out laughing. "That's good, but I don't see the connection to what we were talking about."

"Yes you do. You're coming on to me. You still want me to pose nude." I crossed my arms defiantly. "Not so fast, Johnson."

He nodded. "Busted." He turned away from me and ambled to the kitchen just off the dining room. "The pizza's already here. Lemme warm it up in the oven. Can I get you anything to drink?"

"Water's fine," I said, following him.

"Really? I've got plenty of beer."

"I'm on the job."

"What are you, a cop?"

"I prefer '*sleuth*'," I said daintily.

Doug turned on the oven, took the pizza out of its box, slid it onto a cookie sheet, and stuck it in the oven, then he poured me a glass of water from the tap and plunked in two ice cubes. He popped the top of a Bud Lite.

"Where's your bathroom?" I asked. "I need to freshen up."

"It's in there," he said, nodding at his bedroom. "To the left."

Doug's bathroom was a tad cramped. I washed my hands and splashed water on my face, then grabbed a hand towel to dry off. As I was checking my hair in the mirror, the portrait hanging behind me caught my eye. There was something instantly familiar about it.

I spun around to get a closer look. Gazing back at me was a painting of an unclothed Marcie Peck.

In the portrait, Marcie sat straddling one of Doug's backward-facing, latticed dining room chairs. In her hands, she held a bunched and crumpled bed sheet against her chest. The top of the sheet curled forward revealing a hint of cleavage. Her shoulders and arms were bare. The sheet flowed to the floor, covering her breasts and abdomen, but her curved left leg was exposed all the way to her ample, rounded bottom. Marcie's raven hair was disheveled as if she'd just gotten out of bed. Her full lips were parted slightly, a coy smile beginning to form. Her almond eyes looked love-sated.

Doug's painting had skillfully allowed Marcie's true beauty to emerge. And, by the look on her face, I could tell she felt unabashedly gorgeous.

It took me a moment to catch my breath and compose myself. Seeing the picture certainly confirmed my hunch that at least *something* was going on between Marcie and Doug. Part of me, I had to admit, was a little hurt and jealous. But it also confirmed to me now more than ever that Doug Mitchell was definitely off limits and that any lustful attraction I might have for him would have to remain private. Extremely private.

I returned to the living room where Doug—beer in hand—was lounging on the sofa, an arm stretched out across the back. If he sensed I was rattled by seeing Marcie's portrait, he didn't show it.

"Take a seat," he said, patting the sofa cushion next to him.

I chose a chair, instead. I'd learned from past experience a chair is a more effective way to keep my host at a distance.

Doug took a deep drink that probably drained a third of the contents. He leaned back, stretched out his feet and crossed them at the ankles.

I dug out my iPhone, activated the voice memo function, and placed it on the coffee table in front of him next to my glass of water sweating on a coaster. "So, why did you agree to a sit-down, on-the-record interview?" I asked as I pressed the record button.

"I talked with my lawyer about it, who, by the way, I have you to thank for lining up."

"Ed got the guy for you. I just gave Ed a heads up."

"Well, thanks for doing that much."

"You're welcome."

"Anyway, my lawyer says that as long as we don't get into the specifics of the cases, it's okay for me to talk to you."

I scowled. "But that's what this whole thing is about."

"No, it's not."

"It's not?"

"No. People need to know who I am and realize I didn't kill either of those young women."

"So, you're sticking by your denial."

"Absolutely, but that's all my lawyer will allow me to say about the cases."

"Okay. Fair enough." I paused to gather my thoughts. "So, tell me about yourself. You know, the basic resume stuff."

"Is this a job interview?" he laughed.

I didn't.

"Okay," he coughed uncomfortably. "Let's see." He leaned forward, closer to the recorder and rested his elbows on his thighs. "I'm originally from Fairport, New York near Rochester. Went to school at Fredonia State."

"Where's that?"

"Western New York, near Buffalo. Majored in communication arts, but specialized in photography. After college I joined the Army."

"Why?"

"My brother was killed on 9/11. He was an investment banker working on the 80th floor of one of the towers in the World Trade Center."

"Do you have a picture of him that I can use in the story?"

"I've got tons." He plunked the beer can on the coffee table, shot to his feet and went briskly into his bedroom. I heard him rummaging around. In a moment, he was back. "Here," he said, handing me a snapshot. "This is of both of us taken back home the last time I saw him."

I looked at the picture. "What's his name?"

"Clarke. With an E on the end," he said as I jotted down the name.

Clarke was every bit as good looking as Doug. In the picture, Clarke wore a deep blue shirt and solid red tie. He had broad shoulders and filled out the shirt nicely. Clarke had his arm around Doug's shoulder. The two of them had broad grins on their faces.

"Older brother?" I asked, looking up.

Doug was standing over me looking at the picture. There were tears in his eyes. He nodded curtly. "Two years older." His voice was tight, strained. "He'd be 39 now."

"I'm so sorry," I said.

He shrugged and scowled. "Thanks."

"I'll get this back to you as soon as I can scan it," I said.

"No hurry."

"So, you joined the Army."

Doug took his place on the sofa and nodded. "Yeah."

"But as I remember, you told me you were a photographer."

"Right. I got assigned to DINFOS—the Defense Information School at Fort Meade, Maryland." He chuckled. "Graduates from there call themselves 'DINFOS-trained killers.'"

I laughed.

"Oops," he smirked. "Better not use that."

"We'll see," I smiled.

"Anyway," Doug said, continuing his story. "I shipped out from there when we invaded Iraq in 2003."

"How come you didn't join the Marines or a special operations unit where you could have taken out your revenge on the enemy?"

"That's a great question. I've just never been the violent type. I hate guns. But I wanted to do something. Maybe it was a vicarious thing. Instead of doing the killing, I was close enough to the action that I could see it and record it."

"You know what I'm going to ask next, don't you?" I smiled.

He got to his feet. "Pictures. You want more pictures, right?"

"You're good."

"No, *you're* good. You realize that journalism is *show* and tell."

"Thanks," I blushed.

The timer bell went off on the oven.

"I'll get it," I said, getting up. "You go find me some visuals."

He returned to his bedroom while I went to the kitchen. The break gave me time to reflect and regroup. I liked Doug. I also took a stern inward look at myself. I realized that I wanted him to be innocent. But I also knew that I couldn't let my personal feelings get in the way of doing an objective job.

I found an oven mitt and, as I extracted the warm pizza from the oven, I remembered something Lionel had said once about objectivity. He'd told me it's human to have opinions, but the professional journalist is able to recognize his or her personal bias and take definitive steps to keep those opinions from crowding out other points of view. Now more than ever, I told myself, I *must* take Lionel's advice.

The cheese on the pepperoni pizza bubbled. I turned off the oven, set the cookie sheet on the stove, slipped off the oven mitt, and found two plates in a cupboard. I noticed that Doug actually did a pretty good job of keeping his place clean.

"Do you have napkins?" I called into the other room.

"No. Use paper towels," he said as he came out of his bedroom carrying a handful of pictures. "We can sit here," he said, placing a pile of black-and-white glossies on the dining room table.

I tore two sheets off his paper towel dispenser and brought the dishes of pizza to the table. "You get the plate with two slices," I said to him.

"You're only gonna have one?"

"For now."

After putting down his pictures, he retrieved our drinks from the living room and brought them to the table where I was already sitting.

"Oh, I need to get my phone," I said.

"I'll get it." He got up before I could, walked to the coffee table, picked up my phone/recorder, and brought it to me. "Here you go." He set it down on the table.

"Thanks." I checked to make sure it was still recording. It was.

He sat down opposite me and took an enormous bite from one of his slices. A string of hot cheese dangled from his lower lip and onto his chin.

I was having just as much difficulty remaining dignified. "This is really good," I mumbled as I savored my first bite. "I didn't realize until just now how hungry I was."

"I know. Me too." He was already finishing his first slice. He washed it down with more beer.

"So these are your pictures from your Army and Iraq War days?" I asked.

"Some of 'em."

I pawed through them, looking for a shot that would best sum up that portion of Doug's biography. Many were pictures of combat—soldiers aiming their weapons and firing, but the one I liked best showed a tired, grimy Doug holding a long-lensed camera in both hands and staring blankly.

"Looks like this was taken on a rough day," I offered, hoping it would elicit another anecdote.

Doug craned his neck to look at the picture. "Oh, that one. Yeah. Long day."

"Care to elaborate?"

"Let's not go there."

"Why not?"

"It was the day my best buddy got blown to bits by an IED." His eyes took on the same haunted look as the eyes of the man staring at me from a battlefield in Iraq.

"What was his name?"

Doug shook his head making it clear he had no intention of saying any more about it.

We ate in silence for a few more minutes. As I sifted through more of the pictures, Doug got up, went to the fridge and got another beer. "Want one?" He held up a Bud. "No thanks. I'm still good with my water." I took a sip for emphasis, but secretly, I craved a beer.

As Doug rejoined me at the table, I became aware of the limp I'd first noticed on the day we met. "Is that limp an old war wound?" I asked, half joking.

"How'd you guess?"

"Is it really?"

He nodded.

"It was just a hunch. What happened?"

"I had my own IED moment in Iraq." He leaned down and lifted the cuff of his blue jean above his right hiking boot. Doug Mitchell had a titanium shin. "The bomb blew off my leg below the knee."

I flinched involuntarily.

Doug must have noticed because he yanked hard on his jean cuff, pulling it back into place. "Thank you, George *Fucking* Bush," he growled.

My reaction to Doug's revelation: shock and awe. My ever-so-brief recoil was in surprise, not revulsion because my fascination with him had just increased exponentially. Dozens of questions rushed into my head, but all I could muster was a meager, "Care to tell me the story?"

"Nope." He pursed his lips.

I could tell I was getting under his skin. I decided to back off. "How long were you in the service?"

"Three years. Two tours."

"Then what?"

"Rehab at Walter Reed near DC. Honorable Discharge. The *Sun-Gazette*."

"And the rest is history."

He smiled ruefully.

"When did you start painting?"

"After I got out. It's very relaxing."

"I can imagine."

"Meaning?" He raised his eyebrows.

"There's nothing like the naked body of a beautiful woman to take your mind off the cares of the world."

"I won't deny it."

"But here's what I don't understand."

"What's that?"

"Here you are, a person of interest in the investigation into the deaths of two young women, and you aren't ashamed to let me—and our readers—see how you spend your free time."

"No. I'm not."

"Why not?"

He sighed, stood, and shuffled to the picture hanging over the sofa in the living room. The scene was too good to pass up. Quickly, I picked up my iPhone, got up and joined him.

"I'm going to take your picture standing by the portrait." I said. It was a statement, not a request for permission.

Doug didn't object, he merely continued to gaze at his artwork.

I began squeezing off shots. When he turned to look at me forlornly, I clicked the shutter. In that instant, I knew I'd just taken the money shot, the shot that summed up my profile piece at a glance: Doug Mitchell standing almost defiantly in front of a nude picture he'd painted.

He didn't seem to mind. Would the general public? I had my doubts. But then I wondered if he might end up having women throwing themselves at him to be one of his models. *That,* I sighed to myself, *seems more likely.*

"So, why don't you have any qualms about letting people see this side of you?"

"Here's why: And I say this without conceit: Even though I'm a gimp, I've always been successful with women. Beautiful women. These women posed eagerly." His voice began to rise in intensity and he jabbed a finger at the painting. "They made love with me *freely.* Why am I telling you this? Why am I showing you this? Because I'm *not* some sexually-repressed reprobate with no social skills who needs to rape and kill to get my jollies. I'm *not.*" Fire and indignation flashed from his eyes.

THIRTY-FOUR

IT WAS AFTER ten when I dragged myself to my desk at the newspaper office. Marcie had alerted an editor that I had an exclusive interview with Doug, so they made room for it in the morning paper.

I worked steadily for the next forty minutes, doing my best to block out the din of a newsroom on deadline: Bleating telephones, squawking police radios, clattering keyboards, shouting people. The deadline for the paper was eleven; I filed my story twenty minutes early, then stayed around until it was edited.

The person in the editor's slot was an older, white-haired, gravel-voiced guy I'd never worked with before. I watched him from across the room as he read my piece. He kept looking worriedly at the clock on the wall in front of him, then back to his computer screen. At one point he slapped both of his hands against his forehead, then plunged his fingers into the keyboard and began doing what looked to me like major surgery—with no anesthetic.

I sidled closer to see how badly he was butchering my story.

He wasn't aware of me until I was almost at his desk. He glanced up.

"I can't talk right now," he barked, impatiently, "I'm on deadline with this piece of shit."

"I wrote it," I said.

"Are you Chadwick?" he challenged.

"I am. What's the problem?"

"What's *not* the problem?" He turned his attention back to his work.

"What do you need me to fix?" I asked, worried.

"Nothing. I'll take care of it." He scowled at my words on the screen.

"Mind if I watch?"

He ignored me, so I circled behind him to see what he was doing. My copy scrolled up as he read quickly. Every now and then, he let out a burst of profanity, but kept reading. When he got to the bottom, he extended his arms toward the ceiling as if imploring the News God to save him from this idiot reporter.

"Where's the *balance?*" he shrieked.

"What do you mean?" I asked, moving to his side.

"You only quote the suspect."

I felt by blood begin to simmer on its way to a rolling boil, but I took a deep breath and tried to answer calmly. "It's a profile piece."

"I *know* that," he said, his voice dripping with derision, "but even profiles have to be balanced with the opinions and insights of other people who've known the guy over the years."

"But I just did the interview an hour or so ago and I'm on deadline," I said more defensively than I would like to have sounded.

"So?" he countered. "That's not an excuse to turn in a halfbaked piece of crap."

"What do you want me to do?" My voice was steel, but he was making me feel like an idiot—and part of me believed he was right.

"If this were the old typewriter days, I'd tear this up and dump it on your desk in tiny little pieces and make you start over."

"Oh, come on. I'm sure there's something in it that can be salvaged."

"Not much," he said, taking another nervous glance at the clock.

"Alright," I said. "Here's a suggestion: I wrote up a piece earlier today, breaking the news that he'd been released and that the GBI is taking over the investigation. How about if we drop into that piece the picture of him in front of the nude painting and his strong statement that he's not a sex-crazed reprobate? We can use that to tease a profile I'll do for the Sunday paper."

Rather than simply react, he paused for the first time and thoughtfully considered what I had to say. "I'm okay with dropping his statement into the other story," he said slowly, "and I think the shot of him with the portrait of the babe is okay, too—we've got room for it. But no teasing." He gave me a stern look.

"Why not?"

"Because at this rate, I can't be sure you're gonna have enough to round out the story in time for the Sunday paper."

"I'm not as pessimistic about my abilities as you are, but okay on the no-tease part. Do *you* want to drop in the quote, or should I?"

"I'll do it." His fingers banged on the keyboard as he pulled up my earlier story, parked it at a corner of his screen, then copied and pasted Doug's comment from my profile piece and dropped it into my earlier story. "There," he said.

"Okay, thanks," I said, as diplomatically as I could. "I'll work on the profile and beef it up for Sunday."

"You do that," he sneered.

I stalked back to my desk, saying in my head all the nasty things I longed to say to his face. I smiled at one point when I realized that Lionel's wife, Muriel, would be proud of me for showing so much restraint. She'd once told me I had "fight-and-flight tendencies" because I would blow up about something and then run away and sulk. It had stung when she'd pointed it out to me, but I could see that she was right. That conversation with her a couple years ago had helped toughen and mature me just in time for my unpleasant encounter with this night's editor.

I got back to my desk about eleven. As wrung out as I was, I knew I needed to get a grip on all the loose ends that were beginning to appear. I felt as if I was on a crazy carnival ride, struggling to hang on as events thrust me up, down, and around. I had to take an objective look at where things stood and try to prioritize what to do beginning first thing in the morning.

I flopped open my narrow reporters' notebook on my desk and started listing things in the order they came to mind. Topping the list was beefing up Doug's profile. Two people I thought of immediately who might be able to supply me with insights, quotes, and new leads were Sam Erickson and Marcie Peck.

Thinking of Marcie reminded me of how complex my feelings had become about her. It was now obvious to me that Doug was the "inattentive" boyfriend she'd referred to when she and I had our get-to-know-you talk the night she let me crash at her place. But tonight's revelation paled in comparison to Priscilla coming on to me and her news that Marcie was telling lies about me behind my back. It irked me that I wasn't sure how I should handle it.

My first instinct was to realize I needed to find a new place to live, but I didn't have time to deal with that just yet. Putting a move on hold, however, would, of course, complicate things. I'd promised Priscilla that I wouldn't rat her out, so I decided instead not to confront Marcie, but to keep an eye on her. It grieved me to realize that I couldn't trust her, yet still had to depend on her as I did my job, so I figured I would be wary and guarded about what I told her, but continue to treat her cordially—unless or until I caught her in the act of another attempt to undermine me. Then I'd confront her and we'd have it out. I wasn't looking forward to that possibility.

I also wrote a reminder to myself to research the Sonny Laskin interview I'd be doing Saturday. Next I wrote *car lights* onto my list, a reminder to check with John, the Notre Dame intern, to see what he'd come up with about car makes that might resemble the one I saw on the bridge just before discovering Luanne's body.

Thinking about Luanne made me realize I still had some hunches to check out. I made a note to interview Bob Black, the guy who inspired Luanne to dump Tyrone Jackson.

And then there was the bag boy, Augie Ackermann—*definitely* an intriguing person. Why had Matt Benson warned me to be careful?

I decided to do a little Googling.

There are about 300 entries for August "Augie" Ackermann on the Internet. Topping the list, a link to the Georgia registry of . . . sex offenders.

THIRTY-FIVE

STAYED RIVETED TO my computer until close to two in the morning reading all about Augie. The one thing that struck me is how "normal" Augie seemed in person, so unlike the man described in the various news accounts, some written by Sam Erickson when he was the cops and courts reporter at the *Sun-Gazette*.

I liked Augie. He seemed like a good and decent man. Reluctantly, I added him to my list of possible suspects—a list that included Doug Mitchell, Tyrone Jackson, Luanne Donovan's father Buddy, Sam Erickson, and now Augie Ackermann.

After getting barely four hours of sleep, I trudged into our fifth floor War Room promptly at eight o'clock carrying a cup of steaming Starbucks coffee. The others were taking their seats at the conference room table.

"So, where do we stand?" I asked. "Who wants to go first?"

Alicia spoke. "Is it true Doug Mitchell's been fired?"

I tried not to let my shock show. "Where'd you hear that?"

"In the hallway. Just now."

"Not that I know of. I interviewed him last night." I turned to look at Marcie, sitting to my right. "Marce, have you heard anything?"

She shook her head. "Nope."

"Maybe Elmer will have something to say about it in the morning editorial meeting in here at nine," I said. "What else?"

John raised his hand and I nodded at him. "I went online and came up with a few car models that could belong to the picture you emailed me. There are a couple of luxury cars, a few sedans, but the one that stands out is a Mustang GT and maybe a Saturn."

"Do you have pictures?"

"I'll email them to you."

"Thanks."

John spoke again. "You asked me to look into possible shrinks for you to interview."

"Right. What'd you come up with?"

He slid a small packet of stapled-together papers across the table. "I found five. Two men, three women. I starred the two I think are strongest and included some relevant background info on each of them."

"Cool." I picked up the packet and quickly thumbed through it. "I'll go over it after the meeting. Thanks. Do you want another assignment?"

John sat up straight. "Sure!"

"Find out all you can about Sonny Laskin."

"How do you spell that?" John asked, opening his notebook

I spelled it for him.

"Who's he?" John asked as he wrote.

"He's the lead investigator on the case for the Georgia Bureau of Investigation. I'm interviewing him Saturday for a profile piece. If you want, you can tag along when I interview him. You up for that?"

"Absolutely!" John beamed.

"The next thing, then," I said to Alicia, "is looking for sex offenders who are living in the area—guys who were sent to prison for sexual offenses who are out now and living among us."

"How can I find out that information?" she asked.

"There's a sex offender registry," I told her. "I'll send you the link."

"So, where do we go from here?" I asked everyone.

At first, I got several blank, alarmed stares in response, but then Priscilla said, "It seems to me that we have a lot of loose ends and no concrete direction."

I scowled. "And it feels terrible."

They laughed, but I wasn't joking.

"Here's a thought," John said. "You could do a piece that lists what we know and what we don't know."

"Good idea," I said, writing it down. I noticed Marcie taking notes, too. "I like this. You guys are great."

More ideas began coming thick and fast. By the end of a half hour, we had a list of possible story ideas that could take up to a month to flesh out. I assigned each intern a story to begin doing the preliminary legwork on—research, mostly. But what they found could result in interviews. I was thrilled to see the enthusiasm in their eyes. They seemed excited to actually be doing journalism, not just answering phones and making coffee runs.

After the meeting, I had a few minutes, so I went back to my desk on the third floor and gave Doug a quick call.

"Is it true?" I asked when he answered on the second ring.

"Is what true?"

"Someone told me you've been fired."

"Not exactly."

"Then what exactly?"

"Are we on the record?"

"Yes."

He let out a long, loud sigh. Finally, he spoke. "Alright, then. I've been suspended."

"Jesus."

"But with pay."

"That's a relief."

"If you say so."

"What happened? How'd you find out?"

"I got a call from Elmer last night after you left."

"What'd he say?"

"He said that under the circumstances, it wouldn't be wise for me to be working while the murder investigation is pending and I'm considered to be a person of interest."

"Is that a quote?" I was taking notes.

"He specifically used the words 'it wouldn't be wise.'"

"What was your reaction?"

"I bit my tongue. I'm on thin ice, here, so I didn't want to make matters worse. He did make it clear that I'd still be getting a paycheck, so that made it a little easier to take."

"Did he say how long you'll be suspended?"

"No. He said it's open-ended, depending on the outcome of the murder case."

"Is that the same as indefinite?"

"No, because he said that the decision would be reviewed on a monthly basis."

"Meaning?"

"Meaning they could stop paying me or even fire me."

"So, you're standing on a trap door."

"Ooooo. Nice image. You're good."

"I try."

"I did call my lawyer, though," Doug said.

"What did he say?"

"He's making it clear to Elmer—probably as we speak—that if I'm fired and someone else ends up being tried and convicted of the murders, that the paper will have a major lawsuit on its hands."

"I wonder how Elmer's reacting to that one."

"Maybe you can find out."

"Maybe. How do you feel, Doug?"

He paused, obviously weighing his words carefully. "I feel innocent. I feel grateful to still have a job. And I hope the cops catch the son of a bitch, because I want to get back to work."

"What'll you do now that you have some spare time?"

"Paint." He paused, then: "And I'm in need of a new model. Got any ideas?"

"None that you'd want to hear."

He laughed. "I thought not."

THIRTY-SIX

I **HAD HOPED TO** grab Elmer in the hallway before the nine o'clock meeting and get a quote from him there so that I could quickly file my piece, but the meeting was just beginning when I arrived with Marcie. We sat in chairs that lined the side of the conference room because all the places at the long, oval conference table were taken.

Elmer was listening to Ed go down the list of possible stories for tomorrow's metro section. When he saw me taking my seat, he interrupted his litany. "I see that Lark's here now, so we can ask. Lark, what will you be working on today?"

I cleared my throat. "Actually, I'm on deadline right now for the Web edition. I've learned that Doug Mitchell has been suspended with pay."

Several people at the table gasped and all eyes turned first to me, then to Elmer.

"So," I continued, "I need to get a statement from Mr. Wiesenthal."

Elmer turned beet red. He looked like he was about to explode.

"Do you have a comment, sir?" My reporter's notebook was open and my pen poised.

He clenched his teeth and bored into me with his eyes. When he spoke, it was slowly and deliberately, as if he was dictating a letter to an addled child. "It is the policy of this newspaper not to publicly discuss personnel matters."

"Even when those personnel matters are related to an ongoing murder investigation?" I asked.

"*Especially* then. You've got a lot of nerve, young lady."

I ignored the ominous tone of his voice and plunged ahead, ignoring the little voice in the back of my head urging me to be sensible and back off. "Can you explain the reasoning behind your decision?"

"Not for the record, no." He was seething.

"Is it true you told Mr. Mitchell that it wouldn't be wise for him to remain on the job right now?"

"Won't confirm, won't deny."

"Has Mr. Mitchell's lawyer been in touch with you?"

Elmer's face was beginning to turn purple. "Really, Miss Chadwick, I hardly think your inquisition is necessary."

"You hired me to do a job, sir. I'm doing it."

The room was dead silent. The tension was electric. No one thumbed a BlackBerry or made bored doodles on notepads. They either looked uncomfortably at the center of the table, or looked back and forth between Elmer and me as if watching a mesmerizing tennis match—to the death.

"I repeat: Have you been contacted by Mr. Mitchell's attorney, warning of a possible lawsuit if Mr. Mitchell is fired?"

"Lark," Ed cut in, "Don't you see that Elmer can't and won't go there?"

"So it would seem," I said, "but I still have to ask the questions." I turned back to Elmer. "Mr. Wiesenthal?"

"Ed's right. I can't go there."

"One final question, then: Is there anything you *can* say, on a *personal* level, about your feelings regarding Mr. Mitchell?"

I was looking for something that would humanize the story and take it out of the bureaucratically impersonal no-comment mode Elmer was in, but he merely sat at the head of the table seething, his mouth agape as he struggled to find a way to avoid a direct answer.

"Is there anything you can say about Doug as an employee, as a person?" I asked softly.

Everyone turned to look at Elmer who was still struggling to come up with something. Finally, he shrugged and slumped against the back of his chair. "Our lawyers have advised me not to discuss this matter in public at all."

I thought about saying *So, Doug's identity is now merely "this matter"?* but, instead, I heard myself ask, "Is this paper still committed to providing its readers with an aggressively unbiased pursuit of the truth in the serial killer investigation even though it has touched one of its own?"

"Yes. Absolutely," Elmer said, softly, almost absent-mindedly, without conviction.

"And can you say, Mr. Wiesenthal, that Mr. Mitchell has been an exemplary employee, that it's your firm desire that he'll eventually be exonerated and that the real killer will be captured?" I hoped the now gentle tone of my voice let him know I was giving him the words for a graceful, face-saving way to end this.

He'd been gazing, dazed, at the center of the table, but when I'd finished asking my question, he looked directly at me. "The lawyers will kill me, but yes, I can say that."

"Thank you, sir." I got up abruptly and went to file my story.

THIRTY-SEVEN

A **FEW MINUTES LATER**, I was at my desk doing a final proof-read of my story about Doug's suspension and Elmer's tepid response when Ed stormed up to my desk.

"Step into my office," he hissed, his voice clipped. He didn't linger to wait for my reply, but turned on his heel and charged across the newsroom.

I hit the *send* button, filing my story, and followed him.

When I arrived, he was already sitting behind his desk looking out the window, his chair with its back to me.

"I assume you'd like me to close the door," I said, signaling my arrival.

Ed didn't respond, but swiveled to face me.

I eased the door closed and took a seat in one of two chairs sitting opposite his desk. Bright light from the window behind him made it nearly impossible to see the expression on his face, but I didn't need to. The anger in his voice said it all.

"I just saved your job, young lady."

I decided the less I say, the better, so I waited.

He went on. "After the meeting, Elmer was so livid he wanted me to fire you, but I talked him out of it."

"Thank you," I said softly.

"But if I were him, I'd want you gone, too. What in the world possessed you to verbally assault the publisher of this newspaper in front of the top members of his staff?"

I felt my anger beginning to simmer. "I didn't 'verbally assault' him."

"Who do you think you are—Mike Wallace?" Ed was shouting now.

"I'm a journalist, on deadline, doing her job," I said firmly. It was a struggle to keep from shouting back.

"And, let me understand this correctly," he continued, his voice steely. "Your job is to embarrass the head of the company, is that correct, Miss Chadwick?" His voice mimicked mine during the staff meeting.

"My job is to get his side of the story. To hold him accountable."

"Hold him accountable?" Ed nearly shrieked. "Lark, Elmer Wiesenthal's not on trial."

"I shouldn't have to explain to you what a journalist does, Ed. I was doing what you pay every one of us to do and that's to get the story. Unfortunately, this newspaper is now part of the story."

Ed slumped back against his chair, his anger seemingly spent, but I couldn't be sure because I still couldn't see the expression on his back-lit face. When he spoke, his voice still had an edge.

"I think you owe Elmer an apology."

"For what?"

"For embarrassing him in public."

"I was on deadline. I asked direct questions. I was polite and I was professional."

"Is that what you learned from Lionel Stone?" Ed's voice dripped with sarcasm.

Ed was getting close to pushing one of my buttons—the one criticizing my former boss, mentor, and best friend. Start attacking Lionel and you ran the risk of making me very, *very* angry.

"Let's leave Lionel out of this," I said as evenly as I could.

Ed stood. When he did, I could better see his face as he glowered down at me. He was doing his best to make me feel small. To make me cower. And it wasn't working. I knew in my heart that Lionel had taught me well not to be intimidated by power. Ever. Lionel had faced down Nixon during Watergate and had earned a place on the former president's infamous "enemies list."

I stood. Ed and I were now eye to eye across his desk.

"Are we through?" I asked.

"The question is, are *you* through?"

"Meaning what?"

"Do I have your word that you will never again rake Elmer Wiesenthal over the coals like you did this morning?"

"No. You don't. First, I disagree with that characterization. I was no-nonsense and direct, but I don't control how he feels."

Ed sighed. "Help me out, here, Lark. I'm trying to keep you from getting fired."

"And I appreciate that. Tell Elmer that you chewed me out. Tell him that I heard you loud and clear. You can even tell him that I will do my best to cover this story fairly and professionally. But I'm telling *you* that it's my *duty* to follow the truth wherever it leads. Do we understand each other?"

His eyes continued to drill into mine. He seemed to be searching for some new way to intimidate me. Finally, he simply said, "We do."

I turned and walked out of his office, knowing that I might be looking for another job before I'd been on my current one for even a week.

THIRTY-EIGHT

I **WAS SHAKING BY** the time I got back to my desk. Several people had given me questioning looks as I left Ed's office. Either they had heard our raised voices, or they just knew something was up.

As I'd headed for my desk, a flurry of little dings pinged like rain on many of the computers in the newsroom, the cyber equivalent of intra-office jungle drums. I could only imagine the terse, snarky, instant messages going back and forth about me, speculating about how much longer I'd last at the paper. I hadn't been here long enough to have made many friends—and my "friendship" with Marcie was dubious, at best—so I could only assume that since people still didn't know me very well, it was easier for them to sit back and watch my fate play out from a safe and impersonal distance.

Being the object of everyone's *schadenfreude*—getting pleasure from my pain—made me feel very alone.

My instinct and desire was to reach out and talk with Lionel, but I had too much other stuff to do, plus I didn't want the entire newsroom listening in on my side of our conversation. I decided, instead, to send Lionel a quick email.

I opened up a new email page, typed in Lionel's address and began to write.

Hi, Lionel.......

I paused to look at the blank screen a moment, then increased the size of the font and added:

ARGH!!!!!!!!!!!!!!!!!!!!!!!!!!!!!!!

After proof-reading it, I put in about a dozen more exclamation marks followed by:

Love, Lark

I looked it over. It summed up everything I needed to say. I hit *send* and moved on, feeling MUCH better.

THIRTY-NINE

WAS GRATEFUL THAT I didn't have any appointments or news conferences to attend, so I had some time to get caught up. But my gut was telling me that life as a reporter at a daily newspaper with a Web presence and a constant deadline would make it seem that I'd never again feel "caught up." It felt as though some unseen hand had sadistically cranked up the speed of the treadmill and it was either run harder to keep up—or crash.

I opened the email John sent containing pictures of cars that resembled the one I saw on the bridge just before I'd discovered Luanne's body. I know nothing about cars, so I looked over what John sent. As near as I could tell, pictures of the Saturn looked similar to the car Sam Erickson drove—just as I expected—but a chill went over me when I realized that I knew another person who drove a Saturn: Augie Ackermann, the sex offender bag boy. But when I saw the Mustang GT, I sat up, stunned. The spacing of the headlights made the car a dead ringer for the one Tyrone

Jackson had been driving when he squealed out of the church parking lot after her funeral, giving me that middle finger salute.

I found the phone number Luanne's friend Tracey Meadows had given me at the funeral and gave her a call. When I got her voice mail, I decided to send her a text message: *Hi, Tracey… it's Lark Chadwick at the* Sun-Gazette. *I'm trying to find Luanne's boyfriend Bob Black. Can you help me?*

I was beginning to surf the Web, looking at my competition to see if I was being beaten by anyone, when my cell phone boinged—a text from Tracey: *Hi!!!…luvd ur story about Lu. In math class now (BORING!!!). I've got lunch at 11:40. Meet me @ the parking lot. I'll introduce u 2 Bob, k?*

I checked my watch—10:15. *Cool,* I texted back, *c u then. Thx!* And, to myself, I thought, *Oh, to be carefree and sixteen again.*

I pulled up Sam Erickson's blog on my computer. I could barely read it without sputtering. He focused on the story of Doug's arrest and subsequent release. He did not use my quote suggesting his charges against me yesterday were the work of a disgruntled former *Sun-Gazette* employee. Instead, he merely reported, "*Chadwick refused to comment directly on the matter*" of my relationship with Doug.

But Sam did mention that I was seen leaving Doug's apartment after his release. So, I realized, Sam was keeping a close eye on me. But I knew in my heart that I had nothing to hide. Our paper had already run the picture of Doug in front of one of the nudes he'd painted, and my name was on the photo credit.

I made another conscious decision not to let Sam Erickson get under my skin, but I knew it wasn't going to be easy and that I'd probably have to keep reminding myself not to stoop to his level. The less I had to deal with Sam Erickson, the better. I decided not to include him in my profile of Doug, even though the two had worked together for a couple years. There would be other colleagues and friends I could track down.

Also, eating into the back of my mind was the realization that Sam may be following me and that a car like his was at the scene of the first crime. But what link, if any, did Sam have to Luanne and Polly? I'd already given the cops Sam's name. That was when Sheriff Parrish, Matt Benson and I were talking at Polly Arceneaux's crime scene. Matt and the sheriff had better resources at their disposal than I did to investigate Sam.

I turned my attention to the research John had given me about possible shrinks to interview. One stood out: Dr. Paul Dobransky, a psychiatrist in Chicago specializing in violent crime and psychological trauma. He had a website. I clicked on the link and found a clip from a recent appearance on CNN's "Anderson Cooper 360." Dr. Dobransky seemed like a rugged guy in his mid-thirties with short, dark hair. He wore fashionable black-rimmed, rectangular-lensed glasses and had a friendly, calm demeanor. I could see myself sitting in front of him pouring out my heart.

I dialed the number on the sheet John had given me. A secretary answered. I identified myself and, to my surprise and delight, she put me right through to Dr. D.

"Hello?" His voice was warm. He didn't sound rushed.

"Hi, Doctor Dobransky. I'm—"

"Doctor Paul," he purred.

"What?"

"You can call me Doctor Paul." His voice had a soothing, mesmerizing effect on me that felt at some deep, ineffable level like an invitation to tell him everything.

"Um, okay. Thanks. Sort of like Dr. Phil, right?"

He laughed. "Something like that, just not as well known."

I told him I wanted to talk with him on the record about the two murders I was investigating.

"Yes, I read something about that," he said. "And you say your name is Chadwick?"

"Yes, sir. That's right."

"Didn't you once live near here, in Madison, Wisconsin?"

"I did. How did you know?"

"Who can forget that dramatic story of how you solved the mystery surrounding your parents' deaths? The *Chicago Sun-Times* picked it up and I saw the YouTube clip of your rescue. You're an impressive young lady."

I felt myself blushing. "Thank you, sir."

"Doctor Paul."

"Right."

"And now you've moved south?"

"That's right." I quickly brought him up to date on my decision to move to a bigger paper and how I found Luanne's body.

As I briefed Doctor Paul on the murder cases and possible suspects, he inserted little "uh huhs" to let me know he was tracking my story. I pictured him in a white lab coat taking notes as I spoke.

"I have two main questions, Doctor Paul: Could the same person have committed both these murders, as the police theorize, and what psychological triggers could prompt the person to kill?"

Doctor Paul cleared his throat. "First, it sounds to me like the police are correct in assuming that the same person committed both murders."

"And why is that?" I was scribbling furiously in my reporter's notebook.

"It's Ockham's Razor."

"What's that? And can you spell it?"

He spelled it for me, then explained, "It's a logical construct that goes back to the 14th century and Franciscan Friar William of Ockham. Basically stated, the most accurate solution to a problem—*in general*—is also the simplest."

I already had my doubts. It seemed to me that the suspects were vastly different from one another, plus I didn't see any common links between them and the victims.

"So, why do you assume a single killer?" I asked.

"Mainly, the chances of two different bodies being found in nearly the same place are infinitesimal."

"What about the possibility of a copycat? Someone could've learned through news reports where the first body was found and then, for whatever sick reason, decided to plant a dead body of his own in the same place."

"Sure. That's certainly possible. But that's not my first assumption."

"But don't police need to look into all the different permutations and possibilities?"

"Of course. But they need to start somewhere."

"Okay."

"And the first step is to find evidence that links one person to both victims."

"Right now, there doesn't appear to be any," I said.

"So it would seem, but you can bet the police are looking for them."

"What else would they be looking for?"

"In addition to common links, they'd be doing lots of interviews with witnesses, suspects, friends, and family. There's much the police can learn by studying a person's facial expressions, body language, and vocal features."

"Does anything about the suspects I've mentioned jump out at you as significant?"

"First, all the suspects are male."

"Does that surprise you?"

"Not at all."

"Could a woman have been the killer?"

"It's a remote possibility, but let's set that aside for a moment."

"Okay."

"Any one of the suspects you've mentioned could have been the killer," he said.

"Who's the most likely candidate? Can you rank them?"

"I'm at a disadvantage, of course, because I haven't interviewed them, but the young man . . ." Dr. Paul paused and I heard him shuffling through his notes. "Tyrone Jackson. I'm intrigued by him."

"Why?"

"He's an impulsive male youth who's been spurned, plus he threatens and postures. In addition, we know he knew at least one of the victims. Those who commit violence usually do so on intimates, with motives being jealousy, rage, shame, or other passion-level feelings which, by definition, trigger impulsive actions."

"Could race be a factor?"

"Could be, but I doubt it."

"Why?"

"Strong, passionate emotions of an intimate usually trump race. I wouldn't read too much into the fact that one suspect is black and the two victims are white."

Again, I wasn't convinced, but Dr. Paul was the expert. "But there's no evidence that Tyrone knew the second victim," I said.

"As far as we know," Dr. Paul replied.

"Yes. That's true."

So far, what Dr. Paul was saying about Tyrone as a lead suspect made sense. I was glad I'd made plans to check into that angle soon. I checked my watch—10:45. I still had plenty of time before I had to leave for my meeting with Tracey and Bob.

"What about the other suspects?" I asked.

"Okay. We have the first victim's father and the sex offender," Doctor Paul said.

"Right."

"The common link there might be pornography."

"Uh huh."

"Does the father have a history of violence, Lark?" Dr. Paul asked.

"None that I know of," I said, making a note to ask Matt or Sonny about that.

"Porn alone doesn't at all constitute the likelihood of the father actually acting out against his daughter. It would only be if the father has a history of violence."

"But what if the dad feared she was going to blow the whistle on him? That could change everything and cause him to resort to violence, couldn't it?" I asked.

"True. Good point. But we know of no link between the father and the second victim."

"What about the sex offender?" I asked half-heartedly, finding it difficult to think that Augie was at all the violent type.

"I know I sound like a broken record," Dr. Paul answered, "but I keep coming back to, A) a common link between the killer and the victims and, B) proximity. Physical closeness. The sex offender's involvement, in my opinion, hinges on a motive that's dependent on a degree of him knowing either—or more likely both—of the victims."

I glanced at my watch—11 o'clock. I needed to wrap this up and get going soon if I wanted to meet Tracey and Bob in the narrow sliver of time they'd be available.

"One more quick question, doctor, and then I'll let you go. You've been extremely generous with your time."

"Happy to do it."

"What about the possibility of a female killer?"

"Oh, right. We set that aside, didn't we? A female killer would be even less likely than multiple males, or one male covering one murder with a second."

"Wait. What do you mean by 'covering one murder with a second'?"

"It's possible," Doctor Paul said, "that the second victim witnessed the first murder and was killed as a form of witness elimination."

"I see." I paused. "How likely is that?"

"It's a stretch, but certainly possible. I wouldn't rule it out."

"But you say it's a stretch that a woman killed both victims?"

"Yes. Extremely remote."

"Can you picture any scenarios?"

"Let's see . . . ." He paused for a moment, then continued. "One possibility would be an older female who knew and killed one of the younger females, then in retribution, a male killed her. That's one remote possibility. A woman would kill another out of rage or jealousy, but by far, most victims know their killer. It is rather inherent in humans not to inflict violence on those unknown to them, unless they're severely depressed, and less likely, psychotic."

"Okay. Good. Any final thoughts?"

"Unless you can find evidence that proves multiple murderers, Lark, you *must* start with Ockham's Razor, that one man with ties to both females committed both murders."

I thanked Dr. Dobransky profusely and hung up. I had just enough time to get to Tracey's high school, now armed with the key question I needed to pursue: Was there a link between Tyrone Jackson and the second victim?

FORTY

WAS PULLING OUT of the parking lot behind the *Sun-Gazette* on my way to meet Tracey and Bob when my cell phone bleeped. It was Lionel.

"Hey, Lionel," I said, putting him on speaker so that I had both hands free.

"'Argh,' you say? Is it Talk Like a Pirate Day?"

I laughed. "I felt better as soon as I sent it."

He chuckled. "So, what's happening that has your undies in such a bundle?"

I told him about my showdown with Elmer and subsequent chewing out by Ed. "Was I wrong, Lionel? Did I cross the line?"

"Well, you've got balls, that's for sure."

"Would you have done it?"

He paused, took a deep breath and exhaled loudly. "If I was on deadline, like you were, I might have strongly urged him to step into the hall where I could grill him without an audience."

I felt my heart sink. "I'm toast."

"You've always got a job here if you need it."

"Thanks. I might have to take you up on it, but I'm not ready to retreat. They'll have to fire me first. Maybe I should apologize to Elmer."

"That's a thought. Don't grovel, though."

"Why not?"

"Because they hired you to dig out the truth and follow it wherever it leads, even if it's into the highest level of your newspaper."

"I know. I heard your voice in my head at the time telling me not to flinch when confronting power."

"Good for you. You should have my voice in your head *all* the time," he chuckled.

"How's Muriel?" I asked.

"She's good. She's right here. You want to say 'hi'?"

"Sure!"

There was a pause and a clunk as Lionel handed off to Muriel. I could see her in my mind, leaning on her elbows on the long counter at the front of the paper office, cardigan sweater pulled tightly around her shoulders to chase away the chill of early spring in south central Wisconsin.

"Hello, Lark!" Muriel called out brightly.

"Hi, Muriel. Are you keeping Lionel in line?"

"I'm doing my best, but I could use your help. We still haven't replaced you, so things have gotten busier here. I've been pressed into service as a reporter."

"Wow. Good for you."

"I'm way out of my element. It's not at all like teaching high school English."

I heard Lionel's voice in the background. "Tell her we need her to come back."

"Lionel says you should come back. And I second that. We miss you."

"Thanks, Muriel. I miss you guys, too."

"I'll give you back to Lionel now. Wonderful to hear your voice, dear."

"Thanks, Muriel."

Lionel came back on the line. "I'm still reading your stuff online, kiddo. Sounds like you've got your hands full with the serial killer story."

"That's for sure. It's like being on a treadmill that keeps going faster."

"Yeah. I know what you mean."

"How did you deal with the daily pressure when you were at the AP and then the *New York Times*, Lionel?"

"There were more people to share the load back then. Now, with all the cutbacks, coupled with technological advances, there's more work for fewer people. You just need to prioritize and work smart."

"That's what I'm trying to do."

"And just realize you can't be everywhere at once. Do your best, but take care of yourself. I learned that lesson way too late."

I knew Lionel had had a drinking problem earlier in his career, plus he'd had heart problems. I began to wonder—and worry—that perhaps his deteriorating health was on his mind.

"You feeling okay?" I asked, trying to keep from sounding overly concerned.

"I'm fine. Just slowing down, that's all."

I was getting close to the school. "I have to go, Lionel, but I'm glad you called. It's nice to know you're there."

"I'm just an email or a phone call away, kid."

"Love you."

"Yeah. Same here." His voice sounded husky, like it did whenever he talked about Holly, the daughter about my age who'd died in a fall off a cliff along the Inca Trail in Peru a few years earlier.

I pulled into the school parking lot—a collection of Camaros, Corollas, and Chevy pick-ups—and checked the time—nearly 11:45. I saw Tracey standing at the curb looking anxiously toward the road that passed in front of the school. Standing next to her and holding her hand was a young man who stood towering over her.

I found a space near the entrance, parked, then hopped out of Pearlie and trotted toward Tracey.

She smiled and waved eagerly when she saw me.

"Hi!" Tracey called as I got closer. "I was afraid you'd forgotten all about me."

"Sorry I was late," I said stepping onto the curb, "I was finishing up an interview."

"This is Bob Black," Tracey said, looking up at Bob. The top of her head came to the center of his chest.

"I'll bet you're on the basketball team," I said, shaking Bob's big, boney hand.

"Yes, ma'am. I am."

His politeness made me feel old, something I wasn't used to and hoped I wouldn't be used to for a long time.

"It's great to meet you," I said to Bob. "Thanks for taking some time to talk with me."

"No problem, ma'am."

"And stop calling me ma'am. You make me feel old."

"Yes, ma'am."

"Let's sit over here," Tracey said, leading us to one of several benches lining the sidewalk leading to the front door of the school.

The day was warm and bright and many of the students had come outside to take advantage of the nice weather. It had been eight years since I'd been in high school, but this place seemed strangely familiar with each clique marking off its own turf.

Some of the more geeky students sat by themselves. One pretty girl wearing glasses sat on the grass, cross-legged, a book propped in the lap of her jeans. Two white ear buds were jammed into her head and a thin, white cord led to her iPod lying in the grass next to her. She took absentminded bites from a sandwich as her eyes raced across the pages.

At the far end of the building, a cluster of Goths—pink and purple hair, black clothing—lounged and laughed as they leaned against a wall smoking. Closer to us stood a group of exquisitely-dressed blondes—short-*short* skirts and tight-*tight* blouses. There were four of them—all wearing a ton of makeup, raccoon-eyed eyeliner, and their glossy-pouty lips slathered with bright-*bright* red lipstick. They pointed, giggled, and gossiped whenever someone walked by.

On a patch of grass across from us, a gang of about four or five jocks passed a football around, each strutting as they tried to get the attention of the giggling Barbies near us.

In high school, I'd usually kept to myself and was probably considered one of the geeks, but I mostly floated and had friends in each group.

"Gee, Lark, didn't you bring your lunch?" Tracey asked as she took a sandwich out of a brown paper bag and unwrapped the cellophane girdling it. "You can have half of mine." She held part of her sandwich out to me.

"No, thanks. I'm too busy to be hungry," I laughed, waving away her kind offering.

"How 'bout some chips?" Bob said, holding the open end of a potato chip bag in front of me enticingly.

I looked longingly at the chips and thought about how much more lard would be added to my butt.

"I know what you're thinking," Bob said, smiling, "but don't worry. These don't have *any* calories."

"Well, maybe just one," I said, plunging my hand into the bag, but being careful to snag just a single chip.

As I delicately placed the chip into my mouth, Bob said, "And even if they have a *few* calories, it'll take way more than one chip before they begin to show up on your figure."

Tracey gave Bob a playful sock on the shoulder. "Hey! No fair flirting with her. I'm still here, y'know."

"So, when did you two become an item?" I asked, looking back and forth between them.

"Yesterday," they said in unison, then laughed together.

"How did it come about?"

"We both miss Luanne," Bob said, "so last night when we were hanging out talking about her, we realized we had something deeper than just friendship."

"I'm sure Luanne would approve," I said. "You seem to make a great couple."

"Thanks," Tracey blushed, leaning her head against Bob's shoulder.

"Have you talked to the police yet, Bob?" I reached tentatively toward his potato chip bag, then dove in again when he gave me a go-ahead nod.

"Yeah, but they told me not to talk to reporters."

I made a dismissive wave. "They always say that. Don't pay any attention. They're just trying to cover their butts."

"That's what I thought." He took a bite out of his sandwich. "What do you want to know?" he asked, savoring what looked like roast beef and lettuce.

"Several things. I'm wondering if Luanne had ever confided in you about her, um, relationship with her father; I'm trying to find out if you witnessed any menacing behavior of Tyrone Jackson toward Luanne; and I'm wondering if you know of any link between Luanne's dad or Tyrone Jackson and the second victim, Polly Arceneaux."

As soon as I closed my mouth, I rebuked myself for unleashing a barrage of such scatter-shot questions, but Bob seemed unfazed. He slowly shook his head as he chewed and pondered. Finally, he swallowed and spoke. "No link that I'm aware of at all between either Tyrone or Mr. Donovan and the second victim."

"What about the relationship with her dad?" I asked gently. I didn't want to use the word abuse for fear that if he hadn't heard about it, he might repeat my question to someone, fueling more gossip and speculation about something that had yet to be established.

He nodded. "She mentioned that he'd been sexually abusing her. In fact, that's how we ended up getting closer. She sensed she could confide in me and I wouldn't judge her."

For a moment, I wished I'd known someone like Bob when I was in high school. Most of the guys I'd known over the years were either oafish cads who wanted to grope me or gays who are only interested in me as a friend. I longed for someone who got the friend thing, but could fulfill my more libidinous longings, too.

"Had you met her dad?"

"Once."

"What was your impression?"

"That he drank too much and was just plain weird."

"What do you mean weird?"

"I don't know. Just weird."

"No social skills?"

"Yes. That's it exactly. Thank you."

"Did he seem violent? Did Luanne indicate that he had a violent side?"

"No. He just seemed spooky and creepy. She was finally moving toward becoming more herself, I guess. I was really proud of her."

Tracey gave Bob's arm an encouraging squeeze.

As we sat talking, something caught my eye. I turned toward the front door of the school. Tyrone Jackson had just left the building and was sauntering down the sidewalk in our direction. He wore a burgundy football jersey that seemed two sizes too small. He had broad, shoulder-pad shoulders and well-chiseled, muscular arms. The blonde babes swooned as he walked by. He ignored them.

As he got closer to us, his eyes locked on mine for just an instant before he looked away quickly. I knew that he'd seen and recognized me, but he turned his attention toward the jocks throwing around the football as he continued to walk in our direction.

"Throw it here," he bellowed, holding up his hands as a target.

One of the guys heaved the football toward Tyrone, but the ball sailed over his head and bounced onto the grass behind and just to the side of our bench.

Tyrone, still assiduously ignoring us, trotted gracefully to the ball and scooped it up. Then, in one smooth move, he swiveled around and came set in a throwing stance like the quarterback he was.

"Go long," he shouted. His voiced boomed off the wall behind us.

All eyes were now glued on Tyrone as he pump-faked twice before rocketing a pass that arced over the heads of all the boys.

"You turkeys," he hollered. "Ya gotta run faster." His thigh brushed gently against the side of my leg as he passed our bench and trotted toward the boys, his calf muscles bulging. He treated us as if we weren't there.

"He's such a jerk," Tracey said when Tyrone was safely out of earshot.

"Do you think he killed Luanne?" I asked them both.

Tracey looked at Bob who spoke first. "The thought has crossed my mind."

"Why?" I asked.

"Luanne told me she was afraid of him."

I hadn't been taking notes, but that got my attention. I dug out my reporter's notebook and clicked my pen into position. "Is 'afraid' the exact word she used?"

Bob paused and scowled as he tried to remember. "Yes," he said, finally. "She said 'afraid.'"

"Can you remember what prompted her to say that?"

"It was the last time I ever saw her," Bob said, turning serious. "In fact, it was on the day she died. We'd gone to an afternoon movie and then for a walk down by the river. We were sitting on a rock, um, talking . . . ." He glanced furtively at Tracey.

"You were making out, weren't you?" she said, poking him.

Bob smiled, sheepishly. "Mayybee . . . . But we were talking, too," he said in a playful tone that suggested mock defensiveness.

"What were you talking about?" I asked, trying to get Bob's focus off Tracey and back onto my question.

"She told me the same story Tracey told you at the funeral, of how Tyrone had freaked out on her the day before."

"Did she say if he'd ever hit her?"

"No, but she said he was getting more menacing once she made it clear to him it was over between them."

"Menacing in what way? Threats?"

He shook his head. "Not in so many words, but indirectly. Driving by her house and glaring at her. Stalking kind of stuff."

"Did she say what it was specifically that she was afraid of?"

"No. She just said, 'He frightens me.' That's it. She didn't say 'afraid.' She said 'frightens.' Pretty much the same thing, I'd say, but I can see," he nodded toward my notebook, "that you want to get your quote right."

"I appreciate the clarification," I said as I scribbled. "Did Tyrone ever threaten you?"

"No. I think his specialty is intimidation. He's got too much to lose by getting violent."

"What do you mean?"

"He's being scouted by all the big schools and the pros, so it would be stupid for him to give up all that just because of some girl who dumped him."

"It wouldn't be the first time a dumb jock did something stupid," Tracey said.

"Do you think Tyrone killed Luanne?" I asked her.

"Yup."

"Really?"

"Yeah, but it's just a hunch. I can't prove it."

"How did the detective react when you talked to him?" I asked her.

"He took lots of notes, but otherwise, he was a sphinx."

My phone bleeped. It was the desk calling.

"This is Lark," I said into the phone.

"Breaking news," Marcie said.

"What's up?"

"Guess who the cops just arrested?"

"Doug?"

"No. Luanne's dad."

FORTY-ONE

LURCH AND SWERVE. It's an apt description of my life as a newspaper reporter, especially a reporter on a moment-to-moment deadline. Marcie's news was stunning, but the details were sketchy. Too sketchy, I felt, to blurt out to Bob and Tracey that Luanne's dad had been arrested. I felt they would spread the news through the school like a wildfire fueled by the powerful Santa Ana wind of rumor and innuendo.

Tracey must have seen the stunned expression on my face. "What's wrong?" she asked me, alarmed, as I hung up.

I tried to collect my thoughts before I responded.

"Are you okay, ma'am?" Bob asked, touching my arm.

"I-I have to go. Something's come up."

"Has there been another murder?" Tracey asked, clutching Bob's arm.

"No," I said, "but there's been an arrest."

"Who?" they both asked, excitedly.

"I need to find out more first. I'll let you know." Quickly, I made sure I had Bob Black's contact information—and I gave him mine. I thanked them for their time, wished them well in their budding romance, apologized for rushing off, and then bolted—leaving them sitting bewildered on a bench as Tyrone Jackson pranced and preened nearby.

Before I'd even gotten to Pearlie I was already working the phone. I called Matt Benson first.

"Is it true?" I asked when he answered.

"Is what true?" He sounded wary.

"I just heard Luanne's father's been arrested."

"Not by us."

"By who, then?"

"I dunno."

"You don't?"

"Nope. News to me."

"What the hell!" Was it a hoax? Had Marcie been fed some bum information?

"I'm sorry, Lark. I'd tell you if I knew, but I don't. But you certainly have me intrigued. Lemme check around. I'll get back to you."

"Thanks, Matt."

I tried Sonny Laskin.

"Laskin," he said when he picked up.

"Hi, Sonny. It's Lark Chadwick at the *Sun-Gazette*."

"Hey, Lark." His drawl was lazy like a day whittling on the back porch at sunset.

"I've just gotten word that Luanne Donovan's father has been arrested. Is it true?"

"It's true, but not by us."

"Who picked him up . . . and why?"

"The feds."

"The FBI?"

"Uh huh."

"On what charge?"

"Trafficking in child porn."

"Jesus." I hadn't expected that, so it took me a second to re-group. "Tell me more."

"I don't know too much more, other than what the FeeBees shared with our task force."

"Is this related to Luanne's murder?"

"Not directly."

"What do you mean?"

"In the course of our investigation, we got a warrant to search his computer. When we found thousands of pornographic im-ages of underage girls, along with evidence that he'd been selling them across state lines, we brought in the feds and they made the arrest."

"Were any of the images Luanne?"

"Can't say."

"Can't or won't?"

"Both."

"Why not?"

"Too delicate."

"No it's not. It's not like her privacy needs protecting. She's dead. She can't be embarrassed any more."

"You obviously don't have children, do you?"

"No, but what's that got to do with it?"

"I guess the dad in me is being a little protective."

Without saying it in so many ways, Sonny Laskin had just confirmed—whether he intended to, or not—that at least some of the images on Buddy Donovan's computer were of his daugh-ter and that he was selling those pictures to fellow sickos all over the country—probably for beer money.

"Got a number for the feds?" I asked Laskin.

He gave it to me.

"Thanks for your help, Sonny. One more quick question: Do you feel as if murder charges against him are imminent?"

"I wouldn't say 'imminent,'" he said, "but they're possible."

"Likely?"

"I wouldn't go that far, no."

"But it's safe to say that the GBI task force is working with the FBI on the serial killer case?"

"Mmmmm, that's a little misleading."

"Okay. Please clarify."

"You can't say we're working together on the serial killer case. The FBI's case is only about child porn, so we're sharing information on that."

"Okay. Gotcha. When was he arrested and when'll he be in court?"

"I don't have that. Check with the feds."

"Okay. Thanks, Sonny. We still on for Saturday morning?"

"Yes'm. Looking forward to it."

"Me too. See you then."

I called Marcie and fed her what I had. We agreed that she would be the main writer, but we would share the byline.

"Here's the phone number for the FBI." I gave it to her.

"What are you going to do?" she asked.

"I'm out near the Donovans' house right now. I'm going to swing by there and see if her mom will talk to me."

"Ooooo. Good idea."

"Let me know what the FBI tells you, okay?"

"Sure thing. I'll get right back to you."

Part of me hesitated to trust Marcie. I still wasn't sure how much she was doing to undermine me behind my back. It occurred to me that the snipey thing she'd said to Priscilla—that I'd come on to her—happened before she realized that I was championing her cause to Ed and Elmer. Other than that one glimpse behind the veil that Priscilla had given me, I still had every reason to believe that Marcie and I made a good team. I still believed that. Mostly. Or, I asked myself, did I believe it because I wanted to avoid confronting her?

Before I could answer my own question, Marcie called me back as I was just pulling up to the Donovans' trailer. "I've just gotten a lesson from the FBI on all the various ways one can say 'no comment.'"

"Did they at least confirm that they'd arrested Luanne's dad?"

"Yes."

"Did they say when?"

"About six this morning."

"When's he making his initial court appearance?"

"It already happened."

"Damn. When?"

"Eleven."

"Does anyone else have it?"

"Surprisingly, no."

"Okay. Can you or someone get the info from the court?"

"Already on it."

"I'm at the Donovans' now. I'll let you know when I'm done."

Before I went up to the front door, I called Tracey.

"Hey, Lark. We're just heading back to class. What's happening? Who'd they arrest?"

"Luanne's dad."

She gasped loudly. "Oh my *God!* Is he the serial killer?"

Her reaction made me question the wisdom of telling her. "Careful, Tracey. Don't get ahead of the facts. Listen carefully."

"Okay." I heard her take a couple deep breaths.

"Her dad has not—I repeat: *not*—been charged with murder."

"Then why was he arrested?"

"Before I answer that, let me ask you a question."

"Okay. Sure."

"Did Luanne ever tell you that her father had taken pornographic pictures of her?"

Tracey was quiet. In the background, I could hear the hubbub of the school hallway as students jostled to get to class. A bell rang and the hall noise lessened.

"Tracey? Are you there?"

"I'm here." Her voice seemed to echo.

"I don't want to make you late for class, but I need to know. Did he take pictures of her?"

"Y-yes."

"Are you sure?"

"Yes." Her voice was stronger, but she was crying.

"Can you elaborate? What else did she tell you about that?"

"She just said that lately he'd begun to pose her in all kinds of disgusting positions and take pictures. She was so ashamed. She'd told me not to tell anyone. And I didn't."

"You were a good friend, Tracey."

"Wh-what's he been ch-charged with?" she asked between sobs.

"Trafficking in child pornography."

"Oh my God," she wailed.

I shook my head sadly. "Indeed."

FORTY-TWO

IT'S NOT TOO often that I experience butterflies in my stomach, but they were fluttering as I walked up to the front door of the Donovans' trailer home. I had no idea what state of mind Mrs. Donovan would be in, whether or not she'd be angry with me or would even allow me inside—and, if she did, what, exactly I would ask. I just found myself pushing farther and farther beyond the fear barrier the closer I got to her front door.

I noticed the blinds were all pulled giving the place the feeling of having closed its eyes and gone to sleep.

I knocked gently on the door and waited. At first, I didn't hear any sounds inside. I waited a tad longer, then knocked again, a little more loudly this time.

More silence.

I looked around. A big pickup truck was parked in the driveway next to a Toyota Corolla. I assumed Mrs. Donovan was home. Maybe she was taking a nap. It was after noon, but it must have been traumatic to be awakened at six in the morning and have your husband carted off to jail.

I decided to knock one more time before giving up. This time, I rapped on the front door with more authority than my first tentative tries. Almost immediately, I heard some movement inside. In a moment, the haggard and bleary-eyed wife of Buddy Donovan was peering at me through the door window.

She opened the door and stared blankly at me.

"Hi, Mrs. Donovan. I'm Lark Chadwick with the *Sun-Gazette*." She continued to stare at me dully.

I kept chattering. "We met earlier this week when I interviewed you and your husband for the paper."

No response. No personality. No nothing.

I plunged ahead. "I know this must be a dreadful time for you and I'm so sorry to intrude, but may I come in?"

For the first time, a flicker of awareness seemed to dawn behind her dead eyes. She focused on me, perhaps really seeing me for the first time. I wondered: Has she been drinking? Is she drunk?

"May I come in?" I repeated.

She licked her lips, bit her lower one and then swallowed. "Sure. I guess," she said without affect.

Mrs. Donovan opened the door all the way and stepped back.

"Thank you," I said to her as I brushed past and entered her home for the second time. Unlike earlier in the week, the place no longer had on its sunny disposition in spite of the gloomy news she had been trying to absorb that day after her daughter's murder.

I stood just inside the front door as she closed it. It was past noon, but she was wearing a pale green bathrobe and slippers. Her hair was a disheveled rat's nest. She wandered past me into the kitchen where she took a seat at the Formica-topped table.

Even though she'd said nothing welcoming, I followed her and slid into a chair across the table from her. The only light coming into the room was from the window over the kitchen sink, which she sat facing. A framed portrait of Luanne, a box of tissues, and a half-filled cup of coffee sat in front of her. Several spent tissues were crumpled into tight balls next to the box. She fiddled absent-mindedly with the cup, staring vacantly past me, looking out the window behind me.

I got up and moved to the chair to her left so I could be closer to her.

She didn't seem to notice.

On instinct, I reached out and gently touched the sleeve of her robe.

She bit her lower lip to keep it from trembling. Her eyes were bloodshot and baggy.

"How can I help?" I whispered.

In the back of my head I could hear Lionel jumping up and down screaming, *You're not a frickin' social worker. You're a reporter! Get your interview and go.*

It's one of the few times when I mentally told Lionel to zip it.

Mrs. Donovan shook her head, almost imperceptibly, hopelessly.

I knew the feeling. I'd been there, too.

For the next five minutes, neither of us spoke. I simply sat next to her, gently stroking her forearm.

Finally, she sighed, raised her hands to her face, and began to sob, silently at first, but then with a full-throated intensity that caused her whole body to shake.

I placed my right hand on her back and stroked it—a weak attempt at comfort.

"Why?" she wailed. "Why is this happening?"

"I don't know," I whispered.

Finally, she snagged a tissue from the box on the table, dabbed her eyes and blew her nose.

"I'm so sorry, Mrs. Donovan. I'm so sorry."

She nodded, sadly and pursed her lips.

"Can you tell me what happened this morning?" I asked.

"We were asleep," she began, her voice nearly a whisper. "All of a sudden someone began pounding on the door loudly." She spoke as if in a trance. "'FBI,' someone shouted. 'We have a warrant. Open this door *now*.'"

"What did you do?"

She looked at me for the first time. "I was terrified. Buddy went to the door and immediately the place was swarming with FBI agents. They handcuffed Buddy and took him away."

"Did they tell you why?"

She nodded. "One of them did, after they'd taken Buddy away."

"What did they tell you?"

A pained expression crossed her face and her mouth trembled. "They told me that he—" She stopped abruptly and bit a knuckle, but then regained her composure and continued, ". . . that he's a child pornographer."

"Did they say anything else?"

She looked at Luanne's picture. "They said he'd taken dirty pictures of Lu and sold them on the *Internet*." She said the last word fiercely through gritted teeth. "Naked pictures of my baby on the Internet," she shouted.

"Did they say anything else? Do they think he killed her?"

She looked at me, shocked. "No."

I hesitated, then said softly, "Do *you* think he did?"

"Of course not. Don't be ridic—" but then she caught herself, as if considering the possibility for the first time. "At least I don't think so . . . ."

"I don't know how to tell you this, Mrs. Donovan, but I've talked to some of Luanne's friends," I said. "Would it surprise you to learn that she confided to some of them that your husband had been molesting her?"

"Oh, my God!" Her hands flew to her face—and stayed there as she tried to shield herself from the latest bombshell.

"Did you know?" I asked gently. "Did you suspect?"

She shook her head, silently. "Not a clue."

"She never tried to tell you?"

Mrs. Donovan shook her head, took her hands away from her face and reached for another tissue. She clutched it tightly in her hand. "I'm so ashamed," she said. Turning to look at me, she added, "I suppose you're going to put this in the paper?"

"Yes, ma'am. But it gives me no pleasure."

She sighed. "What am I going to do now? I can't face my friends."

I shook my head helplessly. "Who can you turn to right now for support?"

She shrugged. "I don't know." Her eyes were empty. Lifeless. Somewhere, deep inside me, an alarm went off.

"Mrs. Donovan?"

She turned to look at me.

"I have to ask you a personal question."

She laughed bitterly. "Isn't that what you've been doing?"

"This one's different. Have you been thinking of killing yourself?"

She smiled ruefully. "Funny you should ask."

"Why's that?"

"That's what I was thinking about when you knocked on the door. I was probably two seconds away from getting up, taking a knife out of the drawer, and slicing my wrists," she glanced at me as if to gauge my reaction.

I bit my lip and thought immediately of Annie, the Aunt who'd raised me after my parents were killed. For the millionth time, I kicked myself for leaving Annie alone the night she died.

I looked Mrs. Donovan in the eye and said, "Not that long ago, I was about two seconds away from letting myself get hit by a train."

Her eyebrows raised in surprise.

"I've been *exactly* where you are right now." I smiled at her. "But I changed my mind . . . and I'm glad I did."

"I'm glad I did, too—I think." She took my hand and squeezed it.

"Who can you call right now to help you get through this?" I asked.

"My pastor," she said.

I stood, got the phone from a desk in the corner, and brought it to her. "Do you want to make the call, or should I?"

She took the phone from me. "I'll do it." She touched my hand, then gave it another squeeze. "You're a good person, Miss Chadwick. Maybe even a lifesaver. Thank you."

A short while later, as I let myself out, she was on the phone telling her pastor what had happened. I got in my car, strapped myself in . . . and began to cry.

FORTY-THREE

IT TOOK ME several minutes to compose myself. While I was still snorting and wheezing, I noticed a car pull into the cinder parking area of the Donovans' lot. The pastor who officiated at Luanne's funeral, hopped out of his car and scurried to the front door. I sincerely hoped he'd be able to provide the solace Mrs. Donovan so desperately needed. The fact that he'd gotten here so quickly after her call to him was a comfort to me.

I called Marcie at the paper to convey the latest tidbits I'd been able to glean from Mrs. Donovan about her husband's arrest and to see if there were any new developments. There weren't.

Next I called Augie.

"Hey," I said when he picked up. "It's Lark Chadwick."

"Hey, yourself."

"Are you at work?"

"I start at two."

I checked my watch: Quarter to one. "Got a few minutes? There've been new developments. I want to talk with you."

"Sure." He sounded eager. "Wanna stop by here?"

Being alone with Doug was risky enough, but being alone with a sex offender I barely knew didn't seem like such a swift idea.

"How 'bout we meet somewhere close to work?" I suggested.

"We could meet on the Georgia side of the 12th Street Bridge. There are some benches along the River Walk."

"I can be there in fifteen minutes."

"Cool. See you then."

He was waiting for me when I arrived, sitting on a green, metal bench overlooking the river.

"So, what's up?" he called when he saw me approach.

I sat next to him and pulled out my iPhone recorder and notebook. "Thanks for meeting with me, Augie."

"Sure. No problem. What's the new development?"

"Luanne Donovan's father has been arrested."

"Has he been charged with murder yet?"

I told him what I knew and what Mrs. Donovan had just revealed.

"So, why do you want to talk with me?"

I hesitated, not sure yet if I should be subtle or direct.

"Don't tell me," Augie said, interrupting my reverie, "let me guess. You Googled me. You know I'm a sex offender and now you want to know if I killed Luanne Donovan and/or Polly Arceneaux."

"Now that you mention it . . . ."

"I didn't kill them. Okay?" He was pissed.

"Look, Augie. Let's back up. You're a reporter."

"I *was* a reporter. Those days are over for me. Forever. When I got busted, I became the story. Gives one a whole new perspective."

"Tell me."

He gave me a skeptical look.

"Really," I said. "I want to know."

He took a deep breath. When he exhaled, some of his anger seemed to go with it. "When I was busted, reporters were staked out at my house, trying to get an interview with my wife."

"I didn't know you were married."

"I'm not any more."

"Can you tell me what happened?"

He looked at my phone. "We on the record?"

"Yes."

He scowled and swore softly under his breath.

"Augie, most people only hear about sex offenders when they've been arrested. They don't know the rest of the story—I certainly don't. And, frankly, I think most of us—including my-self—don't understand what causes someone to, um, offend."

Augie continued scowling as he watched the water flow lazily beneath the old stone bridge to our left.

"Maybe you can help people understand," I nudged.

He shrugged. "Maybe, but going public is a little frightening."

"Could you lose your job?"

He nodded. "I had to reveal my conviction when I applied for the job, so my boss already knows. But once it's out there, there's no telling how people will react. I had a sales job right after I got out of prison. My boss knew about my past and believed in second chances, but then a rival sales rep Googled me. When he found me on the sex offender registry, he complained loudly and I was toast."

He stood and walked to the railing at the edge of the river. For a long moment, he leaned against it with his forearms crossed. Finally, he pushed himself back and returned to his seat next to me on the bench, his chin jutting out, determined.

"I'm willing to do this," he said, "but only if you agree not to use my name." He looked at me and studied my face. "No one other than my therapist, parole officer, and the guys in my group therapy sessions knows any of this."

I nodded gravely. "Okay." I hit *record*. "Tell me your story, Augie."

What do you want to know?"

"What happened to you?"

"I don't like the way you phrased the question."

"Why not?"

"It makes it sound like I'm a victim. I'm not the victim. I'm a victimizer."

"Fair enough. In what way did you victimize people and how did you get caught?"

He paused and seemed to be collecting his thoughts. When he started speaking, the words came out slowly, haltingly, but then he picked up his pace. "I started out in radio about twenty years ago up in Rhode Island. Bounced around the country every two years or so as a reporter, then got into TV six years later, gradually working into management."

"When'd you come to Columbia?"

"Five years ago. Started a family and settled down."

"Supposedly, that's the idyllic life."

"Yes," he nodded. "I had it all. And I blew it."

"Why? What went wrong?"

"The 'what' is easier to answer than the 'why,' but I'll try to answer both questions for you," he said.

"Okay."

"One thing I learned during my therapy sessions in prison was that for as far back as I can remember I didn't know how to be authentic. My life was layer upon layer of lies."

"Why?"

He shrugged. "I don't know. Low self-esteem is at the root of it, but it makes no sense because I had a good upbringing, loving parents, no trauma or abuse. I was normal, but for some reason, I couldn't accept myself. Compared to everyone else, I felt like a psychological pygmy."

"So what did you do to compensate for those feelings?"

"Drank. Took drugs—marijuana, mostly. And learned how to spot and prey upon people with lower self-esteem than me."

"Women?"

He nodded.

"How'd you find them?"

"The Internet. It's a Godsend."

I gave him a look.

"Was," he added quickly. "And maybe Godsend isn't the best choice of words, either, but that's the way it felt at the time."

"How'd you use the Internet?"

"Chat rooms worked best."

"How so?"

"No matter what your deviance, there's a chat room for it."

"And it's anonymous, right?"

"That's a huge plus. *Huge.*"

"So what would you do?"

"Find someone who wanted to hook up."

"Was it hard?"

He shook his head. "Like shooting fish in a barrel. We'd banter back and forth and pretty soon I'd suggest we get together. I could be an entirely different person online because the anonymity gave me a sense of power and confidence that I lacked in my daily life."

"How old were these women—or were they girls?"

"At first they were women pretty much my own age. I became a serial adulterer."

"Why didn't you leave it at that?"

"Good question. I suppose it's the law of diminishing returns. I needed to push the envelope toward bigger and bigger thrills. My victims kept getting younger and younger."

"How young?"

"My youngest hands-on victim was thirteen."

I shook my head in disgust.

Augie picked up on my body language right away. "I'm not proud of myself," he said.

"How'd you get busted?"

"I got overconfident. I didn't listen to the little voice in my head telling me to be careful. I lined up a rendezvous with what I thought was a thirteen-year-old girl. Even talked to her on the phone. Turns out she was an FBI agent who was able to sound just like a ditzy kid. When I showed up at her address, I was surrounded by a score of federal agents, guns drawn."

"Geez," was all I could manage to say.

"It was probably the best thing that ever happened to me."

I looked at him, surprised. "What do you mean?"

"At the rate I was going, there's no telling what might have happened."

"Are you saying you were capable of killing someone?"

He nodded. "I've thought a lot about that," Augie said. "My therapist asked me that same question during one of our first sessions."

"What did you say?"

"I was quiet for a very long time," he said. "It occurred to me that if I'd been cornered or feared the girl might blow the whistle on me, that I just might be capable of, say, strangling her in order to keep her quiet."

"Had you ever come close to doing that?" I asked.

He shook his head. "No, thank God. But I understand how it can happen and I'm so thankful I never got to that point."

"But aren't you still at risk of sliding back into that lifestyle?"

"Yes. I've learned that I'll never be cured of being attracted to young girls, but I have learned how to manage it."

"How'd you learn that?"

"I was very lucky. I pleaded guilty to one charge of using the Internet to entice a minor into immoral activity. In exchange, they sent me to the federal prison at Butner, North Carolina. It's one of the only prisons in the country that has a program that treats sex offenders."

"Treats, but doesn't cure, right?"

"Right. There's no pretense that a person is ever 'cured' in the clinical sense of the word. It's a rigorous program. If I'd broken any of the prison rules, or been found with contraband pornography, I would have been kicked out of the program and been forced to spend the rest of my time in the general prison population."

"And that would have been bad because why?"

He looked at me and smiled. "The short answer is the general prison population has a special level of contempt for sex offenders. Let's just say you don't want to accidently drop the soap when you're in the shower."

"So you were able to stay in the program?"

"Yup, for all of the two and a half years I was there."

"How are you different now?"

"I think I'm more self aware. I know what my triggers are."

"Triggers?"

"The feelings that could cause me to reoffend."

"What are your triggers?"

"Stress . . . fear . . . ."

"Fear of what?"

"Fear of rejection. Fear of losing my job. Stuff like that."

"Have you experienced those things since you've gotten out?"

He nodded. "A lot at first."

"What would cause it?"

"At first, it was the fear of reoffending and getting sent back to the slammer. I had to take a lie detector test every three months. Evidence of evasion would be enough to have my parole revoked. So I would catastrophize."

"What's that?"

"It's a term my therapist used to describe my thinking. I could imagine the worst-case scenario in any given situation and then, in my mind, magnify the negative consequences. It was psychologically paralyzing."

"But stress and fear are normal in most people. What do you do now to keep those feelings from triggering a re-offense?"

"I've got people I can talk to."

"Have the cops talked to you about the current serial killings?"

He laughed. "Oh yeah. They were on my case right from the beginning. It comes with the territory of being an ex con."

"Are you bitter?"

"A little. But I brought it on myself. I think what really bothers me is having to keep paying for my crime even after I've paid for it."

"What do you mean?"

"I can understand and even accept that I need to register with the police whenever I move. I realize I'll always be an initial suspect when a woman gets raped or murdered. But what makes it hard is when politicians like the governor pander to the public's fears by restricting where we can live."

"How's he doing that?"

"One of the provisions in the Safe Streets Initiative makes it illegal for a sex offender to live within two thousand feet of a bus stop or park, or church or a school."

"What's wrong with that?"

"Do you realize how many bus stops and parks there are? It would mean I'd have to live out in the boonies somewhere. I've read that in other states where this kind of law has gone into effect, people lose their jobs just because the workplace is too close to a restricted area. It's draconian."

I realized Augie had just used the same word I'd used to challenge the governor about his bill. Now I needed to challenge Augie. "But you understand society's concern, don't you?" I asked.

He turned and glared at me. "Of course I do. But here's the inconsistency: I can't work at a place that's across the street from a church, but I can become a *member* of that church. The law may *mean* well, but its restrictions—especially in this economy—condemn me over and over again, even after I've paid for my crime."

"I see what you mean," I said. I checked my watch: 1:40. He had to be at work in twenty minutes. "So, who do you think killed Luanne and Polly?"

He shrugged. "I don't have the slightest idea."

"Same person for both?"

"Dunno. Your guess is as good as mine. What do you think?"

"The cops think it's the same person, but they won't tell me why. A shrink I interviewed also goes along with the single killer theory. But I'm still leaning toward two separate killers."

"Why?"

"I can't find the common link between the two women. There are a couple strong candidates for Luanne's murder, but neither guy seems to have a connection to Polly."

Augie nodded thoughtfully and looked at his watch. "I've got to get going."

"Thanks for your time, Augie. I'm glad we talked."

We stood.

"Let me get a quick picture of you with my iPhone," I said.

Augie blanched.

"Don't worry," I said. "I can photoshop it so your features are blurred. Let's stand over here by the railing." I moved to where he'd been leaning earlier.

Augie walked over to me while I fired up the camera app.

"I don't feel much like smiling, Lark."

"That's okay," I said. "Why don't you just lean against the rail and look thoughtfully into the distance?"

"I do that a lot, so that won't be a stretch." He put his right elbow on the concrete railing, cupped his chin in his hand and squinted into the sun as it got lower in the western sky.

I squeezed off a few shots. As I did, I couldn't help but notice how sad and haunted Augie's eyes looked.

FORTY-FOUR

AFTER INTERVIEWING AUGIE, I hustled back to the paper just a few blocks away. The newsroom was on deadline, with much scurrying and shouting.

I parked myself at Marcie's cubicle and looked over her shoulder as she brought up the story on Buddy Donovan's arrest that we'd been writing together. It looked good. I suggested a few tweaks and then we filed it.

From there, I went to my desk and wrote up the Augie profile. It wasn't budgeted for the paper going to press now, but I wanted to get a first draft written while the conversation was still fresh in my mind.

Late in the afternoon, about 4:30, as I was finishing the piece, an email went out from Elmer's secretary to the entire staff with the words "IMPORTANT MANDATORY MEETING" in the subject line. It was simple, terse, and ominous: "All staff will gather in the newsroom at 5:30 for a **mandatory** meeting."

I filed my story. I had an hour to hang around, so I thought I'd make some quick phone calls to get additional quotes about Doug to sprinkle into the profile piece about him.

Against my better judgment, I called Sam Erickson. As much as I didn't like him, he had worked with Doug for a long time and might be good for a quote or two.

"Erickson," Sam said brusquely when he picked up on the first ring.

"Hi, Sam. It's Lark Chadwick."

His voice switched immediately to something resembling the triumph of a hunter finding prey in his trap. "Well, hello. I was just going to call you."

"Oh?"

"What's up with Elmer's mandatory meeting?" Sam asked.

"You saw the email?"

"Someone forwarded it to me. I still have friends there," he said. "Lots of them."

"I don't have a clue about the meeting. What's your hunch?"

"The paper's hemorrhaging money. Probably more layoffs, or they just won a Pulitzer—or maybe both." He laughed. "It's been nice knowin' ya."

"But they just hired me."

"Doesn't matter."

"It does to me."

"They don't care about you. They care about the bottom line."

I was stunned into silence, trying to process what Sam was telling me.

"You still there?" Sam asked.

"Y-yeah. Just thinking about what you said." I let out a sad sigh. "I hope you're wrong."

"You'll find out soon enough. But that's not why you called, is it?"

"No." I shook my head to jog myself back to the reason for my call. "I'm doing a profile on Doug. I need a few quotes to round it out. You worked with him for a long time. What's your take?"

"On Doug?"

"Uh huh."

"On the record?"

"Yes."

"Good photog." He paused. "But . . . ."

"But what?"

"I'm trying to choose my words carefully so as not to slander the poor boy."

"You have some reservations about his personal life?" I offered.

"You could say that."

"What gives you pause?"

"He likes the ladies."

I laughed. "Don't most men?"

"I mean he *really* likes the ladies."

"He's already shown me some of the nudes he's painted."

"Yeah. I saw the picture you took."

"Did you know about the nudes?" I asked.

"No. Not surprised, though."

"Why not?"

"The guy's a player, Lark. Pure and simple."

"Do you have a problem with that? You sound a little envious."

Sam laughed a mirthless bark.

"Did Doug's being a player affect his job performance?"

"No. Not at all. The guy's a consummate pro, I'll give him that."

"Do you believe he's the serial killer?"

"Anyone's *capable* of murder."

"You're ducking the question."

"Yes. I am," Sam said. "Do *you* think he's capable of murder, Lark? Or are you too . . . *close* to him to be objective about it?"

"I'll duck the question, too. Thanks for the quotes, Sam. I'll see you later."

"Lemme know what happens at the meeting."

"We'll see." I hung up as quickly as I could, pulled up the story I'd written about Doug and dropped in Sam's quotes, including the one about Doug being a player who really likes the ladies.

People were starting to gather in the main newsroom. Marcie came to my desk and pulled up a chair. She looked worried as she tugged absentmindedly on her hair.

I'd never seen the newsroom this crowded. People from other departments were now crammed into what had been a spacious area. The room had almost a party-like atmosphere as people who hadn't seen each other in a long while began to get caught up. A few people laughed loudly, while others looked nervous and kept to themselves.

Elmer, looking flushed and glum, entered the room flanked by Ed, who looked grim and ashen. Immediately, the buzz in the room heightened, then fell silent.

"Thank you all for being here," Elmer began. "I'll make this brief. As you know, the *Sun-Gazette* has been through some hard times. And it was founded in hard times back in the 1970s when the morning *Sun* and the evening *Gazette* merged into the current entity."

"Christ," someone muttered behind me. "Is he gonna give us another freakin' history lesson?"

"The eighties and nineties were the paper's best years," Elmer went on. "We won a Pulitzer back then, remember?"

I looked around. With the exception of Ed, everyone else in the room had probably been in grade school or hadn't even been born back then.

"Anyway," Elmer continued, "the newspaper industry has been going through some tough times. When we were bought out by Leigh Enterprises a few years ago, things began to change. The bottom line seemed to become more important than the craft of journalism. But we soldiered on." Elmer was smiling, but his voice caught.

The room was dead quiet.

"You all know that the last few months have been tough," Elmer continued. "We had to lay off some good people. But I always hoped we could make it. Well . . . " he paused and looked around the room. "You are some of the finest people I've had the privilege of working with." He paused again and then chuckled. "I know. I know. I'm burying the lead. But here it is, folks. There's not a good way to say this, so I'll just say it: Leigh Enterprises is cutting its losses and closing us down. The last issue of the paper is Sunday."

"Oh, no!" several people said in unison.

A few expressed their anger with terse expletives.

Marcie buried her head in her hands and sobbed.

Ed was choking back tears. Tears were now streaming down Elmer's face. He waited until the wave of grief made its initial pass through the room.

"I'm sorry for the short notice," Elmer continued, "but I didn't get much of a heads up myself. We have an excellent Human Resources department that will meet with all of you to discuss your personal situation. The general policy is that you'll get two weeks of severance for every year you've been with the company."

"That means I get about six *minutes* of severance," I said bitterly to Marcie. I don't think she heard me because she seemed too shell-shocked to react, but it felt good to say it.

Someone spoke up. "But we've been kicking ass on the serial killer story. Don't our corporate handlers care?"

"Obviously not," Elmer said. "Obviously not. It's now all about the bottom line. But, as for us, let's resolve to go out with dignity because for *us* journalism—really good journalism—still matters. It would serve them right if our last edition was Pulitzer-worthy. We have two more days together, folks. Let's make it happen."

Someone started to clap and soon the room rang with loud applause. Elmer gave Ed a bear hug, then lingered in the newsroom, shaking hands and talking with people informally.

I felt numb. I'd just moved more than a thousand miles from my home in Wisconsin to a job in Georgia that was now a dead end. I stalked out of the newsroom without speaking to anyone.

FORTY-FIVE

I **HAD MY CELL** phone out and was speed-dialing Lionel's number by the time I hit the door.

"We never talk twice in the same day," Lionel said without saying hello. "Don't tell me you're toast already?"

"The whole paper's toast," I sputtered.

"What are you talking about?"

I told him about Elmer's bombshell.

Lionel let out a long, slow whistle and his voice softened. "You okay, kid?"

Tears were welling in my eyes. "No. I'm really angry." I was now seething *and* crying.

"Just let it out. Talk to me."

I sagged against a retaining wall just outside the building and, for the next five minutes, poured out my frustrations. They started with an extremely articulate, but expletive-laden diatribe against corporate America, then transitioned to a point-by-point analysis of all the reasons why my reporting on the serial killer story is extremely important and shouldn't be truncated just because of a silly little technicality like the paper not being able to make payroll.

Lionel listened for about a minute—the amount of time he considered to be patient—before trying to interject, but I bulldozed through him and continued ranting. He finally got a word in when I paused to catch my breath.

"As I said this morning," he said gently, "you can have your old job back."

"Thanks, Lionel. That's good to know, but I'd feel like a failure if I had to return in disgrace."

"What's so disgraceful about working for me?" he asked with a touch of indignation and hurt.

"That's not what I mean, Lionel. It's just I feel like I need to keep moving forward. Going back is too . . . well . . . easy."

"I understand," he grumped.

"But I don't know where forward is," I sighed.

"You want to keep working that story, don't you?"

"Absolutely. I've got to find out who killed Luanne and Polly and maybe—"

"And maybe personally stop the guy?" Lionel interrupted, completing my thought.

"Yeah. How'd you know?"

"Just a hunch. I *know* you."

"But I don't know what to *do*." I sounded whiney and hated myself for it.

"Well, you could solve the murders in the next two days and save the paper."

"Lionel, you're not helping."

He chuckled. "I know. Sorry. I'm just trying to cheer you up."

"Did you ever lose your job? I asked.

"Sure. Hundreds of times."

"Really? C'mon."

"Seriously. When I was at the AP, I used to clash almost daily with an editor. He'd fire me, but then call me the next day when he discovered he was short-staffed and in a jam. Our relationship was like a dysfunctional marriage."

"Hmmmm," I said. "You've just given me an idea."

"I did? Couldn't have. I wasn't even trying."

"The AP in Atlanta has picked up some of my stories. Maybe I can convince them to take me on full-time after the paper goes out of business Sunday."

"Great idea."

"I think so, too," I said, my mood brightening. "I'll call you back."

"Okay, kid. You hang in there. You're doing great stuff. Keep up the good work."

"I will. Thanks, Lionel. I always feel better after talking with you."

"Well, of course," he laughed. "It's to be expected."

After hanging up, I speed-dialed the number of the Associated Press in Atlanta. As the phone rang, I realized I had some leverage. Since most of my colleagues at the paper were still absorbing Elmer's stunning news, perhaps no one had yet thought of reporting on the story of the newspaper's collapse.

I got through to an AP editor who identified himself as "Wilson." When I told him who I was, he immediately recognized my name.

"We just saw your piece on the arrest of the father on porn charges," Wilson said.

"I've got another story for you," I told him, then gave him the details from Elmer's mandatory meeting.

"Thanks, Lark. We'll check it out."

"One more thing," I said.

"Yeah?"

"Starting Monday, I'm going to need a new job. I'd love to keep working the serial killer story. Got any openings?"

"That's above my pay grade," Wilson said, "but lemme kick it upstairs. At the very least, I'm sure we could use a stringer."

I thanked Wilson, got his name, number and email—and made sure he had mine—then thumbed a reminder note to myself in my iPhone to send him my resume and some of my published clips. For the first time since the mandatory meeting, I felt at least a glimmer of hope about my future. That is, until I got to my car.

I could tell something was amiss right away. Pearlie seemed to be sitting at a slightly crooked angle as if on bended knee. Then I saw that the left front tire was flat. So was the left rear.

"Oh, no!" I wailed. One flat tire was annoying enough, but at least I could change it. Two tires meant getting towed. I dashed across the street to where Pearlie was parked and went around the front to the passenger side, anxiously looking at the tires there. Both flat.

Crestfallen and angry, I circled around the back of the car thumbing my iPhone to see if I could find a nearby towing service. I was about to lean against the driver's side door when something caught my eye. My door was dented, and gouged into it was this angry scrawl: *BACK OFF!*

FORTY-SIX

THE ATTACK ON my precious Pearlie felt like an attack on me—a kick in the gut. I immediately thought back to the day Ross Christopher nearly raped me and all at once I was re-experiencing those feelings of helplessness and rage.

And fear.

I looked around quickly. Was I being watched? Was I about to be attacked?

The street was nearly deserted. Thank God it was still daylight, but the sun was pretty low in the sky, casting long shadows from the warehouses on Front Street. Soon it would be dark.

I had my cell phone in my hand. I thought about calling Sonny Laskin, but reconsidered. He'd dismiss me as some hysterical female making a federal case out of a minor act of vandalism. But this could also be an ominous warning from the serial killer himself. I called Matt Benson, instead.

"Benson," he said when he answered.

"Hi, Matt. It's Lark Chadwick."

"Hey, Lark."

At least he didn't sound annoyed to hear my voice. I plunged ahead. "I'm in front of the newspaper office. Someone just slashed all four of my tires and then used a key or something sharp to scratch a warning note into the driver's side door."

"A note? What's it say?"

"It says 'back off.'"

"I'll be right there. Don't. Touch. *Anything.*"

"Should I call 911?"

"I'll take care of that. Are you okay?"

"I'm fine, but pissed. Very pissed."

In less than two minutes, a squad car, lights flashing, siren blaring, screeched to a stop next to Pearlie and me. Two patrolmen got out.

"Are you the person who phoned in the complaint?" the cop sitting shotgun asked as he closed his door.

"I called Detective Benson and he contacted the dispatcher," I said. "He told me he'd be here any minute."

As if on cue, Benson pulled up in an unmarked Crown Victoria while I was still talking with the two patrolmen. A blue light strobed on the dashboard of his car.

"Show me," Benson said to me brusquely as he got out and strode to me.

I pointed at the tires and the scrawl that filled the side door.

Benson turned to the other cops. "This could be related to the serial killer case. Block this area off and tape it," he ordered. "And let's get a crime scene detail here pronto."

Both of the cops sprang into action. The driver got on his radio and called for assistance, while the other cop opened the trunk, got out a big roll of yellow plastic crime scene tape and began to wind it around a light pole, the car parked behind mine, a newspaper kiosk on the curb next to Pearlie and then back to the light pole. Pearlie was the center of attention.

As all that was going on, Benson took me aside. "Tell me everything," he said.

"There's not much to tell. I came outside and this is what I found."

"Have you gotten any threatening phone calls or messages?"

I shook my head. "Just this."

"How long's the car been parked here."

"Since about two. I'd just come from an interview with Augie Ackermann."

Benson looked up at me, a surprised look on his face. "Oh?"

"He didn't do it, Matt."

"I didn't say he did."

"But you were thinking it."

He shrugged and nodded at Pearlie. "Who do *you* think did *this*?"

"Tyrone Jackson."

"You seem pretty certain. How come?"

I told Benson about my unpleasant face-to-face with Tyrone at Luanne's funeral, punctuated by his middle-finger salute as he squealed out of the church parking lot. I also told him about my meeting with Tracey and Bob Black earlier in the day at the high school.

"Tyrone saw me talking to them," I said.

"Did he say anything to you?" Benson asked.

"No. He pretended not to see me, but he brushed right past me after throwing a football."

"Why do you think it's him and not Augie?"

"It's just a gut thing. The talk with Augie wasn't at all confrontational. He opened up to me. But Tyrone seems to be a hothead and used to getting his way. He's used to adulation, not critical and suspicious questions from a woman. My guess is he's more accustomed to having women on their knees in front of him—figuratively AND literally. Plus he's got a lot to lose."

"How so?"

"I understand that a lot of universities are scouting him for their football teams in the fall. Negative publicity could ruin all that."

Benson nodded knowingly. "Does he know where you live?"

"I don't think so."

"I'll have a squad car parked in front of your place tonight, just in case."

"That would be great, but it's probably not necessary."

"It'll make *me* feel better," Benson said.

Just then Marcie called out to me. "Lark! What happened?" She'd just left the newspaper office and was standing at the curb.

I looked up and waved her over to us.

She trotted across the street and came up to Benson and me. "Are you okay?"

"I'm fine, but Pearlie's not." I pointed at my forlorn and wounded car.

"Oh, my God!"

"This is Marcie, my roommate," I said to Benson.

"Ma'am," he said, nodding his head.

"Detective Benson is working the serial killer case," I said to Marcie as the two shook hands. "It looks like I'm gonna need a ride home," I added, giving Marcie a helpless look.

"Sure. No problem." She began digging in her purse, but instead of pulling out her keys, she hauled out a tiny camera. "We need to do a story on this."

Both Benson and I winced.

"I'm not so sure that's a good idea, Marce," I said.

"Why not?" She continued fiddling with her camera's settings.

"Maybe we shouldn't call attention to this," I said.

She took a picture of my vandalized car. "Maybe we should," she said.

"Why?"

"If someone's trying to intimidate you, then this is the way to show him that you've brought in the heavy artillery. That you're not gonna back down."

She had a point. I'd only been thinking of my personal safety and the damage to Pearlie. "Go ahead," I said, waving my hand, "but let's see what an editor says."

Marcie continued to snap pictures of the scene as I finished talking with Benson.

"Once we're finished processing the vehicle, we'll have it towed for you, Lark," Matt said. "Frankly, I don't think we're going to find much, but maybe Marcie is right: this could spook whoever did this by giving him even more attention than he was getting, but not the kind of attention he may want."

"What do you plan to do?" I asked.

Benson looked around, then pointed toward the roof of the newspaper office. "See that?"

I craned my neck to look.

"That black bulb is a security camera," Benson explained. He was pointing at an unobtrusive ball suspended from the eave at the corner of the top floor of the *Sun-Gazette* building. "We may have caught the punk in the act."

"Let's hope."

Marcie, finished snapping pictures and came back to where Benson and I were talking. "Now then," she said, pulling a reporter's notebook from her purse, "I'm Marcie Peck from the

Sun-Gazette. Would you care to make a statement, Detective Benson?"

"We have a suspect in the case," Benson said, winking at me, "and we feel confident that an arrest will be made soon."

"Is this related to the serial killer case?" she asked.

"It might be, but it's too soon to tell."

Marcie turned to me. "Any comment, Ms. Chadwick?"

"I feel violated, but I have no intention of backing off our investigation," I said. But I spoke with more conviction than I actually felt.

FORTY-SEVEN

AFTER BENSON AND I had finished talking and Marcie had completed her interview with us, we all went back into the newspaper office. Marcie wanted to file her story right away and Benson wanted to track down the surveillance tape recorded by the security camera mounted on the building. Marcie went up to the newsroom while I tagged along with Benson.

He whipped out his badge and showed it to Flo, our receptionist. "I'm Detective Benson, Columbia Police. I'd like to talk with your head of security."

Flo, a pleasant woman in her fifties, always wore pastel-colored outfits accented with fluff and bows, and wore so much make-up she must have put it on with a trowel. She looked over the top of her half-moon glasses and studied Benson's badge. Her hands trembled as she picked up the phone and dialed an extension.

"Mister Thomas? There's a Detective Benson here to see you." She paused, then hung up. "He'll be right out," she said to Benson.

"Thank you, ma'am."

We only had to wait a moment before Mr. Thomas burst through a door behind Flo. He had a crew cut, wore a crisp white shirt, plain dark blue tie, and a dark suit. If he'd been wearing an earpiece and sunglasses, he would have looked just like a Secret Service agent. His bearing was ram-rod straight as he shook hands with Benson.

"I'm Brian Thomas, detective. How can I be of service?"

"There's been some vandalism out front," Matt said, showing his badge to Thomas. "I'd like to look at your surveillance tapes."

"Certainly. Follow me."

Thomas did an about-face and led us through the door behind Flo. As we walked through a bewildering warren of narrow, unadorned hallways, Brian Thomas tried to build rapport with Matt Benson. "I was the head of MPs at Fort Benning when I retired from the Army five years ago. How long have you been with the force?"

"Gettin' close to twenty years, now," Benson said.

"Gonna retire soon?"

"That'd be nice. I need more time to fish."

Thomas laughed. He stopped in front of a nondescript, unmarked door. "Here we are," he said, placing his ID badge against a black pad on the wall adjacent to the lock. There was a beep and he pulled the door open.

The room was much smaller than I expected, dimly lit, and claustrophobic. An African-American man sat at a desk facing a huge bank of television monitors. Each monitor reflected images from various parts of the building—hallways, elevators, the newsroom.

"You say the vandalism happened out front?" Thomas asked Benson.

"Uh huh. Someone vandalized Miss Chadwick's car," Benson said, nodding at me.

Thomas ignored me and turned his attention to a monitor showing the street outside the building. He tapped on the screen. "Zoom in on that car there, Horace," he said to the man sitting at the console.

Horace clicked on a mouse, then maneuvered a toggle switch. The camera zoomed in for a close-up of Pearlie. A crime scene unit had arrived and appeared to be dusting the driver-side door for fingerprints.

"Did you notice any suspicious activity around that car earlier?" Benson asked Horace.

"No, sir."

"When do you think the vandalism happened?" Thomas asked.

"Sometime after two this afternoon," Benson replied.

"Okay. Let's check it out." Thomas sat down at a console next to Horace and began tapping the keys on his keyboard. "What camera is that, Horace?" he asked.

"It's, um, camera twelve, sir."

Thomas tapped more keys and soon he was able to pull up the recorded image of the street scene. Superimposed at the bottom of the screen was a bunch of gobbledygook that I figured out was the date and time.

Benson and I leaned closer to the monitor to get a better look. The shot was wide and grainy and showed the entire street, including the entrance to the building. We watched as the camera panned steadily to the left. Its sweep extended to the intersection, then continued its arc to survey the cars parked on the street around the corner. Then the camera swept back to its starting point. The entire arc took about a minute.

When the camera panned back to its starting point, we could see that I had just parked Pearlie and was getting out of the car.

"There she is arriving," Benson said.

As I walked across the street and into the building, the camera panned again to the left.

Thomas clicked on something and the images sped up. The camera swept back and forth rapidly showing nothing but an empty street with only occasional car and pedestrian traffic. This went on for several minutes.

I was beginning to get impatient when I saw a car pull up next to mine and stop.

"Slow it down now," Benson said to Thomas. "Let's see what we have here."

The car that stopped alongside mine was a Mustang GT. The time code on the monitor read 16:14:32.

"Almost four-fifteen," Benson said helpfully, writing in his notebook.

"That looks like Tyrone's car," I said to Benson. "And take a look at the headlights. They're spaced a lot like the ones on the car that passed me as I approached the bridge the other night."

"Uh huh," Benson said.

The camera continued its sweep and we lost sight of the Mustang for a moment. When the camera cycled back, the Mustang was still there, but the driver's door was open. At first, I couldn't see anyone, but as the camera began its pan to the left, a person came into view at Pearlie's right rear fender. The person had been crouching by the tire. When he stood, I recognized him.

"That's him! That's Tyrone Jackson," I said angrily.

The camera continued its slow-steady sweep. When it returned, Tyrone was bending down at the driver's door. If viewed from the front of the building, no one would have seen Tyrone because he was crouched between my car and his—the Mustang concealing what we could see clearly from the oblique side angle where the security camera was mounted.

As the camera cycled away from the scene, we could see Tyrone using what looked like a key to carve his Etch-a-Sketch handiwork into my side door. He stood and gave the door a sudden, violent kick as a way of punctuating his message to me.

By the time the camera returned to Pearlie, Tyrone and his car were gone. The whole incident took less than two minutes.

"Can you burn me a DVD of that?" Benson asked Thomas.

"Not a problem, sir."

"Shall we pay Mr. Jackson a visit, Lark?" Benson said to me, a wry smile on his face.

"I'd *love* to," I beamed.

FORTY-EIGHT

WHILE BRIAN THOMAS burned a DVD for Benson, I called Marcie.

"Hey, Marce."

"Hi," she sniffed.

"You okay?" It sounded like she'd been crying.

"I'll be fine."

"What's wrong?"

"I'll be fine. We can talk tonight."

"That would be good." I thought to myself that it might also be a good time to clear the air with her about the lie she told about me to Priscilla. "Is it the whole thing about the paper folding?" I asked.

"Yeah. Something like that." Her voice was still quavering.

"I've got an update on the vandalism piece you're writing up."

"Okay. I'm ready." Her voice sounded puny and wee.

I began to dictate: "Surveillance tapes of the scene appear to show star high school quarterback Tyrone Jackson using a sharp object to deface Chadwick's vehicle. Jackson is the ex-boyfriend of Luanne Donovan, one of the victims of the Columbia serial killer. Chadwick has been investigating the story. Police have not named Jackson as a suspect in the case." I stopped and turned to Benson. "Matt, would you say that Tyrone Jackson is a suspect in the serial killings?"

He shook his head vigorously. "I wouldn't go that far."

"A person of interest?"

"Yes. I'm extremely interested in talking to him—again."

"Add this sentence, Marce: Police say they are—and this is a quote—*extremely interested* in talking to Jackson."

"Okay. Got it. Anything else?" Her voice sounded a little stronger.

"I think that's all you need. I'm going with Detective Benson to pay a visit to Jackson so I'll send you an update if anything else develops. I think I'll be getting a ride home later from the detective . . ." I looked at Matt hopefully and he nodded, ". . . so I'll see you back at the apartment."

"Okay." Her voice sounded weak and wistful.

"We can talk then, alright?"

"Yeah. I really need to talk, Lark."

"We do, indeed."

When Benson and I left the building, a tow truck had arrived and a guy was hoisting Pearlie onto the truck's flatbed. He had me fill out a form, then gave me a copy along with a business card with the address of the garage where Pearlie would be towed.

While I dealt with the bureaucratic issues surrounding my damaged vehicle, Matt Benson talked earnestly with the two police officers who'd been processing the scene. At one point, he also used the two-way radio in his unmarked Crown Vic.

"You ready?" he asked as I approached his car after finishing with the tow truck driver.

"All set."

He opened the passenger door for me and I got in.

I noticed tension in his face as he went around the front of the car and got into the driver's seat next to me and turned on the ignition.

"You look nervous," I observed.

He shrugged. "We're gonna bring in Jackson for questioning in the Donovan case. It could get dicey."

"Dicey?"

He checked his side mirror and pulled away from the curb. "The kid's a hothead. He might resist. So, I've called for a SWAT team as backup just in case."

"A SWAT team?"

He nodded. "They'll be nearby. Plus some black and whites. I want overwhelming force to show him I mean business."

"Do you even know where he is right now?"

"Not yet. Sent out an APB on his car, so we should find him soon. In the meantime, we'll swing by where he lives to see if he's there. He lives with his gramma."

"What do you want me to do?"

"Keep me company."

"Anything more official?"

"Yeah. I figure you might want to talk with him."

"You've got that right." I felt my blood pressure go up a notch as I began to compose the scolding I wanted to give Tyrone.

Matt Benson was a man in a hurry. He turned on his blue flashers and gunned his engine as we raced toward the north side of town. Traffic was fairly light. Only occasionally did he need to make his siren squawk as we approached an intersection with the traffic light against us. Otherwise, we were traveling fast, but silent. Once when I glanced at him, I noticed that his jaw muscles were flexing as if he was grinding his teeth.

He must have been able to discern something intelligible out of the gibberish coming from his police radio because a few minutes into our speed-drive, he picked up a microphone and spoke into it. "This is Benson. Go ahead."

The raspy voice of a woman came from the radio. "Suspect's vehicle is parked at 1124 Garden Avenue. Please advise."

"He's home," Benson said to me, then, into the mic: "Ten-four. How soon will the SWAT team be in place? Over."

"They're on the way. About five minutes."

"Roger." He paused. "And the black and whites? Over."

"One is parked a block away. Officers are monitoring the vehicle. Another team is enroute, ETA one minute. As per your instructions, sirens are off. They will be moving into position in the alley behind the house."

"Ten-four. I'm almost there. Will advise." He hooked the mic to the side of the radio, put both hands on the wheel and floored it.

The car's power pressed me against the front seat.

FORTY-NINE

AS MATT BENSON and I sped to Tyrone's house, I found myself thinking of the situation I'd gotten myself into. I was being given a police escort to a confrontation with the jerk who'd not only keyed a threatening message into the door of my car, but who might also be a murderer of two young women.

And there was the very real possibility that I'd be an unarmed, unprotected bystander in the middle of a firefight. The sissy in me wanted to jump out of the car at the first opportunity—even if the car was just slowing down, but not stopping. But the tomboy in me was getting excited.

"I've got a question," I announced to Benson.

"Shoot."

"Interesting choice of words," I said more to myself.

"Huh?" he glanced at me, confused.

"If the situation is so dicey, why are you bringing me along?"

"You want out?" he asked.

"Not at all."

"I'm bringing you along for two reasons," he said. "One: You're tough, no nonsense, and brave. I think you'd relish the opportunity to confront him."

"You got that right."

"Two: You apparently evoke a strong response from him. I figure he might say something incriminating if you're in his face. Three:—"

"I thought you said you had two reasons."

"I lied."

I chuckled.

"Three: I assume you want to be treated like the boys."

"I do."

"Good. Then it's settled?"

"Totally." I could still feel the butterflies circling in my stomach, but they were being anesthetized by my adrenalin-fueled anger at Tyrone Jackson.

Benson made a right turn off Veterans Highway onto Garden Avenue. He turned off his blue flashers, but continued to move at a pretty good clip.

Garden Avenue is quiet and tree-lined. The branches of budding elm trees formed a canopy above us. A middle-aged black man with snow-white hair and wearing a sleeveless white T-shirt was mowing his lawn; two little Latina girls played hopscotch on the sidewalk.

We drove another block before coming to a stop next to a squad car parked on my side of the street. In the distance, I could see Tyrone's red Mustang parked at the curb facing us, its quad headlights taunting me.

Benson double parked next to the cop car, got out and, leaving the engine running, walked around the front of his car to the driver of the squad car. I rolled down my window, so that I could hear their conversation.

"We'll pull up and park in front of his house," Benson was telling the cop. "I want to make sure he knows I've got company."

I heard a whirring sound and looked up. A police helicopter was hovering above us.

"If I need you to come in, I'll let you know," Benson said to the cop.

"Roger that," the uniformed policeman said. He was a young guy, about thirty. He looked at me and winked.

I smiled and rolled up my window.

As Matt headed back to the car, a black SUV pulled alongside us. It was full of muscled guys with crew cuts and wearing Ninja black. Matt talked to the SWAT team through their passenger side window. I couldn't hear what was said, but the conversation didn't last long. The SUV pulled to the opposite side of the street and parked at the curb while Matt opened the trunk of his car and rummaged around. A moment later he was standing next to my door holding something black in his hands.

"Here. Put this on," he said.

"What is it?

"It's a bullet proof vest."

"Where's yours?"

"I'm not gonna wear one. I don't wanna spook him."

"Then I'm not wearing one, either. Same reason."

Our eyes locked. Then he shrugged. "Suit yourself."

He walked back to the trunk, tossed the vest inside and slammed the lid, then got behind the wheel. "It's showtime," he said, putting the Crown Vic into gear. He looked at me and, for the first time in my memory, grinned.

FIFTY

GOT MY FIRST glimpse of 1124 Garden Ave. when we rolled to a stop in front of it. Tyrone lived with his grandmother in a nice place. The house was a handsome two-story brick structure with a spacious front porch. Tyrone's Mustang GT was parked across the street.

As Benson and I got out of the car, I saw him slip his right hand inside his sport coat. I presumed he was just checking to make sure his weapon was within easy reach. I wondered if all cops try to draw a bit of strength or courage from their weapon by caressing it briefly as a talisman just before going into a tense and potentially dangerous situation.

A three-foot high stone retaining wall, interrupted by a few concrete steps, stretched across the base of the yard. Benson and I walked side by side up the stairs and along the sidewalk that sloped up to Tyrone's house. Birds chirped and I heard the comfortingly domestic sound of the lawnmower we'd passed earlier. The idyllic setting reminded me of Pine Bluff, Wisconsin. I missed it.

Benson and I climbed a few more stairs that led onto the stone porch. A couple of wicker chairs sat against the front wall facing the yard and street. Beyond the chairs, a porch swing hung listlessly facing us and at a right angle to the wicker furniture.

Benson rang the doorbell.

In a moment, an older black woman wearing a dingy apron over her blue and white patterned housedress answered the door. She wore wire rim glasses and had grey hair pulled back in a bun. Her face was pleasant, but she looked tired.

"Hello, Mrs. Jackson," Benson said, showing her his badge. "It's good to see you again. I'm Detective Benson." He nodded at me. "This is Lark Chadwick with the *Sun-Gazette*. We have some questions we'd like to ask Tyrone. Is he here?"

"Oh, he's here alright." She pushed open the door, but instead of letting us in, she came out onto the porch. "What's he done *this* time," she asked wearily.

I thought it best to let Benson take the lead rather than blurt out my indignation to Mrs. Jackson about her grandson. I silently congratulated myself on how well I was doing taming my impulsiveness.

"We'd just like to ask him some questions," Benson said, sidestepping her question.

She walked past us and sat on one of the wicker chairs and gestured to us to join her. I sat on the porch swing. Benson leaned up against one of the wooden pillars that supported the porch ceiling. He *looked* nonchalant, but I saw his jaw muscles tensing.

"I see you brought the police with you this time," she said, nodding toward the patrol car parked in front of the house. She said the word police with the emphasis on the first syllable and a long O—PO-leece. "You gonna take him in?" Her tone was almost hopeful.

Matt shrugged, but said nothing.

I spoke. "Mrs. Jackson, maybe you've already covered this ground with Detective Benson, but I'd like to know how long Tyrone's been living with you."

"Too long, chile. Way too long. That's the short answer. His daddy's my son. He got sent up 'bout ten years ago. Armed robbery. Tyrone's momma needed my help, but then she met up with some no-count and ran off to Atlanta or somewheres."

"When was that?" I asked.

"Not long after Rufus got sent up. Rufus is my son. I'm all Tyrone's got."

"And your husband?"

"Dead almost ten years. I think he died of a broken heart when Rufus went off to prison."

"And it's been a struggle?" I prompted.

"Oooo-weeee yes," she chuckled. "Tyrone's all boy and then some. I lost control years ago." Her voice had a sweet, gently rolling lilt.

Just then, a loud voice boomed from inside the house. "Hey, Gramma. I'm hungry. When we gonna eat?"

"You hush now, boy," she hollered sharply, "We've got comp'ny."

A moment later, Tyrone appeared at the screen door. He glared at the three of us as he pushed the door open. It swung toward us. He stepped onto the porch and leaned against the edge of the door as he held it open. He was still wearing the sleeveless burgundy football jersey he'd been wearing when I saw him a few hours earlier at the high school. His hard-muscled arms, clearly his most distinctive feature, were enormous.

"Hello again, Tyrone," Benson said, calmly pushing himself away from the pillar. He showed his badge to Tyrone. "I'm Detective Benson. Remember?"

"Oh, I 'member," Tyrone said, belligerently. "I tole you I didn't kill that bitch."

"Tyrone! You stop that kinda talk," Mrs. Jackson admonished. "And shut the door. You'll let in flies."

Tyrone shrugged, let the door slam, then leaned against it. "So, whatchoo want?" He glowered at Benson.

"Miss Chadwick and I want to ask you a couple questions," Benson said.

"What about?"

It was all I could do to keep myself from springing from the porch swing and getting into Tyrone's face, but I held my fire as my blood pressure ratcheted up another notch.

"Where'd you go after school today?" Benson asked. His voice was soft and smooth.

Tyrone shrugged and scowled, apparently his only means of response. "Hung out with some friends and then came home."

"Did you make a stop at the *Sun-Gazette*?" Benson asked.

"No. What's this about, anyway?"

"Miss Chadwick has reason to believe that you vandalized her car."

"Well, Miss Chadwick is a *liar*," he sneered at me.

I couldn't wait any longer. I had to get into the fray. I stood. "Are you denying that you keyed my car today, Tyrone?"

"I'm denying it. I don't even know what you're talkin' 'bout."

"How can you say th—" I began to say, enraged, but Benson interrupted.

"Where were you at 4:15 this afternoon, Tyrone?" Benson's tone was still calm and reasonable.

"I was here."

Benson turned to the gramma fanning herself with her apron. "Is that true, Mrs. Jackson?"

She shook her head sadly, but said nothing.

Benson looked back at Tyrone. "Wanna try again, son?"

"I ain't your son," he hissed.

"Your gramma disagrees with your story. Wanna try again?"

"Then I must've been with my posse."

"Where? You got names?" Matt took out a notebook and pen.

Tyrone shrugged. "Tiny, Pee-wee, the usual guys. We hung out in the school parking lot."

"That's your story?"

"And stickin' to it. You've got nothin' on me, dude."

Matt put away his notebook and pen. "Actually, I do, Tyrone." He took out his handcuffs, then, in one quick move pounced on Tyrone, spun him around and pressed him against the screen door.

"Lordy!" Mrs. Jackson said, trying to struggle to her feet.

Benson had Tyrone's hands cuffed behind him before he could react or resist.

"You're under arrest, Tyrone Jackson."

"What for?" Tyrone hollered, sounding more hurt than indignant.

Benson put his right hand on the back of Tyrone's neck and pressed him hard against the door. The screen bulged inward. Benson spoke firmly into Tyrone's left ear, teeth gritted. "You're under arrest for vandalism and lying to a police officer. And that's just for starters, you punk."

"I'm not lying," Tyrone whined. "I didn't vandal her car."

Benson continued. "You're also under suspicion for the murder of Luanne Donovan. You have the right to remain silent. Anything you say can and will be used against you in a court of law. Do you understand, Mr. Jackson?"

"I tole you—I didn't kill her." Tyrone's tone was less belligerent this time.

"Are you waiving your right to remain silent, Mr. Jackson?"

"I'm not waving at anybody. I'm handcuffed, you idiot. I ain't done nuthin' wrong."

"Tyrone," I said, walking past Mrs. Jackson who had her face buried in her hands. "I don't know what you've got against me, but I saw you drive up beside my car, slash the tires, and gouge a threat into my door before kicking it in."

"Tyrone!" Mrs. Jackson wailed.

He turned to look at me and his gramma. "Did not. She's lyin', Gramma."

"Surveillance tapes don't lie, Tyrone," Benson said.

"Whuh?" Tyrone mumbled, a confused look on his face.

"The surveillance camera mounted on the outside of the building saw everything you did to her car. Plain as day. You're toast . . . *dude*." Benson laughed.

Tyrone swore under his breath and banged his forehead against the aluminum frame of the screen door. "She's always nosin' 'round, axin' questions."

"Look, Tyrone," I said, more gently this time. "I don't have anything against you personally, but you did some serious damage to my ride, man."

"Do you wish to press charges, Miss Chadwick?" Benson asked, nodding his head vigorously at me—a not-so-subtle prompt to do the right thing.

I thought about it. Tyrone Jackson was, for all practical purposes, an angry orphan. A child. He couldn't help it if life had dealt him a crummy hand. I turned to look at his grandmother, now crying softly as she sat slumped in her wicker chair. She was doing the best she could with her angry, strong-willed grandson, but it wasn't good enough. And never would be.

"Do I *want* to press charges?" I got next to Tyrone's right ear and talked into it. "You may be hot stuff on the football field. You may have colleges all over the country giving you fancy cars and wanting to sign you up. You may be able to use your strength to intimidate people, including girls like Luanne. But you need to realize that the world doesn't revolve around you, Tyrone. You can't always have your own way. You need to learn there are consequences when you cross the line."

Tyrone turned his head away from me in defiance.

"Do I *want* to press charges against you, Tyrone? No. But I will. Why? Because the sooner you realize there are consequences to your actions, the sooner you might get it and begin to turn your life around. By pressing charges, I'm doing you a *favor,* Tyrone."

He turned to look at me. His eyes were fierce and bloodshot. Then he hacked up a wad of phlegm and spit it in my face.

"Tyrone!" his grandmother wailed.

Benson swore loudly and, his hand still cupped around the back of Tyrone's neck, jerked him violently away from me and jammed Tyrone's head against the brick wall next to the door.

"Oh, Lordy. Don't hurt him, now," Mrs. Jackson said excitedly. She slipped off her apron and handed it to me. "Here, chile. Let's wipe you off with this." She pressed the cloth against my left cheek where Tyrone's gob caught me. After wiping it away, she folded the apron over it, found a clean, dry surface and rubbed the remaining spittle from my face. "Lordy, lordy," she cooed as she wiped.

"Thanks," I said to her. Tyrone's act of defiance had numbed me. I didn't feel anything for him any more. Nothing.

While Mrs. Jackson tended to me, Benson did a quick pat down to make sure Tyrone wasn't carrying a concealed weapon. Satisfied that he was clean, Benson slapped his hand onto the back of Tyrone's neck again and spun him around so the two of them were facing the street.

"Okay, big shot," Benson said to Tyrone, "let's take a ride downtown."

I handed the apron back to Mrs. Jackson. "Thank you," I said, adding, "I'm so sorry."

She shook her head, sadly, tears dampening her cheeks.

As I turned to follow Benson and Tyrone down the front steps, something on the street caught my eye. I looked. An old beat-up, mustard-colored Cadillac with a black top was racing down the street from the right. A young black man leaned out the passenger window, his head and torso extended above the top of the car. It looked as though he was sitting in the open window, his feet on the front seat. His two arms were extended across the top of the car.

I didn't see the gun cupped in his two hands until the muzzle flashed.

FIFTY-ONE

"MATT! LOOK OUT!" I screamed.

Bullets tore chunks of concrete out of the porch stairs in front of me.

I heard glass shatter and Mrs. Jackson scream as I dove to my right behind the cinder block balustrade that fronted the porch, skinning the palms of my hands. As the fusillade continued, I crawled on my elbows to the far end of the porch and cowered in a corner. I curled into the fetal position and covered my face, praying I wouldn't be hit by ricocheting bullets or stone fragments.

The chattering gunshots came too fast to count. I heard more breaking glass and the sound of lead tearing into stone and brick. The gunfire was deafening. It seemed to go on forever, but must have lasted only a few seconds.

Then it stopped.

A beat later, the whirr of the lawnmower down the street stopped.

The sound of chirping birds was replaced by barking dogs.

Cautiously, I sat up and peeked over the stone railing just in time to see the Cadillac, which had apparently come to a stop in front of the house, accelerate rapidly. It careened down the street, but only got about half a block away before the driver slammed on the brakes when he realized he was heading directly toward the SWAT team's SUV.

Two SWAT team members stood behind the open front doors of their vehicle, M-16s leveled at the Cadillac. As its driver hit the brakes, the two Ninjas opened fire in another deafening fusillade.

The shooter who'd been hanging out the passenger door of the Cadillac was hit. I saw him fall backwards and into the street. He rolled to the gutter and stayed still.

The SWAT team continued to pump bullets into the Cadillac, riddling, then smashing the windshield. The car, its driver either dead or mortally wounded, continued to move forward slowly until it bumped into a parked car and came to rest.

The shooting stopped and at least six military-clad SWAT agents swarmed out of the SUV. Some surrounded the Cadillac and others raced toward the Jackson house.

I stood up and looked around.

The front of the house was pock marked with bullet holes. Mrs. Jackson lay crumpled in a heap in front of her wicker chair.

I screamed and ran to her.

She lay face down, but I saw no blood or injuries.

Gently, I turned her over. Her face was ashen. Her eyes were open in a dead stare. I checked for a pulse, but found none.

One of the SWAT agents clamored onto the porch and laid his weapon down next to Mrs. Jackson.

"It doesn't look like she's been shot," I said, "but she doesn't have a pulse."

"Might be a heart attack," he said.

He checked her airway and immediately began to pump her chest.

I stood and looked down onto the walkway where Matt and Tyrone had been when the shooting started. Both men were down and were being tended to by two more SWAT agents.

I scampered down the steps and ran to Benson. He lay writhing and cursing in the grass next to the sidewalk, his bloody left hand clamped over his right shoulder.

"I didn't even have a chance to draw my goddam gun," Matt was telling the agent.

Tyrone Jackson lay dead, face down in a heap on the concrete, his hands still cuffed behind him. The back of his head was missing and at least three bullets had torn jagged exit-wound holes in the back of his jersey. A widening pool of blood fingered its way slowly down the sidewalk flowing toward the street.

Next I looked down the street at the Cadillac. Three SWAT agents stood around it, their weapons all trained on the back seat. As I ran closer to get a better look, I passed behind Benson's unmarked car and in front of the police car that had pulled up behind us when we'd first arrived. I looked inside. The young cop who'd winked at me just a few minutes earlier sat dead in front of his steering wheel, a bullet hole where his left eye had been.

"Oh, God," I cried, putting my hand to my mouth.

I continued running toward the Cadillac. The driver's bullet-riddled and bloody body was slumped against the steering wheel. Another person—he looked like a teenager, actually—was slouched against the back seat.

With a free hand, one of the SWAT agents opened the Cadillac's left rear door, stood back, and once again trained his weapon on the boy. The kid wore a white T-shirt, a deep red patch of blood widened along his left side. He was conscious.

His hands rested helplessly in his lap. A pistol lay next to him on the back seat.

The SWAT guy on the far side of the vehicle opened the other back door, leaned inside and picked up the pistol, plucking it out of the kid's reach.

As I watched the tableau unfold, I could hear sirens in the distance, getting louder as they got closer.

"Step out of the vehicle and put your hands up," the SWAT agent shouted at the boy.

The kid lolled his head and looked up the barrel of the rifle, his eyes wide with panic. He appeared to be too weak to move. I assumed he was dying.

I took a step closer so that I was next to the SWAT agent.

"Why did you do this?" I shouted at the kid.

He looked at me. "We was just gonna shoot up his house ta scare him," he replied.

"But why?"

"He was sellin' drugs on our turf."

"But you killed him."

The kid winced. "It wasn't spozed to be like that, but they went berserko when they saw him."

"Who went berserko?"

The kid nodded toward the body of the dead driver. "He did." He paused and coughed. "It was all them. I didn't do no shootin'," he said.

"Yeah, that's what they all say, punk," the SWAT agent said. He reached into the vehicle, took a fistful of bloody T-shirt into his gloved hand and pulled the boy out of the car and pushed him violently face down in the street.

Just then, two ambulances and several squad cars converged on the scene from both ends of Garden Avenue.

Quickly, I snapped into reporter mode and took my iPhone out of the pocket of my jeans. First, I flipped it on video mode and squeezed off a twenty-second panorama of the scene. Then, I changed it to still-pic mode and began to snap shots of everything.

A team from one of the ambulances rushed to the wounded boy lying in the street while another one ran up the first set of steps at the retaining wall and came to Matt's aid.

Matt was now sitting on the grass, wincing, legs bent, holding onto his shoulder, now bathed in blood. I followed the EMTs up the stairs.

"Are you alright, Lark?" Matt called out when he saw me.

"I'm fine."

"Thanks for hollering," he said. "It gave me the split second I needed to get *almost* out of the way."

I smiled ruefully and continued taking pictures. When I looked up at the porch, one of the EMTs had just gotten to Mrs. Jackson and the SWAT agent trying to revive her.

The agent stopped pressing on the woman's chest and shook his head helplessly. The EMT looked at his watch to note her official time of death, but it occurred to me that Tyrone's grandmother had actually died ten years earlier.

FIFTY-TWO

I **WAS STILL TAKING** pictures of the scene, when, to my surprise, Doug Mitchell and Sam Erickson arrived almost simultaneously, no doubt hearing about the commotion on their police scanners.

I was kneeling by Matt, tending to him, when Sam scrambled up to us. As he photographed the carnage, he lobbed questions at Matt and me, trying to find out the who, what, why, and how of it all. Matt, though in excruciating pain, managed to give Sam a few details.

"What about you, Lark?" Sam asked. "Are you okay?"

I shrugged and nodded.

"What happened?" he asked me.

"You heard the man," I said, nodding at Matt. "He saw more than I did."

"What did *you* see?" Sam prodded.

"Not much." I really had no desire to help Sam with his story. He'd long ago proved he was no friend of mine.

I watched as Doug systematically sprayed the scene, darting from one grizzly tableau to another, pausing only to size up a scene and then shoot it. His face was grim and impassive as he methodically went about his work. He had just taken a picture of me tending to Matt, and was about to approach us, when it seemed like the rest of the Columbia Police Department descended onto the scene. Several cops roughly manhandled Sam and Doug away from us to a place on the other side of the yellow police tape that was being erected to establish a perimeter.

As a cop pushed him back and away from me, Doug put his hand to his ear. "Call me," he yelled to me above the din of sirens and shouting.

Later, I did call him. We met at the paper and worked together choosing which of our pictures to use for the newspaper and for the website.

"I thought they suspended you," I said at one point.

He shrugged. "What the hell. The paper's going down the tubes and this is a big story. It seems to me all bets are off."

His best picture was a close-up of Matt, gritting his teeth in agony, clutching his bloody shoulder as I leaned in to offer comfort—concern and fear etched on my face. A wider shot of the two of us also revealed Tyrone lying face down. We cropped it so that only Tyrone's legs were in the shot, not his grotesque head wound. The edited picture took up almost the entire top half of the front page of the paper.

My best shot was of the dazed kid, bloodied, lying face down in the street next to the Cadillac, two SWAT team members leveling their M16s menacingly at him. We had to reject many of my pictures because they showed too much gore, but we did use a wide shot I took that showed a panorama of the whole scene: the house, Matt and Tyrone on the ground in front of it, the cop car at the curb, and the bullet-riddled Cadillac just beyond it by the SWAT SUV.

It felt good to be working alongside Doug. We didn't talk much, but sat at adjoining computers so we could coordinate our efforts more easily. At one point, I paused to watch him work. His eyes scanned the computer screen as the digital images passed like a speeding passenger train. Every now and then, he'd pause the pictures in mid-journey, then lean in to study the people inhabiting the windows before clicking his mouse to bring an image full screen. His hazel eyes scanned and appraised. Sometimes he'd scowl. Other times he'd bite his lower lip as he worked to crop an image. Once, he nodded approvingly at a shot I took. "Nice," he said to himself, not aware that I was watching.

I banged out my story, pausing from time to time to provide Doug with a caption for a picture he thought good enough to put in the paper or onto the Web. We both finished about eleven o'clock.

"Buy you a drink?" he asked, his eyebrows wiggling expectantly.

I thought about it. Really wanted to. But he was still a suspect in the serial killings. I personally thought he was innocent, but felt it better to keep my professional distance—at least until things got resolved.

"Thanks. Maybe some other time."

"You sure? Don't you need to talk, or something?"

"Yeah. Probably. But I think what I really need is to be alone right now."

He started to say something, then stopped, unsure of himself.

"Thanks for your help tonight," I said, not wanting the moment to die. We were sitting next to each other at our computers. The office was nearly empty. The hum of the printing press had just begun.

"Not a problem," he said. "I should be thanking you. You took some great shots and I really needed help on those captions."

We sat in silence a moment, neither of us in a hurry to leave.

"It's good to see you again," I said, finally. "How've you been?"

He scowled. "I've moved on."

"What do you mean?"

"With the paper folding, I've got to."

"So, what're you gonna do?" I asked.

"I've been stringing for AP. In fact, I sold them some stuff right after the shooting," he said.

I nodded. "I've got some feelers out with them, too," I said.

Doug looked at me and his mood brightened. "Hey! Maybe we'll be working together there."

"Maybe," I said, trying to hide the enthusiasm I felt. "But . . . ." My voice trailed off.

"But what?"

"But what about that sword of suspicion hanging over you?"

His face fell. "I hate that. I wish it would just end." He turned to look at me. "You don't think I'm guilty, do you?" His eyes were pleading.

"It doesn't matter what I think."

"It does to me."

"Why?"

"Because what you think matters, that's all." He said it with an edge, as if he needed anger to cover up feelings of tenderness.

"I better go," I said reluctantly.

"I'll walk you to your car."

"That, my friend, would be a long walk."

He looked at me quizzically and I told him the story of Tyrone keying my car and slashing the tires. It now seemed such a long time ago.

When I'd finished my story, Doug nodded glumly, lips pursed. Finally, he said, "At least lemme drive you home."

I thought a minute. Part of me wanted to be with him, but the paranoid side of me thought it prudent not to get into the car of someone still under suspicion of being a serial killer.

"What's the matter?" Doug asked, interrupting my internal debate.

"I don't live that far away, I think I'd rather walk. But thanks for the offer. Let's consider the thought the deed."

"Want company?"

I smiled at him. "Aren't *you* the persistent one. What I want right now is to be alone with my thoughts. But thanks." I stood and slung my messenger bag over my right shoulder. As I passed behind where Doug was sitting, I gave his shoulder a playful poke.

"When will I see you again?" he asked, his eyes sad.

"We'll play it by ear," I called as I pushed the button for the elevator.

The bell rang and the door opened. "Want me to hold it for you?" I called.

"Nah. Thanks," he said. "You go on ahead. I've still got a few things to do."

As I stepped into the elevator and pressed *lobby*, I felt a deep and inexplicable longing and sadness for Doug. He sat hunched in front of a computer, scowling at the screen. The last thing I saw as the elevator doors closed was his right hand on the mouse lazily tracing arabesques on the desk.

FIFTY-THREE

THE SUN WAS just coming up Friday morning as I strolled pensively along the Riverwalk. I'd tried to sleep after filing my story, but there was too much inner turmoil and I merely tossed and turned before giving up and going for a walk before dawn. Marcie, on the other hand, must have slept soundly because the door to her room was closed when I got home—and when I went out.

At the 12th Street Bridge, I turned left and walked slowly across the river, pausing at the middle to watch the water pass swiftly beneath me. After a moment, I pushed myself back from the concrete railing and continued my stroll across the bridge to the Alabama side. I'd never had any time to explore over there, so I let my curiosity woo me.

The sun was already warm on my back as I walked. Some traffic had begun to materialize—cars swishing past me, heading to offices behind me in Columbia.

A small, narrow island near the Alabama shoreline diverted a portion of the river and compressed it against the west bank, causing the water here to run wild. The riverbed is littered with boulders and the water careens over and around the big rocks and through a narrow chute that runs alongside the ruins of an old mill.

I picked up my pace as I neared the end of the bridge. The riverbank is lined with tall trees, their gnarled root systems exposed by years of rushing water eating away at their base. I was intrigued by the rapids and the old mill so, rather than explore the Alabama shoreline, I rounded the railing at the end of the bridge and stutter-stepped down an incline that led me to a three-foot wide stone ledge by the water.

The ledge appeared to be the top of the western stone wall of the millrace which, more than a hundred years earlier, would have channeled this portion of the Chattahoochee to the mill's waterwheel. The wheel and the top floors of the mill had long since disappeared.

I climbed onto the ledge and walked downstream. The farther away I got from the bridge, the wilder the water got. It roared as it exploded through the narrow chute and threw itself against the rocks littering the channel.

I continued walking. Soon the ledge ran along the crumbling stone wall of what was left of the mill. I was feeling a bit wobbly, so I decided to sit and dangle my legs over the side. A refreshing mist from the blasting, churning mini Niagara Falls rose five stories to cool my face. Warning signs dotted the area. It would have been deadly if I'd fallen, but I knew my butt was pressed securely against the stone ledge and my back was snugged against the remains of the mill wall.

I loved the sound of rushing water. I let my mind drift as I watched various streams spurt and foam through the myriad rock-strewn channels that had been carved throughout the centuries. The roar of the water blocked out the rest of the world and I could finally be alone with my thoughts.

The first thought I had was a realization that my life was not unlike the chaotic swirling water careening below and beyond me. But as I looked farther downstream, I could see that the island ended and the rapids eventually dissipated and rejoined the wider river as it relentlessly made its way to the Gulf of Mexico. That gave me some hope that peace and placidity might be in my future, too.

I let my focus return to the foaming, angry water below me and let the roar shut out everything else. It was mesmerizing. I let my mind drift.

As the water gushed and thundered, the drive-by shooting once again popped into my mind, unbidden, unspooling in slow motion. I saw flashes of fire from gun muzzles pointed in my direction; chips of concrete exploding at my feet as bullets slammed into the step where I stood; I heard the terrified scream of Tyrone's grandmother; watched as wildly aimed bullets punched splintering chunks of wood from the front of the house. I remembered the brief silence followed by the deafening SWAT fusillade that ended the lives of Tyrone's executioners. Then there was the gore and Matt's angry cursing. I sighed, knowing I'd probably never exorcize the images and noises.

At one point in my reverie, as I sat squinting into the rising sun and dangling my legs above the rushing rapids, I said the word "thank you" out loud. I could barely hear it even in my head as the thundering water drowned out all other noise. I realized that my thank you must have been directed to God. A feeble thank you to an unseen Intelligence that somehow I knew was looking out for me, even though I didn't deserve it.

But I also found myself philosophizing about what seemed like God's capriciousness. Why did bullets find Tyrone, Matt, and the cop in his patrol car, but somehow miss me? Why did I survive? What did it all mean?

I shrugged at the futility of trying to figure out the cosmic scheme of things. I was thankful to be alive. And that was enough.

FIFTY-FOUR

THE VIBRATION OF the phone in my pocket against my leg rudely interrupted my thoughts. I stood so that I could more easily pull it from my pocket—and so that I wouldn't accidently bobble it, causing the phone to squirt from my grasp and tumble into the turbulent water below.

The call was from Marcie, but before I could answer, it had already gone to voice mail. I tried listening to her message, but the roaring water made it impossible to hear her.

What's up? I texted her.

Where ARE u? I REALLY need to talk!!!! she replied almost instantly.

On the Ala. side of the 12th St. Bridge, I wrote. *I'll call you ASAP.*

I trotted along the ledge, jumped onto the grassy knoll alongside the bridge, then scrambled up the embankment to the sidewalk. As I walked over the bridge, the roar of the water receded enough so that I could call Marcie.

"What's up?" I asked when she came on the line.

At first, she said nothing. As I squinted into the sun, all I could hear were what sounded like muffled gasps.

"Marcie? Are you okay?"

More gasps.

"Marcie!" I shouted, alarmed. "Talk to me."

"I-I n-need . . . . " is all she could say before the sound of her labored breathing returned. It sounded like she was sobbing.

"Take a deep breath," I ordered.

She obeyed, inhaling deeply.

"Do it again," I said.

She did.

"Are you in any danger?" I asked.

"No. I'm home."

"What's the matter?"

"I need to talk with you."

"I'm walking over the 12th Street Bridge right now. Do you want to meet somewhere?"

"I'm not far from there. I'll head toward you and we'll talk when we meet."

"Okay. But we can start talking now as we walk. Tell me what's wrong. Why are you crying? Is it because the paper's folding?"

She began to cry again. "It's that. But it's more than that."

I found myself quickly taking stock of our relationship. Marcie was my first friend at a new job in a strange place; she'd graciously opened her apartment to me; she'd been a solid backup for me as I tried to navigate my way through the swirl of events surrounding the serial killer story; but she'd also talked behind my back, something she didn't know I knew—and something I still didn't know how to deal with.

Marcie was talking again. "Everything's so mixed up, Lark."

"Tell me," I said, as gently as I could.

"I don't know where to start."

"Start anywhere," I said. "I'm listening." I looked toward the end of the bridge, but still didn't see her.

"I feel so . . . *guilty*," she wailed.

"What's making you feel that way?" I coaxed.

There was a long pause, followed by a deep breath. "Well," she said, "I've said some things to other people about you that aren't true."

"What kind of things?"

"It doesn't matter."

I fought the anger welling up in my gut. "Actually, it does, Marce." My voice felt brittle.

The other end of the line was quiet for so long I thought I'd lost the connection, but then she went on. "I told one of the interns that you're a lesbian and propositioned me."

I tried to sound surprised, but the anger in my voice was genuine. "Why'd you do *that?*"

"I don't knowwww," she wailed.

I saw her at the far end of the bridge, walking toward me. I waved and she waved back.

"I think you do know why," I said, stopping at the center of the bridge and watching as she continued walking toward me.

"It was before I realized how nice you are. I was jealous of you. You're so pretty and you had just stumbled onto a huge story. I was afraid I'd be eclipsed by you. But then you spoke up for me and, ever since, I've felt like such a loser for what I'd done to you."

By the time she finished her last sentence, she was just a few steps from me. Her voice in my phone came a nanosecond after she spoke the words directly to me.

"Can you ever forgive me?" she said, tears streaming down her face.

As she stood in front of me, phone still to her ear, "forgive me" echoed in my phone.

Simultaneously, we ended our calls, and pocketed our phones. I held out my arms to her and she fell weeping into my embrace.

"But there's more," she said, as she shuddered and sobbed in my arms.

"What's that?" I cooed.

"I'm pregnant," she whispered in my ear.

FIFTY-FIVE

MARCIE CRIED SOFTLY on my shoulder as we embraced at the center of the 12th Street Bridge over the Chattahoochee River. The structure shuddered slightly as rush-hour traffic swished past us.

She hugged me tightly as if she was drowning and I was her life preserver. Gently, I rubbed her back as I softly whispered, "It's okay. It's gonna be okay. Just let it out."

We must have stood that way on the lightly swaying bridge for at least two or three minutes before she finally caught her breath and her sobs became less pronounced. Eventually, she pulled away from me. As she did, I dug into my pocket, fished out a tissue and handed it to her.

"Thanks," she sniffed, then blew her nose and dabbed at her bloodshot eyes. Her face was a contorted wreck. She had bags under her eyes and it looked as though she hadn't slept.

"Okay," I said, putting my arm around her shoulder and guiding her to the railing so we could lean against it and look downstream, "tell me about it."

"Oh, Lark. I'm so ashamed of myself."

"Seriously, it's okay."

"No, it's *not*," she pouted. "I don't know what to do."

"Do you know who the father is?" As soon as the words were out of my mouth, I regretted them because I was implying she was some kind of hussy who had so many sex partners, the identity of the bio dad might be lost in the shuffle.

Marcie picked up on my inartfully phrased question, too, and gave me a reproachful look. "Of *course* I know who the father is. I'm not some kind of slut, Lark."

"I know. I'm sorry. I didn't mean to phrase it that way," I replied, trying to salvage things. "What I meant to say is who's the father?"

She leaned against the railing with her elbows on it, hands cupped at her mouth and gazed down at the lazily flowing river and shook her head. "That's not important," she nearly whispered.

"Sure it is. Does he know?" I asked.

I remembered back to the night when Marcie and I met—the night I'd found Luanne Donovan's body. Marcie'd told me she "sort of" had a boyfriend, but he was being "inattentive." At the time, neither of us knew each other well enough to trust the other with extremely personal details of our lives. And ever since that night, we'd not really had time for much girl talk.

There was the nightcap she and I had after the cops hauled in Doug from the diner. I remembered the ashen look that came over her face when I'd told her about Doug's arrest, and how she'd ducked my question when I'd asked if they were close. I also remembered the longing look she gave him when we were at Ed's barbecue when Doug passed by us with his arm draped around the platinum blonde who would become the killer's second victim.

And then, of course, there was the suggestive portrait of her that hung in Doug's apartment.

I really didn't think Doug was a serial killer, but I knew for a fact that he was capable to getting his way with any woman he wanted. In fact, it was Marcie herself who told me he'd "bagged" just about every woman at the paper. "Including you?" I'd asked, but she merely said, "that's classified," and the conversation moved on.

It hurt to conclude that Doug was the father of Marcie's baby. *Really* hurt. I was beginning to like Doug. A lot. I wanted to believe he was changing. That he really desired to mature and move on to something more fulfilling than one night stands, but if he was the father of Marcie's baby, that would certainly complicate things between us, assuming he would eventually be cleared of the suspicion of killing anyone—which I still thought could and would happen soon.

Marcie hadn't responded to my question, so I asked again, "Have you told the father?"

She shook her head. "Not yet." She looked at her watch. "We're meeting in a few minutes. I was going to tell him before work."

I glanced at my watch. Eight o'clock.

Just then the ringtone on her cell went off, the first bars of Sade's "Smooth Operator." She pried the phone out of the front pocket of her too-tight jeans.

"Hey," she said weakly into the phone. She was quiet a moment then said. "I'm on the 12th Street Bridge with Lark. Can you swing by and pick us up?"

Oh, great, I thought to myself. I didn't relish the thought of coming face to face with Doug right after hearing Marcie's bombshell that had my own emotions churning.

"See you in a few," Marcie said into the phone before hanging up and putting the phone back into her pocket.

"So, what do you hope to accomplish by telling him about the baby?" I asked as we turned away from the railing and began to stroll toward Columbia.

Marcie shrugged. "Maybe this'll get things off dead center," she said. "Maybe now he'll pay attention to me."

"Maybe," I said, unconvinced.

"Or he'll dump me and run away."

"It wouldn't be the first time *that's* ever happened," I nodded.

She gave me a look. "At least I'll know the truth once and for all. Right now, where there's doubt, there's hope."

A car approached us from town flashing its lights.

"There he is," Marcie said, waving at the driver.

To my astonishment, the vehicle wasn't Doug's jeep. It was a hunter green Jaguar and, at the wheel was Ed Richards.

FIFTY-SIX

STOPPED IN JAW-dropped astonishment, as Ed turned on his flashers and made a U-turn at the center of the bridge. There was a screeching of brakes and honking as cars heading toward Columbia were forced to make a sudden stop so that Ed could have his way.

The window on the passenger side whirred open and Ed leaned over so he could see us. "Morning, ladies," he said more jauntily than he'd been since the day he hosted the barbecue at his house in my honor.

Marcie made a move toward the passenger door.

I stood rooted to the spot.

"Hop in, Lark," Ed said.

"N-nah. That's okay. I need to clear my head. You two go on ahead."

The honking behind us intensified.

Marcie got into the car and slammed the door. "Thanks for everything, Lark," Marcie said, looking up at me. "You're the best."

"You sure?" Ed said, looking at me, oblivious to the cacophony he was causing behind him.

Suddenly, I realized I still didn't have a car and needed to pick Pearlie up at the garage where it had been taken after yesterday's keying and tire-slashing.

"Actually," I said, moving to the car and leaning down to Marcie's window, "Would you mind dropping me off so I can pick up my car from the garage where it's being repaired?"

"Not at all," Ed said. "Hop in."

I opened the back door and clambered in.

Ed jack-rabbited away from the curb before I even had the door closed.

"Where do you need to go, Lark?" Ed asked, looking at me in the rearview mirror.

"Hold on. Let me check," I said, rummaging around in my pocket for the address the tow truck driver had given me.

"So, what did you want to talk about that was so important?" Ed asked Marcie.

"I'm pregnant," Marcie blurted out.

I pretended I didn't hear by intensifying the noisiness of my rummaging. "It's gotta be here somewhere," I muttered. *Why the hell is she telling him now with me in the backseat listening?*

Ed didn't say anything, but his grip tightened on the steering wheel.

"Lark and I were talking," Marcie went on, "and talking to her gave me the courage to go ahead. It's sort of like the day she confronted Elmer in the staff meeting. Lark inspires me."

Oh, great. Just great. Why don't you drag me into your messed up life, Marce.

I was feeling more and more uncomfortable as Ed's silence overpowered everything.

Finally, I snagged the piece of paper I'd been looking for. "Here it is," I announced with exaggerated excitement. I waved the slip of paper excitedly.

"What's the address?" Ed asked. All the jauntiness had been sucked from his voice. He was back to being his sullen self.

I read the address aloud off the sheet of paper. It was in Nixon City, Alabama, the town across the river from Columbia. "I'm sorry," I said. "It's out of your way, Ed. Just let me out here and I'll find some other way to pick it up."

"Nonsense," he said. He checked his mirrors and did another sudden U-turn, prompting more brake-squealing and horn-honking. Now we were headed back toward the 12th Street Bridge where we'd just been.

Marcie used the opportunity to continue her I'm-pregnant monologue. "You're the father, Ed," Marcie said bluntly.

"Um, Marcie. Wouldn't it be better if you two talked about this *alone*?" I said through gritted teeth.

"Not at all," she said, looking at me with doe eyes. "I think it's important for Ed to know that this isn't just a she said, he said situation."

As I made a move to put the sheet of paper back into my pocket, it slipped from my hand and fluttered to the floor, but as I leaned down to pick it up, something shiny caught my eye. I reached down to pick it up. It looked like a silver fishing lure.

"Ed, are you a fisherman?" I asked, holding up the lure for his inspection. I was desperate to change the subject until I could get to my car and let Marcie and Ed finish their way-too-personal-for-me discussion which, up until now, was merely Marcie's awkward monologue.

Ed looked into his rearview mirror, a quizzical expression on his face as he glanced at the lure dangling from my hand.

Then, he swung his head around, a look of horror on his face. He looked at it closely.

So did I.

As we both looked at it dangling between us from the thumb and forefinger of my right hand, I remembered where I'd seen something like this before. Its duplicate had been attached to the earlobe of Luanne Donovan the night I found her dead at the water's edge.

Ed looked up from Luanne's earring and his eyes locked onto mine.

FIFTY-SEVEN

THE EARRING DANGLED between us for only an instant. Every nerve ending in my body jangled in alarm. In a flash, I remembered the Jag's flashing lights as Ed had approached Marcie and me. His car had four headlights, spaced in the same way as the car I'd met on the bridge the night I discovered Luanne's body.

I dropped the earring to the floor and began to jabber innocuously, hoping that Ed didn't realize that I understood all too well the importance of the item I'd just found.

"Anyway," I said as breezily as I could, "I'll bet you can catch some big fish with a lure like that. What kind of fish do they have in these parts?" I asked rhetorically, not bothering to pause to wait for an answer. "Back in Wisconsin a lure like that would probably attract something big like a good-sized catfish or maybe a northern pike."

As I babbled nervously, I found myself sounding strangely unlike myself, but more and more with an exaggerated Scarlet O'Hara Southern accent.

Ed returned his attention to the road. Did he know that I knew? I hoped he didn't, but I couldn't be sure. I'd never told anyone else about the earring.

I continued my addled rambling about fishing in Wisconsin as I desperately dug for my phone. I thought about sending an emergency text to Sonny Laskin or Doug, but my hands were shaking so badly that I didn't think I could send anything but gibberish, plus I was trying to jabber at the same time.

"Damn," I said, suddenly. "I just realized the garage might not be finished with my car, yet."

Hurriedly, I punched 911 and held the phone to my ear.

Ed was shooting me suspicious looks in the rearview mirror.

"Nine One One. State your emergency," the voice said in my ear.

I prayed that the guy on the other end wasn't a dim bulb and would pick up on the urgency of my situation as I tried to couch it in terms that wouldn't arouse Ed's suspicion. His glances at me were getting longer.

"Hello," I said sweetly, my voice a jittery drawl. "This is Lark Chadwick calling. You've probably heard of me. I'm the reporter whose been covering the serial killing story? Right now I'm in a car approaching the Alabama side of the 12th Street Bridge and it occurs to me that my car, the one you're repairing because it got keyed and the tires got slashed by the guy who was gunned down yesterday in that drive-by?" I paused, hoping the guy would pick up on my plight without me having to state it bluntly.

"Is this an emergency, ma'am?" the dispatcher asked, uncertainly.

"Yes. Lark Chadwick. That's right."

"Are you in some kind of trouble, Miss Chadwick?"

"Yes. Exactly."

"Are you able to talk freely?"

"No. Not at all."

"Tell me your location again?"

"Anyway," I spoke as rapidly, but calmly as I could, "I'm heading toward Nixon City, just approaching the 12th Street Bridge when I realized you might not be finished fixing my car yet," I gushed in my best Southern belle sweetness.

"I'm dispatching units there now. What kind of car are you in?"

"A Jaguar?" I laughed. "Don't be silly. My car's a yellow VW Bug." I drew out the word bug so it sounded more like buhhhhg.

"Are you in a VW bug, ma'am?" the dispatcher asked urgently.

"Oh my, no," I laughed, trying to sound blithe.

"The Jag?" His voice was tense. All business.

"Yes, sir. That's correct."

"Is a weapon involved?" the dispatcher asked.

"No. Don't be silly. Not at all."

"But you believe you're in danger?"

"Uh huh."

"Is the car you're in being driven by the person you believe is the serial killer?"

"Yes. Absolutely. I'm so glad you understand."

We were at the center of the bridge, but slowing down because traffic was beginning to congeal. Some people were apparently also heading to jobs in Alabama.

I glanced at Ed, but it was hard for me to read his expression. He'd been glancing at me worriedly, but apparently my spirited babbling had convinced him that I was unaware I'd been holding Luanne's missing earring.

"I want you to keep the line open, ma'am. Everything you're saying is being recorded. Stay calm. Help is on the way."

I could have hugged him. "Of course I'll wait while you check and see. Thank you so *verah* much," I Scarlet O'Hara-ed.

"Gimme that phone," Ed suddenly demanded.

Marcie let out a sudden scream. "Ed! What's wrong with you?

He hit the brakes, bringing the Jag to a neck-lurching stop, then swiveled in his seat and jabbed his right hand toward my phone. With his left hand, he reached into the car's center console, pulled out a gun, and pointed it at my head.

FIFTY-EIGHT

MARCIE SCREAMED. "ED! What are you doing?"

"Put down the gun, Ed Richards," I said, loud enough to alert the 911 operator that things had taken a sudden turn for the worse. I pressed myself against the back seat and held my cell phone as far away from his reach as possible.

He swore at me and swiped at the phone, but I continued to hold it out of his reach. He glanced furtively at Marcie cowering in the passenger seat, then sat back quickly against his door to keep the gun out of her reach.

"Why are you doing this, Ed? W-what's wrong with you?" Marcie began to cry.

Ed looked around wildly. Traffic was stalled in both directions. We were still on the bridge, but only a car length or two from the Alabama side. When he turned to look at me, I could see the panic and confusion in his eyes. The gun shook in his hand as he wobbled it vaguely in my direction.

This wasn't the first time I'd been on the wrong end of a pistol, and the muzzle of this one seemed especially large and intimidating. I tried to ignore it and looked into Ed's eyes, instead. I needed to find a way to subtly, but effectively, communicate to the 911 dispatcher what was going on in the car without further agitating Ed.

"Holding a gun on Marcie and me is only making matters worse, Ed. It's not going to solve anything," I said.

He focused on me.

"What's wrong with you?" I asked, looking him in the eye.

"I-I don't know," he replied, shaking his head uncertainly.

"Did you kill both girls?" I asked.

"Uh huh," he said, simply.

"You *what?!*" Marcie shrieked.

"Marcie!" I said, sharply. "Calm down. You *have* to calm down."

She was trembling uncontrollably as she sat as far away from Ed as she could get, her back pressed firmly against her door, her eyes bugged out, staring at the gun in his hand as if it was a poisonous snake ready to strike. In a weak, quavering voice, she asked, "Are *you* the serial killer?"

Ed nodded, almost imperceptibly.

"But whyyyy?" Marcie squeaked, tears coursing down her cheeks.

Slowly, he shook his head. "The pressure at work's been unbearable, my wife's a frigid bitch, and we're mortgaged to the gills." He raised the gun, his finger on the trigger.

I took a deep breath. "Okay, let's try to stay calm now," I said as gently as I could. "Why did you kill them, Ed?"

For the first time, a smile crept over his lips. "Still workin' the story, aren'tcha?"

"No," I smiled—more serenely than I felt. "Now I just want to understand."

For a moment, his face relaxed. "I needed to take control again. I needed to have control over *something*. I picked up the first girl at a 7-Eleven. Stood behind her in line. Got to talking with her and asked if she wanted a ride. She was impressed by my car. 'I've never been in a Jag before,' she said. Took her to a secluded place, but she panicked, so I had to strangle her to shut her up." He looked up at me, a pleading expression on his face. "I never meant to kill her."

I kept my eyes locked onto Ed's, hoping I was successfully able to muster the most nonjudgmental expression I could. "What about the second one?" I asked.

"She was my neighbor. Had had my eye on her for a long time. I went for cigarettes after the party and saw her out walking. Offered her a ride. We got to talking. Was telling her all about the stress I was under at work. And at home. She listened. She understood. I felt powerful. I felt in control. I felt *invincible*." His voice was getting more agitated, edging toward a Hitlerian frenzy.

I wracked my brain, trying to find a way to calm him down, but my relentless curiosity kept pushing me to find out what happened next. Then I found a line of questioning that seemed like a safe detour. "But why, Ed? How did you get to this point in your life?" I was genuinely curious and he must have sensed my sincerity.

He shook his head and took a deep breath. "I don't know, Lark."

If it weren't for the gun between us, it was just like a normal conversation between two people over a beer.

Suddenly, we became aware of a whirring sound. Ed squinted as he looked out the front windshield to see where the noise was coming from. He looked up and swore. "A police helicopter," he spat contemptuously.

I looked out the right rear window and saw the chopper hovering just to the side and above us. In the distance, I heard the swell of several sirens approaching.

Ed swore again. "C'mon," he growled. He turned to his left, briefly shifted the gun to his right hand, then unlatched his door and kicked it open. As he turned back toward Marcie, he put the gun in his left hand and pointed it her. "Open your door and get out."

Tentatively, Marcie swiveled and pushed open her door.

"Now get out," he shouted.

As Marcie stepped out of the car and onto the bridge, Ed pointed the gun at me and snarled, "You, too."

He eased himself out of the car, all the while keeping his gun trained on Marcie and me.

I thought about saving myself by tumbling out of the right rear door and running away, putting more distance and other cars between us, but something inside told me that abandoning Marcie would be the selfish and cowardly thing to do. Meekly, I did as I was told, praying that somehow I'd be able to stay calm and say just the right thing that could keep the situation from ending badly.

Ed bolted around the front of the car and grabbed a sizeable hunk of Marcie's jacket in his right hand. "Let's go," he said to us.

"Noooooo," Marcie wailed helplessly.

He maneuvered her so that she was standing in front of him, his right arm tightly around her neck in a chokehold.

The wind from the helicopter's whirring rotors blew my wild hair in front of my eyes.

"St-stop. You're choking me," Marcie gagged. "I can't breathe."

Ed ignored her and looked up at the helicopter, his face a combination of terror and menace.

The sirens were getting louder, but the traffic jam in both directions was hindering them from getting closer.

"This way," Ed ordered. He gestured at me with the gun and then pointed to the end of the bridge at a spot on the other side of the lane leading out of Alabama.

I held my hands up. I was still holding on to the cell phone. I prayed the line to the 911 operator was still open.

Ed pointed the gun at me, then at the other side of the bridge.

Slowly, I walked toward where he'd been pointing.

Ed followed using Marcie as a shield between himself and the hovering helicopter.

"He's got a gun," someone hollered from one of the cars. "Call 911."

I walked between two cars, Ed and Marcie following. When I got to the railing of the bridge where it met the Alabama shoreline, I stopped and looked back at Ed for more directions.

He was breathing heavily. Sweat poured from his florid face. His thinning hair was wild and unkempt. His darting eyes rapidly sized things up.

"Over there," he pointed.

I looked. He was pointing at the ledge five stories above the churning, boulder-strewn rapids where I'd been meditating less than an hour earlier.

"No, Ed. That's a dead end. How about under the bridge?" I suggested.

He looked.

"You'll be safer and out of sight down there," I said. *And Marcie and I won't be at such a risk.*

For a moment, I thought he just might go for my idea, but inertia—or something powerfully self destructive—kept drawing his eyes longingly to the roaring water.

"That way," he ordered. He pointed the gun at me and nodded toward the dead-end ledge.

FIFTY-NINE

I **FROZE, ROOTED TO** the spot as I looked in terror at the ominous precipice in front of me. The sound of the roaring water mingled with the whirring of the helicopter, which had moved from its initial location next to Ed's Jag and was now hovering over the water about fifty yards in front of us. A police officer sat in the open door of the chopper with a sniper rifle trained on Ed, ready to take him out.

A second helicopter—a news chopper—was now on the scene, hovering behind the police.

Ed jabbed the muzzle of his pistol between my shoulder blades, sending me stumbling toward the ledge.

"Get going," he growled.

I tried to stall by walking as slowly as possible, but Ed kept prodding me along roughly with the barrel of his gun pushing me in the back.

Marcie whimpered softly as Ed kept her close to him so that the sniper wouldn't have a clear shot.

We made our way down the grassy embankment alongside the bridge. I paused at the stone ledge. It stretched out to my right, parallel to the Alabama shore, forming the western edge of the narrow channel of roiling water. I turned to look at Ed.

"Ed, don't do th—" but before I could say anything more, he backhanded me across the face with the barrel of his pistol.

"Ow!" I cried. I saw stars and my glasses were ripped from my face and flew over the side and down to the water cascading fifty feet below us.

I pressed my hand against my now-numb right cheek. When I took my hand away, a bloody smear painted my palm.

Ed leaned his face close to mine and shouted, "Get moving!"

As I turned my back to him, I allowed tears of rage and fear to course down my cheeks. My legs turned to rubber. I could barely walk. What felt like a dead weight seemed to settle in my stomach, a paralyzing certainty that I was doomed.

I felt the gun muzzle dig sharply into my back again, pushing me forward. I took a tentative step onto the ledge.

"Keep going," Ed ordered, pointing the gun along the ledge toward the mill and beyond.

With each slow step, I felt more and more helpless. Mist from the churning sluice drifted upward. It felt cool against my sweat-and-blood-smeared face. My emotions were churning, too, teetering on a razor-thin balance between mindless panic and gritty determination. I knew if I gave in to the feelings of helplessness, there would be no chance for escape. I had to keep my wits about me.

Unbidden sobs began to well up from deep within me. I struggled to regain control. I'd trusted Ed. I'd sympathized with him for the pressures he was under at work. Never in my wildest imagination did I ever think that he had been the one who killed

Luanne Donovan and Polly Arceneaux. What kind of self-loathing rage would bring a person to that point?

As I walked, I began to pray, muttering under my breath, "Help me, God. Give me the words. Give me the strength."

I heard Marcie wailing behind me.

I stopped near the spot where I'd sat earlier leaning against the mill wall, but Ed nudged me in the back with the gun. "Keep moving," he bellowed.

I took another step. In another five feet we'd be beyond the mill and at the end of the ledge. I was penned in by a six-foot-high wall of stone to my right, an insane gunman behind me, and certain death in the rocky rapids fifty feet below me.

My head throbbed and my cheek began to burn as I continued to inch my way along the narrow perch. Gradually, I realized that I was no longer battling my sobs. That I was being girded with a firm sense of resolve that somehow, *somehow* I was not going to give in to the fear. I knew I might die, but I was determined that if I died, I would die *trying* to find a way out rather than simply giving up and giving in.

I stopped and turned to face Ed and Marcie. Marcie stood in front of me, eyes closed, lips trembling, crying softly, her cheeks drenched in her tears, snot dangling from her nose. Ed held onto Marcie, clutching a big clump of the back of her jacket in his left hand. He held the gun in his right hand at chest level. I was relieved to see that at least he no longer had his finger on the trigger. But the weapon was still trained on me.

As I looked into his eyes, I saw desperation and uncertainty. He was making it up as he went along, but his choices had literally taken us farther and farther down a dead-end path.

Silently, I continued to pray that God would keep up a steady supply of strength and give me the words to somehow change

Ed's mind. All I had were my mouth and my mind, but so far neither of them were doing me much good.

"Look at me, Ed," I heard myself say with more confidence than I felt. I had to shout to be heard above the noise of the water and helicopter.

He turned away from looking down at the thundering water and met my gaze.

"It doesn't have to end like this." I was groping, looking for anything I could say that would somehow get him to see things differently.

Slowly, Ed shook his head in disagreement, but he said nothing.

Suddenly, I remembered the cell phone I was still clutching in my hand. Now it didn't seem to matter if Ed knew I'd been on the line to 911 because the area was now swarming with police.

I put the phone to my ear. "Hello? Is anyone there?"

I heard a voice talking into my ear, but it was unintelligible. The roaring water drowned out whoever was on the phone. I'd been hoping a professional hostage negotiator was on the line, but it would be futile because Ed wouldn't be able to hear the person.

It was up to me to say the right words to get Ed to surrender. I'd been in situations like this before and they hadn't ended well. I prayed that this one would be different.

"I'm sorry," I yelled into the phone. "I think someone's there, but I can't hear you well enough."

I gave Ed a helpless shrug.

Whatever light had once been in Ed's eyes was out. I remembered how jovial he'd been just a week earlier at the barbecue in his backyard, welcoming me to the paper. So much had happened in such a short time—a second murder, a drive-by shooting, the sudden announcement that the paper was folding. And now this.

Ed's eyes were dull, lifeless. Sadly, he shook his head, put the muzzle of the gun in his mouth, closed his eyes tightly, put his finger on the trigger, and began to squeeze.

SIXTY

NO!" I SCREAMED.

Instinctively, I reached past Marcie and grabbed his hand with one of mine and jerked the gun out of his mouth and tilted it straight up.

The gun went off with a roar that overpowered the cacophony of the thundering water.

Ed's eyes popped open in surprise.

Marcie screamed.

A blast of gunpowder slapped me along the right side of my face and my ears were ringing, then everything went silent. The concussion of the gun blast so close to my ear deafened me.

Just as I had instinctively grabbed for the gun to pull it out of Ed's mouth, I also spontaneously let go of his hand rather than try to wrestle the gun from his grip and risk a tug of war that could throw us all off balance and into the tumultuous water.

The lack of the distraction of other sounds forced me to use the remaining senses I had. Sight seemed to dominate.

Ed looked genuinely surprised that he was still alive. The expression on his face changed from surprise to quizzical—a look that said, *WTF, Lark. What the hell do you think you're doing?*

"Look at me, Ed. Keep looking at me," I yelled.

His lips moved, but I couldn't hear him.

"Ed. I can't hear you," I said, pointing at my ear. "The blast deafened me." I felt my voice resonating inside my head, the words sounding muffled.

Ed glanced away, looking longingly at the water foaming below us.

"Ed!" I shouted.

He turned to look at me.

"Keep looking at me. And listen."

I had no idea of what I would say next, but I knew my only hope now was to keep talking.

Come on, God. I need you NOW.

Suddenly, instead of saying anything, I reached up with my right hand and put it firmly against the side of his cheek. It was a touch of both firmness and gentleness.

His eyes flickered in surprise.

I leaned closer, trying to fill his line of sight with my face. I lasered my eyes into his.

"Listen to me, Ed." I began. "Marcie and I don't belong out here with you. We don't deserve to die. You've gotten out here safely. You don't need Marcie out here any more. You've got me. Let her go."

Marcie was whimpering softly, her right hand gently massaging her ear. She, too, had apparently been deafened.

Ed looked down at Marcie.

"Let her go, Ed. Let her live."

He looked back at me. His eyes, though somewhat disoriented, seemed to have a flicker of understanding. He bit his lip.

"Let her go, Ed. *Please* let Marcie go."

He looked at me, almost begging for permission.

"It's okay. You don't need her out here. Let her go. Okay?"

Ed nodded curtly. His lips moved. "Okay," it looked like he said.

He took a step back, pivoted slightly, turning Marcie around. He pointed her back toward the bridge and gave her a gentle push.

Marcie, tears streaming down her contorted face, trotted several steps toward freedom, then stopped and turned to look back at me.

I motioned for her to go on.

She hesitated a second, uncertain.

"Go!" I shouted.

She began sobbing, then turned and ran toward safety.

Ed still held the gun between us, but he wasn't really pointing it.

Slowly, I was getting my hearing back. The sound of the water and helicopter began fading back in.

"Thank you," I smiled.

Ed's lips moved. I couldn't hear what he said, but the expression on his face seemed almost trustingly childlike. No longer menacing or terrified.

"Ed. By doing that, you've just begun to turn your life around."

He scowled, uncertainly.

"You've shown me—and the cops—that you still have the capacity to empathize. You've done some bad things. But you're not all bad—even if you might feel that you are."

He curled his lip, considering my words.

"You weren't always this way, were you?"

He shook his head.

"I believe you still have a spark of good in you, Ed."

He scowled.

"A spark. You're not Mother Theresa."

He actually laughed.

And his laugh made me cry.

He reached out and touched my cheek. I put my hand on his hand.

"Now it's time to end this, Ed." I looked him in the eye. "Throw the gun away. Do it *now*."

He followed my head as it nodded down toward the rapids.

"Toss it away. Start over. Let's walk off this ledge together, okay?"

He closed his eyes. He'd lowered the gun so that it was resting harmlessly at his side. Time seemed to stop as Ed weighed his options.

"Let's go, Ed." I stroked his right arm with my hand.

He opened his eyes.

"Let's go," I repeated.

He raised the gun and in one swift motion he tossed it as far as he could away from the ledge. It arced briefly, then plummeted down into the sudsy water.

I took him by the arm and turned him around. "Let's go. There's still hope, Ed. There's *always* hope."

Slowly, we trudged arm in arm off the ledge where Sonny Laskin waited with handcuffs.

SIXTY-ONE

ABOUT SIX SUNDAY evening I was walking past a pub on Broad Street a couple doors down from Marcie's apartment. I looked inside and saw Doug Mitchell sitting alone at a table against a side wall near the front door.

A half-filled pint of beer was on the table. The wooden chair he was sitting in was tilted back on two legs. His hands were full of the spread-open final edition of the *Sun-Gazette*.

It was the first time I'd seen him since he'd been cleared of the murders, so I decided to go inside to say hi—and maybe have a beer with him. But just as I was about to open the door, I noticed a beautiful woman walking from the bar toward Doug's table.

I stopped to watch.

The woman was in her mid-twenties and Maxim-Magazine stunning. She had luxurious blonde hair that fell to her shoulders. Her pink scoop-necked cashmere sweater was at least one size too small for her 36-C build. She wore tight jeans and fringed 6-inch-heeled black boots that made it look like her legs would never end.

I stood mesmerized, feeling frumpy in my baggy sweater and unwashed hair. I watched and waited to see how Doug would react.

He looked up at her.

She smiled at him.

He smiled back, then returned to reading the paper.

She glided past him toward the door, but stopped abruptly, bit her lip and made a face as if she'd suddenly realized she'd forgotten something. She turned around and pranced past Doug again.

Doug looked up and, for the briefest moment, watched her shapely rear end as Miss Maxim waltzed leggily to the bar. Before she got there, Doug had returned to reading his paper.

The babe paused at the bar a moment, but it didn't look like she retrieved any forgotten item. In a moment, she turned around, and walked toward Doug again, slower this time. When she got to Doug's table, she stopped.

Doug looked up from his paper and smiled politely.

She had a beautiful oval face, high cheekbones, and full, luscious lips that revealed perfect teeth when she returned Doug's smile.

She spoke, but I was on the street looking through a closed glass door, so I couldn't hear what she was saying.

She stood in front of Doug, hands on her hips, one knee slightly bent. As she talked, she absent-mindedly shifted her weight, alternately throwing one hip, then the other toward Doug.

My blood was coming to a rolling boil.

Doug tilted forward so all four legs of his chair were on the floor. He listened politely, elbow on the table, a hand cupping his chin. His eyes, I noticed, stayed above her neck the whole time, even when she'd glance away.

After only a moment, she took what looked like a business card from the front pocket of her jeans—as near as I could tell, it was the only thing that would fit in them. She handed the card to him.

Doug studied the card for a moment before handing it back. He spoke to her, a sympathetic look on his face.

She scowled, pouted, and blushed, then stuffed the card back into her pocket, said something to him and walked quickly toward the door.

I had to move fast to get out of the way as she shoved the door open. There were tears in her eyes.

"That's *never ever* happened to me before," I heard her mutter angrily as she brushed past me and stomped down the street.

I caught the door before it closed and went inside.

Doug was reading the paper again. He glanced up, looked down, did a double-take and clumsily got to his feet.

"Lark!" he beamed. "It's great to see you."

"Hi, Doug. Is this seat taken?"

"No. No. Not at all." He pulled out the chair on his left and held it for me. "Have a seat."

I sat down and put my messenger bag on the empty chair to my left.

Doug sat down and folded up his paper. "It's great to see you again," he repeated.

"You too. Who's the babe I just saw you talking with?"

He shrugged. "She's a model. She gave me her card. Said she wanted me to paint her."

I smiled. "Is that *all* she wanted?"

Doug chuckled. "Probably not."

"What'd you tell her?"

"I said I'm moving on."

"Moving on?"

"To landscapes."

"Really?"

"Don't sound so surprised, Lark. I told you I'm turning over a new leaf."

"Very funny."

He look at me, confused.

"Leaf. Landscape. Try to keep up."

"Oh." He laughed hard. "I mean changing my ways. Settling down."

I ordered a beer and we talked for awhile. Then I ordered another and we talked some more.

I told him I'm glad his name had been cleared. I told him I'd always had a strong hunch he was innocent.

He thanked me for trusting him and believing in him. He said he enjoyed working with me. He said he was glad to finally get a chance to sit down over a beer and get to know me.

We talked some more. We worried out loud about what we'd do next now that the paper had folded.

Two hours later, we were each finishing our third beers. At one point, I put my right hand on the table at the same time he put his left hand there. The back of our hands touched. Neither of us did anything to move apart. The moment was subtle. And electric. I felt an emotional tectonic shift inside me.

Or was it just the alcohol?

Doug must have felt something, too, because he took my hand and leaned slowly toward me, his eyes on my lips. I've had to feint to one side or the other plenty of times to avoid The Lunge.

This. Was not. The Lunge.

Doug's lean was slow and deliberate, but then he stopped and looked at me, eyebrows raised. He was signaling his intent, but asking for permission.

I gave it.

I gave it with a smile, parted lips—and a lean of my own.

His kiss was firm, authoritative, giving.

I gave as good as I got.

"Let's pay up and get out of here," he said, when we came up for air.

"No." I squeezed his hand.

He looked at me stunned.

"I like you, Doug. Really. I do. But I need to go slow."

"But this might be our only chance to be together," he said.

"Or it might be just the beginning."

He tried again. "We may end up in different parts of the country."

"All the more reason to go slow."

Doug leaned back, but continued to gently hold my hand. He was clearly disappointed, but puckered his lips and sighed through his nose, seeming to give serious thought to what I had said. He was no more used to someone turning him down than was the perfectly-put-together blonde earlier that night.

"Okay," he said, finally. "But, for the record: I like you. A lot. It's no secret I've been with many other women, but there's something different about you, Lark. Something solid. Real." He looked deeply into my eyes. "You're worth the wait, Miss Chadwick. You're worth the wait."

Then he kissed my hand.

EPILOGUE

ED PLED GUILTY to the two murders. He's in prison serving life without the possibility of parole. He uses his journalistic skills to write and to assist law enforcement in its study of the mind of a serial killer.

Marcie put her baby up for adoption and has gone back to school to get a Master's degree in journalism. She volunteers at a women's counseling center.

The profile piece I did on Augie ran in the last edition of the paper. Governor Gannon's Safe Streets Initiative got watered down in the special session of the legislature. Augie was promoted to cashier and, last I heard, was being considered as a manager of the produce section.

Luanne's dad, Buddy Donovan, is serving a 15-year prison term—the maximum. His wife divorced him and she's now dating a millionaire widower who adores her.

Sam Erickson continues to be bitter about how he was treated by the *Sun-Gazette*. He regularly lashes out at the news media in his blog, which now has a national following. I hear a major publishing house is interested in the manuscript of a book he's writing.

Doug got a job as an Associated Press photographer based in D.C. He's been embedded in Will Gannon's presidential campaign. We talk and text regularly, but don't see each other nearly as much as I'd like.

A news helicopter filmed the dramatic moment when I pulled the gun muzzle from Ed's mouth. They used audio of my 911 call in which I talked Ed into throwing away the gun. The reporter supplemented the 911 audio with the compelling pictures of Ed's surrender. The story got international attention and, once again, landed me on front pages and talk shows including "The View," Leno, Letterman, Conan, and even "The Daily Show with Jon Stewart" and "The Colbert Report."

I wrote a first-person account of what happened that ran in the last edition of the *Sun-Gazette*. A couple of agents have approached me about writing a memoir. I'm thinking about it. I'm also giving serious thought to going back to grad school to get a Master's in psychology. We shall see.

A few days after the events of Friday morning, I was driving back to Wisconsin talking with Lionel on speakerphone.

"Great piece," Lionel said. He was reacting to my first-person account of the dramatic denouement on the ledge with Ed.

"Thanks. It pretty much wrote itself." I was somewhere in central Illinois, the scenery flat and uninteresting. "But ya know what I just found out?"

"What?"

"Remember the day I talked to you about grilling Elmer during the staff meeting?"

"Uh huh. That's when you thought you were toast."

"Right."

"Didn't Ed tell you he'd saved your job?"

"Yes, but it turns out it was *Ed* who wanted to fire me, but Elmer overruled him."

"How'd you find that out?"

"Elmer told me. After the dust had settled and the last edition of the paper had gone to bed, Elmer took me aside and made it clear he had no hard feelings about the day I was trying to get him to comment on Doug's arrest."

"Uh huh."

"I told him that Ed had said: 'I just saved your job, young lady.'"

Lionel chuckled. He loves stories and was definitely getting into this one.

I went on. "Elmer told me that after the staff meeting, Ed said to him, 'don't worry, Elmer. I'll go fire her ass right now.'"

"Whoa, baby!" Lionel exclaimed.

"Elmer told me he said to Ed, 'you'll do no such thing. I admire her spunk. She's just doing her job. If she can get me to squirm, then she's got the courage to make the sheriff—or any other public official—squirm, too. She's just the kind of person this paper needs, so don't you *dare* fire her ass.'"

"So, Ed was going to use your aggressiveness against you to justify getting you out of the way and off the story."

"Exactly."

"You dodged a big one, kid."

"I know."

"And it seems like you played it just right with the cops," Lionel said.

"I guess I did. Thanks for your guidance on that."

"Don't mention it." He paused. "Hell. Mention it as much as you want."

I laughed. "Just before I left town, I visited Matt Benson in the hospital and he actually apologized to me."

"What for?"

"He said they should have released the 7-Eleven surveillance tape when I'd asked for it because Ed would have been recognized talking with Luanne. He said they probably would have released the tape eventually, but he'd hoped they could discreetly ID the guy without tipping him off publicly."

"So," Lionel asked, "do you want your old job back?"

"I'd love it, Lionel, but I need to keep moving on. You know that."

He sighed. "I know. But I can at least ask—and hope."

"I just got hired by the Associated Press in Washington."

"Really?"

"Don't sound so surprised."

"That's great, Lark," Lionel laughed. "Paul will be thrilled."

Paul is Lionel's son who covers Capitol Hill for AP. We've only met once, but I could tell right away he has a "thing" for me. Unfortunately, the attraction's not mutual, but I can't explain why. I just know.

"When do you start?" Lionel asked.

"In a few weeks. They want to put me in the Homeland Security unit with an eye on maybe covering the White House someday because they liked my coverage of Gannon the day he came to Columbia."

"Excellent!" He paused. "And what about that Doug photog guy?"

"He got picked up by AP, too, based in DC."

"Nice. You'll be in the same city—and Gannon, too, if he's elected president."

"I *know!* Isn't that *great?*"

"You tell me. I thought you had serious doubts about both of them."

"I do, but they're both *extremely* attractive, Lionel."

"But the prez--"

"He'd be off-limits. Yes. I know. He's happily married and I'm a reporter. Sadly, it'll never work out between us." I sighed and giggled.

Lionel laughed, then turned serious. "But with Doug?"

I thought for a moment. "But with Doug, it just might work, Lionel. It just might."

ABOUT THE AUTHOR

Journalist and novelist John DeDakis is a former Senior Copy Editor on CNN's "The Situation Room with Wolf Blitzer." During his award-winning 45-year career in journalism (25 years at CNN), DeDakis has been a White House Correspondent and interviewed such luminaries as Alfred Hitchcock, Jimmy Carter, and Ronald Reagan. He is a writing coach, manuscript editor, writing workshop leader, and teaches journalism at the University of Maryland – College Park. He lives in Washington, D.C.

A NOTE TO BOOK CLUBS

Troubled Water is excellent for your book club. If you're not in a book discussion group, then I encourage you to either form one and invite a few of your book-loving friends, or contact your library or a nearby bookstore to see if there's a group already meeting in your area.

After your book club has read *Troubled Water* – or if you're about to tackle it – I'd love to meet with your group via Skype, e-mail, speakerphone, or in person to discuss the book, the creative process, or anything else that's on your minds. You can contact me through my website: www.johndedakis.com.

Here are a few suggested questions to get your book club talking:

- How did you like the book?
- Who are your favorite and least favorite characters? Why?
- What did you learn about journalism that you didn't know before you started the book?
- How do you feel about the relationship dynamics between Lark and Doug?
- Do you feel the sex offender issue was handled fairly?
- How effective was Lionel as a mentor to Lark?
- Who were/are the mentors in your life and in what ways have they helped you?
- How well do you feel Lark handled the office politics at the newspaper where she worked? Did you pick up any tips from her on how to communicate more effectively with your co-workers?

CURRENT AND FORTHCOMING TITLES FROM
STRATEGIC MEDIA BOOKS

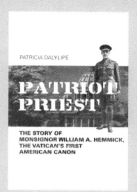

PATRIOT PRIEST
The Story of Monsignor William
A. Hemmick, The Vatican's First
American Canon

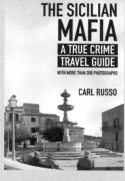

THE SICILIAN MAFIA
A True Crime Travel Guide

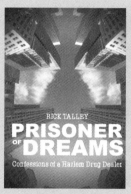

PRISONER OF DREAMS
Confessions of
a Harlem Drug Dealer

**THE GOSPEL
ACCORDING TO PRISSY**

AVAILABLE FROM STRATEGICMEDIABOOKS.COM, AMAZON, AND MAJOR BOOKSTORES NEAR YOU.